SHATTERED BONES

MAYA BARTON #BOOK 2

KATE BENDELOW

BLOODHOUND
— BOOKS —

www.bloodhoundbooks.com

Print ISBN 978-1-914614-61-3

ALSO BY KATE BENDELOW

Definitely Dead (Maya Barton #Book 1)

NON-FICTION

The Real CSI: A Forensic Handbook for Crime Writers

To Dorothy & Kenneth Bendelow,

Also known as Mum #2 and Daddy. I'm truly blessed to have you as my in-laws.

Thanks for everything you do. Including all the gorgeous food, stunning hanging baskets, babysitting and causing minimal damage when you've set fire to my Christmas table (Dad).

I love you both.

Purge me with hyssop, and I shall be clean;
wash me, and I shall be whiter than snow.
Let me hear joy and gladness;
let the bones that you have broken rejoice.
— Psalm 51:7-8

PROLOGUE

Trevor Dawlish had never been an angry man. It wasn't in his nature. He was renowned for being mild-mannered. He was studious, polite, thoughtful, dependable, and honest.

Honest? Well, most of the time...

The majority of the time.

He had his 'little-white-lies'. Okay, and one filthy black lie. That didn't make him a duplicitous person, surely.

He protected secrets and held his counsel, but didn't everyone?

He wasn't harming anyone with the confidences he kept.

Up until now.

Now he could harm someone.

Now, he was raging with an intensity so strong it was a physical burn. A pain so raw and visceral, nothing he thought or did could shake it off.

He was hurting.

He was shaking, fists clenched so hard, his fingernails buried into the palm of his hands leaving half-moon furrows in the flesh.

Right now, Trevor felt like he could kill.

And, as God was his witness, he'd smile while he was doing it.

As God was his witness, he would sing his exaltations as he squeezed out every last breath of the person who had wronged him. And then he would shatter every single bone in their body...

1

The biting wind plucked and twisted the crime-scene tape. It had been strung across the canal bank from a fence post to the remains of a burnt litter bin. It hung miserably, like a piece of pathetic party bunting. Moody, plump clouds chased each other across the skyline casting watery shadows onto the towpath. The weather was typical for late October, the sun barely a pallid smile as if it knew an hour's daylight was about to be snatched away, and it resented the prospect.

Next to the crime-scene tape, a uniformed police officer was stamping his feet in a desperate attempt to stay warm. He was also willing the pressure in his bladder to subside. The sound of water lapping against the canal bank was doing nothing to take his mind off the mounting urge to piss. Had he been alone, he would have relieved himself against the bin, but the presence of two SOCOs, CID, and the underwater search unit meant he couldn't.

Plus, it would be just his luck that the minute he whipped his dick out, the press would descend on the otherwise secluded location. He would have to wait until he got back to Beech Field police station, which he suspected would not be happening any time soon.

'You're going to have to be really careful when you pull the body out. From what I can see, he looks like he's about to pop.'

SOCO Maya Barton's voice was muffled behind the face mask, as she addressed Steve Bower, the sergeant from the underwater search unit. Bower was lowering himself gingerly into the canal as the wind battered against him. Maya didn't envy him the task in hand as she watched him submerge into the murky water. It wasn't just the biting wind tearing across the canal bank that caused her to shiver violently, it was the thought of the foreboding water, swirling menacingly below.

Maya took a small step back, so she could shelter against the crime-scene tent. DC Mike Malone stood stalwart, feet firmly planted on the canal bank, seemingly immune to the biting wind. Late fifties, with grey hair and a stocky build, Malone had pretty much seen and done it all during his extensive career and was rarely flustered; if anything, like now, he carried an air of perpetual boredom.

Maya's colleague, Chris Makin, had already taken refuge inside the tent and was peeping sullenly from the confines of the white canvas. Despite his bulky frame being ensconced in a scene suit, he was shivering. His thickset eyebrows were furrowed in a frown, and he exuded irritability. His dark hair, peppered with silver, and his thick-rimmed, black glasses made him appear older than his late forties.

'How long does it take to get a body out of the water for fuck's sake? God, they do some pissing about.'

Maya grinned beneath her mask. 'Don't take it out on them. It's a crap enough job as it is, without you having a go. You're just hangry.'

'Hangry? What are you talking about, woman?'

Maya laughed. 'It's a word used to describe someone who is

irritable and in a shitty mood just because they're hungry. It has something to do with your blood sugar being low and your body releasing certain hormones that cause you to feel tetchy. I told you before, I've got an apple in the van. You should have eaten that before we got suited up.'

'An apple? A fucking apple? Who's ever eaten an apple and felt full?'

Maya ignored him as she watched Bower steady himself. At six foot three he looked like he could just about stand on the surface as the water touched the top of his shoulders. Despite the choppiness, there was no chance of the body floating away, as it had been snagged securely against a piece of shrubbery that stretched into the canal. Bower's colleague, Mel Gregory, was crouching on the towpath close to the cadaver, ready to lower the orange, plastic body scoop into the water.

'You all right, Steve? Can you get him on from there or do you need me to come in too?' Mel called.

'Nah, you're all right. Don't break the habit of a lifetime by getting wet, eh. You're better staying up there, so you can help heave him out once he's strapped on.'

'Do you want the body bag?'

'No, we're secluded enough here, I'm happy to keep him on the scoop. That okay with you, Maya?'

Maya considered it a moment. The underwater search unit used a mesh body bag to remove cadavers from the water, but in view of the fact the body had clearly been there some time and, as Steve had said, they were in a secluded location away from prying eyes and cameras. 'It's fine thanks, Steve. He can go straight into the tent when he's out.'

'Get ready with your camera then, Maya.'

Shivering again, Maya stepped away from the tent and approached the edge of the water.

Maya adjusted her camera settings. 'Where the hell is Jack,

he should be here for this.'

Malone shrugged. 'The DI should be here for this too, but have you ever known Redford turn out in wet weather? Jack has gone to phone him. In other words, he's keeping his arse warm in the car while we do all the donkey work. I'll ring him on his personal number and see if I can chivvy him along.' He fished down the front of his scene suit, so he could reach for his mobile.

'Can you shift him okay, Steve?' asked Mel.

Maya heard a grunt of confirmation as Bower disappeared behind the shrub. She could see the foliage bending and heard a handful of branches breaking.

'Got him. His hood was snagged on the lower branches. Fucking hell, he really is ready to pop. He's as bloated as a toad. Hold it steady, Mel, while I fasten him on.' There was another grunt and the foliage dipped violently. 'Right, he's ready, start to pull him up.'

Maya watched as the body scoop, now filled with the decomposed corpse, was heaved out of the water. The plastic scraped across the stones of the towpath, like a child's sledge over slush and ice. Mel backed away allowing Maya to take several photographs.

'Come on, love. It looks like it's going to start pissing it down any minute, we better get him in the tent.' Chris was at her shoulder surveying the cadaver.

'Yeah, we don't want him getting wet, do we?' Maya rolled her eyes.

Bower emerged from the water, and he and Mel heaved the body scoop towards the crime-scene tent. From there, they carefully lifted the cadaver and placed it on the waiting body sheet on the floor of the tent. His clothing was worn at the edges, the current having made light work of the hems. Maya took a series of initial photographs before carefully removing the bags that Steve had placed over the cadaver's head, hands, and feet for preservation purposes.

He was dressed in jeans, black socks, and a nondescript black hooded top. He had one trainer remaining, the other most likely removed by the swirling water. The exposed foot hung oddly in his sock suggesting the bones had been shattered when the current had dragged him along the coarse riverbed. Maya took a few more photographs before placing her camera carefully out of harm's way. She crouched down to survey the corpse more closely.

He was severely bloated. His face and neck had been eaten away, leaving no facial features. Instead, his teeth, nasal cavity and eyes remained crudely exposed without the aesthetics of lips, nose and eyelids. The remaining flesh was a shining, marbled grey colour. Maya suspected that under his clothing, the skin would have begun to peel away. His hands were exposed and due to prolonged contact with water, the epidermis was becoming detached.

Maya knew this would make fingerprinting the cadaver difficult but not impossible. If need be, they could employ a technique called double-glove. If the epidermis became completely detached, the SOCO or fingerprint technician would 'wear' the cadaver's skin over a nitrile glove, while inked fingerprint impressions were taken.

'What do you think of what's left of his eyes?' asked Maya.

'Beautiful windows to the soul,' Chris murmured.

'Sod off.' She grinned. 'Seriously, does that look like petechial haemorrhaging to you?'

Chris looked closer at the glazed, exposed eyeball and noticed the red spots she was referring to.

'Well spotted, mate, but it may also be post mortem pooling which can look like asphyxiation. It's a bit too faint to say for sure because of decomposition.'

'Would drowning cause that?' Maya straightened up to peruse the rest of the corpse, looking for more clues.

'Not usually. If he'd been coughing or vomiting excessively, that could account for it. Likewise, if he'd been–'

'Strangled,' Maya said, finishing his sentence for him.

Chris inched forward from where he was still squatting, to move the clothing further away from the neck area, but the front had been too eaten away to provide any obvious clues.

'Fucking hell, he stinks,' said a voice. Maya turned away from the corpse to see DS Jack Dwyer framing the entrance to the crime-scene tent next to Malone. He was ensconced in a white crime-scene suit, which Maya noted with amusement made him look incredibly stooped and uncomfortable. It was hardly surprising as Maya had supplied him with a small size, knowing full well he would need a large because of his height. Still, there was no love lost between the two of them and although it was a childish prank, Maya counted her victories where she could. She scored this up as strike one.

'Have you photographed him?' Jack asked Maya unnecessarily.

'No, I've committed it to memory so I can interpret what I've seen later by the medium of dance.'

'So, what are we thinking?' he said, clearly unwilling to venture any further into the tent. Maya straightened up to face Jack and beckoned him closer, forcing him to take in the full Technicolor and accompanying scents of the cadaver. She knew full well Jack despised being around bodies, let alone one that was so severely decomposed. She knew if it was up to him, he would avoid getting too close where possible. Strike two.

'Well, if this was his Tinder profile picture, I certainly wouldn't be swiping right.'

'You've got a high opinion of yourself when it comes to men.' Jack raised an eyebrow below the hood of his scene suit.

'You think? I'd still much rather go to bed with him than you, any day of the week.'

'Ouch,' Chris muttered from under his mask.

Strike three.

Jack chose to deliberately ignore Maya's comment as he took a perfunctory look at the body. 'I can't tell if it's our missing person on account of the fact this fella has no face. He's described as wearing jeans and a dark top when he was last seen so it could be our man judging by the clothing. He's described as average build and height. He was last seen on the 5 October, just over a fortnight ago. How does that match with the rate of decomposition?'

Maya nodded. 'It'd fit. We had a warm spell about a fortnight ago, so that's something to be taken into consideration. Cold water would normally slow decomposition down but it's a fast-moving body of water, so he's been bashed about a bit as you can tell by the wear and tear of his clothes. He's been snagged near the bank which has made him partially emerge from the water. That's allowed the local wildlife to start feeding on him and decomposition to take place.' She looked to Chris for confirmation.

'Obi Wan has taught you well,' he said in his best Darth Vader impression. The exchange was lost on Jack who eyed the pair uncertainly.

Maya extended a hand toward the body. 'It's difficult to judge his build. Do you want to search his pockets? He might have a wallet or some form of ID on him.'

Jack looked at Chris pleadingly, but he appeared to be concentrating avidly on something in the corner of the scene tent. Malone muttered something about asking Steve and Mel to collect a water sample and left hastily. Sighing, Jack crouched down to gingerly search the pockets of the swollen cadaver.

Maya smiled to herself as she heard him attempt to mask a retch. Strike four.

'Bank card,' Jack announced bluntly as he rose quickly and hurried to the doorway of the tent. He wafted the proffered bank card in Maya's direction as he greedily gulped the fresh, chilled air, desperate to clear the fetid stench of decomposition from his nasal passages.

Maya took the debit card, which displayed the name of Mr Trevor Dawlish, and placed it on the floor so she could photograph it.

'Bingo! Looks like it's our man,' she announced to Chris.

'Yeah? Let's check his back and get that photographed. Jack, mate, if I roll him over and support his weight, can you lift his top up while Maya photographs?'

Jack reluctantly stepped back into the centre of the tent, sulkily muttering something incoherent. Chris knelt and gripped the cadaver by the shoulder, grunting as he carefully rolled the body towards him and allowed it to rest on the top of his legs. Maya was ready and poised with the camera as Jack gingerly lifted up the man's hooded top, revealing a navy-blue T-shirt that also needed pulling upwards.

As Maya had suspected the epidermis had begun to peel away. The body let out a gurgling sigh and a fresh waft of fetid odour was released into the confines of the tent. Jack, who had been about to pull the clothing back down, suddenly retched again, this time not making any effort at all to mask it. He dived out of the tent and Maya and Chris exchanged amused eye contact as they listened to him vomiting noisily onto the canal bank.

'Someone's got a sensitive stomach,' Chris laughed as he carefully placed the cadaver back on the floor.

'More of a sensitive nose,' Maya replied.

'Eh?'

'Well, I might have suggested he apply some Vicks VapoRub under his nose and on his face mask before he came into contact with the body.' She shrugged.

'What did you do that for? It's an urban myth. It doesn't mask the smell, it actually clears the nasal passages, so you can smell more clearly.'

'Oh really? Never thought of it like that. I was only trying to help. Poor Jack.' Maya widened her eyes innocently. Strike five.

'You've a wicked streak, Maya Barton, reckon that's why I like you. I'll go and ask Malone to get the undertakers en route. When Jack's feeling better we need to decide whether we need a Home Office or standard post-mortem, although I know what we'll be recommending. I'll give Kym a quick call and keep her in the loop.'

Jack was swaying unsteadily on his feet and looked as white as the crime-scene suit he was wearing.

'Are you okay?' Maya called sweetly. Jack didn't even dignify her with a response.

Steve Bower was peeling his wetsuit off, and Mel Gregory was filling out a yellow exhibit label ready to be attached to a container filled with water.

'There you go.' Steve nodded towards it. 'A sample of fresh spring water. Nearly as pure as Evian that, you know.'

'Much obliged.' Maya began to sign, time, and date the back of the exhibit label attached to it.

'What's the water for?' Jack gingerly approached her. He had shrugged off the top half of his scene suit and removed his face mask.

'Diatoms.'

'Eh?'

'They're a type of algae unique to the body of water they are taken from. The presence of diatoms in the body can indicate that death was caused by drowning here.'

'How?'

'Diatoms can only enter the body by being ingested through the stomach or lungs while the heart is still beating. Traces of diatoms can be found in the blood, bone marrow, kidneys and brain, post mortem.'

Maya looked at Jack, but his face held no comprehension. 'By comparing the diatoms from the body to the diatoms at the scene, we can ascertain whether someone was drowned in the same body of water they were discovered in. For example, if he was drowned in the bath at home and brought here, we'd know because the level of diatoms in clean water is significantly lower.

'Alternatively, if he was already dead then pushed in the water, the lack of circulation means the diatoms can't be transported around the body, so won't be present.'

'Right then.' There was a pause as Jack processed the information, reluctant to show his lack of knowledge and experience.

'Fancy some fish and chips when we get back?'

Jack paled again at the mention of food and shook his head. 'I feel like you're having a laugh at my expense today, Maya.'

'Really? Not at all. I don't know what on earth makes you think that.' Once again, she was wide-eyed with innocence.

'Hmm. Well, you might want to think about having a little more respect in the future.'

'Really?'

Jack's sickly pallor faded as his face flushed with pinpricks of colour, a self-satisfied grin spread across his face. He was a tall man, lean with a shaven head and stubble on his chin. He had dark eyes and an easy smile. He was always stylishly dressed and charismatic. Jack had a reputation for being a womaniser. Maya had once succumbed to his charms, which had resulted in a disastrous date, never to be repeated.

'I was on the phone to DI Redford before...'

'Yeah, your absence was noted as Mr Dawlish was being fished out of the canal...'

Maya was interrupted by Malone's sudden return, Chris hot on his heels. She was disconcerted to see two of the most laid-back people she knew so visibly flustered.

'What's the matter, what's happened?' Maya turned to them, concerned.

'We've got a situation,' Malone announced. 'I've just overheard an update on the radio from comms.' Malone told them what he knew, and they all turned towards the scene tent, gobsmacked.

The call handler braced herself as she heard hysterical crying down the phone. It was never a good sign. The caller was incoherent in between sobs.

'I'm sorry, madam, I need you to try and stay calm and repeat yourself a little more clearly so I can understand what you're saying. Then I can get help on the way to you.'

'It's my husband. He's been missing but he's just returned home and he's assaulted me.' The tears came heavier over the phone.

'Do you need an ambulance?'

'No.'

'Is your husband still in the house?'

'Yes, and I'm scared,' she whimpered.

'Okay, I'll get patrols on the way. Can you give me your address?'

The call handler updated the log with the location.

'And what's your husband's name?'

'Trevor Dawlish.'

2

'If Trevor Dawlish has just returned home, then who the hell is that?' Maya said rhetorically. 'And what is he doing with Dawlish's bank card?'

The heavens suddenly opened causing the four of them to be pelted with sharp, stinging rain. Despite the horrendous stench emanating from the scene tent they had no choice but to huddle at the doorway, clinging to its scant protection. Jack pulled his scene suit back up, shielding under the hood.

'Mike, can you ring the office and see who's in?' He raised his voice against the bellowing rain. 'Dawlish was a low-risk missing but I want uniform there now speaking to him. Get someone to phone the wife back and makes sure he stays put. I want to see if he knows who this guy is and if he has any involvement in the fact he's been doing a shit impression of breaststroke for Christ knows how many weeks.'

Malone nodded, braced himself for the heavy downpour and ran to his car where he could orchestrate the calls.

Maya puffed out her cheeks as she stared at the corpse. 'So, you're not Trevor Dawlish,' she mused aloud.

'No, I'm not, Maya. It's me, Lord Lucan!' Chris answered in a high-pitched voice which caused Maya's booming laugh to echo across the canal towpath.

'Do you two ever take anything seriously?' Jack said disparagingly.

'Oh, relax, man. It's just a bit of gallows humour.' Chris sank to his haunches and began to pat down the sopping wet clothing. 'Let's just check Detective Sergeant Dwyer hasn't overlooked any other ID in your pockets.'

'Okay,' Maya laughingly replied, mimicking the voice Chris had used. 'It's highly likely. Jack doesn't seem very competent to me.'

They laughed again, and even louder as Jack left the tent with a disgusted tut. The rain battered him as he attempted to examine the canal towpath. The stretch of water was surrounded by fields. It was isolated and desolate, with zero chance of providing any CCTV coverage this far along.

Chris emerged from the tent squinting in the rain. 'He really is going to pop. I think we're going to do more harm than good trying to get a look at him here. I think we should reconvene at the mortuary and see what Doctor Granger thinks.'

'Are you suggesting a Home Office post-mortem?' said Jack. 'Why not a standard coronial one?'

Chris frowned. 'Maya has observed what might be petechial haemorrhaging in his eyes, which could, amongst other things, suggest strangulation.'

'Maya would.' Jack rolled his eyes.

'Meaning?' Maya snapped.

Jack ignored her caustic look and shrugged. 'We all know you like a good conspiracy theory. Sudden deaths that don't appear suspicious to anyone but you,' he said, referring to previous events.

Maya opened her mouth to speak but Chris beat her to it. 'And Maya was right about all that. Look, Jack, we've got a John

Doe in possession of a bank card that we know isn't his. Like I said, he has what *might* be petechial haemorrhaging to his eyes and...'

Jack let out a laugh as he interjected. 'Nothing else on his body that appears to be consistent with any form of trauma. And I'm sorry, Chris, but "might be" isn't enough. Is it petechial haemorrhaging or not?'

'I... well, we don't know for certain. The fact that he's so decomposed means that any obvious trauma isn't immediately visible. I agree with Chris. We should call in Doctor Granger,' Maya said adamantly.

'Well, I'll run it by DI Redford, but I'm happy, under the circumstances, that he'll agree with my call,' he said smugly.

'Doubt it,' said Maya with a derisive snort.

Jack glowered at Maya. 'I was saying before, about how you should think about having a bit more respect...'

Maya raised an eyebrow questioningly before he continued. 'DI Redford phoned me to confirm that I have been successful in my recent application for an Acting DI post.'

'Fantastic, I'm sure we'll be working on the night of your leaving do though.' Maya made no attempt to hide the sarcasm in her voice.

'Who said anything about leaving?' He straightened up; a smug expression spread across his face. 'I'm filling in the vacant DI post at Beech Field.'

'Congratulations, I really hope it works out for you,' Maya said genuinely.

Chris nodded. 'So do I. Congratulations, mate.'

Jack raised an eyebrow at Maya. 'What, no sarcastic retort?'

'No. I'm not your enemy, Jack. We're colleagues, on the same side. We've had our differences in the past, but we need to work together in this job. It's hard enough at times as it is without in-fighting. I know how much it means to get a job you've been wanting to do for so long. Let's call a truce, eh? No more piss-taking, let's make a fresh start from today.'

Jack eyed her steadily for a moment before finally replying. 'I appreciate the sentiment.' He was about to comment further but was distracted by the sound of Malone returning and looking uncharacteristically harassed.

Jack frowned. 'What's happened?'

'I've just been on the phone to the office. We've had another update from comms. Trevor Dawlish has gone and done a bloody runner again.'

3

Beech Field police station was a modern building of three storeys. The SOCO office was situated at the back on the first floor adjacent to the CID offices and above the cells. If a troublesome prisoner was in custody and persistently banging on the door, the sound would echo like a drum through the office. Today it was quiet, and the usual bubble of conversation and ringing phones accompanied Maya and Chris down the corporate blue corridor that always smelt of coffee.

Elaine Hall was sat at a computer and greeted them when they walked in.

'Ah, you're back finally. Want a brew?'

Without waiting for the inevitable answer, she began preparing mugs and clicked the kettle on. Elaine was the eldest of the SOCOs. She had fading blonde hair, a plump face and rosy complexion. She was known for her mercurial temperament and had a propensity for saying what everyone else was thinking. She kept all her keys on a carabiner clip on her belt buckle and usually sounded like Marley's ghost as they rattled when she moved around the office.

'Sounds like you've picked up a right ball of shit. What's the score with it?'

'The deceased looks like he's been in the water for a couple of weeks. We assumed he was going to be a chap called Trevor Dawlish and it was looking nice and straightforward as he had a bank card on him in that name,' Maya said.

'And?' Elaine frowned.

'Our Trevor Dawlish has returned home, assaulted his wife and done a runner again. At the moment we have no idea who our John Doe is, but it certainly isn't Dawlish.'

'Nothing's bloody straightforward in this job, is it? You're not the only ones staying on late. Kym's still here,' said Elaine, nodding to the senior crime-scene investigator's office.

Included within the large open-plan office, Kym had her own private room albeit cramped, with space for no more than three people. Three side rooms led from the main office, one of which housed the forensic drying cabinet. This was used to dry out items of clothing recovered from crime scenes which were wet or heavily bloodstained. It protected items from cross-contamination because of the thorough cleaning process between uses and helped contain any particulates on clothing.

The other room was a secure storage facility for exhibits including a fridge and freezer and the third was where the staff kept their cameras and personal effects.

'I spoke to Kym before to update her about the job, but I thought she was due home. She told me Paula Newall was duty CSM this evening.' Chris peered in the direction of Kym's office. 'What's she up to?'

'The usual. Trying to get us more staff but it doesn't appear she's having much luck. Heads-up, she's in a foul mood. Not only has she been on the phone all day, but she forgot her lunch. She went to get some biscuits from the cupboard, but it appears some fat bastard had eaten the last of them and left the packet behind.' Elaine cackled as she stared pointedly at Chris.

Chris had the good grace to look ashamed as Maya's booming laugh flooded the office. Moments later Kym emerged looking uncharacteristically flustered. Short in stature with a trim figure, Kym Lawson had a reputation for being formidable when needed. She was an attractive woman, with large, wide brown eyes and dark hair styled in an elegant pixie cut.

'Thought I heard voices. Where are we up to with the job?'

'The body has gone to The General for a coronial post-mortem much against our advice. I believe it's happening now,' Maya reported. 'We conducted a search of the canal bank once the body had gone.'

'Anything fruitful from the canal bank? Although I appreciate the weather is far from ideal.'

Maya wrinkled her nose. 'Nothing so far. It's such a fast-moving body of water though, he could have fallen in anywhere, not necessarily where he was found. One thing Jack did agree on, was to keep the scene open until after the PM.'

'At least that's something. Incidentally, I've emailed everyone about this weekend's overtime. If you could let me know by morning.' She turned to head back to her office, but paused, running her hand through her hair.

'Sorry, that sounded unintentionally curt. It's been a long day for all of us,' she mumbled by way of apology.

Chris beamed at her. 'It's all right, boss. You're just hangry.'

'Excuse me?' Kym's brow furrowed and her chestnut-brown eyes looked thunderous.

'Hangry...' faltered Chris. 'Maya said it's a term to describe you when you're irritable and in a shitty mood because you're hungry. Something to do with your hormones.'

Kym's cheeks were flushed, and she made no attempt to mask her annoyance as she turned to Maya. 'You've been telling people I have issues with my hormones and it's making me "hangry"?'

'No. Not *you* specifically. It's a term I was explaining to Chris before...' Maya was desperate to explain but Kym was clearly in no mood to listen as she cut Maya off mid-sentence.

'Negative and positive responses to overtime please.' She turned on her heel and gave her customary double clap before returning to her office.

Elaine's plump face was puce as she sat doubled up, silently laughing at the encounter.

'You bloody gobshite,' Maya hissed at Chris as she shook her head.

He was also trying to mask his laughter, whilst waving his hands apologetically at Maya. She flipped him the middle finger and was about to follow it up with a mouthful of abuse when Mike Malone appeared at the office door.

'Not interrupting anything, am I?'

'Only Chris acting like a knob as per usual. What can we do for you, Mike?'

'Jack has just had an update from The General. It looks like you were right to think it was suspicious. The pathologist has paused the post-mortem. Preliminary indications suggest that our chap was dead before he entered the water.'

4

Trevor Dawlish still lived in his childhood home with his wife, Bernadette, and his elderly mother, Rose. The house was a shrine to the seventies with its abstract wall art, garish patterned wall-to-wall carpet and even a glass coffee table. The only hint of modernism was the forty-two-inch flat-screen television balanced precariously on the teak-coloured sideboard.

Bernadette Dawlish's pale cheeks were streaked with tears. She was a petite, bird-like woman in her mid-thirties, with tiny, darting eyes and a narrow, pinched mouth. She was dressed conservatively in an ankle-length, pleated brown skirt and high-necked floral blouse. She sat on the edge of the sofa, wringing a sodden, well-worn tissue in her hands. Flighty and nervous, she couldn't bring herself to look the detective in the eye as she answered his questions.

'When your husband returned home, did he give any indication why he'd gone missing originally?' DC Sean Stevenson was an experienced and efficient detective, much to the surprise of anyone who first met him. He was blessed, or cursed, depending how you looked at it, with boyish looks.

Visitors to Beech Field CID would catch a glimpse of Stevenson, with his unkempt ginger hair and freckles, and wonder with amusement, which of the exhausted saps in the office had been press-ganged into "bring your kid to work day".

'Mrs Dawlish?' Stevenson prompted, tugging at his oversized collar as he tried to mask his impatience.

Bernadette gave an imperceptible shake of her mousey-coloured head. 'Once I told him I'd rang the police to report him missing, he panicked. He said I shouldn't have done that.' She sniffed and shook her head sadly. 'He said I'd made things even worse, and he'd have to go away again.'

She twisted the tissue, oblivious to the torn pieces that snowed onto the garish carpet. It was obvious to Stevenson that she was struggling to maintain her composure as she continued. 'He pushed me out of the way and ran upstairs. I was too scared to follow him. That's how much he was panicking. Something is clearly worrying him. He must be in serious trouble. He's never, ever shouted at me like that before and he's certainly never hurt me. He was so angry. I was stood waiting in the hall. He came back down with the holdall we use when we go on holiday.'

She paused as she smiled wistfully. 'We love the seaside.' The change in mood was brief as she collapsed into fresh, guttural sobs, which seemed to last for an age, before she eventually composed herself enough to continue.

Stevenson looked away discreetly as Bernadette swiped at a snot bubble that protruded from her beak-like nose. 'He took some food out of the kitchen, and all the money out of our rainy-day tin. I begged him to tell me what had happened, but he wouldn't. He said I wouldn't understand. I tried so hard to stop him from leaving again. I was pulling on his arm and he pushed me. Slammed me against the wall, really hard.'

She shook her head. 'It was awful. I reached for him again and he swore at me. I've never heard him swear once in all the years I've known him. Then he pushed me again, to the floor this time. He had his fists clenched; he was going to punch me. Thankfully his mum called from upstairs. He went up to see to her and I ran into the kitchen. I phoned the police from there. After a while I realised it had gone quiet. I crept out of the kitchen and realised he'd gone again. I've never been so scared in my life.'

Fresh tears streamed down her face, and not for the first time since arriving at the address, Stevenson wished he could be anywhere else. She was a terrible witness.

'Would you like to press charges?' Stevenson asked.

She shook her head frantically. 'No! I don't want to get him into trouble. I just want him to come home.'

'I can see how distressing all this is for you, Mrs Dawlish, but a new line of enquiry has come to light. I'm going to have to ask you to talk me through what happened when your husband first went missing.'

Bernadette looked pained as she shook her head. 'I told the uniformed officer everything. The one that had a look around and took Trevor's toothbrush. I don't understand why you need me to go through it all again. Why are you here and not out there looking for Trevor?'

'As I said, there's been a development...' Bernadette had begun to let out a low keening noise. She had visibly paled and started to shake. If she was like this now, how could he even begin to tell her...

'Your husband's bank card was found in the pocket of a dead body we have just recovered from the canal.' The words fell so unguardedly out of Stevenson's mouth he was as shocked as she was to hear them spoken out loud.

Bernadette stopped sobbing and wailing. Her now soundless mouth dropped open. She sat up poker straight, her eyes owl-like. Then she began to shake and scream in hysterics.

Stevenson tried to hold the trembling woman still in an attempt to calm her.

Just when he thought things couldn't get any worse, a tiny, woolly-haired woman wrapped in a maroon dressing gown and wearing sheepskin slippers shuffled into the room. She joined in the wailing.

5

The mortuary was known as Rose Cottage. It was discreetly situated within the outskirts of The General's hospital grounds, slightly off the beaten track so as not to unnerve visitors or attract the attention of any local necrophiliacs. Whereas the viewing gallery could be accessed via a long and winding hospital corridor, the main door was situated at the back. Visitors announced their arrival using the intercom fixed to the door, whilst an imposing fisheye camera unblinkingly observed and recorded each and every movement.

Maya pressed the intercom and gave her and Chris's name as she held her ID up to the camera and waited to be buzzed in. They headed towards the reception room to be met with utter chaos. It was clearly corpse-collection o'clock. A group of jocular undertakers were queuing up to take their customers to their waiting parlours. In addition, due to a fatal pile-up on the motorway, three bodies, covered with sheets, were stacked in the corridor waiting to be placed into the freshly vacated fridges.

Maya attempted to move out of the way, so she didn't block any of the comings and goings. In her haste to avoid a particularly speedy undertaker, she stumbled against one of the sheet-covered gurneys. The brake hadn't been applied correctly, so it jarred violently against the corner of the wall, taking her with it. She put her hand out to steady herself and half-landed on the corpse. She was mortified to feel the body shift forcefully underneath her and noticed that a heavily bloodstained arm was now protruding from the other side of the trolley.

'Oh shit,' she said, wincing. She righted herself and muttered 'sorry' to the corpse under her breath, as she stepped forward to try and discreetly tuck the bloodied arm back in place. Unfortunately, the unyielding limb flopped straight back out. Looking round to check nobody was looking, Maya tucked the hand under the buttock to pin it to the trolley, desperately hoping no one would notice.

The mortuary assistant was thankfully oblivious to her blundering antics, as she was too busy wheeling out the undertaker's clients, causing the corridor to become even more congested as the fetid scent of death continued to build around them.

'Fuckin' stinks,' said Chris from further down the corridor and in the throes of the mayhem. He indicated his head towards Maya. 'C'mon, let's go to the kitchen and get a brew. Is that all right with you, Morticia?' he called to the cheery raven-haired woman who was wielding gurneys with practised efficiency.

'Mine's tea, three sugars and a just a kiss of milk,' she replied with a wink.

'Cor, she'd get it,' said Chris with a lascivious grin.

'Behave,' Maya countered with a playful slap.

Chris looked at her and frowned. 'Have you got blood on your hands?'

'Yeah, but don't worry, it's not mine.'

'I'm not even going to ask!'

Maya frantically scrubbed her hands at the sink as Chris

made the drinks. Then they headed towards the viewing gallery while they waited for Dr Granger, Jack, Malone and DI Redford.

'I told you we were too early,' grumbled Chris. 'We had plenty of time to pick up a McDonalds' breakfast on the way.'

'You, my rotund friend,' said Maya leaning forward to pat his stomach affectionately, 'need to think about eating a bit healthier or you'll be splayed out on one of those gurneys next.'

'Ooh, please let Morticia ride my naked corpse before I'm sent to the smokehouse,' he replied with a wiggle of his eyebrows. They were laughing so hard they didn't realise DI Redford, Jack and Malone had joined them.

'Morning, boss,' said Chris as he addressed Redford. 'We weren't sure if you'd be picking this up or passing it on to the major incident team.'

'Chris, Maya.' Redford nodded in greeting. He was tall and lean, his buzz-cut hair revealing enough stubble to hint at his auburn colouring. He was dressed immaculately in a tailored suit and highly polished Italian leather shoes. 'It's staying with us for now, although MIT are aware. This investigation will be headed under the name Operation Mermaid.' Redford didn't flinch as the irony caused Maya and Chris to chuckle like schoolchildren.

'We should be good to go soon, I spotted Dr Granger's Jaguar pulling up behind us,' said Malone.

'Overcompensating for something,' Chris mumbled to Maya as he gesticulated with his little finger before adding loudly, 'Either of you want a brew?'

The detectives shook their heads and settled down to organise their paperwork.

'Boss, Sue from the Fingerprint Bureau is coming over once the post-mortem is finished so we can try and get a good set of prints off him,' Maya said. 'There is a lot of skin slippage, but hopefully there's still sufficient ridge detail for an identification, we'll do what we can.'

'Very good. Ah. Doctor Granger, good to see you.'

The pathologist bustled in, weighed down by his briefcase. He was a squat man, with wild, eccentric grey hair. Large, round gold-rimmed glasses perched on the top of his hooked nose and every mannerism exuded a pompous air. A conversation ensued to bring Granger up to speed and enable him to view the scene photographs taken at the canal during the body recovery.

They then headed to the changing rooms and climbed into shapeless green scrubs. Maya selected a pair of white wellingtons in her size and joined Chris and Dr Granger in the mortuary. DI Redford remained in the observation gallery where he carried on working whilst being on hand to be relayed information by the two-way mic.

Jack and Malone entered the room, also in scrubs. Malone looked bored already, whereas Jack's face had taken on a sickly pallor. Maya couldn't help but feel sorry for him and gave him a reassuring smile. 'Why don't you sit on the stool over there, so it doesn't get too crowded,' she muttered discreetly and he nodded his thanks.

She prepared her camera and waited until Morticia wheeled in the dissection bed which carried the star of the show. Morticia began to wipe down the whiteboard which would be used to record weight and measurements of the organs.

If they thought he smelt bad when they had examined him on the canal path, it was nothing compared to the overpowering fetid stench that greeted them now, especially as his body cavity had been opened and exposed. Even so, Maya was too preoccupied to see what clues the post-mortem would reveal to be bothered by the smell.

Doctor Granger opened his oatmeal-coloured cloth roll to reveal his personalised cutting instruments. 'Right then, let's see shall we,' he murmured as he gripped his PM40 scalpel as he perused the deceased, flanked by Maya who already had a myriad of questions.

It was strange to see a cadaver that had already been subjected to the preparation stage of evisceration. The body had already been cut open and the thoracic and abdominal walls had been dissected to expose the internal organs. The cracked ribcage gaped like a maw and the contrast of salmon-pink tissue and buttercup subcutaneous fat made Maya think of Battenberg cake.

Morticia approached the body to slide the neck block under his shoulders, causing the body to be raised so the cavity could be further exposed. Maya winced involuntarily as the back of the head made a whumping sound as it struck the aluminium bed.

Maya photographically recorded each stage of the post-mortem as Dr Granger relayed his findings into a voice recorder. The two worked in an almost dance-like harmony. Granger sliced through skin and organs, holding aloft anything of interest, while Maya dipped forwards with her camera, recording each stage.

'...no sign of pulmonary oedema in the airways. Lungs are not over-expanded...'

Maya was absorbed in the procedure, hanging on Granger's every word. Chris worked as 'dirty SOCO' being on hand to receive any contaminated evidence from the body with the added assistance from Morticia.

'Ah,' Granger announced authoritatively as he beckoned Maya forward with a wave of his scalpel. 'Broken hyoid.' He gestured towards the exposed neck area.

'See it there, the horseshoe-shaped bone? Did you know that it's also known as a floating bone as, unlike other bones in the human body, it isn't articulated to other bones but anchored by muscle, ligament and cartilage?'

'Fascinating,' Maya said as she studied the exposed area.

Jack edged forward reluctantly, wincing at the sight of the open body cavity. 'In layman's terms if you will, Doctor?'

'The cause of death appears to be strangulation, detective.'

6

Sean was greeted at Bernadette's front door by a woman with the build of a shot-putter, ensconced in a grey velour tracksuit. She looked to be early forties, approximately ten years older than Bernadette. Her peroxide-blonde hair was sliced to her jawline, she wore heavy make-up accentuated by false eyelashes and lips that were blistered with fillers.

'Laurel Miller!' she announced as she took a vice-like grip of his hand and pumped it vigorously. She towered over him. Stevenson tried not to wince as her cerise acrylics dug into his skin. 'I'm a neighbour and friend of the Dawlish's,' she explained self-importantly as she guided him down the Anaglypta-covered hallway. He choked on a cloud of Chanel perfume as he followed in her wake.

'Take a seat, inspector. Bernadette is just seeing to Rose; she should be down shortly.'

'Thank you. It's actually detective constable, but please call me Sean.'

Laurel lowered her voice in a conspiratorial stage whisper. 'Bernadette is much calmer than yesterday. The doctor has given her a prescription, poor love. She's always been one for her nerves. Trevor going missing has knocked us all for six if I'm honest, and I'm not one who's easily fazed, inspector.'

'Detective Constable...'

'And then there's dear old Mother Dawlish,' Laurel continued as she twirled an ostentatious gold crucifix on a necklace between her clawlike fingers. 'That poor woman... poor, poor woman.' She didn't elaborate further, choosing instead to worry away at the crucifix as she shook her head.

'Anyway,' she suddenly announced gayly as she spun towards the door. 'Here's Bernadette! Darling, the inspector is here.'

Stevenson stood to greet Bernadette, his hand extended, but she merely smiled at it, glassy-eyed, apparently swathed in the comfort of prescription sedatives before she allowed herself to be swallowed up by the armchair. She was wearing shapeless black trousers and ensconced in a beige wrap-around cardigan that drained her already pale complexion.

'I'll go and prepare some drinks. Inspector?'

'It's detective constable. A tea would be lovely, thank you. Not too strong, white, no sugar.'

Laurel bustled out of the room leaving Bernadette gazing vacantly at Stevenson. He made polite small talk with her until Laurel returned with a tray of drinks. He hid his discontent at the sight of a muddy cup of coffee. Nevertheless, he brightened at the accompanying foil-wrapped Viscount biscuit.

'So, Bernadette, I appreciate how stressful yesterday was for you. Are you happy to answer a few more questions today?'

'She's fine. More than happy to help. Aren't you, dear?' shrilled Laurel as she plonked herself on the pouffe next to her neighbour, an encouraging hand on her knee. Bernadette just continued to grin inanely.

Stevenson wiped his hand across his mouth before addressing Bernadette as delicately as he could. 'As I told you yesterday, your husband's bank card has been found in the pocket of a deceased male whose body was recovered from the canal.'

Bernadette nodded dumbly. Tears pricked her eyes as she looked to Laurel for guidance.

'Do you know who the deceased is?' Laurel asked.

Stevenson shook his head. 'Not at the moment, but we're doing everything we can to find out.'

'That's why he took money out of our rainy-day tin,' Bernadette said. 'He must have had his bank card stolen by that man.'

'Enquiries with your husband's bank have confirmed that his card hasn't been used since the day before you reported him missing.'

'Oh.' Bernadette looked confused, her eyebrows puckered into a frown as she tried to think, her concentration clearly addled by the sedatives.

'The man, the body, with Trevor's bank card. Do you know how he died?' Laurel's lips pursed with distaste as she asked the question.

'He... erm... well, I'm afraid to say he was, has been, strangled. He's been in the water a while and was in the advanced stages of decomposition.' Stevenson faltered.

Bernadette gasped and Laurel reached again for the crucifix. They sat in silence for a moment as they processed the situation.

Bernadette eventually broke the silence as she sat erect, a steely expression on her face. 'I hope, inspector, that you're not suggesting Trevor had anything to do with this individuals' demise?'

'As I said, we're doing everything we can to find out who the deceased is. Our enquiries are very much in the early stages.'

'You'll have DNA and fingerprints, surely. I watch a lot of crime dramas and know how it works. Why haven't you checked for those things?'

Stevenson felt the colour rise in his cheeks as he bristled at being questioned by an armchair detective. 'Those enquiries are currently ongoing, I'm afraid in real life investigations, such results don't come back as quickly as they do in fictional dramas.'

Laurel nodded but looked doubtful.

'You have Trevor's DNA,' Bernadette stated.

Stevenson nodded. 'A DNA profile has been extracted from your husband's toothbrush and loaded onto the vulnerable person's database. When a body is recovered, their DNA is compared to the databases so we can establish if they are one of the many missing people who are reported to us and other police forces across the country.'

'Which is all very well, but a moot point on this occasion, as Trevor only returned home yesterday,' Bernadette added with a hint of annoyance as she eyed Stevenson in a way that suggested she doubted his ability as an investigator.

'Does your husband have access to a car?'

'Well, mine obviously, but he doesn't drive. I'm the only one in the house who does.'

Stevenson cleared his throat. 'Okay. Let's go back a bit. I know you've already provided us with this information when your husband first went missing, but I need to build a picture in my head. Can you tell me what happened prior to Trevor first disappearing?'

Bernadette sniffed, nodded and sat up resolutely. 'He was late home from work...'

'He works at the town hall as a janitor,' Laurel interjected. 'The place would simply fall apart without him.'

Stevenson ignored the interruption and waited for

Bernadette to continue. 'He's normally home by seven at the latest. When he didn't come home by eight, I started to get worried. Then the following morning he still wasn't back and that's completely out of character for him. He's never done that before. I didn't know what to do.' She turned to Laurel for confirmation.

Laurel nodded. 'I'd been away that evening. When I returned and heard Trevor was missing, I told Bernadette she should have phoned the police the minute he was late home.' Acrylic nails plucked at the crucifix again.

Stevenson frowned. 'With respect, Mrs Dawlish, I've not read anything that suggests your husband has any medical issues or other concerns. Eight in the evening isn't late for a grown man to have not returned home. What was your immediate concern?'

'It was our wedding anniversary. The night he went missing. We had a table booked at Leo's for 6.30. He booked it weeks ago and had already promised he'd be home by five at the latest. We were planning on exchanging presents and having a quick Cinzano and lemonade with his mother before we left.'

'I see. And remind me, how long have you been married?'

She smiled diffidently as her eyes flickered towards a wedding photograph proudly displayed on the mantelpiece. 'Five years.'

'May I?' Stevenson gestured towards the picture and Bernadette nodded consent before he stood to examine it. The newly-weds were beaming into the camera, their arms were linked and there was a smattering of primary-coloured confetti peppering their shoulders. Bernadette was a vision in white tulle and lace, her cheeks flushed with a rosy glow. Trevor was of average height and build. He wore a bashful smile and an off-the-peg shiny grey suit that didn't quite stretch to the end of his limbs.

'How would you describe your marriage?' Stevenson asked delicately as he returned to his seat.

Bernadette smiled, despite her obvious distress. 'Oh, we're very happy. That's why yesterday was such a shock, his sudden flash of anger, the fact he hurt me. He's usually such a gentle man. Trevor says we're soulmates. That we go together like fish and chips. Doesn't he say that, Laurel?'

She let out a giggle while Laurel said through gritted teeth, 'Trevor is a true gentleman. He wouldn't harm a fly.'

'Our records state that your husband's phone was found on his desk at work, is that right?'

'Yes, it appears he left it behind. I assume that's natural behaviour for someone who wants to go missing, even though we have no idea why,' Laurel stated with a solemn shake of her head.

Stevenson nodded and made a note. 'And you'd not noticed any changes in your husband's behaviour prior to him going missing?'

Bernadette looked hesitant. 'No.' She paused, her gaze dropped to her hands and she began to wring them anxiously. 'Well, not really...'

Laurel rolled her eyes elaborately at this point before making a mouth-zipping gesture with her fingers, which he chose to ignore.

Stevenson again nodded at Bernadette to encourage her to elaborate. 'He had been quieter than usual, but I just thought he was tired. He's not been sleeping well the last week or so; he's been up pacing at all hours. He's even been a bit snappy which isn't like him. He works so hard, though, too hard, so I just thought it was that.'

'Does Trevor have any mental health problems or addictions that may have been a catalyst for why he left?' Sean asked.

Bernadette shook her head. 'What about friends. Does he

have much of a social life? Could he have become embroiled in something by a third party?'

Again, Bernadette shook her head. 'He's not like that although I am worried that he's involved in something he can't cope with though. That's why he was so angry when I told him I'd reported him missing, it shows he's scared of something or someone. I just don't know what.'

'Tell me about him,' Stevenson urged.

Bernadette smiled. 'He's a quiet but complex man. He's a thinker too, my Trevor. When he's home he's always working away, busy at his computer.'

'His computer?'

'Oh yes. He has one in the study upstairs. It's the box room really, but I always think it sounds a bit posher to call it the study.'

'What sort of things is he interested in?'

'He's in the Masons, so that takes up a lot of his time. There's a lot of learning and rehearsing scripture. Mother says he's always had an enquiring mind since he was a little boy. He's very, very clever. Not like me.' She grinned inanely whilst Laurel pouted so severely it looked like she had a clapper board wedged in her mouth.

The smile fell from her face as her eyes sunk towards the floor. She looked confused again and it was as if the conversation had drained her. 'I honestly can't think of anything else to tell you. I just don't know why he's gone. I don't understand any of it. I can't think why he'd leave home, why he'd leave me and his mother, she's in such a state without him.'

'Right.' Stevenson stood up and straightened his unwrinkled tie.

'Thanks for your time, ladies. If you can think of anything else that might help us find Trevor, then please do give me a call.' He extended his card towards Bernadette, but Laurel's cerise talons intercepted it. 'If he does return home again or gets in touch, let us know straight away.'

Bernadette's eyes suddenly brimmed with tears. 'You will find him for me, won't you, Mr Stevenson. Please bring my Trevor home.'

'We're doing our very best, Mrs Dawlish.' Stevenson paused for a moment. 'Could I just have a quick look in the study you mentioned.'

Bernadette nodded, crying too hard now to be able to speak. She merely gestured towards the stairs. Stevenson headed up the floral staircase, inching past the stairlift at the top. A quick peep through the first door revealed a chintz-covered bedroom, with puffed headboard and a ridiculous abundance of cushions and soft toys – teddies and rabbits clutching love hearts.

He padded softly towards the built-in wardrobes. There was an obvious gap in the collection of male clothes, but a sufficient amount remained. Did that mean Trevor was planning on returning soon or just hadn't had time to pack everything?

Adjacent, Mother Dawlish's bedroom was evident by the sound of snoring that drifted through the gap in the door. At the end of the landing lay the 'office', its door clamped shut. Stevenson had to strain the door open against the thick resistance of carpet. A computer sat on a large desk which faced the door.

A battered office chair had its back to the window. Shelves were lined with all manner of books, from engineering manuals to encyclopaedias, science books and computing and an abundance of books about the Masons. Quite an array for a man who worked as a janitor.

Stevenson sank into the chair and surveyed the room, tapping his lips with his forefinger as he tried to get a sense of the kind of man Trevor was. Looking down, he noticed a pair of cabinets tucked under the desk, either side of the chair. He tried each door, but they were locked. He fished around for a key, searching the pen holders which stood neatly on the uncluttered desk, but there was no sign. Curious.

What was so important to Trevor Dawlish that he kept it under lock and key?

7

Marcus Naylor, Maya's estranged father, returned to his cell in C-wing of HMP Ranby with a sense of relief and optimism. Since his parole hearing had been approved, he was praying that it would only be a matter of time before he was released on licence. He thanked God, quite literally, for every day since he had arrived here from the more ominous HMP Nottingham. It had offered him more normality and a sense of freedom that he hadn't realised he had been craving so desperately. He had been incarcerated and institutionalised for so long that he had conditioned himself to dismiss any thoughts of release.

He had first thought of life outside prison after seeing Maya at a crime scene. The footage had made the news after the journalist, Dave Wainwright, had interviewed Maya about comments she had made when she assumed he was a detective. Despite not seeing her since she was a child, Naylor would have recognised her anywhere. She was the epitome of her mother, Dominique.

Naylor washed his face in the little sink and stood back to survey his reflection. Since moving to Ranby, he had become more involved in educational activities and eased off the gym. As a result, his physique looked toned and athletic. Previously his pumped-up muscles looked imposing and added to his intimidating demeanour. He had grown his hair to cover the map of scars on his head, and despite the silver strands, the effect made him look, if not younger, certainly softer.

He smiled to himself as a sense of well-being consumed him. For the first time in so many years he was at peace. Despite being incarcerated he was high on life, whereas years ago he would have been high on drugs or alcohol. He felt clean. Lighter. So much more aware.

He realised how much he missed his family. On the day of his sentencing, he had told them he neither wanted to see or hear from them. He could only countenance doing his time if he forgot about the outside world. Now, he regretted it. Especially the thought of his now elderly mother. He hated the amount of stress and pain he had caused for her. And there was Anthony. The older brother he had revered. So many years had passed, and he still missed their friendship. Naylor knew he would never be able to build bridges with Maya and Dominique, he just wanted them to know he was no longer a threat to them.

He shook his head, ridding it of any negative thoughts and smiled again. He moved to his desk and scooped up his Bible. He pressed his lips briefly to the leather-bound cover and hugged it to his chest. He left his cell with a spring in his step, nodding to one of the wardens as he made his way towards the prison chapel. Marcus Naylor was a man on a mission, he was going to rebuild his life once he was released and nothing was going to stop him.

8

After spotting the broken hyoid, Dr Granger had continued the post-mortem and confirmed death by strangulation. He had praised Maya on recognising the signs of petechial haemorrhaging in the cadaver's eyes, however slight due to decomposition. There were no other apparent injuries, but the state of decomposition certainly masked any potential soft-tissue wounds. Granger had confirmed that the numerous broken bones in the foot and ankle had been caused after death.

Once the post-mortem was over, with the assistance of Sue from the Fingerprint Bureau, they had managed to obtain a full set of inked tenprints which would be autoclaved to sterilise them, before searching them against IDENT1 in the hope of obtaining a match. If the deceased were on the database, it was hoped they would have a confirmed identification by the following day. The canal towpath, which had been kept as a crime scene, had been thoroughly checked by specialist search officers from the Tactical Aid Unit.

SOCO Nicola Warne had also attended in anticipation of being able to record and recover any pertinent evidence. It was such a fast-moving body of water, there was no indication that

43

the cadaver had entered at the point he had been recovered from. He could have been dumped at any point elsewhere along the winding stretches of canal. DI Redford had appointed DC Adila Laghari with the arduous task of searching for potential CCTV along the route.

Maya and Chris had returned to the office exhausted after their stint at the mortuary. Elaine was on the late shift but was already out at a job and once again, Kym was in the office frantically trying to juggle, amongst other things, a desperately understaffed rota.

'Fancy coming back to mine for some food. I don't mind cooking, or we can share a takeaway if you prefer?' Maya asked Chris, whose pale, drained face mirrored her own exhaustion. Despite the tiredness, she was still consumed with thoughts of the post-mortem as she pondered relentlessly over who the deceased might be and why he had been strangled.

He gave her a weak smile. 'No thanks, love. I've got a very quick statement to do before I finish tonight.'

'You're choosing a statement over food? And after a post-mortem, too, they always make you hungry afterwards, you meat-eating bastard.' She raised an eyebrow in his direction, hoping he would change his mind so they could spend a bit longer discussing the case.

'Yeah, I know.' He gave a dry laugh. 'It's overdue, that's all. If I get it finished now, then there's less to do tomorrow.'

'Okay, fair enough. I'll see you in the morning,' she said, trying not to sound too despondent.

Maya called goodnight to Elaine and Kym before she left. Normally, after such a busy day, the thought of climbing on her Triumph Bonneville and riding home would be a source of therapy for her. Tonight, though, as she stepped out into the car park and felt the first pinches of biting wind, she shuddered.

It wasn't just the cold; she had a sense of foreboding that she couldn't place. The thought of going home alone didn't appeal. She tried to shrug the feeling off, she always felt out of sorts after being at the mortuary and she knew it was frustration about not being able to talk about the body. She considered riding to Dominique's on the way home. Time with her mother always helped. Just as she pulled her helmet on, her phone chirruped. A message from Spence. She grinned as she read it, marvelling at the fact he always seemed to know just the right time to message her.

It was just a general message asking how she was and wondering if she was free to meet up sometime. He worked at The Eagle pub a stone's throw away from Maya's apartment, and had even, several weeks ago, moved into the accommodation above the pub since securing the permanent bar manager's position. They had once grown close romantically, but Maya had experienced a trauma at work, she had witnessed a murder-suicide, which had led to her having to take time off work. Spence had supported her while she had received counselling and they had settled into a platonic relationship.

Maya was still attracted to Spence but had shared so much with him about her past, she worried that he was no longer attracted to her. Did he see her as damaged and flawed? His job and her shifts meant that they didn't spend as much time together as they once had.

Perhaps now was the chance to readdress that and to explore the fact that if there was still something between them, it needed to happen before it was too late. There was a risk that the longevity of their friendship remained the priority over any potential romance. Feeling decisive, she grinned to herself as she responded, letting him know she'd grab a quick bite to eat and drop in the pub to see him. Many a time she had propped up the bar and kept him company while he served customers.

She rode home feeling buoyed and was fed and ready in no

time. She appraised her reflection before she left. Late twenties, she was tall and slim. She had honeycomb-coloured skin and a swathe of dark-brown corkscrew curls that hung below her shoulders. She applied a slick of lip gloss, and a final squirt of perfume before heading for The Eagle. It was busy for a Wednesday night and her heart sunk slightly at the prospect. Busy meant that she wouldn't see as much of Spence as she wanted. Still, she couldn't stay late anyway as she was on earlies the following day.

She grinned as she spotted Spence. He was draped across the bar chatting to a group of women. He was dressed casually in a navy polo shirt with orange trim, a hint of tattoo showing just below the sleeve. His dark, wavy hair was gelled back, and his electric-blue eyes flashed as he chatted back animatedly. Spotting her as she approached him, Spence gave Maya a huge grin and blew a kiss. He raised his hand indicating he'd be a couple of minutes.

She settled herself at her usual spot at the end of the bar. Lisa Cohen, who worked with Spence, came over carrying an array of empty glasses.

'Hey, stranger. He'll be pleased to see you.' Lisa smiled, nodding in Spence's direction.

'You think? He looks like he's enjoying himself over there,' Maya replied wryly as she glanced in Spence's direction. One of the women, wearing a plastic tiara, was squeezing his bicep and laughing raucously. She was clearly flirting, and Spence appeared to be enjoying every minute.

Lisa shook her head. 'It's just work. The happier the customer, the bigger the tips. Apparently, they're celebrating a birthday and have money to burn. I'll go and take over. What can I get you to drink?'

Maya asked for a Diet Coke and watched as Lisa approached the party. She said something to Spence and nodded towards

Maya as she skilfully squeezed herself in at the bar, and began admiring one of the women's manicures. Spence poured a Diet Coke and handed it to Maya, leaning to kiss her cheek as he did so.

'You're a sight for sore eyes. How's things?'

'Good thanks. Work's been busy but interesting. How are you?'

'I'm good. We were having a quiet shift until this lot waded in,' he said, grinning towards the group. Lisa had turned the music up and they were now gyrating to Beyoncé.

'Do you not want something stronger?' he asked, nodding towards her drink.

'No, thanks. I'm on a day shift tomorrow. You can tempt me another time,' she said with a lascivious grin.

'Actually, I've been meaning to say...' He was interrupted mid-sentence as the birthday girl reached for Spence's hand, insisting he dance with her. He smiled apologetically at Maya as he was whipped away and joined in the group of partygoers. Maya sighed and sipped at her drink feeling like a spare part. She busied herself on her phone, deciding to text her mother, Dominique, rather than watching Spence gyrating against a beautiful woman. Even she wasn't that thick-skinned.

After what felt like an age, the song ended and Spence disappeared back behind the bar, priming a bottle of champagne and a tray of glasses. Maya attempted to catch his eye but was suddenly met with the full onslaught of the birthday girl as she swayed in front of her.

'Hiya, sorry to bother you, I'm Helen.'

'Hi, Helen, happy birthday. I hope you're enjoying yourself?'

'I am, thanks,' she slurred. 'I just wanted to ask you about Spence.'

'What about him?'

'I just wanted to check I wasn't stepping on any toes. I saw

47

you kiss when you came in. He says you're just friends, though, right? I just thought I'd double-check, though, you know what men can be like, right?'

'Erm, yeah. Friends. If that's what he... Sorry, Helen, what did he actually say?'

'That you weren't his type, and you were just good friends. That there was nothing going on between you.'

Despite the Diet Coke, Maya's throat felt dry, and she struggled to swallow. Shame engulfed her like a wave. 'Yes, exactly that. Like he said, we're just friends.'

'So, you wouldn't mind if I made a move on him?'

It took a gargantuan effort to plaster a grin on her face. 'Go for your life, he's a free agent.'

The birthday girl squealed as she flicked her hair at Maya before returning to her friends. Spence was carefully placing the tray on a table in the middle of them all when she flung her arms around his neck and ground her mouth against his. Maya couldn't watch as Spence's arm wrapped around the woman.

Her face burnt with embarrassment at the thought of Spence's words. She fished about in her purse for money for the drink. She threw money on the bar and left The Eagle, head down, ignoring the tears that pricked her eyes.

9

Dominique Barton was a tall, black woman with close-cropped hair that accentuated her bone structure. She was an attractive woman, and it was clear to anyone who met her that Maya had inherited her looks. She kicked her shoes off in the hall as she returned home after a busy shift. She scooped down to collect the post before heading into the kitchen and switching on the lights before clicking on the kettle.

She hated the autumn months, the way the cold and damp felt as though it would seep through to her bone marrow. She gazed out of the kitchen window watching the rain pouring like tears down the glass. The waterproof cover that protected the patio furniture was being tugged at by the wind. The sight of it made her shiver. She wondered whether Maya fancied taking a week off work and booking a holiday somewhere hot for a bit of winter sun.

She poured boiling water on a teabag, leaving it to stew as she turned her attention to the post. The usual Matalan brochure, insurance renewal and a formal-looking envelope. She reached for a knife to slice it open and felt her blood run cold at the sight of the familiar headed paper. It was from the

Victim Contact Scheme, part of the probation service. They were writing to advise her that Marcus Naylor's application for parole had been successful and his release was imminent.

She threw the letter from her, as if it were on fire. She closed her eyes, fighting back tears. It wasn't a complete shock. She had known this was coming several weeks ago when a letter from Marcus himself had scuttled across the hall mat. Now she could no longer bury her head in the sand. She needed to tell Maya he was going to be released. Hands shaking, she tipped the tea down the sink and reached for the gin.

10

It was only when Maya arrived at work the following morning, she remembered there was an office meeting. She was running late, which was out of character for her, but she'd struggled to sleep the night before. After leaving The Eagle she'd lain awake, blocking out all thoughts of Spence and instead wondering if they'd missed any clues from where the body had been pulled from the canal. She was consumed with thoughts about John Doe as she wondered who he was and how he had come into possession of Trevor Dawlish's bank card.

Had Dawlish killed him and was that the reason he had left home? She also thought how sad it was that he'd clearly been in the water some time but nobody had reported him missing. As a result, it had taken an age to fall asleep, and when she eventually did, she slept fitfully, plagued by disturbing dreams that haunted her long after she'd woken.

She mumbled her apologies to Kym and the others. Amanda Mayhew, the office administrator, welcomed Maya with a wink and gestured to the chair next to hers, where a hot drink was waiting.

'Everything okay?' Kym asked over the top of her glasses. She was perched on the edge of the desk like a vulture.

'Yes, I had a bad night and overslept. Sorry again.'

'Hmm. Well, you've not missed anything. Just the usual reminder to make sure you follow the weekly and monthly van and equipment checks. I've emailed you all with the dates for your next UKAS assessments so please be prepared, and while I remember, we're late with the environmental swabbing in the consumables room so can we please make that a priority?'

'Moving on to recruitment...' The dramatic pause and wry smile on Kym's face caused everyone to straighten up in anticipation. 'You'll be pleased to know top office has finally filled our vacancy.'

There was a collective cheer.

'There not sending us a newbie, though, are they?' grumbled Elaine. 'Not being funny, but we've not got time to train someone. We need someone who's ready to go or we're no better off.'

Chris and Nicola mumbled agreement, while Maya and Connor stayed quiet. As the newest recruit to the team, Maya couldn't comment. Connor was a volume crime-scene investigator, which meant he currently only attended burglaries. He had shadowed the others at more serious scenes, though, and had expressed an interest in attending more serious incidents once a vacancy arose.

'Don't worry, I'd already argued that point. It's someone who's been on the transfer request list for a while and is very experienced.' Kym pulled a face.

'What's that look for?' Chris leaned forward in his chair; an eyebrow arched in Kym's direction. 'Who are we getting, boss?'

Uncharacteristically, Kym gave a nervous cough, unable to look anyone in the eye before she answered. 'Tara Coleman from Pine Grove,' she finally informed the top of the desk.

There was a collective groan. Even Amanda tutted, and she rarely had a bad word to say about anyone.

'Who is this Tara?' Maya asked, intrigued.

'You must have heard of her,' Chris replied incredulously.

Maya shook her head.

'Not even when you worked at Alder Street?' asked Nicola.

'No, but I'm dying to know. What's wrong with her?'

Kym interjected any potential responses by giving her customary double clap. She straightened up and eyed the group with a steely expression. 'I'm aware Tara's reputation for being somewhat of a... Let us just say her personality precedes her, but the fact remains she will be coming to work here. She moved early last year and has been on the transfer list since then so she can work closer to home.'

Nicola opened her mouth to comment but was silenced by a raise of Kym's hand.

'As with every new member of staff, she will be greeted warmly and treated with respect. Although she's not new to the job, we all know it can be difficult to adjust to the dynamics of a new office environment, but I'm confident we will all pull together to make her feel welcome.'

'Maya!' Kym said with a clap. 'As the newest member to the team, I'm putting you in charge of helping Tara settle in. Show her around the station, equipment stores, etc. I'm sure you'll get on like a house on fire.'

Maya ignored the pitying sidelong looks from the others as Kym continued to ramble on about staffing and movements.

'Which brings me to the fact there will be a force-wide vacancy for an enhanced crime-scene investigator.' Kym beamed wildly in Connor's direction. 'This obviously means you have a chance to apply.'

Connor reddened at the mention, but Chris clapped him avuncularly on the back. 'Let's get working on that application, matey. I'm sure between us we can all think of enough suitable lies and waffle to get you through to interview stage.'

'Yeah, just don't mention the time you fingerprinted a car at the garage that was in for a service and not an outstanding stolen.' Elaine laughed.

'Or the time you exhibited and packaged your own mobile phone instead of the offender's!' Nicola's remark was met with a two-fingered salute from Connor. The meeting threatened to descend into banter and chaos until a phone call interrupted the team. Efficient as ever, Amanda answered before extending the receiver to Maya.

'It's Sue from Fingerprints asking for you or Chris, she's got an update on Operation Mermaid,' she mouthed.

'Oh, fantastic!' Maya reached for pen and paper as she took the phone from Amanda. She listened intently as she doodled away, before thanking Sue and hanging up.

Chris looked at her hopefully. 'Well?'

Maya shook her head and held up the paper where she'd doodled a question mark, surrounded by asterisks.

'Our John Doe's not on the system.' The frustration in her voice was unmistakable. 'We're still no closer to knowing who he is.'

11

Jack had arrived at work that morning eager to settle into his new office as Acting DI. His initial enthusiasm at finally having his own space waned when he saw that the door was not yet adorned with his name plaque. Instead, admin had seen fit to crudely laminate an A4 piece of paper endorsed with his name and collar number. *Bloody cutbacks.* It looked cheap and amateurish, and if he wasn't mistaken, the word 'Acting' was in a slightly larger font than the rest of his title.

He swore under his breath at the slight, then cheered as he nudged open the door and was greeted with the sight of his large imposing desk and chair. His predecessor, Alison Mitton, had kept the office in a state of what she used to call 'organised chaos'. Haphazard piles of paperwork had been separated with gaudy seashell paperweights. The desk was often marred by coffee stains and littered with crumpled Post-it notes and scraps of paper.

He smiled to himself as he looked at the freshly vacated office. The empty bookcase and desk awaited his presence. He pushed open the window, letting in the fresh autumn breeze, imagining he was releasing years' worth of odour from Alison's stale ready meals and cheap instant coffee. He placed his box of belongings down, ready to unpack at his leisure. He was pleased to see there were folders already waiting his attention. DS Mark Turner, once the same rank but now technically his subordinate, had clearly been busy the previous evening.

'Settling in?' Jack looked up to see Maya stood in the doorway.

'Yes thanks.'

'I just came to tell you that we've had a call from Sue in the Fingerprint Bureau. Our John Doe isn't on the database. I'm going to review the photographs I took and see if there's anything we may have overlooked at the scene. His clothing is currently in the forensic drying cabinet, but it'll take a few days until they're ready for removing.'

'What are the chances of us getting anything from the clothing due to how long he was in the water?'

'Slim to be fair. I've been thinking about the bank card. Trevor Dawlish looks to be the most likely suspect, doesn't he?'

Jack shrugged. 'Too early to say. He's certainly a person of interest. Sean has been to speak to the wife and a neighbour, but we're no closer to tracking him down.'

'Well, it certainly looks like you've got some investigating to do. A baptism of fire in your new job.'

Jack nodded primly and straightened his tie. 'Thanks for the update, leave it with me.'

Maya nodded and left the office. Sighing, Jack sat back in the chair and rubbed his eyes. His earlier enthusiasm waned as the enormity of his new role struck him for the first time and he realised he was out of his depth. Still, he was a great believer in the expression 'fake it till you make it'. He'd keep any trepidation he felt to himself, nobody needed to know how daunting his new promotion felt. Least of all Maya Barton.

12

Spence was sat at the bar, sipping a hot coffee and enjoying a moment of serenity. He loved this time just before opening. It was good to have the place to himself, the calm before the storm. The cleaner had just left so the place was spotless and sweet-smelling. For once it was quiet and peaceful other than the occasional jingling sound emanating from the games machine. Everything was prepped ready for the first customers. His regulars, who he and Lisa referred to as the barflies, were usually through the door within five minutes of opening and were quite demanding.

He toyed with his phone, thinking of Maya. He had texted her to ask why she'd disappeared without saying goodbye the other night. She had said she was tired, but that was out of character for her. He suspected he was being fobbed off.

He ran his fingers through his thick, wavy hair. He recalled what Helen, the persistent birthday girl had said to him, and his heart sunk to his soles. Buoyed by alcohol, she had demanded a birthday kiss. He had to put an arm around her to steady her as she ground her mouth against his. He had resisted and declined as politely as he could, removing her face from his as he looked round, frantic to see if Maya had witnessed the exchange.

She had drunkenly purred that it was okay. She had seen his earlier exchange with Maya and had been to speak to her to make sure there was nothing going on between the two of them. She told him that Maya had reassured her that she had no interest in Spence. Not like *that*.

That had come as a shock to Spence, as he had hoped they were more than just friends. For a while now he had become frustrated by the fact their relationship hadn't progressed and was beginning to worry that Maya was no longer attracted to him. He decided he would find out once and for all and text her.

Would be good if we could meet up soon. Maybe tonight? Talk about how things stand between us. Or not... x

He needed to know once and for all how things stood between them. He wasn't going to hang around like a lovesick puppy waiting to be kicked. If she wasn't interested, then he needed to know so he could get over her and move on.

He was broken from his reverie by a banging on the door. Startled, he checked his watch and realised he was ten minutes late opening up.

'Shit,' he muttered as he ran to the door. Swinging it open he was met with the flushed, meaty faces of two of the barflies. They were huddled against the wind and did not look happy.

'You're bloody late,' the younger one grumbled as he bulldozed past Spence into the pub, carrying in the chill air. The older one prodded a finger in Spence's chest, a wry, all-knowing expression on his face. 'Here's a life lesson for you, cocker, you snooze you lose.'

Yes, thought Spence. It was beginning to look like that was exactly what he had done.

13

Oakwood was a large, detached house on the leafy Byron Lane. Even with a satnav it had taken an age to find, mainly because neither name nor number of the property was adequately displayed. This was always frustrating. If the homeowner ever needed the emergency services urgently, the assistance could be hampered by not being able to locate the correct address.

Maya had eventually arrived at the property by chance after driving up the same road several times. She had pulled over, deciding to phone Amanda in the office and ask if she was familiar with the place and if she could give her directions. Despite the rain battering the van window, Maya could make out a sign hidden below an overhanging evergreen which was being lifted by the wind.

Bracing herself against the horrendous autumnal weather, Maya had reluctantly peeled herself away from the warmth of the van to read the tarnished plaque which stated this was indeed Oakwood. The wind and rain pushed and pulled her as she buzzed the intercom and waited at the electric gates. After what felt like an age, the gate swung open, and Maya heaved her kit up the azalea-lined drive.

A man appeared at the front door. Early sixties, he was tall and slim, wearing chinos and a khaki gilet over a long-sleeved cream shirt. He had grey hair cropped close to his head and an impeccably trimmed goatee beard. He was scowling as Maya approached. Dropping her kit, she reached for her lanyard and ID.

'Mr Hanford? I'm SOCO Maya Barton from Beech Field police station.'

He barely acknowledged her ID as he glowered at her, still eyeing the driveway. 'It's *Councillor* Hanford,' he growled. 'Are you on your own? I was expecting a man.'

'My apologies, Councillor. I am on my own. Would you mind showing me where the offenders got in and what they've touched?' Despite the wind stinging her cheeks and the homeowner's pompous air, she was determined to remain professional and not allow herself to be riled.

'I was expecting you hours ago.'

'I do apologise, we've been really busy today. Perhaps I could make a start now I'm here?'

Grumbling incoherently, he gestured for her to follow him in, demanding she wipe her boots properly on the mat first. He took her through to an expansive lounge with huge sash windows. The room was adorned with expensive antique furniture, figurines and paintings. In pride of place on the wall in the middle of the room was a tapestry depicting a square and compass which Maya recognised as representing the Masons.

'They've jemmied the window here.' Hanford gesticulated to the splintered wood. 'They've taken an iPad off the sofa then come through to here.' Maya trailed behind him as he marched her down a wood-panelled, ornate hallway into a farmhouse-style kitchen.

'There was a mobile phone and my wallet next to the fruit bowl. I had approximately £150 in cash in that drawer. The keys were in the kitchen door, and they've used them to let themselves out.' He puffed his chest like a pigeon. 'Bloody idiots are clearly clueless. You could pay a chunk of your mortgage off with some of the furniture and ornaments in this house.'

Maya nodded. 'They don't tend to be that sophisticated. They want cash or small items like jewellery that they can pocket and sell on. Usually, vehicles too, if they get lucky. I'd guess your electric gates have deterred them from taking your car. Have they been upstairs?'

'No, they've obviously not wanted to chance it with me being in bed,' he growled. 'You lot would have been carrying them out in a body bag if they had. I'll be up on a murder charge if I get my hands on the thieving bastards. I bet you'd turn up on time then, wouldn't you, eh?'

Maya ignored the comment, she'd heard similar too many times for it to necessitate a reply, instead she informed him she'd start examining the lounge window.

Oblivious of her need for personal space, he hovered over her and watched closely while she opened her fingerprint kit. 'Do you know what you're doing?'

'Yes, Councillor,' she replied with as much dignity as she could muster.

'That torch doesn't look right.'

'I can assure you it's more than fit for purpose.'

Maya continued her examination regardless of the continued criticism. There was no chance of enhancing any footwear marks due to the thick, heavily patterned carpet below the point of entry. She was about to inform him that glove marks were evident on both the glass and the window frame when her mobile phone began to ring from the confines of her trouser pocket.

'I hope you're not going to answer that,' he said, tutting.

Maya began to explain about the glove marks when the sound of a voicemail message chirruped from her phone, which she also ignored.

'What about outside?'

'I'm going to search out there for any evidence, but I can't fingerprint the exterior point of entry because of the wet weather. The powder obviously doesn't work on wet surfaces.'

'Well, what about the kitchen drawer. And the door...'

'I'm afraid there's nothing I can do with the handles because they're such a small surface area and regularly touched. The same applies to the keys.'

'Shouldn't you be looking for fibres or something?'

'That would only be relevant if we had an offender in custody and we'd been able to seize their clothing.'

'Oh, for Christ's sake, girl, stop making bloody excuses,' he blustered. 'I'm fully aware of the type of forensic examples you people can recover, I've watched enough episodes of *CSI*. I could probably teach *you* a thing or two. What about a paint sample from the window frame, or a tool cast?'

'Again, that's only useful if we have a tool to compare against, which unfortunately we haven't.'

It wasn't the first time a member of the public had questioned Maya's competency whilst she was working. The CSI effect was a result of the exaggerated portrayal of crime-scene investigation on crime shows, which influenced the public's perception so much so, it even had negative connotations on jurors.

Councillor Hanford's face was growing puce, and whilst Maya had every sympathy for him being a victim of crime, his inability to listen was beginning to grate.

'Perhaps, sir, if I could offer some crime prevention advice...'

'I don't need patronising by a slip of a girl like you,' he

hollered. Unfortunately, at that moment Maya's phone chirruped with a text message. 'Especially not one that can't get off her bloody phone. That's what's wrong with your generation, always got your bloody faces in a screen with no regard for what is going on around you.'

He was clearly working himself up to a full-blown, clearly well-rehearsed rant now and Maya tried to interject.

'Councillor Hanford, if I could just...'

He raised a hand to silence her, causing her to clench her jaw in annoyance.

'When will the policeman be here?' he demanded.

'Hopefully soon. There are a number of incidents ongoing at the moment. Patrols are currently dealing with a serious car accident and a violent domestic as well as trying to locate a suicidal male.'

If looks could kill, Maya would be stone dead there and then. The councillor glowered at her, his mouth quivering with rage.

'All I've heard from you is excuses. It's not bloody good enough. I can't believe they've dared to send me an incompetent bloody female.'

'I agree. It's not good enough. Something needs to be done.'

'Excuse me?' Hanford hesitated, momentarily perturbed by her response.

'Government need to recognise that the police are desperately under-resourced and overworked. That we don't have enough people to do the job we love effectively. The forensic branch lost forty per cent of its staff a few years ago. Where was your outrage then?

'Where is your outrage when police officers are working at dangerously low numbers and are being sent single-crewed, to violent incidents which then leaves them vulnerable and at risk of being seriously injured. Perhaps you didn't know. Well, you do now and as a local councillor, that's something you need to start taking responsibility for and feed back to the local authority. If there's nothing else I can help you with, I'll show myself out.'

He slammed the front door so hard she could hear the windows rattle as she carried herself down the driveway.

Maya climbed back into the van and took a few calming breaths before she began to write up her job sheet. She had three more burglaries to attend before she could head back to the office and see if there was any update in the investigation into John Doe's murder. She desperately hoped there would be as the lack of progress so far was incredibly frustrating for all involved in the case.

Before she started the engine, she reached for her phone and smiled to see she'd missed a call from Dominique. She listened to the voicemail message and was perturbed to detect a note of worry behind her mother's overly cheery message.

'Hi, love. Hope you're having a good day. Nothing to worry about, but if you get a chance, could you call round on your way home tonight? Okay. That's all. Bye then.'

Frowning, Maya listened to the call again. Despite her words, the tone of Dominique's voice indicated she was clearly worried about something. She tried to call back, but the phone went to voicemail, which wasn't unusual. Dominique worked as a district nurse, so like Maya, couldn't always pick up. Maya sent a text to let her know she'd call after work.

Then she read the text Spence sent her:

Would be good if we could meet up soon. Maybe tonight? Talk about how things stand between us. Or not... x

She felt like she'd been winded. She closed her eyes and sat back in the driving seat. The memory of Spence and Helen the birthday girl was incredibly vivid. She could see them together, Spence wrapping his arm around her and then...

She shook her head, ridding herself of the image. It was too much. Too painful. And what did this text mean? She didn't have the time to catastrophise over the meaning of the message. It was clear he was going to tell her he was seeing someone. That there was no longer any chance of them being an 'us'.

Stoically, she composed a reply.

Sorry. Can't tonight, got something else on.

Her main concern right now was whatever Dominique wanted to talk about. She was worried that something serious was amiss. That had to be her priority. Meeting Spence to be officially told that he had no romantic intentions towards her could wait. And ideally, it could wait a lifetime. There were some words she never wanted to hear.

14

'It's your dad... sorry... Marcus. The probation service have written to me. There's no easy way to tell you this, so I'll just come out and say it.' Dominique took a deep breath and closed her eyes. 'He's due to be released soon.'

The words she had dreaded for years – the ones she never wanted to hear, hung in the air like a noxious gas.

Maya shook her head. 'No.'

'I'm sorry, love. I know this isn't easy.' Dominique took another deep breath. 'I was as shocked as you are. But there'll be rules. He'll not be able to–'

'NO!' Maya repeated.

She stood, swaying slightly as she steadied herself with a hand on the table. 'I'm sorry, Mama. I can't deal with this right now.' She dropped a kiss on Dominique's cheek.

'I'll ring you. I just need time.' Maya fled down the garden path, flinching as a flurry of fireworks exploded over head. The bangs caused her frayed nerves to heighten even more; her hands shaking as she pulled on her gloves and helmet.

She caught a final glimpse of Dominique standing on the doorstep looking concerned. Not for the first time, Maya was struck by how much she reminded her of her late grandad. As always, her heart ached with loss for the man she had loved so much.

In thinking of him, she was also reminded of how much pain and hurt Marcus Naylor had inflicted on the old man. Naylor was evil and the mere thought of him made Maya feel tainted and repulsed. She felt an emotional pull towards her mother. She wanted to run back to her. To allow Dominique to soothe and comfort her and reassure her that everything would be okay. But the mention of Naylor had opened a chasm between them.

She fired up the ignition and without giving Dominique her usual last wave goodbye, she accelerated away from the house with reckless abandon, determined to outrun the memory of the demon that lived in her mind.

15

Laurel was in her front room, polishing the pristine window ledge as she listened to breakfast television. She glanced out of the bay window at her front garden and tutted at the sight of even more leaves. She had only cleared a pile up the previous day and the compost bin was already nearly full. She despised autumn; it was such a messy time of year. She thought of Trevor and her heart sank. Clearing the leaves was normally the kind of job he'd help her out with. She missed him terribly and still couldn't fathom why he'd gone missing.

Hadn't she always made it clear she was a good listener? It wasn't as if he could share any worries with his mother. The poor dear was away with the fairies half the time. As for Bernadette, she wasn't much different; she was simple-minded and weak. She stood gazing out of the window, consumed by thoughts of Trevor, when suddenly, she caught a flash of movement from across the road. She took a sharp intake of breath, stunned. It was him, Trevor. It was as if she'd summoned him with her thoughts!

He'd slipped out of the garden gate at the side of the house and was headed towards the path that led to the back of the estate. From there, she knew he could pick up several other avenues, or even follow the path that led down to the canal. He had a rucksack slung over his shoulder and his hood was pulled up, partially shielding his face, but not enough to disguise the fact it was definitely him.

She tore the front door open, screaming his name. Regardless of the fact her slippers were soaking up autumnal mulch, she stumbled across the road. Neither her body nor her footwear were made for running. By the time she'd made it to the path, there was no sign of him. She pounded the top of her legs in annoyance as her eyes darted everywhere and she continued to call his name.

Frustrated, her sodden feet carried her back to the Dawlish's, soles slapping as she walked. She rang the doorbell impatiently. After several moments of no response, she rattled the letter box flap and pounded on the front door for good measure. Bernadette eventually appeared, wrapped in an oversized, fluffy, unicorn dressing gown, looking as dim-witted as ever.

'Darling, what did he say? Where's he gone now?' Laurel bustled into the hallway, nearly bowling Bernadette over and walking wet footprints down the hall.

'What did who say?'

'Trevor, of course. Who on earth do you think I meant?'

Bernadette shook her head stupidly and it was all Laurel could do not to slap some sense into her.

'I've just seen him. I saw him walk out through the side gate and cut through to the back of the estate.' Laurel gestured wildly to the door. 'I tried to catch up with him. I shouted his name but he... he... oh, he's gone again.'

Laurel slumped across the hall table despondently. 'Where were you? How did you not hear him come in? Were you even up?'

Bernadette flushed at Laurel's accusing tone. 'Yes, of course I was up. It's the pills. They make me so drowsy. I must have nodded off on the couch...'

'Check in the kitchen and upstairs. See if he's taken or left anything. The police will need to know.'

Laurel trailed behind her into the kitchen. Trevor's brown leather wallet lay forgotten on the Formica worktop.

'His wallet, look; he must have been in a rush.' Laurel tutted.

Bernadette reached for it. She opened it up and looked at the two ten-pound notes inside, before showing it to Laurel. 'He won't have any money now,' she muttered desolately.

'Which means he'll have to come back for it, darling, that's something, at least. Leave it there for him,' Laurel said buoyantly.

Bernadette padded mutely to the kitchen door, which was pushed to, but not shut. She sighed and rested her head against the door before softly clicking it shut. She held on to the handle a moment longer than necessary, as if clinging to her husband's hand.

Then she made her way up to her bedroom. Laurel followed behind, tutting as she inched past the stairlift – there was barely room for it on such a narrow stairway and she nearly always caught her leg on it when she had used the bathroom or on the few occasions when Rose had been laid up in bed. She had long since suggested it would be better if they moved Old Mrs Dawlish's bedroom downstairs and they had a wet room installed, but of course, neither Trevor nor Bernadette listened to her.

Bernadette was stood at her bedroom door frowning. Laurel peered over her shoulder into the obscenely chintz room. She tutted at the sight of the unmade bed and gestured for Bernadette to check the wardrobe. She watched as her neighbour swung the door open, before shaking her head mutely, tears beginning to well in her eyes.

'It looks like he's taken some more clothes. There are definitely a couple of jumpers missing.'

'What about his study?' Laurel suggested.

She began to follow Laurel down the landing, pausing at the sound of Rose Dawlish calling from her bedroom.

'I'll go,' said Laurel, leaving Bernadette to search the study.

Rose was propped against a mound of pillows, her white woolly head barely visible beneath the swathe of duvet. Laurel winced at the tang of unwashed skin and urine that permeated the air. Clearly Bernadette wasn't coping well with caring for her since Trevor's disappearance. Rose gave Laurel a huge gummy grin once she saw her. Laurel's stomach lurched at the sight of the old woman's familiar smile also beaming at her from a glass on the bedside table.

'It's Trevor,' Laurel explained. 'He's been back.'

Rose attempted to reply but it was unintelligible without her teeth. Laurel passed her the glass, then turned away discreetly as the old lady popped her gnashers back in. Just then Bernadette dashed in the room, dots of colour pinching her cheeks.

'He's been in one of his cabinets. One of the doors is open and it looks like something's missing, but I don't know what. I'm not really sure what he kept in there, it's always been his private place.' Bernadette was wringing her hands anxiously, waiting for Laurel to tell her what to do.

There was a mashing of gums before Rose spoke. 'Trevor!'

Laurel nodded. 'Yes, dear. I was just telling you.' She paused before elevating her voice more exaggeratedly, 'Trevor has been home.'

'Oh, I know.' Rose nodded to the armchair at the side of her bed. 'He popped in for a chat. I thought he was bringing my breakfast, he promised me he would.'

———

16

Kym Lawson reached for her cup, took a sip of coffee, and banged it back down on her desk frustratedly when she realised it was cold. She could have sworn Amanda had only just brought her the brew minutes ago. She wiped the splashes of spilt coffee on her pants, choosing to ignore the dribbles that marred the side of her desk. She didn't have the time or inclination to wipe it away. Glancing at the clock, she swore under her breath as she raked her fingers through her hair and continued to plough through the ceaseless chain of emails.

She could feel the familiar cramping in her stomach that signalled another bout of IBS. 'Fucking stress and mither,' she muttered under her breath as she continued to flick through the emails, chancing the ones she could delete without even reading, going off the predictable subject heading.

Her cramps intensified as she read a long-winded email from a member of the public who wanted to lodge an official complaint about one of her staff. She scribbled a note to herself to deal with it, before leaning back in her chair and taking a moment of calm. All the staff were due a performance review and she couldn't stand the thought of all the paperwork that entailed. It was also an opportunity for them to discuss any options for career development which would be futile as there wasn't enough money or resources to send people on courses or specialist conferences.

She glanced at the whiteboard which listed everyone's contact details. She pondered the list thoughtfully. She didn't need the Myers-Briggs test to categorise the personality of each individual, she knew them all too well. She smiled at the board as she thought of her staff. They weren't without their faults, God knows, neither was she, but she was lucky to have each and every one of them. They were a good team who worked like clockwork and supported each other. There were genuine close friendships amongst her team, and she was proud of the fact they were more than just colleagues.

'Have you got a minute?'

Her reverie was broken by the arrival of Jack who had suddenly appeared at her doorway.

'As long as it is only a minute, I'm up to my eyes in it. Please take a seat.' Kym winced as he sat on the chair, legs spread as he rolled up his sleeves to accentuate his muscular forearms. If this was a David Attenborough documentary, she thought, he'd be beating his chest and pissing on the desk to prove his masculinity.

'It's about the body Chris and Maya helped me recover from the canal.'

Kym opened her mouth to contradict the recovery process but decided she didn't have the energy.

'Ah, yes, Operation Mermaid. I believe we've drawn a blank on fingerprints and DNA.'

'Yes. I'm wondering what forensic opportunities we have left to identify him. I was thinking facial reconstruction and wondered how soon we could get the ball rolling with it.'

'Woah, Jack. Take a breath.' Kym raked her hand through

her hair again. 'There's a huge cost implication involved in facial reconstruction. It would have to be approved by top office and you've a long way to go before it's even considered.'

Jack puffed out his cheeks. 'You're saying no?'

'No, listen to me. I'm saying you need to exhaust *other* lines of enquiry first.'

He raised a questioning eyebrow and her stomach cramped again, momentarily taking her breath away before she could carry on. 'Have John Doe's dental records been checked against all our current missings? Has he got any tattoos or scars – any identifying features at all that could be used to identify him? Did Dr Granger identify any operations he may have had that we can make enquiries about? Consider another press release appealing for information. Check the clothing – is there anything distinct about it we can work with?'

'It's still drying out. Maya said she'd let me know once it was removed.'

'That will give you a new area of work to consider. Get the usual investigative legwork out of the way and then if we've still drawn a blank, only then will we consider our other options.'

Despite the fact he nodded, he was clearly dissatisfied with her response. Kym sighed as she leant across the desk, her demeanour softening as she appraised him. 'I appreciate that the DI role is a huge step to take. It's a massive learning curve for you and I appreciate it's not ideal being thrown into your first job, which is complex to say the least. I don't want to appear like I'm criticising or patronising you, my team and I are here to support you as and when we can, but honestly, Jack, facial reconstruction is the last resort. You've lots of other boxes to tick before we even consider it.'

His face flushed as he stood up. 'Just so you know, that sounded very patronising,' he hissed as he stormed out of the office, banging the door shut behind him.

Kym swallowed down a Buscopan as her phone rang. She listened intently to the caller as she scribbled down some details. A suicide had come in that appeared suspicious. She desperately hoped it wouldn't be or that meant she wouldn't be seeing much of home for the next few days. Still, it was preferable than dealing with office politics. Anything was better than that.

17

Marcus remained in the prison chapel long after the service had finished. He knelt in the pew, head bowed, hands clasped. If the chaplain could see his face, he would have observed Marcus's lips moving in silent prayer. He walked lightly amongst the pews, collecting the prayer books, and then settled himself at the front, submerged in his own silent contemplation until Marcus appeared ready to talk.

'You seem troubled today,' said the chaplain as Marcus eventually joined him. 'Is it the parole? You wouldn't be the first person to have reservations about being released. I can arrange for you to talk to someone about it if it helps.'

Marcus's gaze remained fixed on his feet as he shook his head solemnly. 'I took your advice. About trying to reconnect with family before I'm released.'

'And? Did it not go as you hoped?'

Marcus sighed again. 'Better. I had a reply from Anthony, my older brother. He seems genuinely pleased to have heard from me. He'd like us to meet up once I'm out. He offered to come and visit before I'm released, but I don't want him to see me in here. We've been speaking on the phone, though, and writing.'

'That's great news, isn't it?'

'Yes. It is. So much more than I could have hoped and prayed for. I don't deserve his love and forgiveness.'

'Jesus teaches us to forgive, Marcus. That includes being able to forgive ourselves for our sins. Your brother is...'

'Our mother died.'

Naylor's words stopped the chaplain in his tracks. He opened his mouth to offer words of comfort but hesitated when he noticed Marcus had more to say.

'She died two years ago. Apparently, she dropped dead of a heart attack. It would have been quick. Relatively painless, I believe. He did try to contact me in here at the time to let me know, but I'd already made it clear I didn't want to hear from him.'

'Would you like to pray for her?'

Marcus shook his head. 'I have been ever since I read Anthony's letter. I didn't expect it to hurt so much after so long apart. I was so arrogant to think it wouldn't happen.' He coughed back a sob as he ran a hand across his face. 'I just imagined she would be carrying on out there, without me. I never considered how she would be feeling or coping. Never thought about what would happen if she got ill, how she was coping financially, if she was in any trouble. I've been so selfish.'

The chaplain nodded, holding his counsel while Marcus held his head in his hands.

Suddenly he sat up and eyed the chaplain with a wild desperation that caused him to draw back against the pew. 'Do you know what hurts more than grief?'

The chaplain shook his head numbly.

'Guilt.'

18

'Inspector Stevenson?'

Sean winced at the familiar shrill voice of Laurel Miller. He kicked himself for answering the office phone and glowered at Malone who was sat, oblivious to his pain, as he happily munched away on a bacon sandwich, whilst his own seemed to stale in front of his very eyes.

'Mrs Miller, it's detective constable,' Sean said, not bothering to mask the irritation in his voice. He honestly believed he could call her the 'c' word and she would still only hear what she wanted.

'Oh, it's "miss" not "Mrs".' *Oops, maybe not then*, he thought, stifling a laugh.

'How can I help?'

'I have an urgent update. Trevor has been back to the address. I saw him with my own fair eyes. Chased after him but lost track. Out the side gate, down the path, back of the estate and *puff* in a cloud of smoke.' The garbled words flew from her mouth as Sean rubbed at his eyes, trying to keep up.

'Okay, and where...'

'Of course, Bernadette didn't see him. She was out for the

count. On the sofa, would you believe? Honestly, I need to speak to her GP about cutting down those tablets. They're doing her more harm than good, you know. Do you think her GP would speak to me?'

'Miss Miller. Laurel, can you...'

'So, I told her to check if he'd taken anything else or left something behind. I knew you'd want clues. He's left his wallet in the kitchen which I'm sure he'll come back for if nothing else. It appears he's taken some extra clothing and Bernadette seems to think something has gone missing from the study, but she doesn't know what, if you can believe it. Honestly, I despair at times. But more importantly this time, inspector, we have a key witness to Trevor's state of mind.'

Sean, expecting not to get a word in edgeways any time soon, failed to comment quick enough as he waited for the relentless barrage to continue. 'Are you still there? Are you even *listening*?' Laurel harangued.

'Yes, of course. Sorry. I was waiting for you to finish. Who's the witness?'

'Old Mother Dawlish. Rose, for your records. He sat and had a chat with her. Told her he was going to fetch her breakfast, so we're hoping he's not *gone* gone again. He may well be back at any minute this time. I knew you'd want to know. Shall I let Bernadette know that you're on your way?'

'I'm sorry, Miss Miller, but I'm tied up with something more pressing at the moment. I can try and see if a uniform patrol can attend, but if you think there's a possibility he's going to return imminently, we'll wait until he's back then we can attend as a priority and take a missing-returned report. That's our standard procedure.'

'Oh no, inspector. That simply won't do. We need *you* here as soon as possible to speak to Mother Dawlish and to make sure when he does come back, he stays put.'

'I've explained that unfortunately I'm dealing with something that takes precedence right now. If he's gone again there's really nothing I can do. I'll arrange for a response officer to come and see you.'

'Bernadette is used to you now, and it will only upset her if uniformed officers visit again. She finds it very intimidating and that only causes her to go to pieces. Not that it takes much.'

A lengthy conversation ensued during which his bacon sandwich practically decomposed before his eyes. His temples throbbed by the time he eventually ended the call. He glanced across the office to see Malone watching him, looking his usual unharried self, clearly amused by listening to Sean's side of the conversation.

'Don't suppose you fancy doing me a huge favour? Could you go and speak to the family of one of my missings?'

Malone let out a chesty laugh. 'Mate, I'd rather drape me sopping wet, hairy bollocks over an electric fence.'

Yes, thought Sean. *That makes two of us.*

19

Maya had finished removing John Doe's clothing from the drying cabinet. As she had anticipated, it had taken several days for the clothing to completely dry out. She examined each item carefully, wrinkling her nose as the smell permeated her face mask. Due to the body's heavy state of decomposition, this was the first time she'd been able to scrutinise the clothing properly.

Owing to the prolonged exposure to water and maceration from the body it was unlikely they would yield anything forensically, yet she continued to fastidiously examine each piece as she photographed it before repackaging. Her mind was consumed with thoughts of John Doe and particularly the fact he had been strangled. The majority of strangulation cases involved females who suffered from domestic violence, and it was unusual for a male to be strangled. She wondered if John Doe had been murdered by his partner. She pondered yet again on how Trevor Dawlish's bank card had ended up in his pocket, and if he was involved in the murder.

After cleaning the drying cabinet ready for its next use, Maya de-suited and placed the repackaged clothing into the exhibits store. As she headed back into the main office hoping for some lunch, Kym saw her and beckoned her over.

'Shut the door, please, Maya.'

'Oh God, that's never a good sign.'

Her comment was met with a raised eyebrow. Kym removed her reading glasses and raked her hand through her hair before she spoke. 'I'm not going to beat about the bush, but I've had a complaint about your conduct.'

Maya let out a hollow laugh. 'Oh, let me guess, *Councillor* Hanford? Honestly, Kym, it wasn't me. I didn't do anything wrong. The guy's a massive prick with a *CSI* box set and a shitty attitude!'

'He claims you were rude, appeared incompetent and took personal calls while you were at the scene.'

'No.' Maya shook her head incredulously. 'He was the rude one. He was arrogant, patronising and wouldn't listen to me from the moment I got there. And yes, my phone rang while I was there, but of course, I didn't answer it. You can check my call record.'

Kym smiled, shaking her head. 'I don't need to. I believe you. As with any complaint, I just needed to discuss it with you first before I provide a written reply. I have no doubt your integrity is without question. Right, forget about all that. How are things generally?'

'Okay.'

'If you're going to lie to me, Maya, at least do me the courtesy of making it convincing.'

Maya felt suitably chastened and began to pick at her cuticles with her teeth, unable to look her boss in the eye. She knew she could confide in Kym. She knew she could trust her implicitly. She worried that once she said the words out loud, they would become a reality. For now, she felt safer living in denial.

'Maya, don't,' Kym said softly as she reached for Maya's hand, pulling it away from her mouth. She was shocked to see blood beading at the cuticle where she had bitten too hard. She felt the sting as Kym passed her a tissue. The kind gesture was overwhelming. Maya felt as if she had a golf ball in her throat as she choked back tears, her lip trembling so much she could barely make herself heard.

'Naylor's being released.'

Kym's eyes widened and she let out a small gasp as she reached again for Maya's hand. 'Oh God, no. When?'

Maya shook her head. 'I don't know. That's all my mum told me. It was such a shock; I couldn't cope with hearing the rest. I said I needed time for it to sink in. I don't know any of the details.'

'Whilst your reaction is understandable, forewarned is forearmed. There will be conditions to his release.'

'That's what Mama said.'

'And has she told you what they are?'

Maya began to shred the tissue. 'No. Not yet.'

'Okay, finish your shift as early as you need to and go and see her. Find out what's what. Then, ring me or come and see me tomorrow, whatever suits. Keep me in the loop. We will support you as much as we can. Whatever you need, you've got it.'

Maya nodded her thanks, the lump of emotion in her throat left her unable to speak.

'Also, Jayne from Welfare has been in touch with me. She said she's been emailing you to arrange a follow-up appointment now you've been back to work for a while. She was concerned that you'd not replied.'

Maya grimaced. She had deliberately ignored Jayne's emails. As wonderful and supportive as her counsellor had been after her previous incident, she had shied away from the idea of going back and talking about things. She felt like she'd talked and shared enough. She felt drained at the thought of being so emotionally exposed again. She would prefer to just put it all behind her and move on.

'Oh, it's just been tricky trying to arrange time to see her.'

Kym eyed her sternly. 'Maya, I have made it perfectly clear that regardless of your shifts and operational requirements, your appointments with Welfare remain a priority. Particularly in light of what you've just told me. I am *telling* you to make an appointment with Jayne by the end of the day and I want to see proof of it, please. No excuses.'

'Yes, Kym.'

'Anyway, Tara will be joining us shortly, so staffing will soon ease. She's collecting her things from Pine Grove this morning and should be with us in a couple of hours. Are you still okay to shadow her? I can ask one of the others if it's too much in light of what you've got going on.'

'No, honestly, it's fine. It'll be a nice distraction meeting someone new.'

'I assume the others have told you about Tara?'

Maya shook her head. 'I'd rather not know to be honest. I'd much rather just meet her and make my own judgement. She's clearly got something of a reputation judging from everyone's reaction when you mentioned she was moving here, but people can change. I'm giving her the benefit of the doubt and I'll see for myself what she's like.'

Kym smiled. 'That's refreshing to hear. We just need to convince the others of that.'

Maya stood to leave, thanking Kym as she tucked her chair under the table.

'One last thing,' called Kym as she reached for the door handle. 'Jack seems to be out of his depth in his new role as DI. I appreciate you two have had issues in the past, but just be mindful that his change in rank denotes respect.'

'I cleared the air with him when he first told me about his promotion. He knows he's got my support if he needs it. Unfortunately, his arrogance might be his downfall.'

'I'm afraid you might be right. Be nice to the bastard. Trust me, it'll unnerve him even more.'

Maya's laugh ricocheted around the room.

20

Anyone who didn't know the Naylor family, would never suspect that Marcus and Anthony were brothers. They looked absolutely nothing alike. Whereas Marcus was a tall mountain of a man, Anthony was short and skinny. Where Marcus had once been dark-haired and swarthy, Anthony was fair with pale, alabaster skin. Marcus had a gruffness to his voice that immediately put people on edge, and Anthony, even as a grown man, sounded as if his voice had never broken.

Despite being the elder of the two, it was Anthony who had always been the runt of the litter. In his earlier years, he had been the butt of the playground jokes. Childish banter that had quickly descended into kicks, slaps and worse. That was until his baby brother, Marcus, had reached an age where, physically advanced, he had stood toe to toe with his brother's antagonists. He revered his brother, and, whilst they had their moments, Marcus was adamant that no one but him could slap Anthony about. Once he learnt about the bullying, he had swung for anyone who had ever slighted his brother verbally or physically.

What Anthony couldn't achieve with his weedy arms and legs, Marcus managed with ease as he delivered black eyes, chipped teeth and even a broken arm. Their parents had mixed views on the violence. Brian Naylor had never been an aggressive man and didn't believe violence was the answer. A sworn pacifist, he had never raised a hand to either of his children, choosing instead to defuse a situation through conversation and encouraging empathy.

Lily Naylor, however, was a powerhouse of a woman who thought her husband was a wimp and disagreed with his views. She claimed there was no way she could have raised two boys without taking a belt to them when needed. She had worried for Anthony when he had started showing signs of being weak like his father. She couldn't countenance the thought of a son of hers being bullied. It was embarrassing.

She badgered him to take a stance and fight back. She told him in no uncertain terms that punches spoke louder than words, but the boy was a gutless wimp, just like his father. Her heart had burst with pride when Marcus delivered a beating on Anthony's behalf. From that first incident, the bullying had stopped, and Anthony had earnt respect by proxy of his brother.

The family settled into a harmony of their own. The only fly in the ointment was Brian's insistence that Marcus's violent tendencies were unacceptable. Nobody else in the family agreed. Anthony was living his life without having to look over his shoulder for once and Marcus had found a way to regularly let off steam.

For Lily especially, Brian was proving to be as much a disappointment as a father as he was as a husband. That was why, when he was killed by a drunk driver one evening on his way home from work, neither thirteen-year-old Anthony or eleven-year-old Marcus were too upset. As for Lily Naylor, she didn't shed a single tear. She was much happier as a widow than she had ever been as a wife.

21

After her meeting with Kym, Maya took a walk round the car park, hoping the fresh air – however cold – would help to clear her head. She leant against her motorbike and called Dominique. Just as she thought the call was going to go to voicemail, she answered.

'Hi, are you okay?' Dominique sounded breathless.

'Yes, thanks. How are you? Are you at work, I couldn't remember what shift you said you were on today?'

'I wish I was. It'd be easier. I'm cleaning and sick to death of lumping this bloody great hoover up and down the stairs.'

Maya grinned. 'I've told you before, get rid of that antique.'

Dominique kissed her teeth. 'I'm not getting rid of something that works perfectly well. I'm not made of money.'

'Okay, well how about you buy a smaller, cheaper one to keep downstairs. Then you don't have to keep lugging that monstrosity about. You could just keep it on the landing to do the bedrooms with.'

'I'll think about it.' Maya could hear Dominique sigh and could picture her sitting down on the stairs. 'How are you? I've been worried about you.'

'I'm okay. Sorry I left like I did. It was just a shock, that's all.'

'I understand. Have you had enough time to come to terms with it?'

'Yeah. I'll call round later if you're in, and you can tell me what happens next.'

A sudden gust of wind ripped across the car park, the stinging chill causing Maya to shiver. 'Look, Mama, I'm going to have to go. I'll be round later.'

She said goodbye and hung up before zipping her coat higher, burying her chin into the material which gave scant relief against the frigid wind. Just as she reached the station doors, she noticed someone struggling to lift bags and a box out of the boot of the car. The wind was tugging at the bags, making it difficult to keep hold.

'Are you okay there?' Maya called.

She came face to face with a tall woman with black hair and stunning grey eyes. Her uniform, similar to Maya's, suggested this must be the new SOCO.

'It's Tara, isn't it? Hi, I'm Maya.' She extended her hand and was momentarily stunned as Tara squealed, dropped her stuff back into the boot of the car and engulfed Maya in a hug like she was long-lost family.

'Oh, it's so good to finally meet you. I've heard all about you,' Tara effused.

Maya laughed nervously. 'Okay, well, let's get you settled in. Can I help?' She gestured towards the boot.

'Oh, thanks,' said Tara as she began to load Maya's arm with the box and bags, picking up her handbag as she locked the car. 'Lead the way!'

Maya stumbled under the weight of Tara's belongings as she led her through Beech Field police station.

'Tara's here,' announced Maya breathlessly as she dumped everything on the nearest desk. She caught Amanda giving her a bemused look as she took in the sight of Tara carrying nothing other than her handbag.

Kym emerged from her office to greet Tara. 'Hi, Tara, good to see you. Give me a couple of minutes and then pop in for a chat.'

Tara turned to Amanda and smiled. 'How are you? I've not seen you in so long I thought you'd retired. You must be due to, surely? You're like, what, sixty-five?'

'Fifty-seven and still here,' Amanda replied with a rictus grin as she busied herself with the kettle.

'You've a drawer and some shelf space through here,' Maya began as she indicated the back office, but Tara ignored the invite to settle herself in. Instead, she perched on the edge of the desk, her unflinching grey eyes boring into Maya.

'So, tell me everything. I mean, I've been to a few murder-suicides over the years, but to have actually seen one. How did it feel? Were you scared? I bet you feel guilty, don't you, like survivor's guilt? I wouldn't be able to sleep at night. Can you? I bet you're terrified of being haunted. I would be.'

The words poured from Tara leaving Maya like a rabbit caught in the headlights.

'I... it was...'

'And then there's the whole thing with your dad. Is that true? What's he inside for? Do you ever speak to him? It must be embarrassing. If my dad was...'

Tara was cut off mid-conversation by Kym delivering her customary double clap. 'Tara, I think it's time for that chat. *Now* please.'

'Eugh, she's like an ice queen,' Tara hissed to Maya as she followed Kym into her office, shutting the door behind her.

Maya slumped into a chair. 'Christ, what the hell was that?'

Amanda stood to finish making the tea, giving Maya a hug on the way past. '*That* is Tara. Absolutely zero filter, I'm afraid.

And to give you the heads-up, she's the most work-shy SOCO on the force. But don't worry, Kym will put her in her place.'

'I hope so.' Maya sighed.

Amanda grinned. 'I'm sure she'll settle down soon enough.'

Maya frowned as she began to pick at her cuticles. 'I hope so, because if that's what it's going to be like, I'm not sure I can work with her.'

22

Spence let out a low whistle as his colleague, Lisa, walked into The Eagle. He could tell by the way she was fidgeting with her clothes that she was nervous.

'Miss Cohen, you look lovely.'

'Thanks,' she said shyly as she approached the end of the bar.

'Hey, where are you going?'

'To get a drink. I'll pay, obviously.'

'You're staying strictly behind that side of the bar tonight, lady. What would you like? And the first drink is on me.'

'Thanks, Spence. White wine please.' She rearranged her necklace and checked her lipstick as he fetched her drink.

'Here, it's a large to settle your nerves. What time are you meeting him?'

Lisa glanced at her watch. 'Half past. Will he think it's weird that I'm here first, this early?'

'No, it's fine. This is your manor, so just relax.'

'What if he doesn't show?'

'He will. And the minute he claps eyes on you he'll realise what a lucky bugger he is.'

Spence was surprised to see Lisa so nervous. She was usually such an extrovert; it was part of the job description working behind a bar. She may only be petite, but she could handle herself and mastered the art of banter. He really hoped this date worked out for her, she deserved to be happy.

He managed to keep her chatting and distracted so her nerves would ease. Eventually, her eyes lit up as a man built like a rugby player walked in. He was dressed smartly in jeans and a long-sleeved black shirt, his muscles straining against the fabric. He looked to be six foot two, easily a foot taller than Lisa.

'Cor, he's a big old unit,' Spence said.

'He's gorgeous,' hissed Lisa as she stood up to greet her date. He stooped to kiss her cheek, and Spence was amused to see her practically swoon in front of him.

'Jason, this is my friend, Spence.' The two men shook hands and Spence prepared them a round of drinks before busying himself at the other end of the bar to keep a discreet distance.

After a couple of drinks Lisa waved him over. 'We're moving on, mate. Going to try a new bar near the precinct.'

'Okay, have a great night. Don't do anything I wouldn't do.'

He waved them off, smiling as Jason slipped an arm casually around Lisa's shoulder as they left the pub.

23

___

Dominique was waiting for Maya on the doorstep when she arrived. The rain was pelting down mercilessly, but she seemed immune to the weather. Maya removed her helmet, shook her curls free and dashed up the path.

'What are you standing there for, it's freezing,' Maya said as she gave her a kiss.

'I heard you coming, I swear that exhaust is getting louder. It needs looking at.' She hung Maya's biker's jacket up and bustled her through to the lounge where a pot of tea and banana bread were waiting on the coffee table.

'Thanks, Mama.' Maya smiled as she settled herself down on the sofa. They exchanged small talk for a while, before Dominique set her cup down and wiped her mouth.

'We need to discuss the huge elephant in the room, it's starting to dirty the carpet.'

'Ha! It wouldn't dare, not when you've cleaned.' Maya rubbed her hands across her face. 'So, when is he out?'

'Twenty-sixth November.'

'What! That's only a few weeks away.'

Dominique nodded and moved to the sofa next to Maya, placing a hand on her knee.

'I know. The most important thing to remember is that there will be rules he needs to follow. He's out on licence and the minute he does anything wrong, he'll be straight back inside. No doubt about it.'

'What rules?'

'Well, most importantly, he's not allowed to contact either of us, directly or indirectly, and he can't come anywhere near either of our addresses or places of work. He'll also be subject to alcohol and drugs testing and be on a curfew. Things like that.'

Maya snorted. 'Like any of that will make a difference. He's never obeyed a rule in his life. He's dangerous, Mama, and he's going to be back... out there somewhere.'

Dominique could feel her daughter trembling as she took her hands.

'It might not be that bad.'

'Really! Jesus, even you're not that optimistic, surely?'

Dominique gave her a wan smile. 'I've not told you before because I wanted to brush it all under the carpet before now. He wrote me a letter. Would you like to read it?'

Maya shuddered. 'I don't even want to *touch* anything he's handled. The thought of it sickens me. Just tell me what it said.'

'He wanted to let me know he was going for parole and to apologise.'

'Apologise!' Maya was incredulous.

'He claims he's found God and is fully penitent. He wanted to say sorry to both of us and understands if neither of us, especially you, want to see him again. He's promised to stay away.'

Maya leapt up like a scalded cat. 'And you believe this bullshit? He's the master of lies and manipulation. He's threatened us before, remember? You know he blames us for the fact he was sent down in the first place.'

Dominique shrugged. 'I've exhausted myself thinking about this. The letter had no sway on the parole board's decision. He's served his time for what he did to us and to people inside.' She sighed. 'I can honestly think of no reason why he would lie about it. It's safe to say neither of us want to see him, so what does he have to gain? Are you sure you don't want to read it?'

Maya shook her head numbly.

'Okay.' Dominique sighed again. 'He's insisting that since he saw you on the news, all grown up, that it's made him realise how much he's missed out on. He says he regrets wasting so many years inside and wants to start living again.'

'It's all bollocks,' Maya hissed.

'I'm inclined to agree. But, the fact remains, once he's released, he can come nowhere near either of us. The way I'm looking at it is that nothing's going to change. Okay, so he's no longer going to be in prison, but that doesn't mean he'll be in our lives. He's coming nowhere near us. Understand?'

Maya nodded mutely. The tea and banana bread lay heavy. But it wasn't that making her feel sick to her stomach. She was determined regardless of his impending release not to let it get to her. Her work was more important to her than Marcus, and right now there was the body of a murdered, unknown male lying in the mortuary. If anything deserved her attention, that did, and sod anything or anyone else.

24

S pence had locked up and carried a couple of beers up to the flat. He cracked one open as he reached for the remote control. He frowned as his phone rang, wondering who would ring him so late.

He grinned when he saw her name flash up, but it soon faded as he heard how distraught she was.

'He's what?' He listened intently, colour draining from his face as he banged the bottle down on the table. Frantically, he gathered his coat and car keys. 'Don't worry, I'm on my way.'

He disconnected the call and ran out of the flat.

25

DC Adila Laghari slammed the pile of paperwork down on the desk. 'This is fucking hopeless,' she muttered.

Malone, who was working the late shift with her, popped his head over his computer monitor. 'What's up, Ads?'

Adila frowned at him from under her thick dark fringe. 'Operation bloody Mermaid. Jack has tasked me with trawling through all the missings to see if there's any correlation with our John Doe, as well as obtaining their dental records for comparison. He's also asked me to look at photographs of the clothing Maya took to see if that gives us any clues, but it's like finding a needle in a haystack. Except in this case, I don't even know which bloody haystack I'm supposed to be searching.

'And I wouldn't mind, but he knows I've been busting my arse studying for the sergeant's exam. DS Turner has been a great help, it's a shame other people aren't as generous. Since Jack's been temporarily appointed, he doesn't give a shit about anyone else trying to climb the ladder. Redford would give me some slack with all this if it was down to him.' She gesticulated towards the paperwork with an air of frustration.

Malone frowned sympathetically. 'Take it you got nothing from the CCTV?'

'No. Maya told me before that the underwater search unit have helped to track the most likely entry point into the canal based on tidal flow. We think he's gone in on, or near, Stour Bridge.'

'At the back of the precinct? There's a huge council CCTV mast there.'

Adila nodded. 'I know but apparently it wasn't covering the direction of Stour Bridge that night.'

Malone tutted. 'Fucking typical. They're useless in there, couldn't find their dicks with both hands. Who did you speak to?'

Adila looked in her policy book. 'The supervisor in there, a Patrick Karim?'

Malone nodded. 'Yeah, I've dealt with him before. Bit of an arrogant git. I saw him a few months ago when we had the mugging in the subway off Albert Road. He made a point of telling me the cameras couldn't see through brick. Bellend.'

Adila laughed as she put the paperwork to one side. 'I need a break, I'm starving. Fancy a pizza?'

'You've twisted me arm.'

'Right,' she said, 'you hold the fort and I'll nip out.'

Malone gave her his order then curiosity got the better of him. He sat at Adila's desk and flicked through the paperwork. He was keen to see how far she'd got, and if there was anything obvious he could do to take the slack. He stared at the post-mortem photographs of their John Doe and shook his head, tapping the photo. 'Who the bloody hell are you, fella?' he muttered. 'Who the bloody hell are you?'

26

Spence gave Maya a quick hug. 'Thanks for coming.'

'Not a problem. Where is she?' Spence gestured to the lounge. Maya was shocked to see Lisa in such a state. Her clothing was torn, and as much as her thick make-up was streaked across her face, it didn't disguise the swollen lip and black eye.

'Oh, Lisa!' Maya gathered her friend in a hug and held her while she cried. Spence left them to fetch a fresh glass of water and more tissues for Lisa.

Maya waited for the tears to subside for a while before she pulled away from Lisa and looked her in the eye.

'Tell me what happened,' she said gently.

Lisa gulped, wiping her nose. 'It was great at first. We'd had a couple of drinks here and then we went to a new bar near the precinct. We had a few more in there. I thought we were getting on really well. I liked him. Then he asked me if I wanted to go somewhere else for last orders.'

Fresh tears sprung in her eyes again. 'It's my own stupid fault, I should have realised it was already too late to move on somewhere else.'

'Hey,' said Spence. 'None of this is your fault, Lisa.'

Maya nodded. 'He's right. What happened next?'

Lisa shook her head. 'We were passing near the bridge and he just snapped.'

Maya held up her hand. 'Wait, which bridge, Stour Bridge?'

Lisa nodded and continued. 'He pushed me against the wall and started to maul me. Don't get me wrong, I was really into him. Up until that point, if he'd tried to kiss me, I'd have been elated. But it was the way he suddenly just pounced on me, it wasn't romantic, there was no kiss, just his hands suddenly everywhere. His whole demeanour changed. He was like a different man. Cold and aggressive.'

Lisa started to cry again, so they waited until she was more composed before she continued. 'The way he grabbed at me so suddenly and... violently... it took me by surprise, so I pushed him away. It was just instinct. I started to say something to make a joke out of it, like slow down, and out of the blue he punched me. Next thing I know he was all over me.' She sobbed loudly. 'It was horrible, he was pulling at my clothes and his hands were hurting me. He was grabbing at me like I was just a piece of meat – just an object.'

'Did anything happen. Did he manage to...?' Maya asked tentatively.

Lisa shook her head. 'You know me. I'm only short but I know my moves. I bit him really hard on the neck. It shocked him enough to pull away and I managed to get a throat-punch in to give me enough time to get away. I ran back to the pub, locked myself in the women's toilets and rang Spence.'

Maya nodded. 'I know it's hard, but you really need to report this to the police.'

Lisa shook her head vehemently. 'I can't. They're gonna think I asked for it. Going drinking with someone I don't know. Someone I've met on Tinder.'

Spence shook his head and Maya gently took Lisa by the shoulders. 'They won't think that at all. Trust me. I work with them, don't I? This is all on him. You've done nothing wrong. He's assaulted you.' Maya sighed. 'We've had an incident recently in that same area, so the council cameras should be covering it, which will be great evidence.'

Lisa looked up. 'What incident? Is it the same as what happened to me?'

'No, and I'm afraid I can't say.' Maya paused for a moment. Was there any coincidence to the fact that Lisa had been attacked in the same place John Doe had most likely entered the water? Even if there was, now wasn't the time to think about it.

She turned her attention back to Lisa. 'Just think, what happens if his next victim can't fight him off?'

She thought about it for a while. 'You're right. I can't have that on my conscience. Could you phone them for me? I wouldn't know what to say. I don't have the words. That's why I rang Spence.'

'Of course I will.' She picked up her phone and went into the kitchen to make the call. She stared out of the kitchen window at the street below and thought of the damage that bastard Jason had inflicted on her friend. Then she thought of Marcus Naylor and wondered exactly how many other dangerous people were out there on the streets. More importantly, she wondered how she was going to keep Dominique safe once Naylor was released. She shuddered at the thought.

27

Maya and Chris were both on a late shift and arrived at Beech Field at the same time. As they walked in, she told him all about Lisa's attack.

'What a bastard. Let's hope they find him. Lisa's a smashing girl. Give her my love next time you speak to her, eh?'

Maya nodded. 'I will do. Thank God she knows some self-defence.'

'I can't remember the last time we were in The Eagle. Now I come to think about it, I can't remember the last time you mentioned Spence. How are things going between you two?'

Maya was about to swerve the conversation when they saw Tara heading down the corridor towards them. She squealed when she saw Chris. 'Well, long time no see. How are you?'

Chris gave her a sheepish grin. 'I'm good thanks, Tara. How are you?' Maya could tell he was speaking with forced politeness.

'Oh, I'm fantastic. In more ways than one!' She shrieked with laughter. She pretended to lick her forefinger and pressed it against her hip and made a sizzling sound, symbolically indicating she was hot stuff. Maya and Chris both winced at her shameless conceit.

'You've put a fair bit of timber on since I saw you last. Step away from the doughnuts, Chris.' She waved her hands theatrically around her own slender stomach, still laughing, oblivious to the stony glances she was met with.

'How are you settling in?' Maya asked flatly, determined to deflect the slur away from her friend.

'Okay so far. I think I'm going to like it here.' Her eyes darted towards the office at the end of the corridor. She dropped her voice to a stage whisper. 'Especially since I met the Acting DI. He's quite a treat, isn't he? You could have told me, Maya, or are you keeping him for yourself, you dark horse.'

Maya raised an eyebrow. 'Trust me when I say, I'd rather eat my own shit than go anywhere near him.'

Tara shrieked with laughter and carried on to wherever she was off to. Chris shook his head. 'Tara and Jack? They'd spoil another pair, wouldn't they?'

'Let's just hope they don't breed,' Maya said. 'Can you imagine a narcissistic baby using the baby monitor to take selfies?'

Chris laughed. 'Don't get me wrong, like Jack, she's very attractive. But if her personality was a toilet, she'd be the one from *Trainspotting*.'

'I just love the fact you can compare somebody's personality to a toilet, and I don't find it strange. I think we might be soulmates.' Maya grinned and linked his arm. As they approached the office, Sean walked out carrying a disc.

'Ah, Maya,' he said. 'I've just picked this up off Nicola. She's been to photograph your friend's injuries.'

'Oh, good. Obviously, I couldn't do it because I know her but I'm glad Nic managed to get hold of her.' What she didn't say was that she was glad Nicola had been and not Tactless Tara. 'How's the investigation going?'

'Really well. Lisa's a good witness and we've got contact information for Jason off her phone. Unsurprisingly, he's known to us. Hopefully, we should have him locked up very soon.'

'That's fantastic news. Any CCTV of the attack?'

'Annoyingly, no. You know where it happened, don't you?'

Maya nodded. 'Stour Bridge where they think our John Doe went in the water. Do you think the two incidents could be linked?'

'Too early to tell and even if they are, we have no footage. As per usual, council cameras were pointing elsewhere.'

'That's ridiculous. Surely, they should be covering that bit after what's happened. What's their priority? The precinct is covered by private security cameras, so they're not needed for that.'

Sean rubbed his thumb against his fore and middle fingers. 'If you ask me, it's money. There's an antiques' shop on the main road. It's owned by a local councillor. Bit of a coincidence that the cameras are always fixed on that, don't you think?'

'Absolutely,' said Maya. 'And can I hazard a guess that the councillor's name is Hanford?'

'Yeah, how do you know him?'

'Burglary – long story. Oh, and Sean?'

'Yeah?'

'When you lock that bastard, Jason, up, don't worry if you accidentally bang his head several times as you're putting him in the back of the van.'

Sean laughed. 'It's not *Life on Mars*, Maya. We don't get a confession out of people by beating them, contrary to what the public think. This isn't America.'

'I know, I know. But when it comes to certain people, I really wish we could.'

28

Anthony Naylor finished putting fresh linen on the spare bed and stood back to admire his efforts. He'd given the pokey room a lick of fresh paint and added a new lightshade and curtains for good measure. It was no palace, but it was clean and cosy enough. And compared to years spent in a prison cell, he imagined Marcus would think he was in the lap of luxury.

Humming to the radio, Anthony pottered around the rest of the flat, tidying and polishing as he went. The probation officer was due in two hours to assess Anthony and the flat to ensure it was suitable for Marcus's release. He was looking forward to being reunited with his younger brother and having some company. He glanced at the display cabinet in the corner and carefully removed the framed photograph from it. He wiped it with the duster, then smiling, he raised it to his lips and gently kissed his mother's face.

It was an old photograph taken a year or so before his dad died. He and Marcus were stood either side of Lily, beaming at the camera. Brian was in the photograph too, but as the picture was slightly too big for the frame, his bit had been folded over so it could fit. Nobody had thought to buy a bigger frame. Brian had always been inconsequential.

Anthony carefully positioned the frame in the middle of the fireplace and stood back to admire it. He went back to the cabinet and removed a long plastic lily that his mother had always coveted and lay it at the foot of the frame. That looked nice. They looked better there, the two lilies in pride of place rather than squirrelled away in the cabinet.

'Your boys will be back together soon, Mum,' he told the picture. 'And I know you'll be watching over us. Showing us the way.'

29

Kym was having a weekly catch-up with DI Redford in his office. They were discussing the results of a recent court case, where three prolific armed robbers had each received lengthy prison sentences, thanks to an accumulation of great detective work and the painstaking recovery of a vast quantity of forensic evidence.

'And apparently, everyone involved is to receive a Good Work Minute from the Acting Chief Constable. So, I think we'll book the conference room that day and make a celebration out of it. A bit of finger food and a few bottles of sparkling grape juice.'

Kym swallowed a mouthful of coffee and nodded. 'That would be nice. The job is on its arse with cuts and everything else at the moment, so I'm in support of anything that will keep the troops motivated. They deserve to feel valued and appreciated for the back-breaking work they do.'

'I agree. I heard yesterday that Cedar Lane's response sergeant has handed his ticket in.' Redford shook his head. 'Bloody heartbreaking to hear of a good cop like that walking away from the job because they've had enough.'

'It's politics, Phil. It all turned to shit when–'

Kym was interrupted by the sound of Jack bursting into the office. Uncharacteristically flustered, his arms were full of paperwork and he had a sheen of sweat on his forehead despite the chilled air that seemed to permeate the building this time of year.

'Phil, Kym, sorry I'm late. Just been juggling a few enquiries.'

'So we can see,' Redford said with a raised eyebrow as he watched Jack fumble with the paperwork. 'First off, where are we up to with the arrest of Jason Laing for the assault and attempted rape of Lisa Cohen?'

'Right, okay. Well, so far we've not managed to bring him in.'

Redford raised an eyebrow again. 'I thought Sean was on it.'

'He was. Unfortunately, Laing has done a runner. He left his current digs the night he attacked Lisa. Enquiries are ongoing to track him down.'

Redford frowned. 'Make sure that's being treated as a priority please, Jack. Laing's a predator. In my experience someone on the run like him is bloody dangerous. He knows he's going to be sent away for a stretch and is highly likely to reoffend before he's brought in. Plus, I don't like the coincidence that he attacked Lisa in the same area we know John Doe went into the water.

'He's clearly comfortable with it being somewhere he can get away with God knows what without being incriminated. Deal with the attack on Lisa first, but I also want to know if he knows anything about the body in the water.' Redford ran his hand on his chin. 'And as an afterthought, ask him if he knows Trevor Dawlish.'

Jack scribbled down some notes as Redford turned to Kym. 'We know Lisa Cohen bit Laing before she managed to get away. What are the chances we could still record the bite mark once he's brought in?'

Kym thought for a moment. 'It depends. People bruise

differently as you know. If I recall rightly, she claims she bit him quite hard on the neck, so the bruising would be quite deep over a decent area of skin. That would take the bruising quite a while to fade even on somebody who heals quickly.

'Have him assessed as and when he's brought in, and we'll get any remaining bite mark recorded. Try and locate the clothing he was wearing on the night, too, if you can. If it's not been washed, there's potential for Lisa's saliva to have been transferred from his neck to the shirt.'

Jack nodded and made some more notes.

'Also,' added Kym. 'Just be aware that both Maya and Chris are acquaintances of Lisa Cohen, so, if necessary, somebody else should be asked to photograph him. Utilise another local crime-scene unit if you need to.'

Redford allowed Jack to catch up on his notes before moving the briefing on. 'Where are we up to with Operation Mermaid?'

'Well, the press release brought lots of responses but no positive leads unfortunately. The clothing has taken us absolutely nowhere. Enquiries into all our other missings and relevant checks of their dental records have also drawn a blank.' Jack shrugged and looked at Kym. 'I know we've discussed this before, but facial reconstruction is the only chance we have of identifying this man. I'm pissing in the wind here.'

Kym raked her hand through her hair. 'I understand that, Jack, but like I said, we really need to explore every avenue first.'

'Which I've done.'

'Have you made those same enquires with neighbouring forces? Consider liaising with Interpol too if need be.'

'Seriously! Jesus, that's a lot of work.'

'You mean,' Redford snapped, 'that's a lot of investigating. It's what we *do*. Kym's right in what she says. Forensics support an investigation, but on a case like this, we need to resort to good old coppering before we tie up the experts and deplete the budget.'

Jack mumbled something incoherent as he gathered up the paperwork. 'Right, I'll get onto it,' he said, leaving the office like a wounded puppy.

'Welcome to life as a DI, Jack!' Redford called.

A slammed door was the only response.

30

The rain battered Maya as she ran across the car park. She held her thick curls out of her face so she could see where she was going. She arrived at the front door and pressed the intercom. She stamped her feet as she waited for what felt an age before a tinny voice responded.

'Hi, it's Maya Barton. I've got an appointment with Jayne Harding.'

Maya was buzzed through. She was grateful for the warmth of the Welfare Unit's waiting room as she signed herself in. She stood reading a few of the notices on the wall when she heard a familiar voice call her name.

'Come on up.' Jayne Harding was a tall lady with long blonde hair. She had a mischievous smile and radiated warmth. Maya followed her up the first flight of stairs to her office, where she was invited to sit down in the familiar comfy chair.

The room hadn't changed in the months since she'd last seen her. The comfy chairs were positioned either side of a low desk, which contained a box of tissues and a basket of stress balls and fidget spinners. The room was softly lit and adorned with ferns and posters depicting Buddhist quotes.

The usual smell of lavender was also evident and instantly soothing.

'It's been a while. I was beginning to think you were ignoring my emails,' Jayne said.

'Sorry. I wasn't. I mean, I suppose I was but, it's been hard, the thought of being back here. No offence.'

Jayne laughed. 'None taken. I understand that, honestly, I do. It's a natural response. You're not the first person who's expressed the exact same thoughts.'

Maya looked around the room and thought of all the hours she'd spent in here with Jayne, unravelling, dissecting and analysing every moment of the murder-suicide. She looked in the basket and noticed a new stress ball that looked more like a dog chew. Jayne caught her eye and Maya raised an eyebrow questioningly. 'Do people bring their pets?' she asked.

Jayne grinned and gave a small shrug. 'When we're angry, scared or upset, we can revert to animal state. Everything in there is regularly sterilised, so gnaw away on it if you feel the need to. If it helps.'

Maya laughed, the ice was broken, and she remembered, despite having some harrowing conversations in here, that Jayne was good fun. Had they met in different circumstances, she was the kind of person she'd have loved to go on a night out with. She was funny, straight-talking and good company.

Jayne reached for a folder and began by making a note of the date. 'How have you been?'

'It's good to be back at work. It was exhausting at first, but now I've settled in, it's nice to have a routine.'

Jayne nodded. 'Although routine and familiarity can sometimes feel tedious, it is good for us psychologically to have stability. How are things at home and generally being out and about?'

Maya took a deep breath before she answered. 'I've just

found out that Marcus, my estranged father, is due to be released from prison.'

Jayne chewed the top of her pen as she flicked back through her notes. 'We've not really discussed Marcus in any great detail. By that, I mean, you've never shared what happened in your past. You've never told me exactly what he did to you and why he ended up in prison in the first place. Is that something you think you're ready to explore now?'

Maya felt as if the walls were beginning to close in around her. She felt like a weight was pressing against her chest and a pulse started to throb painfully in her temple.

'I can't. I'm not ready to go into all that. It's too much. And, if I'm honest, there's so much of it that's hazy. My memory of back then is like a Swiss cheese, there are just too many holes. I guess I've just blanked the worse bits out over the years.' Maya's lip trembled as she reached for a tissue and swiped at her eyes.

'Okay.' Jayne held her palms up towards Maya. 'Remember the rules. I'm not going to force you to talk about anything that makes you feel uncomfortable. But perhaps it is something to bear in mind, moving forward.'

Maya nodded, unconvinced.

'Perhaps we could talk about how you feel knowing Marcus is going to be released? That's something we could work on.'

'Sick. I feel physically fucking sick. There are already too many monsters roaming the streets without adding him back into the mix. I'm worried sick about my mum. He's threatened us before from prison, so what's he going to do now he's out? My mum doesn't seem concerned, she seems to have fallen for some cock and bull story that he's born again.'

Jayne sat back and took notes as Maya told her about the claims that Marcus was coming out of prison a reformed man who had found God.

'I'm going to play devil's advocate now, so bear with me.'

Jayne began to chew her pen again. 'Do you not think it's possible that he could have changed? He's been inside a long time. And if he's embraced his faith, that can have a huge impact on how people live their lives.'

Maya shook her head vehemently. 'Don't misunderstand me, Jayne, my faith is important to me. It's seen me through some dark times over the years. Neither he nor Mama were religious, but I went to faith schools. This claim that he's born again adds insult to injury.

'It sickens me, the thought that we would ever have the slightest thing in common. It's bad enough we share the same DNA. It particularly hurts that it's something that's so personal to me. He has never showed an interest in religion in his life other than to mock it.'

Maya sighed and wiped a hand across her face before she continued. 'I understand all about repentance and forgiveness, but this isn't him. There's more chance of Lucifer himself embracing God than Marcus. He's evil, rotten to the core. People like him are incapable of change. A snake can shed its skin, but it's still a snake.'

Jayne nodded and closed the folder. There was nothing left for her to say.

31

Laurel closed the loft hatch. She was breathing hard with the effort of shifting the Christmas tree and storage box bursting with decorations. It was the first time she had ever had to do it as normally Trevor would be round to help. He'd set up the tree for her and later that evening, when the house had been adorned with decorations, the three of them would call round for mulled wine and mince pies.

Sighing, she slumped down on the landing, running her hand over a film of dust on the box. She had always put her Christmas decorations up the last week of November, but this year it just didn't feel right. How could she just carry on, act like normal and even countenance celebrating Christmas with Trevor still missing?

She walked into the guest bedroom and stared forlornly out at the greyness. Dawn had yawned its way to an elephant-coloured sky and the non-stop drizzle seemed to rinse away any hint of colour. The weather mirrored her mood and she sighed heavily.

Her eyes, as always, flickered towards the Dawlishes and she squeezed her hands tight, willing Trevor to appear like he had last time. Despite Rose's claims that Trevor had said he was going to fetch her breakfast, he had not returned. She didn't know who she was more frustrated with, bloody Bernadette for not realising Trevor had been home or that Inspector Stevenson, for not doing what she'd asked and turning out immediately to look for Trevor.

Instead, a female police officer who didn't look old enough to wear the uniform, had eventually arrived and made a show of asking a few questions. She had not been interested in anything Laurel had to tell her, and true to form, Bernadette had been as useless as tits on a goldfish. That had been weeks ago and still no sight or sound of Trevor. She was convinced he would return home for his wallet, but sadly, it remained on the kitchen worktop.

Bernadette and his mother had seemed to settle into a routine around the house without Trevor in it. But not Laurel. She couldn't sleep at night as she listened to the wind and hail hammering the bedroom window, wondering where Trevor was and if he was safe and warm.

Tears filled her eyes as she dragged the Christmas tree and decorations into the guest room and slammed the door shut on them. Tradition or not, she couldn't possibly bring herself to put them up. All she wanted was Trevor back. Even though he would be home with Bernadette, and not with her, where she wished he could be, she didn't mind.

With a heavy heart, she padded to her bedroom, lay on the bed and pulled the duvet over her. Tears streamed down her face and her stomach ached with longing. Years ago, she had accepted that the man she loved was married to someone else. She could just about cope with it as long as he continued to live over the road where she could see him and speak to him every day.

Now and then, she allowed herself to imagine what life

would be like if it was just her and Trevor. No Bernadette and God forgive her, no Rose. She cared for the old woman deeply, but she was becoming a burden and if she was brutally honest, she wanted Trevor all to herself. If he had never met Bernadette, then he would surely have seen, over time, what a match he could have made with her.

A man like Trevor needed a strong woman to support him. And preferably without the constraints of having an elderly parent to care for. She knew, given half a chance, she could make him happy. But that was just a fantasy. The reality was that without him she had nothing.

Each day he remained missing, a little piece of her heart broke even more.

32

Autumn's protracted nights saw the days crawl into weeks. Maya and the team continued to be frustrated by the lack of progress in identifying John Doe. A few false leads initially gave them the boost they needed, only for them to fall into a malaise once they found themselves back to square one. A photograph of the cadaver had been pinned to the noticeboard in CID. Maya felt that each time she glanced at it, the marbled eyes pleaded with her to send him home to his family. The thought that a murdered man remained in the mortuary, unidentified and seemingly unwanted, was difficult to countenance.

She continued to study the scene photographs relentlessly, desperate to spot something they may have overlooked on the day, but it was a fruitless task. She also knew one of the reasons she was obsessing over the job, was to distract herself from Marcus's imminent release.

On the day he was released, Maya and Dominique decided to spend the day together rather than dwelling on the inevitable. They had driven to the local retail park where Maya had managed to persuade her mother to buy a smaller vacuum cleaner to keep downstairs as she had recently hurt her back carrying the heavy, cumbersome one up and down the stairs.

Dominique had also insisted on treating Maya to a new perfume and some books, anything to erase the worried frown that drifted across her daughter's face when she thought Dominique wasn't watching her. After a couple of hours retail therapy, they had headed to their favourite Indian restaurant and were putting the world to rights over chicken tikka madras. Dominique took a sip of red wine as she appraised her daughter over the top of her glass.

'Talk to me darlin'.'

Maya's eyes widened. 'I am talking to you. I was just telling you about how Chris...'

Dominique silenced her mid-sentence with a raised eyebrow and pursed lips. Maya faltered and began to pluck crumbs from the tablecloth.

'Honestly, Mama, I've come to terms with him being out. As long as he stays away from us, then things won't be any different, will they? I have been wondering though...'

'What?'

'Where do you think he'll stay?'

'I can ask the probation if it helps you to know. I assume he'll go back to his mother's. That's if the old cow is still alive. Do you remember her?'

Maya shook her head. 'Very vaguely. When I think back to my childhood it's such a blur. Like trying to recall a film I once watched years ago. It doesn't even feel like it was my life; that it happened to someone else who told me about it. I remember times when I was scared. Of him.' She looked up at Dominique and a smile suddenly lit up her face, accentuating her beauty. 'I also remember feeling happy – the days I spent with grandad especially. I miss him so much.'

Dominique shifted in her seat. 'Lily Naylor was a cold, hard woman. Full of spite. Nasty soul.'

'The apple didn't fall far from the tree then, did it? Do you honestly believe it, that he's found God and has changed his ways? That he's actually repented?'

'He wouldn't be the first.'

'Mama, please. This is Marcus we're talking about.'

Dominique shrugged. 'I just don't know. He's been away a long time. That's bound to change people.'

'Evil can't be undone.'

'You believe that? With your faith?'

'When it comes to him, yes.'

'Playing devil's advocate here but, people can change, Maya.'

'That's what my counsellor said. But he never will. He's rotten to the core. And if you want to know what's worrying me the most, it's that you can't see it. You're not concerned that he's a threat. You're not worried that he might want revenge and come after us. You know he blames us for the fact he was sent to prison.'

Dominique took a large slug of red wine and indicated to the waiter that she'd like to order another glass. 'So, what do you want me to do? Live in fear? I won't do that anymore over that man, and neither will you.'

Maya reached across the table for her mother's hand. 'Not live in fear, no. Just be careful, that's all. For example, start locking your front door when you're in the house. I've been warning you about increasing your home security since I started as a SOCO and you still haven't even got a burglar alarm. You need to take care more now than ever. I couldn't cope if anything happened to you.'

Dominique smiled as she wrapped both of Maya's hands in hers. 'Nothing is going to happen to me, darlin'. You don't get rid of me that easily. I'm going to be around for a very long time, don't you worry.'

Despite Dominique's reassuring words, Maya felt a sense of foreboding. Her worse nightmare was due to be released back into society and she was helpless to do anything about it. For her own sanity she knew she would have to just block any thought of him from her mind, but that was easier said than done. She pushed food round her plate as she pondered yet again, where Marcus Naylor would be sleeping that night and exactly how close he might be to her and her mother.

Anthony watched Marcus out of the corner of his eye as he weaved the car in and out of the city traffic. His brother had barely said two words since they had left the prison. Instead, he was glued to the passenger window, watching wide-eyed at everything they passed.

'Are you okay?'

Marcus nodded; his eyes remained fixed on the world as it whizzed by him. 'It's surreal. I mean, watching television has shown me how much life has changed since I've been away, but this... this is just so alien.' He tapped the window with his forefinger. 'So many people on phones and the number of restaurants and takeaways is unbelievable. The smells too – I don't remember the streets smelling so much of food. Where have all the video shops gone and what's a Polski Sklep?'

Anthony smiled. 'It's a Polish shop and we don't have videos anymore, you dinosaur. They were replaced by DVDs and we have Sky TV and Netflix instead. It hadn't occurred to me how strange it would seem to you. I'm sure you'll soon get used to it. I'm here for you and I'm sure your probation officer has seen it all before with people in your situation.'

Marcus nodded. 'It's just so busy. And loud. Don't get me wrong, prison is loud twenty-four-seven, but this is a different kind of noise. I don't remember there being so many people and cars about. And there's so much light everywhere. I must admit, I feel a bit agoraphobic. I'll be glad to get to the flat. I'm not used to so much space. And all the Christmas decorations, it's only the twenty-sixth of November!'

'That's nothing. They seem to go up earlier every year. The shops start selling them in September, as soon as the back-to-school stuff is finished with. It's the same with Easter. As soon as Christmas is over the shops will be stocking eggs, you'll see.' Anthony laughed at Marcus's incredulous expression. 'Do you want to go past the church?'

Marcus shook his head. 'Not today, mate. Can we just go home?'

'Yeah, course we can. Let's get you settled in and acclimatised. I understand things must seem strange for you but give it a few days and it'll be like you've never been away.'

'I think it's starting to sink in exactly how long I've been away. I mean, I've always measured it by how long I've been *in* prison, not by how many years I've missed being out.'

'Too many years.'

'Yeah. I could cope as long as I blocked the outside world out, so I never realised how much I missed it.' Marcus took a deep breath. 'But now I am out, I'm never going back. Ever.'

The two brothers turned to look at each other and smiled. Despite their physical differences, they both shared their mother's wolfish grin.

33

Maya arrived at Beech Field for her mid-shift. She sighed with relief when she realised Tara wasn't in. Chris and Connor were huddled around Amanda's desk, sifting through some paperwork, whilst Connor scribbled down notes.

'What are you two up to? If you're planning on graffitiing the staff board again, please don't. I thought Kym was going to self-combust last time.'

Connor looked up; a huge grin spread across his face. 'Best behaviour, honest. My written application was successful and I've been invited to attend the assessment for the enhanced crime-scene investigator's post.'

'Ah, mate, that's fantastic. Well done and good luck.'

'The assessment is on a Wednesday and the interviews are scheduled for Thursday the week after, if I get through.'

'Which you will,' Chris said, clapping him on the back. 'I'm just going through a few pointers that might help.'

'Basically, approach the crime scene like Nicola would and not like Chris and you'll be fine.' Maya laughed as Chris flipped her the middle finger.

'Are my ears burning?' Nicola said as she arrived at the office accompanied by Tara.

Maya smiled. 'Connor has got through to assessment. I was just telling him to work the scene like you would rather than bumble through it like Chris.'

Nicola laughed as she fist-bumped Connor and joined him at the desk, reading through the notes he'd made so far, ready to add some of her own suggestions.

Tara pouted as she flicked her hair over her shoulder. 'Don't you think you should learn to walk before you can run?'

Connor frowned. 'Meaning?'

'No offence, Connor, but you're still very wet behind the ears.'

Maya was indignant. 'No, he's not. He's got tons of experience over the last three years. Much more than I had when I was in his role; he's shadowed on all kinds of major scenes. He's more than ready for the position.'

Tara raised a perfectly plucked eyebrow. 'I think you're just being kind because he's your friend. I mean, no offence, Connor, but when I look at you, I just think man-child.'

A crimson flush crept up Connor's neck and bled into his face. Nicola and Chris were frozen, mouths open as they glanced between Tara and Connor. Maya could feel the heat rising in her own face. 'That is so uncalled for, Tara. You've no right to knock his confidence so soon before his assessment. If you've nothing nice to say then just keep your bloody mouth shut, nobody wants to hear it.'

Maya was about to continue but was interrupted as Jack appeared in the doorway.

'Ah, glad you're here.' He nodded towards Maya and Chris. 'Kym's asked if you could both join us in DI Redford's office. We've got an update on Operation Mermaid.'

'On our way, mate.' Chris patted Connor reassuringly on the back as he stood up.

Tara was gazing wistfully at the door, amazingly, she seemed lost for words for once.

'Isn't he lovely, Nicola,' she said with a sigh.

Nicola grimaced as she shook her head. 'Nope, not to me.'

'Oh, please. You're as bad as Maya. You can't deny he's gorgeous.'

'Not my type.'

'Oh, so what kind of man do you like?'

Nicola had a wry grin on her face. 'A wo-man. I prefer women.'

Tara's mouth opened in a perfect O. Her eyes widened. 'You're gay? An actual lesbian?'

'Yeah, but don't worry. I don't think it's catching, is it, Maya? I've not turned you yet, have I?' she replied wryly.

'Nope, I'm still a raging heterosexual.' Maya howled with laughter, high-fiving Nicola as she followed Chris out of the office.

'At least Nic's sexual preferences will take the heat off Connor,' Chris said.

Maya shook her head. 'She's a piece of work. I have never met anyone so rude and tactless.'

They knocked and entered Redford's office. Maya took a moment to savour the smell of fresh coffee and expensive aftershave.

'Ah, thank you both for popping in.' Kym smiled as they sat around the conference table. 'We won't keep you long. I just wanted to keep you in the loop as you were involved in the body recovery and post-mortem for Operation Mermaid.'

Maya sat up alert and writhing with anticipation. 'Have we found out who he is?'

'Unfortunately, no. Not yet anyway.' Kym and Redford exchanged a wry smile.

Jack cleared his throat impatiently. Whatever update was about to be imparted had clearly not been shared to him yet, although, judging from the relaxed expression on Redford's face, he had already been made aware.

Redford leant forward straightening his tie. 'Jack, do you want to get us up to speed on the investigation so far?'

Jack referred to his policy book as he listed all the enquiries that his team had conducted and the subsequent, painful lack of results. The fact John Doe had no tattoos or other identifying features stalled the investigation and they had exhausted every other potential line of enquiry. Kym made a note of everything Jack said before turning to Maya and Chris.

'Forensically, are there any considerations you think we have overlooked so far?'

'I've been through the scene and post-mortem photographs several times to check if we could have overlooked anything and I've drawn a blank. The clothing has taken us nowhere. If we have overlooked something, I'm at a loss to know what.' Maya sighed.

Chris nodded. 'I agree with Maya, we've done all we can.'

'In light of where we are then,' Kym continued after a pause, 'I'm going to liaise with the case management unit and see if they will authorise the cost of a forensic facial reconstruction expert.'

'About time,' Jack muttered, earning him a scathing look from both Redford and Kym.

'Is it a time-consuming procedure?' Redford asked.

Kym shook her head. 'No, it can be completed relatively quickly. You do need to be aware that there are limitations to the procedure, for example, eye colour, hairstyles, facial hair and expressions can only be guessed at.'

'When can we expect this to happen?' Jack asked impatiently.

Kym ignored him and turned to Maya and Chris instead as she answered. 'Once we're given the go-ahead, the process can start straight away.' She turned to Redford. 'With a bit of luck, we should have an image of John Doe to share in the media very soon.'

'Fantastic,' Maya said with a huge beaming grin. 'We might not know who our John Doe is, but at least we'll know what he looks like.' A shiver of anticipation ran through her. They were one step closer to finding out who their John Doe was. And once they knew that they'd be one step closer to finding out who killed him.

And why.

34

Sean hovered at the office door but frowned when he saw Maya. 'Oh, it's you,' he announced despondently.

Maya snorted. 'No offence taken, Sean. What have I done to upset you?'

'Oh, sorry, mate. Nothing. I didn't mean it like that. I need a SOCO. We think we've got eyes on Jason Laing and we're hoping to lock him up today. We want to record the bite mark on his neck if it's still there, but obviously you can't do it.'

'It's okay. I'm on a mid-shift and due to finish soon. Elaine is on the late shift so she can do it. She's just nipped out to buy some food before I leave, she should be back in a few minutes.'

Stevenson nodded, relieved. 'Fantastic. We think he's staying with a mate not far from Stour Bridge where the attack happened. I just need to set a few wheels in motion and we're hoping to bring him in.'

'Good luck, Sean. I hope you get the bastard today. I'm sure I'll hear from Lisa later on if you do.'

Maya smiled as she waved goodbye to Stevenson and started to pack up her things. The thought of Jason Laing's imminent arrest was great news. She desperately hoped it would give Lisa some peace of mind. And it would mean one less piece of shit on the streets.

Stevenson and Malone had their body armour on ready to strike on the address where Jason Laing was reported to be hiding out. They had stopped by the town hall on the way so they could call into the council's CCTV room.

'You go, mate, I'll wait in the car. It won't take two of us,' grumbled Malone.

'What's up with you?'

'Nothing, it's just the supervisor in there is a real arrogant wanker. Can't be doing with him.'

Stevenson rolled his eyes as he got out of the car. 'Thanks for the heads-up, mate!'

He showed his ID to the receptionist who buzzed him in and directed him down the ground-floor corridor to the CCTV room. It was a large, dimly lit office with a vast array of screens which were being monitored by staff with joystick-style controllers. Stevenson could hear the familiar sound of the police radio against a backdrop of other communications.

As part of the CCTV operatives' job, they monitored the police and council security staff's radio so if there was an ongoing incident or they were trying to locate a missing person they could direct their cameras accordingly.

The staff in here were the eyes and ears of the city, which was worrying as nobody had taken a blind bit of notice that Sean had just walked into the room. The atmosphere was oppressive and the whole office seemed to give off the air of one giant, surly shrug.

'Hi. I'm DC Stevenson from Beech Field police station,' he

announced cheerily to the room. Nobody looked up or acknowledged him, until after what felt like an age, a man closest to him with greasy hair and bad skin, nodded to a large desk in the corner.

'That's the boss,' he mumbled disparagingly.

Stevenson thanked him and approached the desk, smiling warmly at the man. He was in his late thirties, with dark hair. He returned Stevenson's smile with an acidic glare that could melt the face off a mannequin. 'How can I help?' he asked mechanically.

He was clearly the social equivalent of what a chicken and mushroom Pot Noodle is to fine dining. And that was if you added lukewarm tap water and skipped the soy-sauce sachet.

'Are you the supervisor?'

An imperceptible nod. 'Patrick Karim.'

Stevenson faltered. The man oozed hostility and it temporarily fazed him. It was bloody typical of Malone to shoulder having to deal with an arsehole like this.

'My colleague and I are hoping to make an arrest at Flat 3a, Stour House. I believe it should be covered by your cameras.'

Karim shrugged.

'I was wondering if you could keep eyes on it just in case our suspect has it away on his toes.'

Karim continued to stare at Stevenson.

'He's wanted for a serious assault and is considered a flight risk.'

Nothing.

'So...' Stevenson tapped the police radio on the man's desk. 'If you could keep an eye and ear out?'

A pulse twitched in the man's jaw.

'I'd be much obliged. Thanks so much for your help. It was really, really nice to have met you.' The sarcasm was clearly lost on Karim, and the rest of the office, as he loudly wished them all a lovely evening.

'Well?' said Malone as Stevenson returned to the car.

'You were right – total wanker. Come on, mate, let's go and lock up another one.'

35

Marcus surveyed his reflection in the bathroom mirror. He had piled on weight since coming out of prison. His appetite was voracious now he could eat whatever and whenever he wanted. He had years of digesting cold, tasteless meals to make up for.

He smoothed down his hair and ran a hand across his new beard. He hadn't been sure at first when he had started to grow it, but now it was starting to take shape, he decided it suited him. Anthony had agreed. He almost didn't recognise himself anymore. He was indeed a new man. Smiling at his reflection, he straightened his shirt and decided he looked good. Being out of prison suited him and it was nice to be dressed smartly for once. And, he laughed to himself, not just because he was due in court.

He spritzed himself with aftershave and marvelled yet again at how good it was to smell fresh and clean. Then he gave himself one last smile in the mirror before heading into the lounge. Marcus plucked his prayer cross and Bible from the coffee table and hugged them to his chest before melting into the sofa. Yet again, he marvelled at the softness and the comfort of it. Had it not been for the impending visit, he could easily have nestled his head back and napped. He was gradually beginning to acclimatise to life outside prison walls.

There were certain things he knew he would never, ever take for granted again. In particular, a decent night's sleep without the chorus of prison noise. He revelled in the appreciation of decent food, fresh air and the ability to take a shower or bath whenever he wanted, for as long as he wanted, with nice soap and fluffy towels.

It was a novelty not to have to wear flip-flops to the bathroom like he did in prison. That was because the floor itself was a health and safety nightmare. He even marvelled at the fact he smelt clean long after he had showered. Usually, by the time he had returned to the cell, he reeked yet again of the fetid smell which seemed to emanate within the prison walls.

Trying to adjust to normal life after being institutionalised for so long was proving difficult. Marcus found he had a pent-up energy, that he now realised was usually spent watching his back. In prison, violence could, and did, erupt at any time. Extreme violence was administered at the most imagined slight or insult.

Away from that environment, he now realised how paranoid he had become. He even found himself watching his loving brother, Anthony, out of the corner of his eye. He questioned time after time, how a man he had been estranged from for so long, could care so unconditionally, without expecting anything back in return. Then he caught the photograph on the mantelpiece and smiled at the image of his mother, and it was enough to ease his worried mind.

Still, the paranoia would take some working on. Only yesterday he'd been in the local shop after volunteering to go shopping for their lunch. It was the first time he'd been out on his own. Anthony had already warned him to avoid the self-service till. 'And not because you're massively behind the times,' Anthony had cautioned, 'but because it'll push you over the edge like the majority of society with its "unexpected item in the bagging area" bollocks.'

Marcus didn't even know what that meant but heeded his brother's words. He entered the breezy looking Co-op, marvelling at the huge array of products available, when he realised a man was stood behind him. He could feel his hackles rise and his muscles tense. He was about to turn around and make a pre-emptive strike against the intruder's head, when the man politely asked if he could reach past Marcus for a jar of pesto. Fucking pesto! What even was that? Marcus had left the shop empty-handed and in tears of laughter, and headed home to a bemused Anthony who wondered where their lunch was.

It was only later as he lay in bed, he realised that if he had acted on his instincts, he would be sleeping in a cell that night. The thought was sobering. And terrifying. It was a stark reminder that he needed to keep a constant check on his anger regardless of the situation or circumstances.

Anthony emerged from the hallway. He was wrapped up in his thick winter coat with a scarf entwined around his neck. Even with the excessive padding of his clothing, Anthony still looked like a strong breeze could blow him over. His bald pate reflected in the glow of the hall light bulb, nearly as much as his glasses did.

'I'm off to church,' said Anthony. 'Are you sure you don't want me to stay? I don't mind.'

Marcus shook his head. 'No, you go, I'll be fine, thanks. It's just a general chat to see how I'm adjusting.'

Anthony nodded. 'I'll pick us a takeaway up on the way home, shall I?'

Marcus smiled. 'That'd be great, bro, thanks.' He watched his brother retreat before calling him back. 'And I mean thanks, not just for the takeaway but for everything you've done for me. I really appreciate it.'

'I know, mate. It's what big brothers do. It's my job to look after you and we've got a lot of time to make up for.' Anthony nodded towards the framed photograph on the mantelpiece. 'It's what she would have expected us to do.'

Marcus smiled as Anthony clicked the front door softly behind him. He placed his Bible and prayer cross carefully back onto the coffee table and snuggled back into the couch, waiting for the probation officer's arrival. He was looking forward to talking about how he had rehabilitated and was no longer a threat to society. He would prove to the probation officer that his violent tendencies were a thing of the past and he had changed.

When he needed to be, Marcus Naylor was a very persuasive man.

36

Stour House was a large, three-storey dwelling situated on the main road. Its external façade boasted of a property that, in its heyday, had been a piece of architectural beauty. Stevenson and Malone eyed the front garden which had been left to run to seed. They noticed the makeshift curtains that clung to the various windows and having encountered such properties before, knew that once they got inside, they would see a property that had been pulverised into a shadow of its former glory.

Such houses had been adapted to become a house of multi-occupancy. The once spacious rooms would have been halved in size so landlords could squeeze in as many tenants as they legally could. Most of the lodgings weren't large enough to swing the proverbial cat let alone house anything larger than a sofa bed. Tenants came and went, often leaving a trail of depravity behind them. In such houses, desperate souls were housed alongside people you would normally cross the street to avoid at night. People like Jason Laing.

'Not even got in the place yet and I can already smell it,' Malone grumbled. He was no stranger to the shocking conditions some people lived in. His biggest trepidation about entering a place like this, from experience, was the prospect of spent needles.

'Safe to say we'll be wiping our feet on the way out,' agreed Stevenson. 'Right, do you want to take the front and I'll head around the back in case he does a runner.'

'Yeah, let's get in there, mate. Curtains are twitching already.'

They exited the vehicle swiftly. Malone headed to the front door as Stevenson used the neighbouring, derelict house as a cut through to the rear of the property. He swore under his breath as he became embroiled in piles of rubbish that had clearly been fly-tipped in the rear garden. He clambered over the debris as best as he could, squelching through a myriad of stinking, rotting mounds.

He was about to reach the rear gate when he heard Malone shout up on the radio and saw a flurry of activity from the neighbouring property. Jason Laing, ensconced in a black hooded top, was heading for the ginnel that ran along the back of the properties.

'Shit.' Stevenson wrestled to open the back gate, but years of rust and piles of rubbish piled against it, meant there was no way it was going to open. He scrambled over the top and dropped lightly to his feet in time to see Laing rounding the corner. Whilst the suspect was built like a brick-shithouse, Sean had the advantage of being shorter, slighter and faster. He quickly recovered from the drop and flew after Laing. He shouted up his progress on the radio, asking for any neighbouring patrols to assist in the search.

Laing was in his sight. Stevenson closed in on him as the suspect turned to look over his shoulder, causing him to stumble. Sprinting now, Laing began to knock the wheelie bins over that lined the back streets, to cause obstacles for his pursuer. Stevenson leapt cat-like around the bins, his eyes on

Laing as he heard Malone shout up CCTV and ask if they were monitoring the pursuit. The response was a deafening silence as Stevenson swore obscenities in his mind. His lungs were burning with exertion as he continued the chase.

Suddenly, a white van pulled out of one of the rear gardens, narrowly missing Sean who was forced to stop abruptly and dive out of the way. He slammed the passenger window in frustration.

'Move now!' he screamed.

'Fuck off,' the driver raged. A middle-aged man wearing a stained high visibility coat glared at Stevenson disparagingly. 'I could have fucking hit you, what are you playing at?'

Ignoring the driver, Stevenson ran around the front of the van. He couldn't see Laing. Desperate, he sprinted towards the end of the row of properties which took him near one of the other housing estates and also backed onto the canal. He heard police sirens heading in his direction and he barked instructions down the radio with Laing's description and letting officers know, from his local knowledge, where to start searching.

He began to limp in the direction of the canal. He had pulled his calf muscle when he'd been forced to stop by the van, and it felt like he'd been stabbed. He got to the start of the towpath and heard a car squeal to a stop behind him. Malone's face in the windscreen, mirrored his own frustration.

'Sorry, mate, I've fucking lost him,' Stevenson panted. 'What's that prick in CCTV up to?'

'Haven't a clue, mate, but trust me, we'll be having a word on the way back.'

Stevenson bent forward, his hands on top of this thighs as he tried to get his breath back. He winced, first at the excruciating pain in his calf and secondly at the smell emanating from the lower half of his trousers, where he'd waded through the piles of rotting rubbish. He felt Malone pat him avuncularly on the back.

'Don't worry, pal. I'll let Redford and Jack know what's happened.'

Stevenson straightened up and eyed Malone gratefully. 'Would you? Do you not mind?'

'No problem. But you can let Lisa Cohen know that that maniac is still out there. Rather you than me.'

37

Something had woken Rose. She didn't know what it was, but she was grateful, as it had roused her from a particularly disturbing dream. She felt shaken and confused. She strained to listen, wondering what had woken her. It felt like there had been lots of strange noises lately. Or had there? She struggled to remember what was real and what she had dreamt.

She squinted at her watch and made out that it was just before nine. She was still none the wiser whether it was morning or evening as the sultry darkness outside her bedroom window meant nothing at this time of year.

She shuffled herself further up the bed so she could sit up. The movement caused her head to swim. It didn't help that the glaucoma meant she struggled to focus, making her feel even more disorientated and as if she were looking through a lens that had been smeared with Vaseline.

A flush of shame spread across her chest and face as she caught a waft of her own body odour. She'd always been meticulous about her personal hygiene, but it was getting so much harder to bathe herself without help these days. Trevor and Bernadette were so busy, she didn't like to ask them for the help she so desperately needed.

Suddenly, her stomach rumbled, and she tried to remember the last time she had eaten. Not only could she not remember, but she also couldn't recall what she'd had. She was so confused. She reached for her false teeth and popped them in, glad to at least have a little dignity back.

Steeling herself, she swung her legs over the bed. She was disconcerted to feel the wetness from her incontinence pad and tried to ignore the smell that emanated from her crotch. Taking a deep breath, she slid her feet into her sheepskin slippers and prepared to stand. A movement at the door caught her eye. Relief and love rushed her like a wave.

'Trevor?'

'I thought I could hear you moving about.'

'Oh, Trevor. Where have you been?'

'Getting your breakfast.'

'But... that was days ago.'

Trevor laughed kindly. 'It wasn't, Mum, it's only been an hour. You're confused because of the water infection. You know they always make you go a bit daft.'

Rose squinted at Trevor, shaking her head. She didn't understand. Trevor kept coming and going. The police had been to look for him and everything.

'You went away...' She tried so hard to concentrate, but her mind was like a book that had been left open in the breeze. Just when she thought she knew where she was up to, the pages flicked to another chapter.

'I did go away, but I'm back now. Come on, let's go and get you fed before your scrambled eggs go cold.'

He supported her arm while she stood up and steadied her balance. He stayed close, supporting her as she shuffled to the landing. Laurel suddenly emerged from Trevor's bedroom and gave her a beaming smile when she saw her.

'What are you doing up here? Why were you in the bedroom?'

'I live here, Mum.'

'Laurel?'

The woman laughed and shook her head. 'Don't be daft, Mum, it's me, Bernadette.'

Rose squinted hard again; her vision swam as she tried to focus. Rainbow lights peppered her vision and her eyes hurt. She shut them for a moment, resting her hand on the banister to steady herself. When she opened them again, she could see Bernadette, not Laurel. How had she got the two of them so mixed up?

'Isn't it lovely to have Trevor home?' she asked her.

Bernadette laughed gayly. 'Oh, you silly old thing. He's been back for days now. Come and get your breakfast, then you can take your antibiotics.'

Rose's stomach growled again with hunger. Antibiotics? She wondered why she was taking them. Then she nodded to herself. Trevor had said she had a water infection. That's why she felt funny. That's why she was seeing things. She'd feel better once she had some food inside her and a nice cup of tea. Then she'd get herself cleaned up.

'Can I have a bath?' she asked Bernadette pleadingly.

'Of course you can. I'll run it for you as soon as you've finished your breakfast. I'll put some of the bubbles in that I use, the flowery scented ones, you like them, don't you? A rose for Rose?' Bernadette smiled kindly at her.

She was so lucky to have the two of them. They were so good to her. She shuffled towards the stairlift, feeling happier already. Then she paused at the top. The stairlift was at the bottom. It should have been at the top from when she'd last used it. That was strange. Or was it?

Her vision started to swim again as the stairway blurred in a rainbow halo. Was this another hallucination? She turned to ask them, but before she could even open her mouth, she felt a hand between her shoulder blades. Quick and solid.

She heard an ear-piercing scream but couldn't tell if it was from her or them. She lurched forward, arms windmilling, feet useless as she pitched forward. Her head ping-ponged between the banister and the wall. The track of the stairlift and the metal banister tore through her paper-like skin as she bounced down the stairs. Her neck snapped back quicker than the spring on a mousetrap.

She was dead by the time her brittle body reached the bottom of the stairs.

38

Maya was on the late shift and had spent her morning researching burglar alarm companies for Dominique and emailing her through details of the more reputable companies that she had found. Since Marcus's release, she had taken to phoning her mother morning and evening to check she was okay. Whilst she knew Dominique appreciated her concern, she could tell she found it wearying and was hoping this meant she would be more persuaded to finally get an alarm just to appease her.

When she arrived at work, she made a beeline for CID rather than her own office so she could speak to Sean. She was in luck as she caught him in the corridor.

Sean looked despondent. 'Lisa told you then?'

'Yes, she did. I wanted to check you were okay and reassure you that Lisa honestly doesn't blame you.'

'Shame Redford and Jack don't feel the same. And for the record, nobody blames me more than myself. We nearly bloody had him.'

'And you'll get him next time. He can't hide forever.'

'Really? Well, if he's gone to the same school of hiding as Trevor Dawlish, I won't hold my breath.'

Maya frowned, concerned. 'Come on, Sean. This isn't like you to be so negative. I understand your frustration but beating yourself up isn't going to help.'

Sean gave her a weak smile. 'I appreciate your support, thanks. It's just been a few shit weeks, hasn't it? We seem to be getting nowhere with any of our cases. John Doe is still unidentified, and I can't help thinking that you may be right about Laing having some involvement in his death. The fact we haven't got him locked up to ask is just so bloody frustrating.'

Maya squeezed his arm reassuringly. 'Keep the faith, eh? We'll get him, Sean.'

She smiled at him and headed to the SOCO office. It was rowdier than usual as everyone was discussing their options for the Christmas do.

'It's too last minute to book anywhere now. We should have done it weeks ago if we were going to eat somewhere.' Nicola tutted.

'I'm not bothered about food; I'd rather just go for drinks somewhere.' Elaine shrugged. 'As long as I can have a sing-song and a dance.'

'Whose turn was it to organise it anyway?' Maya asked.

Connor, Elaine and Nicola turned to look at Chris who had the decency to blush.

'In fairness,' said Amanda, as she rapped the desk to get attention, 'the same thing happens year after year. We all meet at The Lamb & Flag for drinks first and despite the fact we have a table booked somewhere, we end up meeting up with CID and forget about food and go for drinks elsewhere. For the last three years, I've taken a multipack of crisps out with me. My Christmas-do handbag is bigger than your fingerprint kits.'

'I'm surprised you've not prioritised booking a restaurant,

Chris. All you ever seem to think about is food, and you're never not eating,' said Tara with a snort. Everyone ignored her.

'Well, I agree with Nicola,' said Kym. 'It's far too last minute to book a meal now. Drinks are fine with me.'

DI Redford appeared at the office door and Kym smiled at him warmly. 'Ah, Phil. We've just been discussing our Christmas do. It sounds like the usual arrangements for us.'

Redford nodded. 'I'm a creature of habit so it suits me and my lot.'

'Why don't we try a couple of different pubs for a change?' said Chris. 'What about The Eagle? Maya, do you think Spence will give us mates' rates.'

She shrugged nonchalantly as her face flushed. 'Do you need us, boss?' she said to Redford, determined to change the subject.

'Yes please. We've just had a sudden death come in. Elderly lady found at the bottom of the stairs. Paramedics are concerned about the length of time she's allegedly been there. There's a suggestion that she's fallen in the night, but apparently there's no signs of rigor mortis, so they're questioning that. They're not ruling out neglect either. Can you oblige, please?'

'Yes, of course,' Maya said as she scribbled down the details. Her eyes widened when she heard the deceased's name.

'Rose *Dawlish*?'

Redford nodded.

'It's not a common name – is this a relation to Trevor?'

Redford nodded again. 'Yes, it's his mother. His wife found her, and the neighbour rang it in. Bernadette's currently staying with her sister as she's understandably distressed. Let's just say that my Spidey senses are telling me that something's not quite right.'

'An unbiased approach based on fact not supposition...' Kym began, causing Redford to grin.

'I know, I know.' He copied Kym's habitual double clap, which caused Maya to snort with a laugh that quickly died in her throat when Redford added, 'Jack's on the late shift too, so he'll meet you down there.'

~

At first glance, Rose Dawlish looked like a bag of rags abandoned at the foot of the stairs. A closer inspection revealed the shattered body of an elderly lady so frail, she reminded Maya of a baby bird. Her face was streaked with blood. Her neck hung at an oddly hinged angle, suggesting it had been broken by the fall. Her body was covered in a myriad of coloured bruises that blended with lividity.

Not for the first time, Maya was struck by how strange and invasive it felt to be standing in a stranger's home, surrounded by their things. The ominous silence made it feel like the house was holding its breath. It was as if Rose's sudden, unexpected death had ripped a void through the fixtures and fittings.

Maya knew that later on, as she moved through the house looking for any potential evidence, she would be struck by the poignancy of familiar, intimate items that would never be used again. Framed photographs, jewellery, Rose's favourite dress – objects that had once been coveted would hang in limbo until such time as the family decided whether to keep them or send them for bric-a-brac, for someone else to carelessly maul and disregard.

The old lady smelt strongly of urine and unwashed skin. Her woolly hair was matted, suggesting it had been some time since it had last been brushed, least of all washed. She was wearing a nightie, which was stained and dirty. She had one slipper on, the bare foot was twisted and splayed by arthritis and gnarled, yellow toenails looked like they were overdue a chiropodist's attention.

After taking an initial series of photographs to record the scene, Maya stooped down and carefully turned Rose over so she could survey her face and hands more clearly.

'Bless you, sweetheart,' she murmured softly to the old lady.

She was easy to manoeuvre. The fact that her skin was so cold to touch suggested she was definitely dead, despite the malleability of her limbs. Maya noticed a cluster of bruises on her upper arm that could potentially be fingermarks. That said, the elderly tended to bruise easily, so anything could have caused it, and Maya was mindful not to let it mar her judgement.

Her cheeks were hollow, and arms so thin Maya could easily encircle her thumb and forefinger around the bony limbs. Her false teeth looked too big for the flaccid mouth. Maya squatted back on her heels as she considered her frail frame.

'What are you thinking?' asked Jack from a discreet distance. His voice was muffled underneath the face mask.

'I can see why paramedics were concerned about the lack of rigor mortis considering how long she's been here,' said Maya. 'But she's incredibly frail and appears malnourished. Lack of muscle mass can lead to a lack of rigidity in death. It's not unusual for the elderly, or the very young for that matter, to not succumb to rigor at all after death.'

Maya stood up and surveyed the stairs. The chairlift was at the top and she could see the missing sheepskin slipper wedged underneath the footrest. She frowned as she took a series of photographs, before making her way up the stairs and examining the position of the slipper.

'Jack, can you come up here, please, I don't like the look of this.' She watched as he gingerly stepped over Rose, doing his best to avoid looking at the body.

'What is it?' he asked, crouching to survey the chairlift.

'The chairlift appears to have been stopped before it's reached the top. Look at the track, it should be facing the landing, as a safety feature. It'd be tricky for someone elderly and infirm to climb off before they need to, that's the whole point of having one. And her slipper is wedged under the footrest.'

Jack shrugged. 'She's lost her footing as she's climbed off it, obviously. Probably happened because, like you say, the chair isn't all the way to the top as it should be. Maybe that's just how she used it?'

Maya shook her head. 'I disagree. That slipper looks staged.'

Jack frowned. 'If I said water was wet, you'd argue the toss with me.'

Maya grinned. 'Technically, though, water isn't wet per se, it causes other things to be wet.'

'Oh, for fuck's sake!'

She narrowed her eyes. 'Don't make this personal, Jack. I'm using my professional judgement, not having a go. If, like you say, she's lost her footing getting off, the slipper would be on top of the footrest or on the landing. It's really wedged in, but far too tight. Look at the size of the gap – she couldn't have slipped her foot underneath that.'

Before she could stop him, Jack reached out to move it, but it didn't shift. He had to pull harder to release it, causing him to stumble back.

'Shit,' he breathed as the reality dawned on him that Maya was correct.

'Also,' said Maya, 'look at the arms of the chairlift. They're both raised. It makes no sense if she was getting on it from up here...'

'The left arm should be raised and the right lowered,' Jack finished. 'Particularly if she was in the habit of getting off before the top. She'd need to lean on the right to get her balance.'

Maya and Jack exchanged a look. 'I think we should see if we can get Doctor Granger down here,' he said.

Maya nodded. 'I agree with you. I'll phone Kym, too, and ask her to make her way.'

She glanced down the stairs at Mother Dawlish's crumpled body and sighed as she wondered who would possibly want such a frail old lady dead. Surely, she was harmless and no threat to anyone. Then something about the slipper caught her attention. There was a smudge of something buttercup yellow on the heel.

She held it aloft to Jack. 'What's that?'

He squinted. 'Paint?'

'Strange. I'll photograph that later. Shall we take a quick look round?'

They had a cursory look in both bedrooms and the bathroom. Something niggled at her as she looked in there, but it was the study that caught Maya's attention. 'That'll explain the paint,' she said to Jack as she nodded towards the wall. Three different shades of yellow had been painted in thick symmetrical stripes. On the desk, stood three opened tester pots of paint.

'Plans to redecorate,' Jack said.

'It seems a bit strange.'

'Why? You're such a conspiracist. What's strange about somebody wanting to redecorate a room?'

'Because downstairs is like a shrine to the seventies. Surely that would be your priority if you were going to redecorate. And look at the colours they've sampled, quite a contrast to the masculine décor in here.'

Jack rolled his eyes. 'They probably just fancied a change. Obviously, it's been a while since they did any home improvements, so maybe this is a practice room.'

Maya wasn't listening, her focus now was on the desk. In

particular the cabinets below the desk. 'It looks like there could be something missing out of here,' she said. Jack joined her and looked. 'Look at the two empty shelves. The rest of the cabinets are full.'

'Okay, I'll make a note that we ask Bernadette about that as part of our enquiries.'

'And the paint?'

'Oh, Maya, forget the bloody paint. We've got a woman lying dead at the bottom of the stairs in suspicious circumstances and you want my detectives wasting their time chatting about colour schemes like they're in B&Q? I'm going back to the car to make a few phone calls. Give Kym a ring, will you, and tell her I want her to turn out as soon as possible.'

He stalked out of the room, leaving her seething at his dismissive arrogance. If he had turned around, he would have seen her wildly gesticulating with two fingers at his back as he carried his condescending ego out of the room.

39

DS Turner pulled up outside the address he had been given for Bernadette's sister. He had been tasked with attending and taking a witness statement from her. He'd already been given the heads-up by Sean that she was a terrible witness, and he wasn't relishing the prospect of interviewing her.

There had been a debate in the office as to whether Sean should interview her, having already dealt with her previously. It was quickly agreed that as Rose's death appeared suspicious, that the investigation into her death and Trevor's disappearance should be kept separate.

The front door opened before Turner even had a chance to knock. A slim woman with cheaply dyed blonde hair, pinched features and a pale face greeted him.

'Stacey?' Turner asked. She nodded and gestured for him to come in.

Turner's heart sank at the sound of wailing coming from another room. This was going to be bloody painful.

'Follow me, Bernadette's in here. Can I get you a drink?'

'A black coffee would be lovely, thanks. No sugar.'

Stacey introduced him to Bernadette. She was wrapped in

her unicorn dressing gown with the hood up as if shielding herself from hearing any more devastating news. The juxtaposition of such a cheerful piece of clothing against the backdrop of her obvious distress wasn't lost on him. She stopped crying for long enough to ask her sister for a cup of tea.

Then she turned her attention to DS Turner. Her small, darting eyes were shining with tears. Turner was struck how alike the sisters looked. He smiled at Stacey as she left the room, settling himself into a chair opposite Bernadette as he braced himself before starting the questioning.

'Mrs Dawlish, understandably, I can see how upset you are, but it would help greatly if I could ask you a few questions so we can build up a picture of what has happened.'

Bernadette nodded and gulped back tears.

'I believe you found your mother-in-law, is that right?'

Bernadette nodded as she started to cry softly. She swallowed back tears before she began to explain.

'As I'm sure you know, my husband, Trevor, has been missing for several weeks now. It's been such a difficult time and it hasn't been easy looking after Mum. She's been even more confused than normal since Trevor disappeared.

'Anyway, Stacey suggested I come for tea last night, for a break and change of scene. I wasn't comfortable with the thought of leaving Mum at first, but without sounding awful, the thought of a break sounded too good to be true. Oh, I wish I hadn't...'

She burst into tears again and Turner sat back, giving her the time she needed to compose herself before she could continue. 'I mentioned it to my neighbour, Laurel Miller. She said it would do me good and offered to look in on Mum. She has a spare key, you see, and Mum and Laurel have always got on, so I agreed.

'Anyway, after dinner I started to feel a little unwell and had a terrible headache too. I think it's the stress. I was so tired.

Stacey told me I could sleep over here rather than chance driving home. I rang Laurel and asked if she'd make sure Mum got to bed okay, which she said she would. She sent me a text message to let me know everything was okay at home. Not long after that I went to bed.'

Turner made some notes before returning his attention to Bernadette. 'What happened this morning?'

'I had a quick brew with Stacey before I went home. I knew Mum would want her breakfast and need to take her pills. I let myself in the front door and then... I saw her...' Bernadette began to sob, her shoulders shaking as she hugged her knees to her chest. Stacey had just returned with the drinks. She set them down and engulfed her sister in a hug, rubbing her back and murmuring soothing words into her hair.

Turner waited patiently for Bernadette to gather herself. Stacey smiled apologetically at him. 'Laurel rang for an ambulance straight away and they contacted the police. We're not sure why, though, as Bernadette seems to think it looks like she'd fallen down the stairs. She wasn't very steady on her feet, you know. She had a very shuffling kind of walk and was always falling over because she didn't pick her feet up enough.'

Turner cleared his throat as he flicked through his policy book and read through some initial notes, including the observations Maya had made about how the slipper and the chairlift looked staged. 'It's early into the investigation, but our preliminary enquiries have suggested that your mother-in-law's death may not be accidental.'

Bernadette's head shot up, she was open-mouthed and wide-eyed.

'I *knew* I should never have left her.'

'Who would possibly want to harm an old lady? Especially someone as lovely as Rose?' Stacey asked, stunned.

Bernadette stood up suddenly, fists clenched either side of

her, tears streaming silently down her face. The hood of her dressing gown dropped away, and she looked like a determined Jedi.

'Laurel,' she announced resolutely as she eyed Turner. 'Laurel Miller wanted Trevor's mum dead.'

40

Maya had carefully and meticulously taken a succession of tape lifts and swabs from Rose Dawlish. Once she had finished, she and Kym had placed the shattered bones into a body bag ready to be conveyed to the ironically named Rose Cottage where her post-mortem would take place. The sight of the diminutive bulge in the body bag left a lump in Maya's throat and she was glad that this was one post-mortem she wouldn't have to endure.

Kym had told her that Nicola and Elaine would attend, leaving Maya free to stay with the scene. Once the body had left the address, Maya had headed back to Beech Field, relieved that her shift was over as she was physically and emotionally exhausted. She rang Dominique to check she was okay before riding to the supermarket closest to home so she could pick up something quick for her tea. She usually preferred to cook, but decided this evening was definitely a ready meal night.

She ambled up the aisles, gazing dully into the chiller, waiting for something to catch her eye and tempt her appetite. Her heart wasn't in it as she moved along to the rows and rows of freezers which made her think of the bodies stacked in the mortuary. She thought particularly of John Doe and sighed as she wondered how much longer he would lie in there unidentified. The longer they waited to find out who he was meant that his killer could be anywhere by now and she wondered if they would ever have justice for the murdered man.

She thought about the facial reconstruction and wondered how it was progressing. The process was a combination of experts in anthropology and osteology, as well as artistic skill to recreate the face. She knew that a cast would have been taken of the skull by now and that the experts would then apply depth markers to the different areas to indicate the thickness of facial tissue at the various points. Strips of clay would then be used to rebuild the face based on the relevant measurements.

She caught her own reflection in the freezer doors and a movement behind her made her jump. She apologised to a harassed-looking woman who reached past her to grab some items. Her eyes continued to graze across the packets of frozen food, but her mind remained consumed with thoughts of John Doe. What if the facial reconstruction didn't help? What if still, nobody recognised him and came forward. How could someone disappear for this long, and be *murdered*, yet nobody had come forward to report a loved one, friend, neighbour or colleague missing that matched his description?

She knew she shouldn't be too surprised. She'd been to countless burglaries where people didn't know who their neighbours were, had hardly seen them let alone spoken to them. She mused over how Trevor Dawlish's bank card had ended up in John Doe's pocket and not for the first time concluded he could be a vagrant. That would certainly account for the fact nobody was looking for him. And he wouldn't be the first homeless person to resort to pickpocketing or shoplifting.

She let out an audible groan as she thought of how Rose Dawlish would soon be John Doe's neighbour and wondered who was responsible for her death. What if her death turned into another seemingly unsolvable mystery? She shook her head and forced herself to concentrate. She was tired and overthinking things. Now wasn't the time. She just needed to have something to eat, get a bath and a decent night's sleep so she was fit and ready for work again in the morning.

She opened the freezer door closest to her and pulled out a frozen pizza. That would have to do. A bit of comfort food might do her the world of good. She closed the door and jumped again as the glass reflected someone stood behind her. She admonished herself as she turned to see several fellow shoppers amble wearily along the aisle. Their faces mirrored her own exhaustion.

Clutching the pizza, she dashed to the till, keen to be out of the supermarket and back in the comfort and warmth of her own home. As people bustled around her, she didn't realise she was being watched. She didn't realise that Marcus Naylor was discreetly following her from a safe distance. His eyes were devouring the very sight of her, as a wistful smile lingered on his face.

41

Bernadette had composed herself enough to be able to continue her conversation with DS Turner. The flush of anger that accompanied the accusation dissipated as quickly as it had come, leaving Bernadette a sobbing mess who clung to her sister like a life raft.

Turner smiled kindly at her. 'Are you ready to continue?'

She nodded.

'What makes you think Laurel killed Rose? That's quite an accusation. Why would she want to do that?'

'She's obsessed with my husband. I realised it when we first started going out. At first it was just dirty looks when she saw me coming and going. Then, when we got more serious and I started staying over with Trevor, I noticed scratches on my car, slashed tyres, that kind of thing.'

'And did you speak to her about it?'

'Not straight away. It was awkward. First of all, I don't like any kind of confrontation or arguments and secondly, Laurel was good friends to Trevor and Mum. As far as they were concerned, she was a family friend who could do no wrong.'

'And did Laurel's hostility progress?'

'Yes. She'd be all smiles and pally-pally in front of them, but when it was just the two of us, oh, she said some horrible things.' Bernadette took a moment to blow her nose. 'She would tell me how I wasn't pretty or clever enough for Trevor. That I was too stupid...' At this point her voice broke with fresh tears as her sister patted her back encouragingly.

'Surely the others must have picked up on this. Did you not think to say something?'

Bernadette nodded. 'When Trevor proposed I didn't accept straight away, I told him I'd have to think about it. I hated doing that as I knew I was breaking his heart. I also knew if I agreed to marry him, it would mean moving in with him and his mother and having to put up with *her*.'

'So, what happened?'

'I was so nervous, so scared to do it, but I went round to her house and confronted her. Told her that Trevor had proposed and that I wanted to say yes, but I couldn't bear the thought of putting up with her hateful comments. I told her I was going to say yes to Trevor on the condition that we sell up and move away.'

She gave a dry laugh. 'Well, that changed things. She started to cry and apologise. Told me she couldn't help it; she was in love with Trevor and jealous of me. I told her I wasn't her enemy but wasn't going to be her verbal punchbag either.

'The thought of Trevor moving away so she'd never see him again seemed to get through to her. She promised she'd change, and to be fair for the last few years, she has. We've even been getting on, or at least tolerating each other. I know she still thinks I'm a fool.'

'So, what makes you think she killed your mother-in-law?'

'She's been in bits since Trevor went missing. Obviously, we all have. She mentioned something in passing the other day that if something happened, maybe that would bring Trevor home.'

'What sort of thing?'

'She didn't say in so many words but hinted that if Mum was ill and Trevor heard about it, there's no way he'd be able to stay away; it would make him come straight back home.'

'What did she actually *say*? It would help if you could remember the words she used and her demeanour when she said them.'

Bernadette screwed her eyes shut and wrung her hands together. 'I don't know. I just can't remember. It's the pills the doctor has given me, you see. They make me feel so sleepy. I didn't even hear Trevor come home the other day. I only knew because of Laurel.' She tailed off looking utterly despondent.

'When I look back, it's so obvious. Laurel insisting I come here. Even if I'd not felt poorly and ended up sleeping over, I think Mum would still have died. I think Laurel orchestrated the whole thing. She must have let herself in and managed to get Mum to the stairs and then pushed her. I blame myself,' she said as she buried her face into her sister's shoulder and began to cry again.

'There's something else,' she added, suddenly straightening up as she dabbed her eyes with a tissue. 'Something that I think inflamed her jealousy and might also be the reason Trevor has gone away for a while. The reason I wasn't feeling well the night I stayed here.' She exchanged a glance with Stacey.

'And what's that?'

Her hands reached down instinctively to cup her stomach. 'The baby.'

42

Rose Dawlish was laid out naked in the mortuary. She was a pitiful sight, stick thin and with her joints jutting out at warped angles from the broken bones she'd sustained in her fall. Anyone who looked at her couldn't help but wince as it looked so painful. Her sparse, white pubic hair was a startling contrast to the aubergine lividity of her skin. Her drooping breasts and stomach looked like nothing more than pockets of overhanging skin, and with her false teeth removed, her mouth looked sunken. Had she been alive, she would have been mortified at people seeing her without her teeth *and* being naked in front of them.

But sadly, what Rose had once thought or indeed felt was now irrelevant. Nobody knew about the people she had met along her life who she loved deeply. These strangers gathered around her in the mortuary would never know that she used to have the sweetest, most infectious laugh or that she could sing like an angel. They didn't know she'd been a huge fan of The Beatles or that she loved to read Agatha Christie novels of an evening while sipping a port and lemon. That was before her failing eyesight made it too difficult and uncomfortable to read. To them she was just a clue. An exhibit to be pulled apart and discussed. One piece, albeit the most important, of this investigative jigsaw puzzle.

Doctor Granger tutted his way through Rose's post-mortem examination due to the obvious signs of neglect, from the sparse stomach contents and the inflamed skin on her buttocks and genitals where she had been left regularly in sodden incontinence pads. She was clearly malnourished although Granger suggested that neglect appeared to be a relatively recent occurrence as there was nothing to suggest long-term abuse.

This time, Jack remained in the viewing gallery, Adila acted as exhibits officer and Nicola assisted as the 'dirty' SOCO whilst Elaine carried on with the photography. It had been a solemn affair. Even though the death of someone Rose's age was not unexpected, the thought that someone could deliberately harm her was inconceivable.

Granger concluded that death was caused by a major head trauma sustained during the fall. It was hardly surprising that a lady of her fragility and age would not survive such an experience. Regarding culpability, it was not possible to ascertain if death was deliberate or accidental. As far as the post-mortem went, that was so far inconclusive and down to the detectives to investigate.

That was why Malone was approaching Laurel's address with a view to interviewing her, especially after the damning accusations Bernadette had made. If Laurel refused to comply, he would have no choice but to arrest her on suspicion of murder based on Bernadette's claims. Malone hoped it wouldn't come to that. At this stage, until concrete evidence could be found, it was easier to treat Laurel as a witness. He had viewed the scene photographs that Maya had taken and agreed with her belief that the fall looked staged. Rose Dawlish's death was definitely not accidental.

Malone knocked on the door, his eyes scouring the street for any CCTV cameras, either council or private. He made a mental note to get a team to check around the back of the Dawlishes' house to see if that gave any leads when the door was swung open. Laurel was dressed in a black jumper adorned with crystals, and black jeans. Her face was devoid of make-up, her hair unkempt, the gold crucifix already gripped between her fingers.

'Mrs Miller?'

'It's Miss. I assume you're here about Rose.' She sniffed noisily as she examined Malone's warrant card. 'Come on in, detective.'

Malone studiously wiped his feet, before he entered the pristine hallway and was led into a spacious lounge. Weak winter sun flooded the room and accentuated a cupboard storing an array of crystal ornaments, causing rainbow prisms to dance across the walls. The lush carpet was spotless, the room sweet-smelling of beeswax and lemon. The plush sofa he sank into was clearly expensive.

'How is Bernadette?' Laurel asked as she sat opposite Malone, too distressed to even offer him a drink.

'She's being well looked after by her sister,' Malone replied diplomatically. 'Obviously, we're keen to piece together the events surrounding the elder Mrs Dawlish's sudden demise and wondered if, based on the information Bernadette has given us, you could answer a few questions.'

Laurel nodded keenly, leaning forward to concentrate on Malone. He opened his policy book and skimmed his notes. 'What's your relationship with the Dawlishes?'

'Oh, we've been good neighbours for about nine years now. Lovely family. They made me feel so welcome from the day I moved in. They're quiet people. Keep themselves to themselves. Rose and her husband started a family quite late on.' She settled back into the chair as she eased into her tale. 'Mr Dawlish passed away about eighteen months before I bought this house. Heart attack, poor man. Very sudden. Understandably Trevor and his mum were distraught. It was evident they were still grieving when I moved here.'

She shook her head sadly. 'As a family they're not immune to tragedy, I'm afraid. Trevor had a younger brother. They lost him to meningitis when he was only four.'

'And what about Bernadette?'

'Ah, well she and Trevor met at work. She has a part-time clerical job at the town hall where Trevor works and that's where they met. They'd been dating about a year and then she moved in and not long after that, they were married.'

'And you get on with Bernadette?'

Laurel shrugged. 'I suppose so, yes.'

'You sound hesitant.'

'Not at all. She's a quiet woman.' Laurel hesitated as she hunched forward, plucking at the hem of her top. 'I don't mean to speak out of turn, but I can never decide if she's shy or just a bit... dim.'

'Dim?'

'Yes.' She let out a nervous laugh to show she meant no offence. 'The Dawlishes are a quiet family like I said. Trevor is a case of still waters run deep. He's an incredibly intelligent man. He's a keen Mason, you know. I think he could go far in life if he didn't have the constraints of having to care for an elderly mother.

'And, Bernadette, well, she's lovely but not the sharpest knife in the drawer. I could never see what Trevor saw in her...' Laurel tailed off, clearly not wanting to add any more in case she spoke out of turn.

'Okay.' Malone decided it was time to redirect the questioning. 'Can you tell me about the events leading to Rose's death. In particular the night before, up until she was discovered.'

Laurel nodded. She took a breath to compose herself although Malone could detect a slight trembling in her lower lip. 'I'd called to see Bernadette in case there was any word on Trevor. I assume you know he's been missing.'

Malone nodded and she continued. 'She seemed stressed that morning and had stated that Rose had been particularly demanding. The house was a mess which is unusual and it was obvious that Bernadette was struggling to cope. She said her sister had invited her round for tea and I encouraged her to go. I told her the change of scene would do her good. I said I could help out if needed, as Rose had my phone number, and I could be round within minutes.

'Anyway, later that evening, Bernadette rang me, very apologetic. She said she was feeling unwell and didn't want to chance driving home. Her sister had said she could stay over and sleep it off. Between you and me, detective, I did wonder if she'd been drinking. Not that there's anything wrong with that mind, it would just be out of character for her. She asked me if I'd go and check the old lady was settled in bed okay and that she'd be back first thing in the morning.'

'Then what did you do?'

'I let myself in over the road. Bernadette had told me Rose was already in bed, just needed her tablets and a drink. She said she'd fed and helped her change before going to her sister's.'

'And how did Rose seem to you when you visited?'

Laurel paused, a frown darkening her face. 'She seemed okay I suppose. She was a bit drowsy and listless, but when I asked her about it, she told me she was just tired. All the stress of Trevor being missing can't have helped, and she has a few health issues like most people her age.

'I did notice that she seemed, oh I hate to say it, smelly, but it was too late for me to do anything about it. She was ready for bed, so it was too late for me to start running her a bath. Plus, it didn't feel right, like I'd be overstepping a boundary. Instead, I made a mental note to say something to Bernadette in the morning.

'I was even going to suggest that she needed to start thinking about getting carers in to help with the load. We chatted for a while. I made her a cup of tea and she ate a couple of biscuits before she took her pills. I wished her goodnight and left. I told her I'd call round to see her in the morning.' Laurel started to cry at this point, her hands wringing the hem of her top.

'I left the landing and hall light on for her and double-checked the front door was locked. The following morning, I heard a car. I looked out and saw Bernadette come home. I watched her go into the house. I thought I'd give it an hour while they had breakfast before I nipped round, but then suddenly I heard screaming. Bernadette had opened the door and saw her straight away at the bottom of the stairs. I rang for an ambulance, although it was obvious the poor woman was already dead. Bernadette was too hysterical to do it, and the rest,' she said as she splayed her fingers, 'you already know.'

'Can you remember the position of the chairlift? Where was it?'

Laurel pursed her lips. 'Well, at the top of the stairs, obviously, where it always is.'

'You're sure?'

'Yes, because I always bang my shin on the bloody thing and I did it again last night.'

'Which way was it facing?'

'Towards the landing. It turns away from the stairs when she gets on and off it.'

'Can you recall what position the arms were in?'

'Well, I expect...'

'Sorry, Miss Miller. Please take your time. It's important to see if you can recall exactly how it was positioned that evening. Not how you assume it would have looked or how you may have recalled it in the past. Our SOCO who attended the scene has queried its position.'

Laurel sat back, frowning for a moment, before eventually shaking her head. 'I think... I just can't be sure at the moment. As I said, I cracked my shin on it, but I was more preoccupied with going to see Rose.'

Malone made a note then wiped a hand across his mouth. 'Forgive me, but this next question is a little delicate.'

Laurel sniffed. 'I can see from your expression that whatever it is it's important so just ask away, detective.'

'Bernadette has suggested that you have feelings towards Trevor.'

Laurel snorted. 'That's ridiculous. As I have already told you, I've known the family for years, we're just good friends.'

'Purely platonic?'

'Absolutely. To suggest anything else is absurd.'

'Okay,' Malone said as he leaned forward, an eyebrow raised. 'I'm afraid as awkward as this conversation may be for you, I do need to explore this a little further.'

Laurel let out a strangled laugh. 'This is ridiculous. What a waste of time. What on earth do you think you have to gain by this line of "enquiry"?' She used her fingers as quotation marks.

'Because, it would appear that Mrs Dawlish's death may not be accidental.' He took a moment to study Laurel's reaction as her hand flew to her mouth and her posture stiffened in the chair. 'And, as I've already said, Bernadette has suggested that you have feelings for her husband.'

Laurel shook her head as her eyes began to pool with tears.

'In fact, according to her, it's fair to say that you are infatuated, no, *obsessed* with Trevor.'

He failed to add that in his eyes that could well provide her with a motive for murder.

43

'So, what's the verdict on the death of Rose Dawlish?' asked Amanda.

Maya stifled a yawn before she answered. The day after the post-mortem, she had returned to the Dawlishes' house, accompanied by Chris, to examine the scene in accordance with a forensic strategy written by Kym. They scoured the house for any clues that would reveal who was responsible for the old lady's death, but unusually, were left with more questions than answers. Despite a late finish, rather than going straight home, she had ridden past Dominique's just to check everything seemed okay, even though she had already spoken to her earlier that evening.

'We've drawn a blank at the scene,' said Maya. 'It looks like the fall was definitely staged because of the position of the chairlift and where the slipper was discovered. There's no way she could have caught her foot under the gap. The slipper had been deliberately wedged there.'

Maya let out a sigh. 'We've got no sign of forced entry, so it has to be someone she knew well enough to let into the house or someone who had a key. What is interesting is that the last time

Trevor returned home, he left his wallet in the kitchen and that's now missing, which makes him a suspect. The post-mortem has given us a cause of death, but no other clues. We know she died as a result of the fall, but we don't know who pushed her, and I'm in no doubt whatsoever that someone did.' Chris nodded in agreement.

'We've also requested toxicology, but that'll be several weeks until we get the results. The way things are going, we might still not have solved it by then.'

She noticed Jack pass by the office door and called to him. 'We're just talking about the Rose Dawlish job. Any joy your end?'

He perched on the edge of a desk as he shook his head. 'We're going round in circles so far. I'm thinking about bringing Laurel in under caution. She's got no alibi, whereas Bernadette has. If she has got a thing for Trevor, that could be a motive and we don't know anyone else who has a key or is a regular visitor to the house.'

'What about Trevor?'

'That's another hypothesis we're working on. He's certainly a person of interest particularly as we know his wallet has gone. The fact he's been missing but we know he's been back to the house proves he still has a key. He's also going to inherit everything, which, if he's disappeared because of money worries, would be convenient.

'There's been no mention of any serious debts, but they don't appear to be a particularly wealthy family. Sean has been tasked with obtaining a recent photograph and I'm going to speak to the press office later about putting out an appeal for his whereabouts as a matter of urgency.'

'The chances are, she knew her killer and it's most likely someone with legitimate access, so forensics from the house isn't going to progress the investigation,' said Maya. 'From our perspective, we're snookered.'

'Any joy with CCTV?'

Jack rubbed the back of his neck. 'Nothing. No private cameras other than a Ring doorbell at next door but one, which only captures the end of their drive giving us nothing of the Dawlishes or Laurel's. It's frustrating because if it had just stretched a bit further... According to the neighbours, there's no one else they can think of. The Dawlishes kept themselves to themselves. We've got nobody else in the frame. My money is on Laurel.'

'I think it's the son, Trevor,' added Chris, whereas Maya just shrugged.

Jack nodded his head towards Kym's office. 'Is she in?'

'Rest day today, she's back tomorrow. What do you need her for?'

'Just wondered if we had an update on the facial reconstruction for Operation Mermaid.'

'Not that I've heard. I'm sure once we have, you'll be the first to know.'

Jack thanked her and left. Chris eyed Maya suspiciously.

'Go on, who do you suspect? You've got a good nose for knowing *whodunnit*.'

Maya grinned. 'I honestly haven't a clue. The wife sounds like too much of a wet blanket according to Sean and I believe the neighbour seemed to have genuinely cared for the old girl. As for Trevor, who knows, his disappearance is certainly bizarre.

'Like Jack said, he's been back to the house, so we know he's still in the area and has access to the property. To my mind, he's someone we need to locate now even more as a priority. His disappearance is strange and suggests he's up to his neck in something untoward. It's possible he killed John Doe, so if he has killed once, what's to stop him doing it again?'

Chris raised his eyebrows. 'Good call. But why?'

'John Doe had his bank card. Maybe it was a mugging gone wrong, and Dawlish killed him by accident, which is why he then did a runner. Or he took it because Trevor owed him money.'

'Ah, but why didn't Dawlish then take his bank card back after he killed him?' asked Amanda.

'Maybe it didn't cross his mind. If he saw red and acted in the heat of the moment, then I imagine he would have been in a state once he realised what he'd done. He certainly wouldn't be the first murderer to make a mistake and he won't be the last.'

Chris leant forward, spreading his hands on the desk. 'Say you're right, why would Trevor then kill his mum? Plus, why, if he's done a runner after killing someone, accidental or otherwise, does he keep returning to the address?'

Maya shrugged. 'We know he's been going back for clothes and money. Perhaps the wife was helping him. We know he's assaulted her on at least one occasion, so if there's violence involved, she's scared of him and will do whatever she's told.

'This wouldn't be the first relationship which everyone assumes is perfect, when the truth is, there's domestic violence. No one knows what really goes on behind closed doors, do they? Bernadette has told us that Laurel had feelings for Trevor, perhaps they were reciprocated, and something was going on between them? I'm going back full circle to suggest that's why he killed the old lady. Cash or passion. Murder is usually motivated by love or money.'

The conversation turned into a comfortable silence, or so Maya thought, when she suddenly saw Chris and Amanda exchange a look.

'What was that?' said Maya.

'What?' asked Chris, wide-eyed with innocence.

'I saw you give each other a funny look. What's going on, what have I missed?'

'Nothing,' attempted Chris until Amanda gave him a scowl. 'Well, I say nothing, it's just that we've been worried about you.'

'Why, because I don't know who killed Mrs Dawlish? Bit extreme.'

Chris laughed. 'No, because he who shall not be named has been released by now. I bumped into Dominique in Tesco yesterday and she mentioned you were worried that she wasn't taking his release serious enough, but you've not said anything to us about it.'

Maya shrugged.

'And...' Amanda said tentatively, 'we both know that the whole thing can't be easy for you to come to terms with. But, up until now, you haven't mentioned it. To anyone. Which also reminds me that Jayne from Welfare rang to remind you about your appointment with her next week. She said to tell you not to even think about avoiding her by trying to cancel it, because she'll just turn up here instead.'

Maya could just picture Jayne saying that, and it made her smile. 'I know, it's in my diary. Look, I'm hardly going to start broadcasting my business with Tactless Tara in the office,' scoffed Maya. 'I've never met anyone who involves herself so much in other people's business. If I so much as go to the toilet, I think she's going to follow me in. Into the actual cubicle, that is.'

Amanda laughed. 'I know what you mean, but you also know you can speak to either of us away from work. Anytime.'

Maya nodded. 'I do know that and thank you. I love that you care, but honestly, this isn't something I want to talk about. I'm dealing with it in my own way, which is by not thinking about it. I don't know where Naylor is staying or what he's doing, and I prefer to leave it that way. The thought of him makes me feel physically ill, so I need to just block him out. I can almost convince myself he's still in prison if nobody mentions him. As far as I'm concerned, ignorance is bliss.'

'It's not always the answer though, love,' Chris said softly.

'I know, but it's how I want to deal with things. It's the best way I can cope for now.'

Chris smiled at her. A smile that didn't quite reach eyes that were etched with concern. 'Well, like Amanda said, we're here if you need us, anytime. I've grown very bloody fond of you, Maya Barton, so don't suffer in silence, eh?'

As much as Maya appreciated their concern and knew how much they cared about her, she didn't want them to know how worried she had felt since Marcus's release. Talking about him made her feel worse. She wanted to bury herself in work and forget about everything else.

44

Laurel followed DS Turner and Malone along the corridor of Beech Field police station, her eyes as wide as saucers. Just spending time waiting at the front desk had been a hellish experience. Three men had been waiting loudly and impatiently to sign on for bail. Their foul language was nearly as disgusting as the smell of stale sweat and cannabis emanating from their pores.

Despite there being plenty of empty seats, one had plonked himself unceremoniously in the fixed plastic chair next to Laurel and asked her chest what she was there for. She had informed him she was just there to help the police with their enquiries, which led to him menacingly asking her if she was a grass. His loud, vulgar voice, wandering eyes and cocky swagger terrified her.

She could have kissed DS Turner when he opened the side door and beckoned her in, such was her relief at seeing him. She was sweating profusely as she scuttled behind him to the interview room as she shed her winter coat and scarf. The interview room consisted of four chairs and a table, the recording device situated next to the wall and an ominous-looking CCTV camera situated in the corner of the ceiling – an all-seeing eye. The walls were soundproofed and caused Laurel's ears to feel muffled once the door was closed.

'Thank you for coming in today, Miss Miller. This interview will be recorded and once again I would just like to remind you that you're entitled to have a legal representative present.'

Laurel shook her head as she reached instinctively for the crucifix. 'There's really no need, detective. I'm not guilty of any wrongdoing. I can assure you that I'm a person of honesty and integrity.'

Malone muttered something indistinguishable as he prepared to take notes. Turner smiled at Laurel encouragingly as he started the recording, stating the time, date, location and who was present within the room.

'Okay, today we just want to elaborate on a few facts following on from our previous conversation. There's just a few inconsistencies we need to iron out.'

'Inconsistencies?'

'Yes, I'm afraid your version of events doesn't quite match with what Bernadette Dawlish has told us.'

Laurel let out a high-pitched laugh. 'If you speak to your Inspector Stevenson, he will tell you that Bernadette, God love her, isn't the sharpest knife in the drawer, she's more of a spoon. I'm confident you'll realise that any inconsistencies are from Bernadette's viewpoint, not mine.'

'Mm. Well, to start with I just need to ask you again about your feelings towards Trevor.'

Laurel puffed out her cheeks. 'Honestly, I'm beginning to despair with all this. There nothing going on between Trevor and I other than a purely platonic friendship. I don't know where *she's* got this idea from that I was obsessed with him.'

'Bernadette has gone further with her claims. She states

when she first started dating Trevor, she received harassment from you starting with dirty looks and caustic comments and even involving damage to her motor vehicle on more than one occasion.'

'What kind of damage?'

'She states several incidents occurred in the first twelve months of her relationship with Trevor, these included scratches on her car, a cracked windscreen and she has also claimed that her tyres had been slashed.'

Laurel shook her head. 'That didn't happen.'

Turner raised a questioning eyebrow.

'If anything like that had happened on the road, I would have seen it. I'm incredibly observant. A one-woman neighbourhood watch if you will. At no point have I ever seen any damage to her car or anyone else's.'

'But she has said you were responsible.'

'Ridiculous.' Laurel tugged at the crucifix, as she crossed her legs and sat back in the chair. 'I would never do such a thing and nobody else did either. I would have noticed. She's lying.'

'You say you're very observant, Miss Miller.'

She gave a small, boastful smile and nodded, uncrossing her legs.

'Yet on several occasions, you have referred to my colleague Detective *Constable* Stevenson as Inspector, despite repeated attempts by him to correct you.'

'Well... I... Honestly, in the grand scheme of things, is that even relevant?' She folded her arms and clamped her mouth shut.

'Moving on to the last time you saw Rose. You stated you made sure she was settled safely in bed and left her for the night after locking up. Are you absolutely sure the door was locked?'

'Absolutely. I double-checked it to make sure.'

'And did you notice anyone hanging around as you went back to your own house?'

'No. I would have remembered. As I said I'm very...'

'Observant. Indeed.' Turner checked his notes. 'Can you remember what the weather was like that evening?'

'Yes, it was raining. And very cold. Sharp wind, you know.' She half closed her eyes, as she remembered. 'It was actually hail-stoning. I remember specifically because it was stinging my face. It was quite painful. And my hands were red raw because I had no gloves on.'

Malone let out a small cough. 'Is it possible that in a rush to get out of the bad weather and back home, you may not have locked the door properly after all?'

'No! It was definitely locked. I resent that accusation,' she said indignantly.

'My apologies. Going back to DS Turner's earlier question though, you're quite sure nobody else was around at that time?'

'Nobody. I habitually look out regularly prior to going to bed and there was nobody else on the road that night.'

Malone cocked his head to one side. 'But visibility wasn't great, was it? What with the windy wet weather, sheets of hailstones, plus it was dark? On a road that still has sodium street lights, which aren't the brightest, are they?'

'I did *not* see anybody else.'

'So, for example, Trevor didn't return to the address again that night?'

Laurel flushed. She shuffled in her seat. Her bum had started to go numb, and it felt uncomfortable. 'I would have noticed.'

'Is it fair to say then, that you were the last person to see Rose alive?'

Laurel gasped. 'Well, yes. I mean no! Bernadette saw her last. When she came home.'

Turner rubbed his chin. 'Sorry to be crass, but the question was, were you the last person to see Rose *alive*? She was already dead at the bottom of the stairs when Bernadette returned home.'

Laurel started to cry quietly, huge tears splashed down her cheeks. Turner and Malone began to busy themselves with their notes to allow her a moment to compose herself.

'There is something else.'

'I'm listening.' Turner smiled kindly while Malone gripped his pen.

'You asked me yesterday about the position of the chairlift?'

'Ah yes.' Turner tapped his pen on the table as Malone flicked through his notes.

'Well, I've remembered.'

'You weren't sure about that yesterday?'

'Well, I am now I've had time to think. I told you I banged my shin on the bloody thing.'

'That must have been quite painful. Do you have a bruise?'

'Pardon?'

'If you have a bruise on your shin, we can have it photographically recorded by one of our crime-scene investigators. It adds continuity to what you're telling us.'

'I tend not to bruise easily.'

'Would you like to double-check?'

She shook her head, eyes on the table. 'No need.' There was a heavy pause. 'There is no bruise.'

'I see. So, what do you remember about the chairlift?'

'You asked about the arms specifically. The left arm was up. I reached out to steady myself and grabbed the arm and it started to push down. I remember pulling it back to how it had been.'

'Which just to confirm, was how exactly?'

'The left arm was raised.'

'And you're sure about that?'

'Positive.'

'What about the right arm. Was that raised too?'

'No, it was down.'

'You're sure?'

'Yes. It was in the position you would expect to find it when it was last used. It was at the top of the track. The left arm was raised to allow her to exit the chair safely onto the landing, and the right was in the fixed position, to prevent her from falling out of the chair.'

'You seem to recall this vividly now when you couldn't be sure when we last spoke.' Malone made a clicking sound with his tongue as he read through his notes. He jabbed a forefinger at a sentence and appraised Laurel unflinchingly.

'When I asked you about it you replied that you were "more preoccupied with going to see Rose". And yet now, you remember it clearly. In great detail in fact. Perhaps you weren't as preoccupied as you claim. Not as worried about Rose as you originally stated.'

'I've had more time to think. It's all I've thought about. *She's* all I've thought about. Her and Trevor.' Tears began to fill her eyes again.

'Ah, yes, Trevor. The man you have a purely platonic relationship with. If I can play devil's advocate for a moment, can I suggest that rather than a sudden rush of memory, you've actually had time to concoct a version of events that fit?' Malone leant forward, a bloodhound straining at the leash.

'No! Of course not!' Laurel began to cry harder. She plucked a tissue from out of her sleeve and wiped her nose. 'I've told you. I've just had time to think about it in more detail and remembered. I have an eye for detail for things like that.'

'Ah, yes.' Turner gave a sly smile. 'You've said several times, you're very observant aren't you, Miss Miller? Would you say you were an intelligent woman? You've made it quite clear that you don't think Bernadette is. Didn't you describe her as dim?

Whereas you, well, I'd describe you as very shrewd. Wouldn't you, Mike?' he said as he turned to Malone.

Laurel Miller stopped crying. It was as if a tap had been turned off. She sat up straight and eyed both the detectives calmly, not a modicum of emotion on her face. 'I think,' she said in an unwavering voice, 'I'd like to speak to my solicitor now.'

45

Maya detested shopping, but with Christmas creeping closer and because of her shifts, she had no chance but to bite the bullet and head to the shopping centre with a list. Every shop she went in was rammed. The continuous Christmas music was already starting to grate on her nerves, and she was uncomfortably hot.

The bright lights were also giving her a headache, which wasn't helped by a woman outside The Perfume Shop who insisted on dousing her in a tester of what Maya could only think was named Eau de Death. The last straw was realising that a security guard was indiscreetly following her around one of the shops.

She fought the urge to stop and tell him what she did for a living. Irritated, she left the shop empty-handed at the same time as two other women. The security alarm went off and she glowered at the hand on her arm as she watched the two white females scurry off with their loot.

'Nothing says Merry Christmas like a bit of casual racism,' she had called after the security guard. Once he had realised his mistake, he ran, red-faced after the shoplifters.

Aching feet carried her across the car park, and exhausted, she stowed her packages away in the boot of Dominique's car. As much as she loved her motorbike, it wasn't practical for carrying shopping. That said, she found riding the Bonneville incredibly cathartic and would much rather be weaving through the traffic on that than stuck in a tin box on wheels.

Despite it only being lunchtime, it felt like the day hadn't yet got started. The sky was a cloak of sulking grey. Rain assaulted the car windscreen, water reflecting the council Christmas lights that peppered the main road. The effort was clearly half-hearted as Christmas trees, stars and what Maya assumed was supposed to be a robin but looked more like a pigeon, had been attached to every other lamp post.

Normally, Maya loved Christmas but this year she just didn't have the same enthusiasm. And it wasn't just because she was due to work, it all just seemed like an extra hassle. Even today she had spent more than she'd anticipated. She knew it was because she was overcompensating for not spending as much time as she normally did with Dominique and her two best friends, Caitlin and Letitia.

When she arrived at Dominique's, Maya reached for her key to open the door but was annoyed to discover it unlocked.

'Mama!' she admonished as Dominique appeared at the kitchen door. 'You promised me you'd start locking this.'

'Sorry, love. Force of habit. I had a delivery and forgot.'

Maya ran her hand through her hair as she bristled with annoyance. 'We've talked about this. Now he's out you need to take more precautions. You're stressing me out by not taking this seriously.'

Dominique gathered Maya into a hug. 'I'm sorry, love. That's the last thing I want to do. Listen, I'll leave a note on the door to remind myself, okay? And, to prove I do listen to you, I've arranged for someone to come and fit a burglar alarm with a panic button both upstairs and downstairs. The company I've chosen are busy though, so they can't come until after Christmas now.'

'Did you not tell him it's urgent? Try and find someone else?'

'Maya, it'll be fine. Also, I've ordered us both a personal attack alarm online. They'll be here in a few days.'

Maya smiled, satisfied at least that Dominique was listening to her concerns.

'All done?' Dominique asked, nodding towards the shopping bags.

'Yes, thankfully. I'm glad that's over. I've a couple of other bits which I ordered online for Chris, but this is the last of it. Can I leave this stuff in my old room for now? I'll collect and wrap them another time, I've had enough for one day.'

'Of course you can.'

'No peeking though. Your present might be in there too.'

'I promise,' Dominique said with a grin. 'Leave the bags on the floor there and I'll take them up to your room later. Are you staying for lunch? I've time to make us something before I head back to the surgery.'

'No thanks. There's a mid-week communion at St Mary's I'd like to go to. I've not been for a while.'

'Please yourself. But before you go, I've been thinking about Christmas. I know you're working, so how about we bring it forward?'

'I think Jesus might object.'

Dominique laughed. 'For someone with faith, you're very blasphemous. I was thinking about the Monday. Stay over Sunday night after work. You're working a mid-shift, aren't you?'

'Yes. I should be finished by seven.'

'Great. Well, on Monday we can swap presents and have Christmas dinner. Tuesday can be our Boxing Day. I can book leave so I'm off the same days as you. We can just slob out, eat and drink too much and watch rubbish television together. What do you think?'

'I think it sounds perfect,' said Maya, kissing Dominique on the cheek.

'Enjoy church.'

'You could come with me, if you like. It might help you get into the festive spirit?'

Dominique laughed. 'I don't want to risk getting struck by a thunderbolt.'

Maya rolled her eyes and waved goodbye, blowing Dominique a kiss as she rode away.

Twenty minutes later she arrived at St Mary's. It was a pretty church, small but packed with character. Maya nodded hello to a couple of familiar faces, before settling in a pew and bowing her head. The familiar scent of the church enveloped her. The smell of old books, furniture polish and freshly cut flowers. She began to pray silently, sharing her thoughts with God, thinking particularly of John Doe and Rose Dawlish, until it was time for the service to begin.

Mid-week communion was a short forty-five-minute affair. It was an abridged version of the previous Sunday's service. As always, it soothed her soul and passed far too quickly. Reverend Hopwood invited anyone who wanted to stay for tea. Maya was initially going to decline, but the peace of the church following the mayhem of shopping was succour for the soul.

She'd been chatting to a couple of parishioners she knew, when a man standing on the periphery caught her eye. He was unremarkable to look at; short, balding, wearing glasses and dressed in jeans and a conservative-looking anorak, but something about him seemed familiar. He was holding a teacup with a chocolate digestive balancing precariously on a saucer and looking slightly awkward.

She smiled. 'Hi, I don't think we've met before. I'm Maya.'

He blushed slightly, smiling shyly back at her. 'Nice to meet you. I'm Tony. I'd shake your hand, but...' He tailed off as he looked at the cup and saucer in his hands, as if he was surprised to see them.

Maya laughed. 'I can see you've got a juggling act going on. Are you local, Tony?'

'I'm not but my friends live near here. I've just been dropping off Christmas cards and saw the service was on and I thought I'd pop in. It's a lovely church.'

'It certainly is,' Maya agreed. 'I don't come as often as I'd like. I've been Christmas shopping, so after an overdose of commercialism, thought I'd drop in. Just like you.'

They chatted about the service for a while and then Tony asked about her plans for Christmas. She told him how she was working and had just arranged to stay with her mum for a couple of days so they could have an early Christmas.

They'd been chatting for about half an hour when Maya heard teacups being washed noisily in the sink – a subtle hint that it was time to leave.

'It was nice to talk to you, Tony,' Maya said as she shrugged on her coat. She waved goodbye to the others and they walked companionably to the car park.

'Lovely to meet you, Maya,' Tony said as they shook hands. 'I may pop in again sometime. I hope you and Dominique have a lovely Christmas.'

It was only later that evening when Maya was relaxing in a bubble bath listening to an audiobook, that she recalled her conversation with Tony. She frowned as she recalled his parting words as he had wished her and Dominique a lovely Christmas. It was as if the water suddenly chilled around her. During the conversation, she had referred to her as 'Mum'. So, how did Tony know Dominique's name?

46

The office was filled with the mouth-watering aroma of fish and chips. Maya and Chris had been working a day shift together. They'd been at the rota garage examining stolen cars. Although they'd been sheltered from the sheet of rain, the garage had been freezing. The wind had pulled angrily at the metal roller-shutter doors, the sound alone making them shiver. It was easily a couple of degrees colder in there than it had been outside.

Chris had suggested a chippy lunch as a treat to warm themselves back up. He looked perplexed as he took a sip of tea whilst Maya told him about the man she'd met at church.

'Did anything about him seem odd when you were talking to him?' he asked.

'No. He seemed nice.'

Chris rubbed his stubble. 'You must have mentioned Dominique's name,' he said eventually.

Maya shook her head determinedly. 'I didn't. I know I didn't.'

Chris belched noisily as he gathered up the chip paper. 'Look, work has been really busy lately and you've had the added stress of Naylor being released. I think you're either misremembering the conversation or it could be paranoia, which is perfectly understandable. No offence, love, but you do look tired.'

Maya slapped a hand on the desk. 'That's because I've hardly slept with going over it. I appreciate what you're saying, but I *know* I didn't say her name.'

'Did someone else maybe? Did he overhear one of the others asking how she was?'

Maya thought about it, but before she had a chance to answer, Kym came bustling in carrying a large golf umbrella and her messenger bag, which as ever was bursting at the seams. She paused in the doorway, her nose twitching.

'It stinks in here.'

'Chippy,' said Chris succinctly.

Her eyes narrowed. 'I know what it is, I'm saying I don't like it. This is a place of work, not a bloody builder's café. Can you go and see if there's any air freshener in the cleaning cupboard, please?'

'What's up with her?' Chris mouthed to Maya as Kym stalked towards her office.

'I dunno. Shall I go and check?'

'Make her a brew first. And take her a biscuit for Christ's sake. In fact, take her the bloody packet, it might help ward off her evil scorn.'

Armed with custard creams and a cup of tea, Maya hovered uncertainly at Kym's door.

'Oh, you're a star, Maya. Thank you.' Kym removed her reading glasses and gave Maya a listless smile as she placed the cup down.

'Everything okay?'

Kym sighed and gestured towards the chair for Maya to sit down. 'I'm just bloody frustrated. I've been up to top office for a strategy meeting with DI Redford about Rose Dawlish's death.'

'And?'

'I've recommended a number of swabs from the body and scene be submitted but the Case Management Unit are holding them back for the time being. I'm particularly keen for the swabs from the fingermarks on the top of her arm to go off as a matter of urgency.'

'Why?' asked Maya incredulously.

'Because it looks like they were a fresh injury and could well have been made by the offender.'

'No,' Maya said through a laugh, 'I meant why are they being held back?'

Kym finished her biscuit before answering. 'The latest shootings by the Organised Crime Group that Cedar Lane have been dealing with are apparently taking priority. For now.'

'I understand that's serious, but that's shit on shit. We're talking about the murder of an old woman.'

'That's the thing,' said Kym. 'Other than the death *appearing* staged, the investigation is taking us nowhere. There's no motive, no signs of forced entry, no suspects. On paper, it looks like an accidental death.'

'But we know it's not.'

'Agreed. But gut instinct isn't enough, not when it comes to spending money. Rose's death is currently in the neither-here-nor-there category of unexplained. It's not helped by the fact that the family are so bloody solitary and we have absolutely no motive or suspects.'

Kym let out a sigh as she shrugged. 'We might well have to accept that this is one of those jobs we just never get to the bottom of. We do get them now and then. You never know, Maya, thirty years from now a cold-case team might crack it for us.'

'True, but I'd much rather it was us that got to the bottom of it for her sake,' Maya said as she recalled Rose's broken body lying at the bottom of the stairs. She understood what Kym had said, but every inch of her being told her that the old woman had been murdered. Someone had pushed her down those stairs and then done an incredibly piss-poor job of staging it to look like an accident. Even Jack Dwyer believed it, and in her opinion, he was as competent as a paper condom.

Despondent, Maya left Kym to it. She explained to Chris what had happened to put Kym in such a foul mood and the two of them sat in a subdued silence, both occupied by their own thoughts. Their lunch and the warmth of the office compared to the blistering cold of the garage made them both feel listless. Maya was trying to summon up enough energy to start tackling her paperwork when a squeal came from Kym's office.

'Y' all right, boss? You've not switched your love eggs on by accident again, have you?' Chris shouted.

Kym appeared at the doorway flushed, as she gave him the middle finger. 'I've had an email through. It's the results of the facial reconstruction from Operation Mermaid.'

'Have you looked at it yet?' Maya was instantly revived; a fist of excitement squeezed her stomach.

'No. We should all look at it together, it was your job after all,' she said with a grin. 'You better give Jack a shout,' she said as an afterthought.

Maya raced down the corridor, irritated by the sight of Jack's empty office. She made her way down to CID and was relieved to see him leaning against a filing cabinet, brew in hand as he chatted to Sean, Malone and Adila.

'You lot, quick!' she called, beckoning them with her hand. 'Kym's got an email, the facial reconstruction for Operation Mermaid has come back.'

The four of them were hot on her heels as they followed her back to the SOCO office. Kym had anticipated the sudden influx of people into her small office would make it too crammed, so was in the main office, logging on to another computer so everyone could see. Maya was practically hopping from foot to foot. She could have screamed as she watched the log on screen announcing it was 'configuring user profile'. The force's IT was renowned for being incredibly slow and unreliable.

After a long and painful wait, the computer's circle of death allowed Kym to log in to her email account and bring up the message. She double-clicked on the attachment. The image opened in landscape, causing them all to tip their heads to the side in unison, like cats following a beam of torchlight.

There was a heavy silence, broken eventually by Sean.

'Is this some kind of piss-take?' he asked flatly.

Kym turned to look at him, confused as he leaned past Maya, knocking her out of the way as he jabbed a finger at the computer monitor.

'That,' he said decisively, 'is Trevor Dawlish.'

THEN

Trevor

Trevor had his own office in the town hall. Office sounded grander than the reality. It was just the janitor's room. It had a desk and chair, which were artfully arranged. The room was bursting with spare cleaning equipment, gardening stuff, tools, lost property, and an array of other paraphernalia, but it wasn't a mess. Quite the opposite; each item had its own place and was kept tidy and organised.

When Bernadette first came to see him in here, not long after they first started dating, she had coined it his office and the name had stuck. Just like the spare room at home had become his study. There was even a little plaque on his door. A ceramic white tile with the wording 'Trevor's Office' in blue letters. She'd spotted it in a shop at the seaside, the first weekend they spent away together.

He smiled at the memory. She'd looked so sweet dressed in a brown spotted tea dress and cream cardigan, with a floral clip in her hair. Trevor stretched noisily and peered through the small slice of window. He was situated in the basement, which meant he could only ever see feet coming and going along the pathway that encircled the building. He could see that the pavement was still dry. Warm air etched with a pinch of a breeze, the final sigh of an Indian summer, breathed its way through the open window.

It was a funny time of year. He had needed his winter coat when he'd left for work at 7am, but he certainly wasn't going to need it now. His wallet was too bulky to carry. He had no pockets in his lightweight hoodie, so he fished out his debit card and slipped it into his jeans pocket. He only needed it to pay for some anniversary flowers and chocolates.

He looked up as he heard someone at his office door. His face turned into a smile, which froze quickly. Trevor had been about to utter a greeting but the sight of the earnest expression on his visitor's face silenced him.

'We need to talk,' the visitor said intensely and apologetically. 'Now. And somewhere private. Not here.'

Moments later, Trevor's trainers accompanied the clicking of his visitor's shoes, as they trod the path past his office window.

47

The facial reconstruction image remained on the screen and all eyes were on it. Kym had managed to turn it to a portrait display, so their necks were no longer aching.

'That's Trevor Dawlish,' Sean repeated.

'Not judging, mate, but have you been on the ale?' asked Chris as he made a drinking motion with his hand, causing Adila to cackle with laughter.

Malone was looking at Sean as if he'd just defecated on the desk. 'Trevor Dawlish, who's returned home how many times since he's been reported missing? I think you need a day off, pal.'

Jack nodded. 'When he was first reported missing, uniform seized Trevor's toothbrush, remember? His profile was loaded to the vulnerable DNA database and checked against John Doe. Malone's right, it can't be him.' Jack glanced at Maya and Kym suspiciously as if this was all part of some trick being played on him.

Sean's face was becoming flushed as he looked at Chris and Malone. 'Think what you want but I'm telling you that's Trevor. Or it certainly looks like him...' He faltered; his brow furrowed as he turned to stare despondently at the screen. The banter had made him question himself, but he had been so sure.

'He's right,' Maya said eventually. 'Do you remember the wedding photo on the mantelpiece?' she asked Kym and Chris. They both nodded.

'The hair's different...' Sean said tentatively.

'That's to be expected. Facial reconstruction has its limitations with regards to things like that,' Kym said.

'Here.' Sean pulled out his phone and began scrolling through some emails of his own. 'You tasked me with pulling together a recent photograph of Trevor for the missing person's press release,' he said to Jack. 'This is what I sent to the press office for their approval, prior to circulation.'

They all hunched around Sean's phone and looked at the more recent image. Even though it was a cropped headshot, the sky-blue trim of the Masons' collar was evident. Sean was right, the hair in the reconstruction was longer and wavier, but the forehead, nose and jawline, was unmistakably Trevor.

'Bloody hell,' muttered Adila, as she brushed her fringe out of her eyes. 'You're right, guys.'

'Well, that puts a different spin on what we were talking about earlier, Maya,' Kym said as she turned to survey all her colleagues.

'In brief, I was explaining to Maya that the samples collected following Rose's death weren't going to be treated with any kind of priority because we had no concrete evidence that a crime had actually taken place. Obviously, we were concerned with how coincidental Trevor's disappearance was with Rose's sudden death, leaving him as the number one suspect, but obviously there has been nothing concrete to go on.'

The others nodded acknowledgement. 'Even MIT had fired it back to us. There were no lines of enquiry for them to follow. We've never been able to definitively prove Rose's death *was* a murder as opposed to an accident. It's all too circumstantial. Primarily because one of the main potential suspects was on the missing list,' Jack said.

Maya pointed at the image on the screen. 'But we now know Trevor has been murdered. It adds credence to the fact his mother's death must be suspicious, surely? You're the detective, Jack, and I wouldn't want to patronise you for a single minute,' Maya said disingenuously, letting out a breath before she continued.

'My guess would be, whoever killed Trevor, also killed his mother.' The others, including Jack, were vocal in their agreement.

48

DCI Donna Chambers from the Major Incident Team was holding court in the conference room. It was the same corporate blue as the rest of Beech Field and housed a large quantity of chairs with lift-up writing tables attached to the arm. A laptop and screen filled one wall and was currently displaying Trevor's face at three stages: the post mortem image, a recent photograph and the facial reconstruction result. Just seeing the post mortem image again reminded Maya of the shocking stench of Trevor's decomposed body and the way it had gurgled menacingly as they'd placed it carefully in the body bag, as they'd desperately hoped it wouldn't pop.

Chambers was a tall lady with brunette hair tied efficiently in a French plait that hung down her back. Her smart trouser suit and overall demeanour demanded respect. Several detectives had joined her from her syndicate and were taking notes as the DCI brought everyone up to speed with Operation Mermaid, details of Trevor's missing persons enquiry and Rose's sudden and as yet, unexplained death.

Maya, Chris and Kym had been joined by Elaine who'd

arrived for the late shift. Redford was also present, as was Jack and his team.

Chambers studied her notes. 'Who's going to deliver the death message to the wife?' she asked.

Jack indicated his head towards Turner. 'DS Mark Turner interviewed Bernadette after the death of Rose. They have a rapport, so I think it would be appropriate for him to do it.'

'I agree,' said Chambers. 'Our team can supply a family liaison officer.'

'No need, ma'am.' Adila raised her hand. 'I'm a trained FLO. I can attend with Mark and stay with Bernadette for as long as she needs me.'

'Thank you. That pretty much covers everything, doesn't it?' Chambers asked as she glanced around the room to a succession of nods.

'Good, we'll continue to work under the moniker of Operation Mermaid but incorporated in this investigation will also be the unexplained death of Rose Dawlish. I'm grateful to Jack and his team for their efforts so far in relation to Mermaid. Please don't think we're here to take over or step on anyone's toes. Think of us as additional support here to advise, as I'm conscious of the fact we're picking up a job half-cock so to speak.'

'Should have been interested in Rose's death sooner,' Maya muttered under her breath to Kym, who nodded subtly in agreement.

Jack smiled at Chambers. 'Thank you, ma'am. My team are collating the information we have so far and we're combining a list of our TIE subjects.'

He continued to update the DCI and the rest of the team of their progress so far. Maya scribbled a note, *what's a TIE?* and slipped it across to Chris. He replied with, *trace, interview and eliminate* and passed the note back.

'Maya can provide copies of all scene photographs and notes so far,' Kym told the DCI once Jack had finished. 'And we'll make sure we have resources available for any further scenes that may arise. I've already written up forensic strategies for any suspects and their properties. Likewise, if we identify any vehicles that may have been involved, we can have them forensically recovered and arrange an examination ASAP.'

Chambers smiled her thanks before nodding her head towards a tall, attractive, black man sat to her right. 'For those of you who don't know, this is DS Alex Adebayo. He is a tier five interviewer advisor. I believe a nominal known as Jason Laing is a person of interest and we are currently working on a press release to ask the public to help us trace his whereabouts. Who's going to be arresting our other suspect?'

Sean raised his hand. 'Me, ma'am. DC Stevenson,' he said, nodding acknowledgement to DS Adebayo.

'Good, well if you two want to get your heads together sooner rather than later and draw up your interview strategy. How soon are you looking to make an arrest, Jack?'

He checked his notes and looked at Redford, who nodded confirmation. 'As soon as we can, ma'am.'

'Good. You have your actions, ladies and gentlemen, so let's go.'

There was a bustle of activity as everyone gathered their belongings. Elaine followed Maya out of the conference room, cupping her elbow on the way out. 'I'm a bit out of the loop with this job. I know Laing was in the frame but as he's still outstanding, who are they locking up?'

'The neighbour, Laurel Miller.'

49

Laurel was sat in the dark. Only the flickering light from the muted television screen illuminated the lounge. The room was in stark contrast to its usual pristine condition. A takeaway carton had been dumped on the coffee table. Sweet-and-sour sauce had been spilt and left to puddle onto the plush Axminster carpet.

Laurel poured the last dregs of red wine into her glass, tossing the empty bottle away from her onto the couch.

'Fuck it,' she slurred.

She staggered to her feet and into the kitchen. Cupboard drawers and doors hung open with various contents strewn across the marbled worktop. The room looked like it had been burgled. Laurel lifted another bottle of Malbec from the wine rack and banged it onto the counter. Swaying, she peeled back the foil top and reached for the corkscrew. She attempted to dig it into the cork, but the bottle rocked precariously before sliding across the counter. She tried to grab it but was too slow and it smashed to the floor.

'Fuck *you*!' she snarled as she kicked at the shattered remains, cutting her foot in the process. She was too drunk to notice. She reached for a bottle of brandy instead and pulled herself up the stairs, slamming against the banister as she climbed. A creature of habit, she wandered into the spare room. The Christmas tree and box of decorations remained unopened in there. As always, her eyes drifted across to the Dawlishes house. It stood ominous and empty in the darkness. She assumed Bernadette was still at her sister's. The stupid cow had stopped taking her calls.

She rested her head against the windowpane, breathing in the smell of winter air that whispered through a gap in the double glazing. She imagined all the times she'd stood here, waiting for Trevor to look up and see her. She closed her eyes as she pictured his face. Every intricate detail was ingrained in her mind and heart. His hazel eyes, which crinkled at the edges when he smiled. The chickenpox scar on his cheek. The small patch of stubble under his left nostril that he always missed when he shaved. It hurt too much to think of him. Laurel choked back a sob. She ran out of the room as if she had the Devil at her heels, slamming the door behind her.

She slapped on the light switch of her bedroom. Light flooded her boudoir revealing an unmade bed, and a pile of dirty clothes discarded on the floor. She gulped at the brandy, pressing the back of her hand to her mouth and wincing as the liquid scoured the back of her throat.

She sat on the bed, eyeing the cushions resentfully. She had no appetite and couldn't sleep. Every time she closed her eyes, she pictured the last time she had seen Rose. Then she thought of Trevor and the pain was just too much to bear. Keening, she clutched her stomach, stunned that such a physical pain could mirror that of her emotions.

Laurel took another swig of brandy, wincing again as she pulled her phone from her jeans pocket. Her lock screen displayed a neutral image. Her wallpaper however, boasted a photograph of Trevor grinning shyly back at her. A sudden wave of rage engulfed her as she selected Bernadette's number. It rang twice before being sent to voicemail. The bitch was still ignoring her calls. How *dare* she. Who the *fuck* did she think she was? She listened to Bernadette's recorded greeting and the sound of the simpering voice fuelled her anger.

'Bernadette,' she slurred. 'You bitch. You fucking bitch. You've stolen my life; do you know that? He was mine. You were never going to be enough for him. I hope you die a slow and painful fucking death. In fact, I'll make sure you do. Get ready cos I'm coming for you. I *hate* you.'

Laurel hung up and threw the phone across the bed. Then the reality of what she'd done dawned on her. She'd let her temper get the better of her again. The thought was sobering. She scrabbled for the phone, wondering if there was any way she could withdraw the message, but she knew it was futile.

'Shit.' She hit her head with the palm of her hand as she thought about the consequences of her actions. She had already lied to the police. A lot. She'd been a fool to think they wouldn't find out the truth. And now she'd left Bernadette a death threat. It felt like the walls were closing in on her.

She thought of prison and let out a wail. They were going to uncover the truth and send her away for a very long time. She couldn't countenance the thought of prison. The thought of being locked away with violent, insane women. The thought of losing her freedom and being left living in squalor. Depending on others to tell her when she could eat and shower.

She'd be as bad as Rose, left to rot in her own filth. She'd not even been able to watch prison dramas such as *Wentworth* or *Orange is the New Black*, just hearing her colleagues chatting about the programmes had unnerved her. She would rather die than go to prison, she knew she wouldn't survive a day.

Panicked, she ran into the bathroom and rifled through the

cupboard pulling out packs of tampons and paracetamol. She fingered a box of prescription tablets addressed to Bernadette. She had taken some of the sedatives the night she let herself in to see to Rose, knowing how much they were making Bernadette even more incapable of coping. Stupid bloody woman. She dropped the toilet seat down and popped the tablets out of the blister pack onto it as she removed them one by one. She took gulps of brandy as she swallowed them down two at a time.

The packet was soon empty. For good measure, she started on the paracetamol, ibuprofen and anything else she could find. Even the expensive collagen tablets that were supposed to plump out her fine lines and wrinkles. Tears streamed silently down her cheeks as the reality of what she was doing hit her. She didn't want to die. She really didn't. The instinct to live was strong, but she couldn't face the thought of prison. That would kill her anyway and this way at least she was in control.

She thought fleetingly of writing a suicide note, but quickly dismissed the idea. There was no one to read it. She had no family other than an estranged uncle. She thought of her colleagues, picturing the other faceless accountants she worked with. Would they even know who she was when they heard she was dead?

They'd roll out a standard book of condolence. Probably the only person to sign it would be the receptionist with the thick calves. She could imagine her writing, *Lauren, I'll miss seeing you at the water cooler and talking about* Love Island. She just knew the bloody woman wouldn't even get her name right.

She had no other way out. Running away wasn't an option, living rough would be even worse than prison. This way she would do what she'd always done and do things her way. What was the point of life without Trevor? She staggered to the bedroom and pulled the thick curtains shut. She reached for her phone again and, this time, selected her Spotify account and began to play the list of songs that she had compiled because they made her think of her and Trevor.

Nora Jones' soulful voice filled the room. Laurel turned on her bedside light and lit her favourite Jo Malone candle. She watched the flame seemingly dance to the music. It helped her feel calmer, despite the fact her heart was pounding so hard it was echoing in her ears, almost drowning out the music. She connected her phone to her speakers and turned them up.

She continued to drink the brandy, taking even larger gulps now as she imagined the tablets being swept away on a tide to her stomach. She caught a glimpse of her reflection in the mirror and was appalled at what she saw. Her face was alabaster, her eyes red and swollen, mascara streaked across her face panda-like.

She let out a scream as she slapped the mirror off the wall. She threw a kick at it for good measure and was momentarily stunned at the sight of blood on her foot. She shrugged. At least she wouldn't have to worry about the cost of pedicures, manicures, blow-dries and lip fillers anymore.

After all that time, money and effort, it had got her nowhere in the end. She even had a regular bikini wax for Christ's sake. How was that for optimistic? The only person who had seen her fanny over the last decade was the poor cow who she paid to wax it. How pitiful was that? She was desperate and pathetic. She deserved to die. She was doing the right thing. She tore off her jeans and jumper as she carried the brandy into the bathroom. She turned on the power shower. She'd only ever used that alone too. She waited for the water to heat up before stepping in, not bothering to remove her underwear. She didn't want them to find her completely naked. And maybe the forensics, who would undoubtedly come in their white suits, would appreciate the tasteful lingerie. It had cost enough after all.

She was starting to feel woozy. The warm water was comforting as it rained around her. The music echoing mournfully from the bedroom. She picked up her razor from the shower rack. She snapped off the safety blade causing it to slice her thumb. A plump, scarlet line appeared. Neat at first until it began to stream down her hand.

The alcohol and pills were starting to take effect, because all she could feel was a slight sting. Taking a deep breath, her mind consumed with images of Trevor, she drew the blade across her wrists.

She remained standing under the water for several moments. Just when she thought she'd successfully numbed herself to any pain, the cuts began to burn like fire. Overwhelmed with shock, she cried out. This wasn't how it was supposed to be. The pain intensified, causing her vision to swim.

Laurel reached for the shower-cabinet door, but it was moving, and she couldn't make her hand connect. There was too much blood. Suddenly, her jelly-like legs gave way and she dropped to the floor like a newborn foal.

Something in her mind was screaming at her, willing her to get up. To get out of there and call for help. But she had become unreachable. She was too far gone. The voice faded in her mind. Laurel eventually succumbed, allowing herself to be swallowed into the blackness.

50

O nce the MIT briefing was over, Jack and Redford remained in the conference room with DCI Chambers. She gave them both a reassuring smile, which failed to convince either of them. They could sense they were in for a bollocking. Jack felt like a naughty pupil kept back after school, and even Redford was uncharacteristically quiet as he fussed with his tie.

'I just want to touch base again to see where we're all up to. I thought we could take it offline and make sure we're all reading from the same page.' The two DIs winced involuntarily at the use of such annoying business jargon.

'What do we know about Trevor?'

Jack began to inform the DCI where Trevor lived and worked but was interrupted with a raised hand. 'I was hoping to dig a little deeper. We need to start thinking outside the box.' Another wince. 'I want to know the man behind the missing report. What were his hobbies, who were his friends, where was his local? I assume you can collate all of this information for me?'

'I... we...' Jack turned frantically to look at Redford, who was busy plucking an invisible piece of lint from his jacket, making it clear that Jack was on his own.

'Mm?'

'Trevor wasn't considered a high-risk missing person. Obviously, enquiries were made but...'

'But?'

Jack stared wide-eyed at Chambers; his mouth hung open making him look vacant. He was clearly out of his depth and Redford shifted in his seat as if to put as much space between them as physically possible.

'Phil?' Chambers said, her steely eyes turned to penetrate Redford.

'Jack was responsible for delegating all the enquiries,' he said smugly.

'Indeed. But as the substantial, more experienced DI, I assume you've been keeping a close eye on his actions.'

Jack turned to look at Redford, a ghost of a smile tugging at the corner of his mouth.

'I didn't feel I needed to with this particular case. It was nothing outside the remit of a detective sergeant or detective constable for that matter.'

The smile disappeared. Chambers stared levelly at them both in turn. The pursing of her lips made it clear she wasn't prepared to listen to a game of tit for tat. Jack wiped his sweaty palms on his trousers and Redford straightened up in his chair, putting more confidence in his voice than he felt.

'Obviously, ma'am, we will prioritise collating what we know and build a full profile of Trevor Dawlish as a matter of urgency. By the end of the day, you'll know what colour underwear he liked to wear.'

Chambers sniffed derisively. 'Blue boxer shorts, Phil,' she said stonily. 'I recall that from looking at the images from the post-mortem and I've only been on the job two bloody minutes.'

An air of dissension remained as she gathered her belongings, making it clear the conversation was over. Jack stood up quickly, making a fuss as he held out her coat for her while she put it on before handing over her briefcase.

'Leave it with us, ma'am,' he announced energetically. 'We'll synergise, circle back and bring you up to speed ASAP.'

Redford waited until the DCI had left the room before turning to Jack. 'You sound like a prick at times, do you know that?'

Cringing at the words he'd just uttered, Jack nodded a doleful agreement.

Dominique lay languishing in an aromatherapy bubble bath. A candle flickered on the bathroom window ledge and she took a contented sigh before sinking under the water, allowing the warmth to cocoon her. As she emerged, she heard the sound of her landline ringing from the hallway, before the answering machine picked it up. She could guarantee it was Maya. She'd have a soak for ten more minutes and then get out and call her back on her mobile while she cooled off on the bed.

Just as she settled back, she was disconcerted to hear it ringing again so soon. Once again, she heard the answer machine click but the call was disconnected, no message left. She frowned as she stood up and reached for her towel, leaving a trail of soap suds in her wake as she padded into the bedroom. She picked her mobile phone up off the bed and noticed she had no missed calls or messages. She rang Maya straight away.

'Hi, love, did you just phone the landline? I was in the bath and missed a call.'

'Not me, I'm just leaving work. Can I ring you back when I get home?'

'Course you can. Ride safe.'

Just as she disconnected the call, the landline rang again.

Tightening her towel around her, she dashed down the stairs, but it had stopped by the time she got there. With a sense of trepidation, she lifted the phone and dialled 1471. The automated message informed her that the caller had withheld their number. She replaced the phone and was about to head back upstairs to get changed when the phone rang a fourth time.

She paused for a moment, before reaching out a shaking hand and picking it up.

'Hello?'

There was silence on the other end.

'Hello?' she repeated. The silence was deafening. 'Marcus?' she whispered.

She heard a click on the line before a voice replied. 'Good evening, madam, this is Carly from Claims 4 U. Can I ask if you've had any accidents...'

Dominique cut her off mid-sentence. 'No. Please don't call again.' She slammed the phone back down and raised a hand to her chest, taking a measured breath against the palpitations that slammed against her ribcage.

'Oh,' she let out a nervous gasp. She had let Maya's paranoid scaremongering get to her and now she felt incredibly foolish and rather annoyed.

Even so, she deadlocked the front door before heading back upstairs.

51

Turner and Adila had been parked outside Bernadette's sister's house for a while. Both were delaying the inevitable visit.

'Twenty-three years I've got in this job, Adila, and I swear I'll never get used to the death knock.'

'I'll do it if you like.'

Turner shook his head. 'Thanks, mate, but I will. It's more appropriate. It's my issue not yours.'

'I don't think any cop really gets used to it,' Adila said diplomatically.

'It's not that. I ballsed my first one up and it's become a bit of a thing for me ever since.'

'What happened?' she asked curiously.

He visibly winced. 'Forty-year-old suicide. I had to go and tell his elderly parents. He was their only child. I was so flustered about what I was going to say.' He let out a sigh. 'It's a massive responsibility, isn't it? Let's face it, they're going to remember the words you tell them for the rest of their lives. You know it's going to be something they recall again and again.'

Adila turned in her seat, intrigued. 'What did you say to them?'

He ran his hand over his face. 'They let me in, and I started to ask about him, the usual, you know, confirm his name and age. Then I asked when they'd last seen him alive.'

'Nooo.' Adila howled with laughter whilst Turner grinned sheepishly.

'Are you sure you don't want me to do this one? The poor woman's been through enough just lately without you wading in feet first.'

He sniffed. 'I'll be fine. Oh, shit, we better go in. She's watching us through the window.'

Adila looked up and saw Bernadette looking pale and terrified. She let out a groan. 'This is going to be fucking horrendous, isn't it?'

'Yup.'

Bernadette was already at the garden gate by the time they'd locked the car. Her sister, Stacey, hovered on the doorstep uncertainly.

'What is it, what's happened?'

'Mrs Dawlish, this is my colleague DC Adila Laghari. Can we come in for a second?'

'Has she admitted it? Laurel. Has she admitted she killed Rose? Have you found Trevor? You must know where he is by now? He *needs* to be here.'

Stacey reached out for her sister and guided her back inside. 'Let them come in and sit down and I'm sure they'll tell you everything,' she murmured reassuringly. 'I'll put the kettle on. We can have a nice cup of tea.'

'Tea. *Tea?* I'm sick of bloody tea. I want to know who killed my mother-in-law and where my husband is.'

They crowded into Stacey's living room and Bernadette

perched on the edge of the leather sofa looking like an anxious hen.

'You will, of course, recall, Mrs Dawlish, that your husband's bank card was found in the pocket of an unidentified, deceased male, whose body was recovered from the canal.'

'Yes, of course. The man who had been strangled. I'm sorry that person is dead, but they're not my main concern right now. You're not going to suggest Trevor had anything to do with the man's death, are you? That's absurd.'

Turner raised his hand. 'Mrs Dawlish, please. If you could you just let me continue.'

She nodded reluctantly.

'We have been unable to identify the man, and despite various press releases, we have received no information regarding his identity. As a result, we requested that experts piece together a facial reconstruction to enable us to identify him.'

'So?'

'Would you and your sister please look at the image our experts have produced?'

Bernadette started to shake as Turner reached for the picture. He held it out so they could both see it clearly. Stacey gasped and Bernadette began to sob uncontrollably, shaking her head.

'No, no, no, no. That's not my Trevor. You've made a mistake. *They've* made a mistake. Don't try and tell me that's my Trevor.'

'A DNA sample from the deceased is currently being compared to DNA from Rose. For some reason the toothbrush which officers seized when you first reported your husband missing hasn't come back as a match. We're not sure why and there may be several reasons for that error. We have asked for the results to be fast-tracked as a matter of urgency, but I'm afraid you do need to prepare yourself for the worst.'

Turner and Adila sat in an awkward silence until Bernadette, eventually calmed by her sister, was composed enough to continue.

'You're telling me that Trevor has been murdered?'

Adila leant forward, her eyes seeking out Bernadette's as she explained as calmly as she could. 'I know how difficult that is to come to terms with and how painful it is to hear such devastating news, but I can assure you we have a team of detectives doing everything they can to find the person or persons responsible.'

At that Bernadette's head shot up. 'You mean he was attacked by more than one person?'

'It's too soon to say. We're working on a number of hypotheses at the moment. My job is to act as your family liaison officer, and I'm here to support you and keep you updated with how the investigation is progressing. It would also help us massively if you could share as much information about Trevor as you can.'

Bernadette nodded weakly. She looked exhausted and her hands covered her stomach protectively.

'If I could ask a rather delicate question, Mrs Dawlish?' Turned said tentatively.

Bernadette's eyes widened and her pallor grew even paler. 'What now?'

He cleared his throat before replying. 'On the day the deceased was discovered, you rang us to report that Trevor had returned home and assaulted you. A short time later, you rang in again to let us know he had left the address. We now know that that can't be the case. Trevor didn't come home that day, did he?'

Bernadette dropped her gaze to the floor, her shoulders hunched as she muttered something so quietly, it was impossible to hear her.

'Sorry, Mrs Dawlish, could you repeat that please? I can't hear you.'

Her eyes remained trained to the floor as she said slightly louder, 'I lied.'

'Okay. Can I ask why?'

'I thought it would make you look harder for him. He'd been missing for two weeks and nobody seemed to take it seriously. I know he was a grown man, but you don't know him, I was so worried. It's completely out of character for him to disappear like he did, but nobody seemed to care.

'I thought that if I said he'd assaulted me, you'd want to speak to him then. I thought that you'd find him quicker if you believed he was dangerous. I feel so guilty because Trevor has never, *would* never lay a finger on me. I'm so sorry.'

'Thanks for your transparency. We understand how difficult the last few weeks have been for you,' Adila said reassuringly.

'Am I in trouble?' Bernadette asked pathetically.

'Not at all,' Turner reassured. 'Like my colleague has said, it would help us greatly now if you could provide us with as much information as you can about Trevor. The more we can piece together a picture of who he was, the more chance we have of finding out who did this to him and why.'

52

The weather was freezing, but at least it was dry. The air was filled with the smell of frost and wood burners and there wasn't a cloud in the night sky. The moon shone like a beacon as Sean and DS Alex Adebayo pulled up outside Laurel's house. They had stab vests on under their jackets, which was customary when making an arrest, but despite the additional thickness, it did nothing to add any warmth. The car heater was frantically puffing out hot air, but Sean's hands and feet still felt like blocks of ice.

Adebayo was an affable man who had been poking fun at Sean for complaining about the weather. 'You need a good feed,' he said, not for the first time. 'You're skin and bone. And you're very pale. Do you think you might have an iron deficiency?'

'No,' said Sean defensively. 'It's just the way I am. All the men in my family share the same Viking look.'

Adebayo let out a roar of laughter and flung back in his seat causing the car to rock. 'Viking? Fucking Viking? You look like a young Ron Weasley.'

Even Sean had to grin at the comparison. 'Are we going to

waste any more time insulting me, or shall we go and arrest our murder suspect, *sarge*?'

Adebayo laughed again as he unfolded himself out of the passenger's seat. The cold didn't even seem to bother him as they locked the car. 'After you, Weasley,' he said as he stopped at the garden gate and gestured for Sean to go first.

Sean reached for the letter box, intending to give it a solid copper's knock, but it flapped pitifully against the draught excluder barely making any noise at all.

'I don't think she heard that,' whispered Adebayo with mirth as he raised his meaty fist and pummelled on the door so hard, the glass in the front window rattled.

They stood in silence for a minute, straining to hear or see any signs of Laurel approaching. 'I don't think she heard that,' Sean eventually whispered back. Adebayo laughed and clapped him on the back with such force, he nearly sent Sean through the front door. He knocked again, and after regaining his composure, Sean attempted to peer through the gap in the lounge curtains.

'There's definitely some kind of light on. The TV, I think, by the way it's flickering, but I can't make anything else out. I certainly can't see her.'

Adebayo nodded. 'Try around the back, mate.'

Sean squeezed down the narrow path at the side of the house. The bins were blocking the way and he was wary of patches of ice that shimmered in the moonlight. The last thing he needed was to fall flat on his face in front of the MIT sergeant. He'd been the butt of enough jokes already. Ron bloody Weasley indeed. He made his way to the back door and rapped on it, shouting 'police' as he tried the handle. It was locked.

There was a light on in the kitchen and through a gap in the blinds he could make out that the room appeared to be in a state of disarray. Cupboard doors hung open, and from what little of the floor he could see, it looked like signs of a disturbance. He could feel the hairs start to stand on the back of his neck and it was nothing to do with the freezing temperature.

Sean banged on the back door again, louder and more insistently. As he strained to listen for any signs of life, he became aware of a sound. It was running water. He stepped further round the rear of the property and located the wastewater pipe that was gushing hot water down the grid. Steam curled like fingers as it hit the icy air.

A copper's instinct caused Sean to sink to his haunches as he pulled his torch out of his pocket and illuminated the flowing water. He paused for a moment as he noticed a lack of any suds or smell of soap that would normally accompany a bath or shower. It could be the poor light or his overactive imagination, but did the water have a reddish tinge?

He shouted for Adebayo, who clearly detected the note of urgency in his voice as he battled past the bins and was at his side in an instant.

'Something's wrong,' said Sean, the adrenaline evident in his voice. 'There looks like there's been some kind of a disturbance in the kitchen. And I think there's blood in the water.'

Adebayo grabbed the torch and shone it towards where Sean was pointing.

'There's a lock-pulling kit in the car. I'll go and fetch...' Before he could finish his sentence, Adebayo took a flying kick at the lock, busting it open as easily as if he was opening an advent calendar door.

'...or we could just kick the fuck out of it instead. Yeah, I was just going to suggest that,' Sean added weakly, but Adebayo wasn't listening. He was already running through the house announcing himself as a police officer.

Sean followed pathetically behind, taking in the state of

Laurel's house. Its current condition certainly wasn't in keeping with the pretentious, overbearing character he had dealt with previously.

'Sean, get an ambulance!' Adebayo screamed.

Sean began to shout up comms as he ran up the stairs. Adebayo had pulled Laurel from the shower cabinet and was laying her on the bathroom floor. She was unrecognisable, the blood had caused her blonde hair to appear even more auburn than his. It was streaming from her wrists, and a stark contrast to the deathly white colour of her face.

Adebayo turned to him as he began to perform CPR. 'I can't find a pulse,' he said bluntly. 'I think we've fucking lost her.'

53

It was a bright but cold morning. Maya was grateful for her Gore-Tex pants as she sat on the frost covered bench in the garden of remembrance. She'd carefully arranged a bunch of orange carnations in the vase that marked the spot where her grandad's ashes had been interred.

'Happy heavenly birthday.' Maya smiled sadly at the flowers, her heart aching with loss for the man who had meant so much to her. She sat for a while, silently conversing with him in her head. The grief had never faded, she had just learnt to live with it, and she found comfort in sitting here talking to him. It made her feel closer to him and she found it soothing. After a while, she kissed her fingers and pressed them against the brass plaque which bore his name. 'I love you,' she murmured, before reluctantly turning to leave. She checked her watch and knew as much as she wanted to stay another five minutes with him, if she didn't go now, she'd be late for work.

As Maya rode away, she was oblivious of the two men sat in a car nearby, but they were very much aware of her. Marcus turned to Anthony.

'I told you she'd come.'

~

'You look smart,' Maya said as she walked in the office and saw Connor, pacing nervously, dressed in a suit and tie.

He gave her a sheepish grin. 'Thanks. It's interview day. I can't believe I've got this far. I'm so nervous.'

'I can believe it, you're more than ready for the job. Hopefully your nerves will fade once you get in there.'

'Speaking of which,' said Amanda as she walked towards him to straighten his tie, 'you better get going. You don't want to be late.'

Kym emerged from her office to wish Connor good luck and they waved him off.

'Any update overnight from Operation Mermaid?' Maya asked Kym.

'There's a briefing later on. In the meantime, I've got a strategy for you relating to Trevor's office.'

'Sure, what do you need?'

'A fingerprint examination so we can compare any marks from there to the ones taken at the mortuary. I'm told nobody else has had access to his room since he's been missing. A temporary janitor has been brought in from elsewhere, but he's not been in, so go through the contents of the desk, etc. and see what you can do.'

'They were hoping to arrest Laurel last night, so I've got Cedar Lane on standby for the scene at her house. I've also got the fingerprint unit on standby to process any marks you get from Trevor's workplace. The way this job's going, the sooner we can confirm he and John Doe *are* one and the bloody same the better.'

Redford appeared at the office door with perfect timing.

'Ah. Phil. How are you this morning?'

'I've been better. Sean and DS Adebayo attempted to arrest Laurel last night.'

'She's not done a runner has she? Nothing would surprise me about this job.'

'She tried to top herself. She's in the ICU at The General.'

'What's the prognosis?' Maya asked.

Redford shrugged. 'It's not looking good. She's taken a cocktail of drugs and alcohol and lost a fair amount of blood. The consultant has said she should know more by this afternoon.'

The words hung in the air unspoken – if she was still alive by then.

54

Malone accompanied Maya to the town hall. After signing them in and issuing visitor passes, the receptionist led them to the bowels of the building, which was Trevor's domain. They were impressed with his office. There was a desk with a phone on it and a comfortable looking office chair. Next to the phone was a framed photograph of Bernadette and Rose. Bernadette was in her wedding dress, beaming into the camera as she linked arms with her mother-in-law. Rose was sporting a hat which left the observer in no doubt that she was an integral part of the wedding party.

Maya found it endearing that Trevor proudly displayed a picture of the two women in his life. Whatever secrets he may have been harbouring, on the surface, he certainly appeared to be a proud family man. A small fridge sat in the corner of the room with a kettle and an organised tea tray sat on top of it. There was a workbench covering the length of the room, and tools clipped to the wall in size order. It was obvious that a lot of maintenance work, including woodwork went on in here, but regardless of that, the place was spotless. There were cupboards and drawers containing light bulbs, screws, hinges, anything you could think of – all neatly arranged and organised, as well as some cleaning paraphernalia propped carefully in the corner near the door.

Maya and Malone slipped on gloves and conducted a cursory search of Trevor's office together to check there was no pertinent evidence which might indicate his state of mind or provide any clues as to who may have wanted to hurt him.

'Tidy, isn't it,' Malone said.

'For a janitor's room, yes. Trevor was clearly an organised man,' agreed Maya.

'Will you be able to get fingerprints?'

'Definitely, there are a few tins in the desk drawer that could be fruitful, and he's left some books and magazines lying around too. I'll try things like the kettle and fridge. The cabinet doors might be too congested and overlapped, but I'll see what I can do. I'll be a couple of hours easily. I'm just going to powder what I can.'

'Right then, I'll get out of your way and leave you to it. I'm going to chat to a few of his colleagues, see if I can get an insight into our mystery man.' Malone left Maya in the room, and she took a moment to sink into the chair while she got a feel for the place.

Not long after starting as a SOCO, Maya became sensitive to the fact that houses all had a different feel to them. Whilst some could be warm and welcoming, others could seem cold and hostile. It wasn't even necessarily down to the cleanliness or the furnishings of a place either. It was as if the personality of the occupants became absorbed within the walls. This room was no different. Trevor had clearly spent many hours in here fixing things and seemingly working away quite contentedly.

Maya closed her eyes and inhaled. The room smelt of sawdust and had an earthy undertone from oil which had been used. She breathed it in, she was immediately transported back to her grandad's garage. She had spent so many hours with him as a child, and even as an adult before he died, as he tinkered with motorbikes mainly, but also fixing bits of furniture for himself or friends and neighbours. She smiled at the memory, which was bittersweet as she felt the all too familiar heartache of loss.

She opened her eyes and surveyed the orderly room, wondering what it told her about Trevor. She was mindful not to let the sentiments from her grandad's memory sway her judgement. She absorbed the room for a moment longer before coming to a conclusion that led her absolutely nowhere.

The room could represent a person who was content and lived his life at a comfortable, organised pace. Or it could denote someone who had a powerfully insightful mind. Someone who was clinical and educated enough to know that whatever he did in his life, he was adept and efficient when it came to covering his tracks.

A few hours later, Maya left Trevor's office having recovered several good quality fingerprints and palm prints. She was loading her equipment back into the SOCO van when she saw a familiar figure making his way into the town hall. She groaned inwardly as he spotted her.

'There hasn't been an incident has there?' Councillor Hanford asked without preamble.

'No. There's nothing you need to be concerned about.'

'Then why are you here?'

'To collect evidence in relation to an ongoing incident.'

'Which is?'

'I'm sorry, Councillor, I'm not at liberty to say.'

He shook his head disparagingly. 'Bloody useless woman.'

Maya turned on him quick as a flash, her large brown eyes glistening with ire. 'Speaking of useless, *Councillor*. A good friend of mine was recently seriously assaulted near Stour Bridge.'

Hanford grimaced. 'I'm sorry to hear that, but I don't see what business that is of mine.'

'Quite a lot apparently. There is no CCTV footage of the attack, despite council cameras being situated in that location. We had another police incident in that same area prior to my friend's attack, which meant that the priority of CCTV placement should have been Stour Bridge.'

He shrugged, not comprehending.

'Instead, I'm led to believe that the council's priority is an antique shop further up the road. *Your* antique shop.'

Hanford's ears flushed a deep red as he began to bluster. 'I hope you're not insinuating that I'm–'

Maya cut him off. 'I'm not insinuating anything. I'm telling you what information I have been given.' She shook her head. 'Quite a scandal though, using council resources to suit your own needs. It's to be hoped no local journalists get wind of this. It wouldn't be a great advertisement for you when it comes to the next local elections.'

Hanford's face was puce, and spittle was flying from his lips as he tried to gain enough composure to reply. Instead, he stuttered and floundered pathetically.

'Ah, DC Malone.' Maya smiled as she noticed Mike approaching. He was clearly concerned about the dispute he was witnessing and was coming over to make sure she was okay. 'This is Councillor Hanford. He had the CCTV cameras situated away from Stour Bridge on the night of the incident you're aware of.'

'Is that right?' Malone asked, giving Hanford a sharkish grin. 'I wonder if I could have a minute of your time, Councillor.' He held the man by the elbow as he steered him towards the town hall. 'I assume you have access to an office,' Maya heard him say. 'Now, I don't believe you know a gentleman by the name of Trevor Dawlish, do you?'

The reply was clearly affirmative by Hanford's increasingly animated body language. Maya smiled to herself as she climbed into the van and conveyed the fingerprints back to Beech Field police station.

55

Sean was feeling perplexed. He was still reeling from the shock of discovering Laurel half-dead in her bathroom. The thought that their main murder suspect might not pull through would leave the investigation with too many unanswered questions. Like all detectives, Sean didn't like loose ends.

As the investigation into the murder of Trevor ploughed on regardless, he had been tasked with going to speak to a Mason friend of Trevor's. He knew absolutely nothing about the Masons and couldn't help feeling that his lack of knowledge may leave him at a disadvantage throughout the interview.

He was crossing the car park, shivering against the early morning frost, when he was suddenly ambushed by the latest addition to the SOCO office, Tara Coleman.

'Hi,' she shrieked gaily in a way that hauntingly reminded him of Laurel.

'Morning, Tara.'

'Do you know, every time I see you, I always think you should be with an adult. You look so young.'

'Great, thanks for that.'

'I bet a lot of the suspects take the piss out of you.'

'Not really, no.'

'And most of the victims too, eh? Do they ask if your uniform is from the Early Learning Centre?' She cackled raucously, pleased with herself. 'So, where are you off to then?'

'I've got an interview with someone who knew Trevor.'

'Family? I thought it was just the three of them.'

'Erm, no. It's a friend, a fellow Mason.'

'A Mason. No way. Aren't you nervous?'

'No. Should I be?'

'Duh, yeah! You know they're all into funny handshakes and witchcraft and stuff, don't you?'

'I know there's a lot of mythology about the Masons, but I wouldn't necessarily say it was witchcraft.'

Tara shook her head vehemently. 'They're not myths, Sean, it's all true. A friend of my aunt used to be married to a Mason.'

'And?'

She winced and closed her eyes before leaning in and whispering conspiratorially. 'At certain times in the year, he'd come home with blood on his gloves.'

'Blood from what?'

'Animals. Usually goats. They used to sacrifice them. They bludgeon the poor thing to death with a gavel. Then they eviscerate it using other tools. Chisels and stuff.'

She shuddered. 'It got too much for her. She left him in the end. Apparently, he came home one night drunk after one of their "ceremonies" and when he fell asleep, he started bleating like a goat. That was the last straw for her.'

'No way,' Sean said sceptically.

'Yeah, honestly.' Tara nodded, wide-eyed and serious. 'That's why they wear gloves during the rituals, to keep their hands clean. Although, I've also heard that they have more than one handshake and one is really taboo and is actually a way of cursing the other person. I'd keep my hands firmly in my pockets if I were you.'

She walked off, leaving him to find which pool car he'd picked the keys up for. He wasn't surprised to discover it was the most iced-up of all the cars in the car park. Or that the can of de-icer on the passenger seat was empty.

Jonathan Forbes had agreed to meet Sean at his home address. He followed the satnav until it led him to an opulent bungalow on the leafier side of town. Before he'd even had time to turn the engine off, a man in his early sixties appeared at the front door. He was dressed in what could only be coined as seventies' geography-teacher-chic; boot-cut grey trousers and a maroon V-neck jumper with leather patches on the elbow. He was squat, with a prominent beer belly and flushed, porcine face that hinted he liked one too many whiskies. Sean could feel the man's eyes follow him out of the car and up the garden path.

'Mr Forbes?' Sean called.

'Please call me Jonathan,' replied the man as he extended his hand.

Sean froze, panicked. He recalled what Tara had said. He reached his own hand out so they could shake but lost his nerve at the last minute. He was horrified to see himself instead, raise his palm in the air, fingers splayed. A voice that sounded like his and came out of his mouth announced, 'High-five, Jonathan.'

Forbes high-fived him back in a moment that was excruciatingly painful.

'So,' Forbes said, clearly amused. 'You've heard all the lies about our "funny handshakes" I take it?'

Sean winced. 'It's not true, is it?'

'Come on in, son and I'll put you right.' Jovially, Forbes stepped back and ushered Sean into the hallway. His face was burning with shame, and he was inwardly cursing Tara. Sean was led into an airy looking lounge. It was tastefully decorated in pastel colours. In pride of place on the mantelpiece was a decorative picture frame with a wedding photograph of a much younger Forbes stood proudly next to his bride.

'My wife, Adele.' Forbes smiled as he noticed Sean looking at the picture. 'I still can't believe she's gone. I miss her terribly.'

'I'm so sorry,' Sean said sincerely. 'Has she been dead long?'

'I hope not. She's only gone to Runcorn to stay with her sister for the week.'

Forbes' booming laugh filled the room as he slapped Sean avuncularly on the back, gesturing for him to sit. 'Don't look so bloody nervous, son. You've clearly heard the lies about Masons. All the conspiracy theories? I can assure you none of it is true. I'm a semi-retired physics lecturer for goodness' sake. And before you ask, I've never sacrificed an animal.'

Sean grinned. 'Not even a goat?'

'Especially not a goat. Have you ever tried to catch one? Nifty little buggers they are.' He suddenly straightened up; a frown passed like a shadow over his face. 'So how can I help you? Poor Trevor. I can't believe it. It's surreal, I don't think it's even sunk in properly yet.'

'I'm sorry I had to be the one to break it to you. We've had confirmation from fingerprints this morning that a deceased male we found in the canal several weeks ago is Trevor. We had been treating his disappearance as a missing persons enquiry, but now, sadly it is a murder investigation as we believe he was strangled.'

Forbes nodded solemnly. 'What do you need to know?'

'I need to know everything you can tell me about Trevor. So

far, he's a bit of an enigma to us. His wife is understandably distraught and it's difficult to get information from her. Unfortunately, his mother also passed away recently.'

Forbes' head shot up. 'Rose too? When? How?'

'Several days ago. At the moment we're treating her death as unexplained.'

'Jesus Christ,' Forbes exclaimed. 'His poor wife. No wonder she's a mess.' Forbes sat back and Sean allowed him a moment to let the additional news sink in until he was eventually ready to speak.

'I've known Trevor for about eighteen years,' Forbes began. 'His late father was a Mason too and introduced Trevor to the Lodge. They were both so similar; quiet, traditionalists. Both solid, good, dependable men. Trevor was very intelligent. It always surprised me that he didn't have a much better job. I don't mean that to sound condescending, just stating fact. He was humble and quite shy, which I guess is what held him back.'

Forbes sat quietly for a moment as he gazed out through the window. 'It's strange, I've known him for so long, but now you're asking me about him, I suppose I didn't really know him that well at all. He was very reticent. Being a Mason was everything to him. I had to warn him on a couple of occasions.'

'Warn him? About what?'

'How much time he was spending at the Lodge or researching scripture. We're a charitable organisation that's steeped in tradition. Because a lot of our rituals are secret, people view us with suspicion. Our four main principles include integrity, friendship, respect and charity. We believe that a man has a responsibility to behave honourably in everything he does. Morality is our lifeblood.'

Sean could feel his cheeks flush as he recalled the horrible moment he high-fived Forbes to avoid shaking his hand. He was clearly in the presence of a good man, and from what he was being told, Trevor had been one too.

'Trevor contributed so much. Too much, if I'm honest,' Forbes continued. 'Our main priority has always been to put our own families first and I was concerned he didn't always do that. I warned him about neglecting Bernadette. I suggested a few times that he needed to spend a little more time at home with her and also hinted that he didn't need to be so financially... generous. But he insisted there wasn't a problem. He said that Bernadette was more than happy for him to do Mason work and she didn't mind him being out of the house so much.'

'And what do you think, did he seem happily married to you?'

Forbes shrugged. 'I know if I spent as much time on Mason business as Trevor did, my Adele would have something to say about it. But Bernadette is like Trevor, she's shy and reclusive. She strikes me as someone who is content in their own company. She joined him at a few of the Masonic dinners and they always seemed very happy and affectionate towards each other. He was very chivalrous; he'd pull out the chair for her and they held hands and whatnot. They were well suited, made a good pair.'

'Did the fact they lived with his mother ever seem like it might have caused a problem?'

'Not at all. Trevor was always very close to his mum. He was close to his dad too, when he was alive, the two of them were best friends. It sounded like Bernadette was close to Rose too. The three of them all got along well.

'When Trevor met Bernadette, it didn't surprise me when he said she was moving in with them. I know not many women would relish the prospect of living with their mother-in-law. There's no way my Adele would have even considered it. But for

Trevor and Bernadette, well, it seemed natural for them. Let's just say I would have been more surprised if he had told me they were buying a place together and leaving Rose on her own.'

'And what about starting a family. Did Trevor ever talk to you about that?'

'Not to me, no. That sort of thing would have been far too private for someone like Trevor to share.'

'I can believe that from what you've told me about him,' said Sean.

'I'm sorry, detective, I don't feel like I've been much help to you.'

'On the contrary, you've helped me piece together a much clearer image of the kind of man Trevor was. When we were treating him as a missing person, he was something of an enigma to us, so it's useful to have his personality described by someone independent.'

'Doesn't really help with your investigation though does it, son?' Forbes said wearily. 'Now you know what he was like it really begs the question, who on earth would want to kill a man as harmless and inoffensive as Trevor?'

It was nearly dark when Dominique got to the garden of remembrance to leave flowers for her dad. She wrapped herself up against the cold, reluctant to leave the warmth of the car. She didn't find this as soothing as Maya did. She came out of a sense of duty rather than any sentiment. Dominique believed that when you were dead, you were gone. She was merely going through the motions, more for Maya's sake than anyone else's.

Shivering, she dashed along the path that carried her to her father's ashes. She hesitated when she arrived. She looked around confused and disorientated for a moment. She double-checked she was in the right place. Futile really as she knew she was. What she couldn't understand was why the heads of orange carnations had been ripped from their stalks and stamped into the ground.

56

Maya arrived at work to find the office in high spirits. Not only was it the day of the Christmas do but the grin on Connor's face revealed there was even more cause for celebration.

'You got it then? Congratulations.' She gave Connor a huge hug and listened as he told her all about the interview and the call he had received to let him know he'd been successful. Tara sat in the corner with a face that looked like she'd been sucking on a lemon, but everyone chose to ignore her.

Maya made a brew and left hers to cool while she headed to CID to see if there were any updates on Operation Mermaid. Spotting Sean and Malone at their desk, she made a beeline for them.

'Morning, gents. How did you all get on yesterday?'

Sean gave her a sheepish grin. 'I high-fived a Mason who could be an integral witness in Operation Mermaid.'

'What? Why?'

'That bloody Tara got in my head, telling me a load of bullshit about how Masons sacrifice goats and can curse me with a handshake.'

Maya was bent double laughing as Sean continued to explain that the Mason in question was a friend of Trevor's. 'Seriously though, Masons are usually really good people. They do a lot for charity.'

'So I've been hearing. How do you know so much about them?'

'I've met a few Widows Sons when I've been on charity bike rides. That's the name of their Masonic Bikers Association. I've met a few regularly at the Ride to the Wall event.'

'What's that?'

'An annual fundraising ride to the National Memorial Arboretum in Staffordshire. It's to recognise the sacrifice of servicemen and women. It's a huge event.'

Sean nodded. 'It sounds it.'

'Take everything Tara tells you with a pinch of salt,' Maya said. 'She's a bloody gossip.'

'I won't need telling twice,' he said glumly. 'Is she going tonight?'

'Yes. Are you lot still able to make it with Operation Mermaid ongoing?'

'I believe so. DI Redford said MIT are going to hold the reins for what it's worth. The bloody investigation seems to be going nowhere. We've got a murder victim who appears to be the most inoffensive man that ever walked the face of the earth and a murder suspect who's still in ICU.'

'Is there any update on Laurel's condition?'

'The fact that she's still with us is a good sign. She's been heavily sedated up to now, but they're hoping to ease her off it later today and see how she responds. If she comes round and is okay, we'll interview her as soon as the consultant gives us the go-ahead. It's a waiting game at the moment.'

'How did you get on with Councillor Hanford?' Maya asked Malone.

Malone leaned back in his chair, hands clasped, as he raised an eyebrow. 'We had an interesting chat. Despite the fact he presents the façade of a respectful councillor and businessman, personally I think the man's a crook. He's clearly slipping cash and favours to the bloke who works in the CCTV room to make sure his shop is looked after 24/7.'

'Did he know Trevor?'

'Yes. Not just from the town hall though.'

'Oh?'

'Our councillor is also a Mason, although I get the impression it's something he's ingratiated himself into, again to accentuate his respectability and standing within the community.'

'I'm going to speak to Jonathan Forbes again and see if he knows much about Hanford and in particular his relationship with Trevor,' Sean said.

Maya nodded as she recalled seeing the Mason tapestry when she'd attended Hanford's burglary. 'Do you think there could be a connection with Trevor's death? Could he have had some kind of involvement?'

'At this stage, we're not ruling anything out. It's the closest thing we have to a lead. What has intrigued me more after talking to him, is hearing how well he knows Bernadette.'

'Really? I suppose that's not unusual though, she works at the town hall too, and he's probably met her at some of the Masons' dinners.'

'It's not a question of him knowing her,' said Malone with a sly grin. 'It's the fact he speaks of her with some affection. I have a suspicion that Councillor Hanford might know Bernadette a little too well.'

'You think they're having an affair? He's much older than she is.'

Malone shrugged. 'Some women like that.'

'Eugh, but he's a horrible man. Personality and looks.'

'Not judging, but didn't you once go on a date with Jack?'

'Well, yes, but a date that lasted about two hours before I realised what an arsehole he is.'

Malone laughed. 'My old mum used to say that there's someone for everyone.'

'Exactly, and from what we've heard, Bernadette and Trevor were loved up. So why would she be interested in Hanford?'

'That's exactly what I said,' added Sean.

Malone rubbed his chin as he considered it. 'Maybe it was unreciprocated. And could possibly supply a motive. If Hanford does have feelings for Bernadette, wouldn't he have a better chance with her if the husband were out of the way? I'll be having another chat with him soon, once we find out what Forbes can tell Sean about our good councillor.'

Maya nodded. 'It'll also be interesting to know what Bernadette thinks about the type of man Hanford is.'

Maya's mobile rang as she headed back to her own office, she looked at the caller ID as she answered. 'Hi, Mama. Everything okay?'

'Yes, it's fine darlin'. I'd not heard from you so just checking in.'

Maya laughed. 'Because you distinctly told me the other day to stop phoning you every five minutes because it was driving you mad.'

Dominique's husky laugh resonated down the phone. 'I know, sorry, it makes me a hypocrite. I just wanted to wish you a good night tonight. You'll be careful, won't you?'

'I'm out with cops and SOCOs, Mama.'

'That's what worries me.' Dominique laughed again. 'Don't

drink too much and don't go home alone. Make sure you share a taxi with Chris or someone.'

'Yes, Mama,' Maya said as she rolled her eyes. 'Got to go because I'm at work. Speak to you soon.'

Maya hung up, smiling to herself as she shook her head. She couldn't believe that at her age Dominique was still lecturing her on being safe on a night out. She was never anything but sensible when she was drinking.

Mothers!

57

The Lamb & Flag was an old boozer within walking distance of Beech Field police station. It was the distance, rather than the ambiance which made it the go-to option every Christmas or retirement do. The pub itself wasn't much to write home about. It was an old-fashioned pub with dated décor, toilet doors that didn't lock and a landlord who was prone to barring people for the most random of slights.

Maya and the rest of her office had changed at work, before braving the icy wind and rain as they bustled into the pub. CID were already there, and despite only having seen each other an hour or so ago, there was an exchange of kisses, hugs, and handshakes.

It was as if seeing each other in their own clothes, combined with the Christmas ambiance, transformed the colleagues into good friends. Kym, looking stylish in a black dress and killer heels, embraced Redford warmly as she kissed his cheek. The sight of her then rubbing her lipstick mark from his cheek seemed so uncharacteristic, it was almost intimate.

Amanda, as organised as ever, had already collected money off everyone for the kitty and had even produced a rota so each person could take it in turns to queue at the bar. Chris was first to the bar, and whilst he waited for their order, tables and chairs were moved and rearranged, much to the chagrin of the cantankerous landlord.

Chris returned to the table expertly brandishing a tray of drinks and an array of crisps, pork scratchings and nuts.

Elaine eyed a bag of scampi fries warily. 'Is this your pathetic attempt at giving a nod to arranging our Christmas meal?' she said scathingly.

'Might be. Not complaining, are you?'

'Well, it's a piss-poor effort.'

He grinned as he slung his arm around her shoulders. 'Sounds like you've just volunteered to arrange next year's. Minute that, Amanda.' He cackled.

The first round of drinks disappeared in no time and Connor was soon sent back to the bar with the tray and a list. CID were ready for more drinks too, and Sean joined him at the bar. No sooner had they left their tables, they were back, with sheepish expressions on their faces.

'What's up?' asked Chris.

Connor mumbled something but nobody could hear him over the roar of voices and Christmas music.

'Say again?' Chris shouted as he craned forward to hear Connor.

Sean coughed nervously, avoiding the eyes from his side of the table. 'He won't serve us.'

'Eh?' boomed Chris. 'Why the fuck not?'

'Says we look underage.'

They all burst into laughter, oblivious to Sean and Connor's embarrassment as they both stood looking like they wanted the ground to swallow them up.

'I'm twenty-two,' said Connor pitifully.

Sean gave him a scathing look. 'I'm thirty-fucking-one.'

'Have neither of you got ID?' said Tara.

'If we had, we'd be passing the drinks round by now, wouldn't we?' Connor said sharply.

'Oh, come on. Look at the pair of you. This can't be the first time; you must get asked for ID all the time.'

'Not helpful, Tara,' said Kym. 'Chris, will you go to the bar again, please?'

'No point,' said Connor. 'He's told us if he'd clocked us earlier, we'd be on lemonade. Even if someone else goes, he's not going to let us have a beer.'

'Sod it,' said Chris as he downed the rest of his pint and stood up, grabbing his coat. 'Nicola, shove those snacks in your bag, love.'

'Where are we going?' asked Maya.

'The Eagle. Are you lot coming?' he called to CID. 'The beer is better in there and so's the atmosphere,' he said pointedly in the landlord's direction as he shoved his arms into his sleeves.

Before Maya had a chance to debate it, chairs were being shoved back and everyone was getting their coats on, piling back out into the winter air as they all made a beeline for the bus stop. Maya decided she'd make the best of it. It was her work's Christmas do after all, and she intended to let her hair down.

Plus, at least it meant she was only around the corner from home. Spence might not even be working tonight, and even if he was, she was out with a crowd, she didn't necessarily have to speak to him. She linked arms with Chris and Nicola as they crossed the road. Their high spirits were contagious, and she felt lifted. It was a night out for God's sake. What was the worst that could happen?

~

Maya, Elaine and Nicola were all using an empty beer bottle as a makeshift mic and torturing a chorus of Mariah Carey's 'All I Want for Christmas Is You'. The drinks had been flowing continuously since they'd arrived at The Eagle.

Maya had faced the elephant in the room the moment she'd arrived in the pub and greeted both Spence and Lisa warmly with hugs. It seemed that every time she looked up, his eyes were on her, and she was confused by his continued attention. The sight of him, as always, made her stomach flutter. She was determined not to let anything ruin tonight, so decided not to overthink things and pushed him to the back of her mind.

The music moved her. She flung her arms in the air as she twirled like a top to a classic nineties beat. She had her drink in her hand and downed it in one, so she could thrust her empty glass on the nearest table while she continued to lose herself to the music. Eye closed, as she sang along. Every bass throb measured her heartbeat, and for the first time in a long time, she felt her neck and shoulders release their tension as she gyrated to the music. It was like therapy. Better than therapy. No words, no emotions just a pure physical being. She was the room. She was the air within it. She just needed to keep dancing. Just dance.

It was one of the few nights out where she had felt safe. She could not only relax her inhibitions, but she didn't feel on constant guard as she normally felt in a pub since she'd joined the job. Even before then. Normally, she would be the one who exchanged every round with a soft drink so she could keep two steps sober behind her friends. And keep herself safe too. She could never really relax in bars and clubs, she envied her friends who would idly toss drinks, phones and bags aside, while she remained, making sure no one got spiked or had their belongings stolen. She had always been aware of potential risks and stayed sober to protect her friends.

But tonight, surrounded by work friends, in Spence's pub, just around the corner from home, surely, she could afford to let herself go. To dance, sing, and perhaps even drink too much. To just be normal like everyone else and enjoy a night out without worrying that something bad was going to happen. And she did enjoy herself. For the next three songs she continued to sway and gyrate to the music. She felt young, beautiful, and liberated. She glanced towards the bar and suddenly felt like she'd been doused in ice-cold water. She was here. Helen, the woman who had been celebrating her birthday the night she kissed Spence.

Maya stopped dancing. Unable to tear her eyes away. Helen was leaning over the bar, making a show of smoothing Spence's shirt down. The sight of them looking so intimate stung like a physical slap. Her reverie was broken by Chris who suddenly slung an arm around her shoulder.

'Want another drink, love?' he shouted above the music.

'Yes please. Shots, let's do shots!'

'Steady on, it's a bit early, isn't it?'

'It's a Christmas do, lighten up. Who else wants shots?' she shouted to the group. Several hands were raised in the air.

'I dunno, love, you should maybe think about pacing yourself. It's still early and you haven't eaten,' Chris said.

'God, you're not my *dad*,' spat Maya. She regretted the words and her tone instantly the moment she saw the hurt cross his face.

'C'mon, I'm up for shots.' Jack was at her side and gestured towards the bar with his wallet. They headed to Lisa's side of the bar and she blocked any further images of Spence and Helen by deliberately keeping her back to them. The shots arrived and were downed quickly.

'Another?' Jack asked with a twinkle in his eye.

Maya hesitated for a moment as she thought of Chris's warning. 'It's Christmas,' Jack said, and the words were all the encouragement she needed. The drinks continued to flow, and the music played on as the night was swallowed up over the next few hours.

Maya was returning from the toilet when Spence approached her.

'Having a good night?'

'Yes thanks.' She looked into his eyes and could feel the physical pull of him.

'Do you not think you've had enough to drink?'

'Oh, please. You're as bad as Chris. For your information, I'm just getting started.'

He sighed. 'Sorry, I didn't mean to get your back up. I just care about you, that's all.'

'Do you? Do you really, really care about me though? How much?' She eyed him insistently as she waited, longing for his reply. Time seemed to stand still as she waited for him to answer. The hand on her shoulder was enough of a response and the rest of the night melted into a drunken memory.

58

The moment Maya opened her eyes, she regretted it. Her head ached like it was gripped in a vice and her mouth felt like a hamster had died in it. She groaned as she tried to recall the events of the previous evening, but it was all a blur. She vaguely remembered Chris asking her if she wanted to go for a kebab, but she'd declined. She had wanted to stay in the pub. She remembered talking to Spence but things after that were a blur.

That was when she realised someone had been sleeping next to her. There was still an indentation in the pillow, a warm spot in her bed and the unmistakable smell of an all too familiar aftershave. Her heart soared as she heard a noise coming from the kitchen. She was about to get up when she heard footsteps padding down the hallway. She turned her head in anticipation as he appeared, grinning in the doorway.

'Ah good. You're awake. I've just realised I don't even know whether you have tea or coffee, let alone how you take it,' said Jack.

~

Spence was hung-over too. Once he'd called last orders and everyone had left, he'd remained in the bar by himself and had worked his way through the best part of a bottle of vodka. The sight of Maya leaving the bar with Jack, of all people, made him feel physically sick. He had been talking to her, concerned she'd had too much to drink.

He had told her he cared about her, and Maya had asked him how much. He had hesitated too long before he answered her, uncertain if he could tell her how much she meant to him, then risk being rejected. Then bloody Jack had appeared out of nowhere with one hand on her shoulder and a large glass of wine in the other and the moment was lost.

Then she was gone. Whisked away by the master of manipulation. Maya knew better than anyone how two-faced Jack could be, yet clearly the alcohol had clouded her judgement. He regretted that he hadn't tried to stop her leaving with him, but she was a grown woman and it had nothing to do with him who she slept with.

∾

'Jack?' Maya sat up in bed, instinctively covering herself with the duvet, even though mercifully, she had her pyjamas on. 'Why are you here? Oh God, what happened last night? I don't remember a thing. Please tell me we didn't...'

Jack laughed as he approached her. She was mortified as he sat on the side of the bed and dropped a kiss on her forehead. 'Are you hung-over? I'm not surprised the amount you put away last night. You're quite the wild thing, though, aren't you?'

Maya shrunk away from his kiss. 'I'm not feeling great. Would you mind giving me a minute. I'll be out in a bit.'

Jack smiled as he sloped away, and she heard him rattling around in the kitchen. Her mind was racing, and her hangover suddenly felt twice as bad knowing he was in her apartment. She reached for her phone, hoping it would provide some clues and help her piece together the events of last night, even though part of her really didn't want to know. She noticed several missed calls and text messages off Chris asking if she was okay.

She sent a text message back to him apologising for worrying him and letting him know she was fine. She cursed herself for drinking too much and allowing herself to get in such a state. She couldn't even remember what she had done. She wasn't a bloody teenager, getting like that was inexcusable and now she was paying the price. She needed to get rid of Jack as soon as possible so she could feel at peace whilst also trying to piece her Swiss-cheese memory back together. She cocooned herself in her dressing gown and walked tentatively to the kitchen.

Jack grinned when he saw her. 'Fancy breakfast? I could knock us up something here if you don't mind, or we could go out. My treat?'

She shook her head; the thought of food made her feel even more queasy. 'Look, Jack, whatever happened last night...'

'Nothing happened. You were paralytic. You passed out. I may be a lot of things, Maya, but there's no way I'd take advantage of someone in that state. If you ever do feel like hooking up though, you know where I am.'

'No offence, Jack, but I'd rather have a smear test without any lubricant,' said Maya as she bustled him through the front door. She strained to listen for the sound of the lift doors closing so she could be sure he had really gone, then let out a little scream as she sank to the floor in despair.

She made herself a strong coffee and reached for some painkillers. Every movement caused her head to slam and her nausea to rise. She'd wait for the painkillers to start working then she'd strip her bed and get rid of any signs of Jack. She carried her coffee into the lounge and reached for the remote when she heard the buzzer go.

She cursed under her breath. It must be Jack – what had he forgotten? She hesitated, considering ignoring it when it sounded again, seemingly louder and more urgent. Annoyed, she checked the spyhole before unlocking the door and was pleasantly surprised to see Dominique.

'Mama,' she said swinging the door open. 'This is nice, I wasn't expecting you.'

'I tried to ring you, but your phone was off. Are you okay? You look terrible.'

Maya gave a hollow laugh as Dominique followed her into the kitchen. 'I had too many Christmas drinks yesterday,' she said as she started to make Dominique a tea.

'Are you sure that's all that's wrong? Just a hangover? Nothing has happened, has it?'

Maya paused and considered telling Dominique about Jack but decided there were some mistakes she didn't need to share with her mother. She'd heeded half her advice from the last time they spoke – she may have drunk too much but at least she hadn't gone home alone!

'Nothing's happened. Why, you look worried, what's wrong? No offence, but why the sudden visit?'

Dominique reached into her handbag and pulled out a box. 'The personal attack alarms that I ordered online have finally arrived. I wanted to make sure you had yours just in case you need it.'

'What's happened? If you're suddenly taking our security seriously, then it means something's happened. Have you seen him? Has Naylor been in touch with you?'

Dominique attempted a light-hearted laugh. 'No. Of course not.'

'Mother!' Maya's voice was stern, her hangover forgotten as she straightened up, arms crossed.

'Have you been to visit grandad?'

'On his birthday? Yes, of course I did. I took him some carnations. Orange ones, his favourite colour.'

Dominique nodded. 'I called after work. Your flowers... Someone had pulled the heads off and mashed them into the ground.'

Maya's hand flew to her mouth as she gasped. Her stomach lurched violently and her mouth flooded with bile. 'Naylor? Have you told the probation?'

'There's no point darlin'. There's no proof it was him. I checked and there's no CCTV. It could just be coincidence and might not even have been him after all. It's the sort of thing kids do all the time.'

'Were any of the other memorials damaged?'

'No. I don't know. It was getting dark and it was cold. I didn't stop to check.'

'But you're worried enough to just turn up here. To suddenly want to bring this,' Maya gestured to the alarm.

'Not worried as such.' Dominique attempted to sound reassuring. 'I'm just being cautious.'

'Well, I'm glad. Whether it was Naylor or just kids dicking about, I'm glad you're being careful.'

Dominique nodded. 'I am. I promise.'

Maya rubbed her eyes. 'Grandad's flowers though. I'll take some more today.'

'He'd understand. Maybe just stay away for a while.'

Maya saw the concern in her mother's eyes and it unnerved her. Things suddenly felt far too real. Blocking Marcus out of her mind wasn't working as well as she hoped. Her head suddenly started to slam again as she rushed to the bathroom to be sick.

59

Maya remembered once reading an article that stated over a quarter of people regretted their actions on their work's Christmas do. She had felt smug at the time, safe in the knowledge that she would never be one of those people that would make such a mistake. Now, walking into work the first morning after the night out, she was genuinely considering handing in her notice rather than have to face Jack in work again. She just thanked God nothing had happened between them as she didn't think there'd be enough antibacterial in the world to douse her genitals in.

She arrived in the office and listened to the tail end of a story Connor was telling. He was regaling how he had woken up the following morning with a half-eaten kebab on his pillow.

'Breakfast in bed, eh?' Chris cackled. 'Sounds good to me. And to be fair, a much more attractive sight than some of the women I've woken up next to.'

'It was a good night all round,' said Amanda. 'Hey, Maya, where did you get to? I didn't see you leave.'

Maya felt as if everybody's eyes were burning into her. 'Oh, I had far too much to drink. I wasn't feeling great so I thought it would be best to just go home. Thank God I was only around the corner, eh?' she added with a nervous laugh.

'Oh, that reminds me,' said Kym, 'I shared a taxi home with DI Redford, and I don't think I paid my share. I'll settle up with him later.' She ignored the suggestive leering from Elaine as she continued. 'Anyway, back to work. For those of you involved in Operation Mermaid, good news, Laurel is on the mend. She's going to be released from hospital later today and she's been deemed medically fit for interview.'

'Maybe we'll eventually get some answers at last,' said Maya. 'Have we any other updates?'

'Yes. Councillor Hanford is also a person of interest. He's going to be brought in and interviewed under caution today too. New evidence has arisen that suggests he may have been one of the last people to see Trevor Dawlish before he went missing.'

'Where?'

'At Trevor's place of work. There is CCTV footage which shows Dawlish and Hanford taking a walk together away from the town hall on the afternoon of Trevor's wedding anniversary.'

'I knew he was a slippery fucker,' said Maya. 'So did Malone. He seems to think there may have been something going on with him and Trevor's wife, which would have given him a motive to kill Trevor. I always thought strangulation was strange. It's usually a crime of passion, isn't it – which would kind of make sense if Hanford and Trevor were love rivals. Wait, does that mean that Jason Laing is in the clear. He's still missing, isn't he?'

'Yes,' said Kym. 'Laing has been circulated as a priority wanted person across neighbouring forces, not just ours.'

'He can't stay missing for ever. His luck is bound to run out at some point.'

'Could Hanford have pushed Rose?' Chris mused.

'Who knows. Possibly. If he was capable of killing Trevor, it's not unfeasible to want the elderly mother-in-law out of the way too. It'd leave the way clear for him to get with Bernadette,' Maya said.

'But if it was Hanford, how does Laurel fit in?'

Maya shrugged. 'I'm sure we'll know more after her interview. It's starting to sound to me that she has nothing to do with the old lady's death after all. I've said it before, from what we know she seems to have genuinely cared for Rose and it would take an incredibly callous person to push an old lady down the stairs, knowing they'd then have to step over her dead body on their way back out of the house.'

Chris rubbed a hand over his stubble. 'I agree with you. But if Laurel is completely innocent, why did she try to kill herself?'

'That,' said Maya, 'is a very good question.'

60

When Laurel woke up in hospital, she wished she were dead. The pain was too much to bear. The doctor had explained how lucky she was, and that if DS Alex Adebayo hadn't administered CPR when he had, she would be dead by now. She wasn't feeling lucky – far from it. The pain across her ribs where he had conducted chest compressions was unbearable and she was covered in bruises. Her wrists had been bandaged, the cuts felt like they were on fire and her throat felt raw and dry where she'd been intubated.

But the physical complaints were nothing compared to the emotional heartache. As the nurses had brought her round, she had questioned why there was a uniformed police officer stationed outside her room. When they explained that she was going to be arrested on suspicion of murder, she thought immediately of Rose.

However, on hearing about Trevor, she felt her entire world fall apart. She had no details about how he had died and was stunned as to why she was considered a suspect. The nurses explained that once the doctor considered her fit enough, she would be formally arrested and taken to Beech Field police station to be interviewed.

That had been several days ago, and now Laurel was ready to leave one institution for another. She had the humiliation of being escorted through the hospital by two uniformed police officers. One of them held her elbow to guide her down the corridors as her wrists were too heavily bandaged for handcuffs. She had been transported like an animal to the police station in the caged area of a police van that smelt strongly of urine. Sean and Adebayo met her in custody. She acknowledged Sean with a nod as he introduced her to Adebayo.

'I believe I have you to thank for saving my life,' said Laurel.

Adebayo shrugged modestly. 'All part of the job. It's what we do.'

'I don't mean to sound ungrateful, but I really wish you had just left me to die,' she replied sullenly.

Sean had been shocked by the sight of her. She was a shell of the bombastic woman he had dealt with previously. Her face, devoid of make-up, made her look younger and more vulnerable. She was dressed in black jogging bottoms and a shapeless black velour hoodie which drained what little colour she had left in her face. Her short hair was lank and greasy, and the ostentatious crucifix was noticeable by its absence. It had been removed by hospital staff and now remained in prisoner's property. Sean flinched at the sight of her bandaged wrists as he quickly dismissed the fleeting image of her lying half-dead and heavily bloodstained on her bathroom floor.

Once the custody sergeant explained her rights, Laurel was taken through to the interview room along with her solicitor, Colin Purcell. She had already had a pre-interview consultation with Purcell, during which time he had recommended that she make no comment.

Laurel, desperate to know the truth about what happened to Trevor, dismissed his advice with a wave of her hand. 'I just want to get on with it,' she had told him. 'I need to know what happened to Trevor. I had nothing to do with his death, so I have nothing to hide.'

She didn't mention Rose. She'd keep her cards as close to her chest as she could on that one, until any concrete evidence was put towards her.

Adebayo took charge of the interview as he asked her once again about the last time she had seen Trevor. She replied verbatim with the same facts she had shared with Sean after seeing Trevor leaving the Dawlishes' house.

Adebayo nodded his way through Laurel's account whilst Sean took notes.

'I really don't know what else to tell you. Perhaps if you'd have turned out when I rang you, you would have been able to find him,' Laurel said accusingly to Sean. He was amused to see a spark of ire, reminding him that the seemingly vulnerable woman sat before them was not to be underestimated.

'You see, here's the thing,' said Adebayo. 'Nobody else saw Trevor that day. Well, Rose states she did but as she is no longer with us, we can't confirm that. Additionally, she was a poor witness anyway because of her failing memory.' Adebayo paused as he looked at Laurel carefully before delivering his next words. 'We now know that on the day you rang us claiming that Trevor had returned home, he was already dead by then.'

Her eyes widened with shock as she gasped. Her hand instinctively reached for the crucifix that wasn't there. 'No. He couldn't have been. I *saw* him.'

Sean produced the image of Trevor and passed it across the desk towards Laurel. 'For the benefit of the tape I'm showing Ms Miller Exhibit KB3. It depicts the image of a male produced by facial reconstruction experts, following the recovery of the decomposed remains of an unknown male recovered from the canal late October. Fingerprints and DNA have since confirmed that same male is actually Trevor Dawlish.'

Laurel's eyes began to brim with tears as Sean carried on regardless. 'So, Ms Miller, it is not possible that Trevor returned home on the day you claimed to have seen him. Unless it was a ghostly apparition. I need you to start telling us the truth.'

'I am telling you the truth. It was Trevor. I'm sure of it. I'm not lying, and I can assure you I am of sound mind.'

Sean raised an eyebrow as he imperceptibly glanced at Laurel's bandaged wrists. She saw his questioning glance and gave him a scathing look as she put her hands under the table out of sight.

'You said the man from the canal, Trevor, had been strangled. Is that right?'

'I'm afraid so.'

Laurel slumped forward, keening as she clutched her stomach. 'Who would do that? Who would kill him? He was such a lovely man. He wouldn't harm a fly.' Her eyes suddenly flashed with anger. 'All that bullshit Bernadette came out with, that he assaulted her when he came home is a lie. Trevor would never hurt anyone.'

'We know,' said Adebayo calmly. 'Bernadette has admitted to us that she lied about Trevor coming home that day.'

Laurel let out a cruel laugh. 'She's got something to do with all this then. She must have. Why else would she make up such a vicious lie?'

'She was frustrated with what she considered a lack of police action in finding her husband. She decided that if she claimed he'd assaulted her, we'd want to arrest him and would therefore find him quicker.'

'Stupid woman. But then you know that, don't you?' she asked Sean as she sat back. 'You've met her enough times to know the lights are on, but nobody is home. Until the day I die I will never fathom what Trevor saw in her.'

'You hate Bernadette, don't you, Ms Miller?'

Purcell interjected. 'You don't have to answer that.'

Laurel shrugged.

'We know about the voicemail you left her on the night you tried to kill yourself. We've both heard it,' said Sean. 'It came as quite a surprise to our team as in a previous interview with my colleagues, you claimed that your feelings towards Trevor were purely platonic.'

Laurel shrugged again, this time though her eyes brimmed with tears that she blinked back. Despite her efforts to present an unperturbed façade, her lower lip was beginning to tremble.

Adebayo leant towards Laurel and smiled sympathetically. 'Did you have feelings for Trevor?' he asked softly. The compassion in his voice caused her to break as she nodded through her tears. Her shoulders shaking with grief as she muttered something inaudible.

'Sorry, Laurel, can you repeat that please?'

She looked up at Adebayo, face streaked with tears. 'I loved him,' she stated simply. She turned to Sean. 'I lied to your colleagues, about all of it. Happy now? I lied and this is the truth. I was in love with Trevor and yes, when he and Bernadette first started dating, I did cause damage to her car and anything else I could do to make her life a misery. We came to an understanding when he proposed to her. She said she'd convince him to move away if I didn't stop bullying her.'

Laurel let out a hollow laugh. 'It was the first time the stupid bitch ever showed any sign of having a backbone. God, she's pathetic with her simpering face and dull clothes. She always looks so bloody nervous and simpering, like a strong breeze would blow her over. And talk about dull, Christ, you'd have a more stimulating conversation with a house brick.'

'Where were you on the last day Trevor was seen alive?' Adebayo asked.

'Away. I always go away on 5 October. The last thing I need is to have to sit and watch them celebrate their bloody wedding anniversary. It was the same on the day of the wedding. I was invited, of course. I made excuses about work to avoid it; it was a mid-week wedding, so the excuse was plausible. There's no way I could have stomached watching Trevor marry that woman. It was bad enough being forced by Rose to sit through the wedding album.'

She burst into fresh, noisy tears, sobbing uncontrollably whilst the three men shifted uncomfortably in their seats.

Purcell cleared his throat. 'May I remind you gentlemen that my client has only just come out of hospital. I'm concerned that this level of distress may be detrimental to her health.'

'What happened to Trevor was significantly more detrimental to his health,' stated Sean unwaveringly.

Laurel sniffed and placed her hand on Purcell's arm. 'Thank you for your concern, I'm fine to continue. I'm more invested than anyone else here in finding out what happened to Trevor.'

'You said you were away,' Adebayo said tentatively. 'Where did you go?'

'There's a lovely hotel and spa in Liverpool I like. I can provide you with the address, booking reference, credit card statements. Whatever you need. I booked several treatments and meals while I was there, so there'll be plenty of witnesses. I returned home the following day, Wednesday, late afternoon.'

'When did you find out Trevor had gone missing?'

'The moment I pulled up outside my house. I hadn't even taken my seat belt off and Bernadette appeared, bawling her eyes out. Stupid woman hadn't even phoned the police. She only rang you because I told her to.'

'Can you recall the last time you spoke to Trevor?'

'Yes, the day before their wedding anniversary. He called after work and put my bins out for me. He was so good like that.' She choked back a sob. 'He stayed for a cup of tea and a chat.'

'How did he seem?'

'Absolutely fine. Same as always.' She rolled her eyes. 'When you asked Bernadette how he appeared prior to going missing, she hinted he'd not been himself. That's all a lie too, there was nothing wrong with him, nothing bothering him, he was the same as always.'

'With respect, would his wife not know more about her husband's state of mind than you?'

Laurel shook her head adamantly. 'I *know* Trevor. I would have known if something was bothering him. He would have told me.'

'Did he talk to you about the pregnancy?'

'What bloody pregnancy?'

'Bernadette is pregnant. She said it came as quite a shock to Trevor and was initially the reason why she thought he may have gone missing. To clear his head while he came to terms with the idea.'

Laurel was open-mouthed with shock. 'I had no clue. Neither of them told me.'

'Apparently it was the reason Bernadette stayed with her sister the night she asked you to look in on Rose. She wasn't feeling well, she was suffering with morning sickness and a migraine.'

'Neither of them talked about having a family. Rose once told me that the death of his little brother had had a huge effect on Trevor. So much so, apparently, he once commented that he would be terrified of having children of his own in case something happened to them. I just assumed from that conversation, that it was never in the pipeline for them. I can't believe Trevor never told me.'

'Perhaps you didn't know him as well as you thought you did?' said Sean.

Laurel glared at him with sheer contempt. 'There would have been a reason that Trevor didn't tell me something as huge as that. It was probably down to her. I bet she swore him to secrecy. She's just the type to be superstitious about announcing a pregnancy too soon. I've seen her saluting magpies in the garden to ward off bad luck for Christ's sake. She's unhinged.' Laurel made a swirling motion with her forefinger at the side of her head.

'Moving on,' said Adebayo skilfully, 'we also need to revisit the events leading up to Rose's death.'

Sean craned forward. 'Is there anything you'd like to admit to now? Have you lied about that too?'

Laurel turned to Purcell. 'I'd like a consultation with you in private, please.'

Sean and Adebayo exchanged a look as they paused the interview.

61

The Naylor brothers were parked in Anthony's car on the road opposite Maya's apartment block. Anthony shifted uncomfortably in his seat. 'I'm not sure about us being here. You're breaching the rules of your probation being anywhere near her home.'

'I know. Obviously, I'm not going to do anything stupid. I know I've got too much to lose. I'm just curious. I wanted to see where she's living. It looks like she's done well for herself looking at that place.'

'It wasn't enough that you got to see her the other day?'

'No. You don't understand. There's so much about her I don't know. I want to see where she lives, see the streets she walks along, where her local shop is. It's the closest I'll ever get to experiencing her life. This curiosity, it's so strong, like a craving. You're not a parent – you don't understand.'

They sat in silence for a little longer, Anthony deciding it was best just to leave Marcus with his thoughts. Just when he was starting to feel uncomfortable from sitting so long Marcus spoke.

'I'm never going to get the chance to speak to her again, am I?'

Anthony let out a snort. 'Not likely.'

'It's a shame really. There's so much I'd like to say. To both of them.'

'Too much to lose, remember. Don't risk what we've got.'

'I won't. Come on, let's go home.' Marcus twisted in his seat so he could take one last look at Maya's building before it disappeared from view.

~

Maya and Chris were in the car park checking the vans. While it was just the two of them away from Tara's endless gossiping, Maya was telling Chris about the damage to her grandad's flowers.

'It's disturbing, but I'm inclined to agree with Dominique. It might be kids. It's natural for you to assume it's Naylor, but why would he? It's risky for him while he's under probation and then there's the letter he wrote.'

'Which I still think is bullshit,' Maya said as she kicked at the floor. 'I honestly think he wrote that to give us a false sense of security. I know Mama thinks I sound like a conspiracist and I'm catastrophising, but I don't believe for one minute that he's changed. It's all a bloody lie, some sort of twisted trick.'

Chris said nothing, he just smiled at Maya reassuringly. 'What do you think?'

'I don't know him or what's gone on over the years, but I can see what a huge impact it's had on you emotionally. And it's understandable, after all he has threatened you in the past.'

'But?'

Chris reached out and squeezed her arm. 'People do change. He's just got out of prison after a very long time. He'd be mad to risk doing anything to get him sent down again. Would scaring you really be worth it? I wouldn't take the risk if I were him.'

'But you're not him, *he's* a fucking psycho.'

'Look, the main thing is, he's stayed away so far. And the flower thing, well, you said yourself, at least it's made Dominique be more wary about her security. So that's a good thing at least, just in case he does show up, which to be honest, love, I honestly don't think he will. Maybe you should think about going to see Jayne again? Counselling may help.'

Maya couldn't even bring herself to answer as she chewed at her lip and began to kick at the floor again. She was starting to wonder if she was going mad. Nobody believed her when she tried to tell them how dangerous Marcus was. Or were they right and she had it all wrong? Could he really have changed? Perhaps she should go and speak to Jayne.

Her reverie was broken by Malone who was striding across the car park towards them.

'Hey, Maya, have you heard?'

She shook her head. 'Give me a clue, mate?'

'Laurel Miller.'

'What about her?'

'She's confessed to harming Rose.'

THEN

Laurel

'Hi, Rose. It's only Laurel,' she called as she let herself into the Dawlishes' house. She heard the old lady call something back in reply, but her voice was too faint to hear what she'd said. The thermostat was in the hall, and she nudged it up a notch. It was bitter outside, and the wind was wild. She went into the kitchen to fetch Rose's tablets and made her way upstairs. At the top she caught her shin on the stairlift and swore lightly under her breath as she rubbed at her leg.

She plastered on a smile as she walked into Rose's room. The old lady was sat up in bed looking frailer than she'd ever seen her before.

'Hello, darling,' Laurel said as she clicked on the kettle that sat on top of the little fridge in the bedroom. 'How are you?'

'Where's Bernadette?' Rose asked, looking unnerved.

'She's gone to her sister's for tea, remember? She's not feeling very well so she's going to sleep over. She'll be back in the morning, but if you need anything before then just ring me.' Laurel tapped the phone at the side of Rose's bed before she began to fuss at the pillows.

'I haven't had my tea.' She sounded like a petulant child.

'Yes, you have, dear. Bernadette gave it to you before she left.'

'I'm hungry.' Rose's lower lip began to tremble, and Laurel fought back the desire to gather the woman in a huge hug. She resisted the urge. She believed that when the elderly became frail and forgetful, they needed to be treated firmly but fairly, just like you would with a child.

'How about a nice digestive biscuit with your cuppa? Then you can take your pills.'

Rose nodded. 'Do I smell?'

'What? No, you silly goose, of course you don't,' Laurel lied. She had noticed a strong waft of stale body odour and urine when she'd plumped up the pillows, but she certainly wasn't going to help the old woman wash. It would be undignified for Rose and horrendous for her.

'Please can I have a bath?'

'You don't need one now. You smell fine. I'll ask Bernadette to run you one tomorrow.'

'Where is Bernadette?'

'I just told you. She's gone to her sister's.'

She passed Rose the tea, biscuits and pills and sat herself in the chair next to the window, waiting until she had finished.

'Now then, is that better?' she asked jovially as she took the cup and plate.

Rose nodded weakly, nestling back against the pillows with a groan. 'Trevor?' she asked hopefully.

Laurel felt as if she'd been winded. She could feel her hands start to shake at just the mention of his name. 'He'll be back again soon. Remember, you only saw him the other morning? He's gone for another little break.'

'With Bernadette. To her sister's?'

'Yes,' she answered curtly, wanting the conversation to end without having to listen to any more of the old woman's confused ramblings. She shut the curtains and plastered a reassuring smile on her face. 'No more talking now. Off to beddy-byes.' She was aware she sounded like she was talking to a three-year-old but wanted to be out of the stifling room. She felt the old woman draining her, as if age and infirmity was contagious.

She went back downstairs and rinsed the cup and plate and put them away. She stood for a moment absorbing the feel of Trevor's kitchen, glancing wistfully at the wallet he'd left behind last time he'd returned home. She had been convinced he'd have returned for it by now. She was wracked with concern, wondering how he was coping without any money.

She peeped in cupboards, drawers and doors, surreptitiously at first, knowing it was wrong to snoop, then more boldly as she felt that by looking at, and touching Trevor's things, she could magic him back. She opened the cupboard above the kettle and spotted the sedatives the doctor had prescribed Bernadette.

'Well, they can go,' she muttered as she pocketed them, leaving half a strip in one of the boxes. Bernadette was bad enough under normal circumstances, but she was even more of a liability smacked off her tits. If she continued taking them, it would mean Laurel would increasingly be called on to look after the old lady, and that wasn't going to happen.

She went into the lounge and sank into the armchair Trevor favoured. She closed her eyes so she could block out the wedding photograph. She couldn't stand to look at Bernadette's simpering face.

It wasn't enough. Her longing for him was like a physical craving. She headed back up the stairs softly, careful to avoid the stairlift this time. She crept into the study, inhaling the smell of the room. She ran a finger across the spines of his books, then lowered herself into the office chair. There was a well-worn copy of a Mason's handbook on the desk. She picked it up and smelt the cover. Then she flicked through it, picturing Trevor's slender fingers turning the pages. She pressed the book against her cheek, imagining it was Trevor's hand.

It felt daring to be in here. She'd never been in the room before and she could sense his presence. This was his domain, his space, she couldn't imagine Bernadette or Rose would ever come in here, unless it was to clean. She was sat where he had sat countless times. It was as if the arms of the chair were his, embracing her. She writhed in the seat and closed her eyes, picturing him, imagining what it would like to be held and touched by him.

She put the book down, still thinking of his hands, his fingers, as she reached her own down into her underwear. She began to pleasure herself on his chair. The fact it was his chair fuelled the arousal and she climaxed quickly.

She could feel a flush of pleasure spread across her chest as her breathing gradually returned to normal. Still, she wanted more. She crept across the landing to the bedroom. She could see which side of the bed was his, it was empty other than a reading lamp. Bernadette's side was obvious as there was a copy of Woman's Weekly and some floral hand cream.

She reached for the pillow on Trevor's side and inhaled it, hoping for the scent of him, but was disappointed to find there was none. It smelt faintly of fabric softener; Bernadette must have recently changed the bed. She would never have done that. She would have done anything to preserve his smell.

She walked to the wardrobe and opened the doors. His suit was hanging neatly. He looked so handsome in it when he was heading to the Lodge. She could feel passion stirring within her again and she reached for it with a trembling hand. She slipped the jacket on and embraced herself. She could smell him. It was almost as if he was holding her. She knew it was taboo but the physical ache for him between her legs was too much to ignore.

She crept back round to Trevor's side of the bed and lifted the duvet. She was about to climb in when a sudden noise caused her head to whip round to the bedroom door. Rose was stood there looking confused.

'What are you doing?' she asked with a hint of accusation in her voice.

'Why aren't you in bed? Why aren't you asleep?' Laurel scolded. 'Bernadette asked me to straighten a few things up for her, that's all.' She shrugged the jacket off and returned it to the wardrobe.

'Why were you wearing that?'

'Because I'm cold. Coming over here to look after you when it's hail-stoning and blowing a gale outside. Back to bed. Now.' The embarrassment at being caught caused her ire to rise. She gripped the old woman by her upper arm and ushered her back to her room.

'Ow, you're hurting me,' Rose whimpered.

'Nonsense. You're just a whinger,' barked Laurel. 'Just hurry up and get back to bed.' She was practically dragging her along; the shuffling footsteps were enraging her even more. She could feel her fingers digging into the old woman's bony arm but was too annoyed to release her grip.

'Where's Bernadette?'

'You know where she is, she's at her sister's. Try and use your mind.' Her grip on Rose's arm tightened. Ignoring her continued protests, she all but shoved the old lady back into the bed. She noticed tears had begun to fill the milky eyes and couldn't bear to look her in the face. She readjusted the pillows as she made a clicking noise with her tongue.

'Now, no more getting up. Go to sleep and Bernadette will be back in the morning.'

'I'm so hungry,' Rose said weakly as she rubbed at her arm.

'Honestly, you've just eaten. You're just being greedy. No wonder Bernadette can't cope, you always want something. And sneaking up on people. You shouldn't do that, it's naughty, you really startled me.'

Rose opened her mouth to speak, but clearly thought the better of it. She shrunk away from Laurel, cocooning herself under the duvet as she protected her sore arm. The tears were streaming down her cheeks now and Laurel felt a wave of shame engulf her as she heard Rose whimper Trevor's name.

'Right. Well, goodnight, Rose,' she said more cheerfully than she felt. She hesitated at the door wishing she could undo all her actions. 'Sleep well, sweet dreams,' she added in a softer voice filled with contrition.

Then she rushed out of the house, slamming the door shut behind her, fleeing to the sanctuary of her own home.

62

Laurel provided Purcell with an abridged version of events, choosing not to go into graphic detail about how she had masturbated whilst sat on Trevor's chair. There were some things she didn't want to share, and particularly not in this room in front of three men and later in a court of law. Purcell had once again advised her to go *no comment*, but it was important to her and in respect for Rose and Trevor's memory to tell the truth.

'So, there you have it, detectives,' said Laurel as she finished her account. 'I wasn't truthful about the last time I saw Rose. I'm ashamed to say I hurt her. I grabbed her arm and dragged her back to bed. I left an infirm old woman alone in her bed, in her house, knowing she was hungry and suffering with poor personal hygiene.

'And, despite what I said previously, I can't confirm that the front door was properly locked after I left. It is possible that someone let themselves in after me.'

She began to cry softly, unable to look any of the men in the face. She was so bitterly ashamed.

'Did you kill her, Laurel?' Adebayo asked bluntly.

Laurel's head shot up; her eyes widened. 'No. I swear to you,

I did not. I've just told you what happened, the truth. What I did, harming her like that, was cruel and unforgivable. I hold my hands up and deserve to be punished for it, but I did not kill her. There's no way I could do such a thing. She was an old lady. My friend. She was Trevor's *mum*.'

'It's just that the sudden change in heart and the suggestion that the front door wasn't locked after all seems very convenient. Bernadette has also told us that you suggested something concerning to her. She states you intimated that if Rose were unwell, or worse, something happened to her, Trevor would hear the news and have no choice but to come home.'

'And we know how much you wanted Trevor to come home,' added Sean.

Laurel turned to Purcell, shocked. 'I didn't,' she said to him before turning back to the detectives. 'I never suggested such a thing. It's a horrible thing to say. She's clearly deluded. You know the sedatives she's been given are messing with her mind. That and her bloody hormones no doubt, she's imagining things.'

'It's not an implausible suggestion, though, is it? We know you were desperate for Trevor to come home. And to have the elderly mother out of the way too, you've admitted yourself, you thought she'd become a burden. You were the last person to see her alive. You had legitimate access to the crime scene, and you've admitted assaulting her. It's all very convenient. All the evidence points to you.' Sean leant forward. 'Was Bernadette next?'

Laurel let out a bitter laugh. 'Jesus, you're a bigger fantasist than she is.'

'Do you know a man by the name of Simon Hanford?' Adebayo asked.

'No, why, is he dead too? Are you going to accuse me of finishing him off as well?'

'He's a councillor. Also, a Mason. We believe he knew both Trevor and Bernadette.'

Laurel shrugged. 'And?'

'We think he may have had a bit of a soft spot for Bernadette.'

'Is there any man alive not immune to Bernadette's inimitable charm? She clearly has *you* under her spell to believe the lies she tells,' she said to Sean pointedly.

'If you're suggesting an extra-marital affair, then you're barking up the wrong tree. Bernadette hasn't got it in her. For all her many faults and failings, she is devoted to Trevor. Who wouldn't be? And for the record, Trevor wasn't the sort of man to stray either. He was too pure, too good.'

'Did you ever try to seduce him?'

'You're disgusting,' spat Laurel. 'I can tell by your tone. Insinuating something sordid between me and Trevor. He meant more to me than just a quick leg-over. I told you, I loved him.'

'Did he reject you?' Sean goaded.

Laurel turned to Purcell. 'I refuse to listen to this line of questioning. It's abhorrent.'

'My client has been more than helpful so far. She has provided an open and honest account of her relationship with Trevor and Rose. She has been more than candid and I suggest you afford her some respect rather than making such lascivious suggestions,' Purcell said.

'On the day you allege Trevor returned home, when you saw him fleeing from the address, Bernadette searched his study and noticed that some sentimental items had been taken from a cabinet he kept locked. Those items included two rather expensive watches, several pairs of expensive cufflinks and a gold Mason's ring. They've all been taken along with their display cases. Some of the items belonged to Trevor's late father,'

Adebayo said, discreetly steering the interview in a less salacious direction.

'Well, perhaps the man who I saw, who I thought was Trevor, was actually a burglar?'

'Perhaps. Do you know anyone by the name of Jason Laing?'

'No.'

'Okay. We have a good description of the items. Bernadette had been able to describe them quite clearly, despite her obvious distress.'

'Well, isn't she just the hero. Can we get her knighted, do you think?' Her voice dripped in sarcasm. 'I'll even do it. I'd love nothing more than to wield a sword either side of her bloody neck.'

'Ms Miller,' said Purcell as he placed a cautionary hand on her arm.

'Is there any chance we might find any of those items in your address or workplace? Trevor's wallet is also outstanding,' Adebayo said.

'No. I am not a thief, and I am *not* a murderer,' Laurel scoffed. 'Tear the place apart again for all I care.' She turned to Purcell. 'I think it's about time this interview was terminated, don't you?'

She eyed Adebayo resolutely. 'What is it they say on the television programmes? Either charge me or let me go.'

63

Maya was sat with Chris in the SOCO office when Jack appeared. She inwardly cringed and it took all her effort to muster up some professionalism at the sight of his smug face.

'Can I help?' she asked as pleasantly as she could.

'I just wanted to give you both the heads up that we've had reports of a possible sighting of Jason Laing. Log 1447 has just gone on if you want to monitor it.'

'That's fantastic news. Thanks for letting us know, we'll keep an eye out.'

Maya walked over to where Chris was reading through the logs on the computer screen. She saw him hesitate and look at her, before turning the monitor in her direction. 'Look,' he said simply.

'What, Laing's job? It won't be updated so quickly.'

Chris shook his head and moved away so Maya could read the screen. It detailed reports of criminal damage to memorial plots at the garden of remembrance. The informant stated that this was repeated vandalism and had been occurring over the last few weeks.

'Oh,' said Maya as she turned to Chris. She thought again of the damage to her grandad's flowers. She'd have to ring Dominique to let her know. She knew that paranoia could be a symptom of anxiety. She frowned as she continued to doubt herself.

If Naylor hadn't damaged the flowers, perhaps that meant he wasn't interested in causing her and Dominique any harm after all. Perhaps, just as he'd claimed, he really had changed. After all, wouldn't he have done something by now? She decided she'd make a Welfare appointment with Jayne as soon as she could. She needed some clarity as she was starting to doubt her own judgement and she was worried that would leave her vulnerable and erratic.

But before she did anything else, she needed to phone Dominique and let her know about the vandalism. Offer her some reassurance that Naylor wasn't responsible after all.

Whilst Sean and Adebayo collated their evidence to present to the CPS for a charging decision against Laurel, Malone was accompanied by DS Amy Lund from the MIT, and they were preparing to interview Councillor Hanford. Despite his respectful façade, his grandiose composure was fading in the presence of the two detectives.

Hanford was dressed in his usual chinos and khaki gilet, this time over a dark-blue-and-white checked shirt which clashed terribly. He was visibly sweating despite the uncomfortably low temperature in the interview room. He had brought a solicitor with him but was overkeen to point out to the detectives that this was purely procedural and not an admission of guilt.

'For the benefit of the tape, Councillor Hanford, can you just remind me how well you knew Trevor Dawlish.'

'Fairly well. As you know he worked at the town hall, so I bumped into him there occasionally when I was on council business. We were also brothers in the same Lodge.'

'Did you get on?'

'I'd say so. Trevor was incredibly quiet. Pleasant man, inoffensive, you know?'

'Would you go so far as to say you were friends?' Lund asked.

Hanford grimaced. 'Friends would be an exaggeration. Associates would be more apt.'

'One of the reasons you're here today is so we can ask you about the last time you spoke to Trevor.'

'How would I know? We were casual acquaintances. It was hardly worthy of making a note in my diary if I happened to bump into him.'

'Perhaps I can jog your memory then. You saw Trevor on the afternoon of 5 October. We have CCTV footage of you walking away from the town hall together.'

'CCTV footage?'

'Yes, taken from the council cameras. Does that ring any bells?'

'I'm a very busy man. I'd have to think... yes, actually. I think it does ring a bell. We were both headed over to the shopping precinct at the same time and walked over together.'

'What did you talk about?'

'I don't bloody know. The weather, the Lodge. It was Trevor, so it wouldn't have been anything earth-shattering or even vaguely interesting.'

'Nothing worthy of noting in your diary at the end of the day.'

'Exactly.'

'Tell me about Bernadette and how well you know her.'

Hanford smiled. 'A lovely woman. I wouldn't describe her as beautiful, she's quite plain to look at but there's something about her nevertheless that appeals. She's the homely, quiet type. Wouldn't say boo to a goose, subservient, you know? Not like a lot of the women today with their brash make-up, loud voices and slutty clothes. And piercings, there's nothing that'd dampen the ardour more than a woman with a face full of metal,' he said pointedly as he looked scathingly at the array of piercings in Lund's ears. 'I met her several times when Trevor brought her to the Masonic dinners.'

'Are you a married man?' Malone asked squarely.

Hanford grimaced. 'No. Don't get me wrong. I enjoy the company of the right kind of woman, but I've never met one I'd want to be saddled with. More trouble than they're worth.'

'I got the impression last time we spoke that you were quite sweet on Bernadette. Is she your idea of "the right kind of woman"?'

'I told you, she has some redeeming features.'

'A colleague of mine has spoken to another gentleman from your Lodge. He claims that on the social occasions you've mentioned that you always made a beeline for them. Well, particularly her. That seems unusual to me considering you and Trevor, in your own words, were mere "associates".'

'Who told you that? It's not true.'

'I'm not at liberty to say. If we asked more members of the Lodge, would they say the same?'

'Now listen here, you can't do that. You've no right. I've come here today to help you. To talk about Trevor so you can find out who killed him. And now you're threatening to out me socially, as some kind of what, pervert?'

'That's not what we're doing,' Lund said patiently. 'It's not unusual in an investigation as serious as this to have to ask some delicate questions.'

Hanford sneered at her. 'I wasn't asking you. I was talking to him. I don't need to hear your opinion.'

Lund arched an eyebrow. 'I do apologise if my presence irritates you. I was trying to explain that we need to piece together as much information as we can. If we do have to corroborate your version of events with other people in your social circle, I can assure you it will be done thoroughly but delicately.'

'You're treating me as a suspect.'

'You're a person of interest.'

'What does that even mean?' he blustered. 'I'm not talking to you, silly bloody woman. He can ask me the rest of the questions.'

'The reason you're here is because, as I have mentioned, you gave me the impression you were quite taken with Bernadette.'

'For Christ's sake.' He turned and shook his head at his solicitor.

Malone flicked through his daybook.

'When I asked you what you thought of Bernadette, your response was similar to your previous comment. You started to tell me you thought she was attractive. That she was the kind of traditional, homely woman that you like. You also used the word "subservient" then too and commented on how much the thought of her freckles turns you on.'

'All right,' he responded sulkily. 'It's not appropriate to talk that way about a married woman, I know, but I'm a red-blooded male. There's no law against noticing what takes your fancy is there?'

'Absolutely not. But it struck me as strange. Normally when I ask somebody what they know about another person, they tell me about the kind of relationship they have. If they get on or not. What the other person's personality is like. They rarely respond by lauding their physical attributes.'

Hanford began to chew on the inside of his mouth.

'Now, I've not met Bernadette personally but a few of my

colleagues have. One in particular is acting as her family liaison officer and is with her right now. I asked her about the freckles you admire so much, and she has confirmed unequivocally that as far as she can see, Bernadette has flawless skin.

'She has no visible freckles on her face or arms. So that would suggest to me, that if Bernadette has freckles in a more intimate area, you know where they are. Which also suggests she is more to you than just the wife of an "acquaintance".'

Lund made no attempt to mask the smug look on her face. 'I'm going to pre-empt your next question, Mr Hanford, and tell you that yes, it is absolutely fine to have a moment's private consultation with your solicitor. I for one can't wait to hear the next instalment. This is better than an episode of *Coronation Street*.'

'Bitch, you vile fucking bitch.' Hanford flew across the desk and attempted to grab Lund, but she had him secured in an armlock with his face ground into the table quicker than you could say misogynist. And Simon Hanford was certainly that.

64

Marcus was humming away to music as he decorated the small fibre-optic Christmas tree. It was hardly Harrods' standards, but it was enough to adorn the small flat and add some cheer. He tried to remember the last time he had trimmed a tree and could only imagine it would have been Maya's first Christmas. It seemed so long ago. He tried to remember what they did that year, but the memory had been lost in time and probably too much intoxication.

He smiled as he heard his brother's key in the lock. Anthony bustled in clutching bags of shopping. 'Why on earth have you dragged that lot out of the loft?'

'Cheer the place up for Christmas.'

'It's suddenly like living with Buddy from *Elf*. It'll be the two of us and a glorified Sunday dinner, mate. Not a five-course meal in the north pole.'

'I know that, but, c'mon, it makes the place look homely. And we are celebrating the birth of Jesus Christ after all. Plus, the probation officer is coming tomorrow and I'm sure he'll appreciate the effort.'

'I suppose so.'

'Anyway, you can talk. Those bags are bulging, have you been Christmas shopping?'

'Just a few treats while we make plans. And I figured we have a few years of catching up to do.'

'Sounds good to me, bro.'

Anthony plucked two lukewarm cans of beer from the shopping bags and they cracked them both open.

'Cheers,' he said as he clinked cans with Marcus.

'Not too many though,' said Anthony as he nodded towards the booze. 'You don't want to be hung-over when the probation come. And we've still got lots to sort out.'

'We certainly do,' grinned Marcus. 'Failing to plan is planning to fail, and *nothing* is going to go wrong for us.'

65

Bernadette had finally mustered the emotional strength to leave her sister's house and return home. She stood in the lounge cradling her stomach while she gazed across at Laurel's house.

'How could she do it? How could she harm Rose like that?' she asked Adila.

Adila joined her at the window. 'I'm sure it will all come out at the trial. She's been remanded, so you don't need to worry about her coming home. Concentrate on settling back in here. How does it feel to be back?'

'Strange. It's nice though, the familiarity. I just can't believe they're both gone.' She began to cry and Adila guided her to the couch and fetched her a glass of water.

'Will you stay here?' Adila asked Bernadette when she was calmer.

'Oh, yes. It's important to me that I bring the baby up here. I want him or her to know all about their daddy. And their nanna. The thought of it sleeping in Trevor's old bedroom seems right somehow.'

'If Laurel is found not guilty of killing Rose, she will still be prosecuted for common assault, as she has admitted to grabbing her arm. It's a minor charge and the fact she has no previous police record means that it certainly won't result in a prison sentence, probably just a fine.'

Bernadette's eyes flashed with an uncharacteristic show of anger. 'A minor charge? She manhandled my mother-in-law. A vulnerable old woman. I can't believe it's possible that a jury would fail to find her anything *but* guilty of murder. She was the last person to see Rose alive. Of course it was Laurel that pushed her, no one else was here that night.'

Bernadette sat back deflated. 'I'm not scared of her anymore. The two people I loved most in the world have gone. Because of her. Now Trevor isn't here, she's nothing to stay here for. She'll probably be the one to sell up and leave. She'll not like the other neighbours knowing the truth and thinking bad of her. All she cares about is her image.'

Adila had received an update from Malone to let her know how the interview with Councillor Hanford had gone and now needed to ask Bernadette some sensitive questions. She wasn't looking forward to it as Bernadette was emotionally vulnerable as it was without being probed further.

'I believe you know Simon Hanford?'

Bernadette physically shuddered and her face grew even paler. 'Unfortunately, yes.'

'He's currently being interviewed by my colleagues as he has been captured on CCTV, walking away from the town hall with Trevor on the day you reported him missing.'

Bernadette sat and looked at Adila wide-eyed.

'What can you tell me about him?'

Bernadette dropped her head and mumbled into her chest. 'He goes to the same Lodge as Trevor. He's a councillor, too, so it's not unusual for either of us to bump into him at the town hall.'

'Would you say he and Trevor were friends?'

'No.' Laurel let out a hollow laugh. 'Trevor was such a sweet man, he'd get on with anybody, but they were like chalk and cheese. Hanford is a bully.'

'What's your relationship with him?'

Bernadette began to squirm uncomfortably in her seat. 'I haven't had a relationship with him.'

Adila frowned, confused. 'No, I wasn't suggesting that. I meant how do you get on. Do you know each other well?'

'I really don't want to talk about him.'

'I can tell something is upsetting you, but I need to know. He may well have been one of the last people to have seen Trevor alive. He has intimated to my colleagues that he has more than just platonic feelings for you. We also believe he has potential for violence as he tried to assault one of my colleagues.'

Bernadette's gaze remained fixed to the floor.

'Can you think of any reason Hanford would want to harm Trevor?'

There was a long, uncomfortable silence. Adila knew from experience that this caused people to start to talk eventually to fill the void. She knew pressurising Bernadette would only result in making her clam up, so instead, she sat back and waited for her to speak.

'I think it might have been because of me,' she said eventually.

'Did he make it clear he had feelings for you?'

'Feelings,' Bernadette scoffed. 'He doesn't have feelings. The man is a monster.' She started to cry again and Adila struggled to hear her in between sobs, but the floodgates were open again now and the truth was pouring from Bernadette.

'He blackmailed me into having sex with him. Said he would make things difficult for Trevor at work and at the Lodge if I didn't. What would you have done? I'd do anything to protect the man I love.'

Adila was stunned. She'd seen a lot over the years and was hardened by most things, but the thought that someone would force someone as weak and vulnerable as Bernadette into having sex with them was sickening.

'How long has it been going on?'

'About six months. He told me at first that it would just be the once. But it wasn't. After the first time, I thought he'd leave me and Trevor alone. But he set me up.' Bernadette looked fearful as she revealed all to Adila. 'The first time we did it, he recorded me. He said if I didn't do it with him again, he'd send the video to Trevor, everyone at the town hall *and* the Lodge.'

Adila felt a wave of disgust in her stomach as well as overwhelming pity for Bernadette. 'I'm worried now that he may have told Trevor. Once I found out I was pregnant I told him it would have to stop. That I wouldn't carry on sleeping with him while I was carrying Trevor's baby. I tried to turn the tables on him and said I'd tell the council. He was really angry. And now I think he may have told Trevor before he killed him as some sort of revenge.'

Adila held her as she sobbed. 'I can't stand the thought that Trevor went to his deathbed, knowing I've slept with Hanford.'

'Where did this all take place?'

'He has an antique shop. There's a flat above it. We met up either there or at his house.'

'Can you remember when? The exact dates?'

'I'd have to double-check, but it always happened on a Wednesday because I work part-time.'

'Is there any evidence of communication with Hanford on your phone?'

Bernadette sniffed. 'No, I deleted all the messages.'

'Okay, well it's not a huge problem. With your permission, if we send your phone to our Digital Investigation Unit, it may take some time, but they'll be able to retrieve any correspondence between the two of you.'

'I don't want you to take my phone. I've got pictures of Trevor and Rose on there and voicemails off him. It's all I've got left.'

'I understand that. The last thing I want to do is cause you any more distress or force you into doing something you don't want to. I think you've had enough of that. I'm going to make a phone call to my colleagues and pass on this latest information.'

'What will happen then?'

'In view of what you've just told me, he's going to be arrested on suspicion of Trevor's murder and blackmail to start with. We'll get warrants to tear his home and business apart while we re-interview him. Councillor Hanford has got a lot of explaining to do.'

66

'Good morning, people,' Kym said with a clap of her hands. 'I didn't even know she was in yet. Has she shit the bed or what?' Chris muttered to Maya, who stifled a laugh. She had got in early herself, keen to see if Jason Laing had been successfully detained overnight, which thankfully he had. Adila had been tasked with interviewing him and Maya was eagerly waiting an update.

'I've just been in the MIT briefing, and I'm pleased to say that at last we have progress.'

Maya straightened up; interest piqued. 'What's happened?'

Kym filled them in on the latest accusations against Hanford.

'Which means,' said Kym, 'we have two scenes relating to Operation Mermaid today. Hanford's house and his workplace. Tara, you're the only person on this division who hasn't had any involvement with Operation Mermaid, so I'm allocating you to his house. I'm going to put the strategy together now.'

'Oh.' She pouted as her eyes fell to the floor.

'Problem?'

'Would it not be easier for me to do his workplace? That would be a quicker scene, surely?'

'I imagine it would be, but I'm asking for help from a neighbouring division who have to travel, so it's only fair they are given the shorter scene.'

'It's just that I was hoping not to have to finish late tonight.'

'And I was hoping when I get home tonight that Idris Elba would be lying naked in my bed. Looks like we're both going to be disappointed.'

'Oh, Kym, there's no need to be so flippant. I have an appointment later, that's all.'

'And what is it today? Laser eye surgery, carol singing at the old folks' home or just your nails again?'

Tara had the good grace to look away, clearly embarrassed, although she couldn't resist taking a pitiful look at her nails.

'Fine. I'll do it.'

'What was that, Tara, you're actually offering to do the job you're paid for? That plenty of other people would give their right arm to do. Thank you so much. If we had an award for employee of the week, I'd put you forward for it. Can I suggest you go and check your van is adequately stocked while I write the strategy?'

Maya and Chris exchanged a grin. Her work-shy laziness was nearly as annoying as her lack of filter and relentless gossiping.

'What else have we got on today?'

Maya checked her list. 'A stabbing overnight which includes a scene and a prisoner. We can cope between us though, Elaine's on a mid-shift too,' she said, and Chris nodded agreement.

Maya thought about what Kym had told them about Hanford. 'So much for the respectful councillor. He's actually a potential murderer and has blackmailed someone into having sex with him. Bastard.'

'And,' said Sean who appeared in the doorway, 'according to Jonathan Forbes, he wasn't popular at the Lodge. In Forbes' opinion he only joined to try and make new business contacts.

That fits in with everything I've learnt about how decent the majority of Masons are. Like you said, Maya, they spend lots of time involved in charitable acts, something which Hanford never, or rarely contributed to.'

'And considering the size of his house and knowing his line of business, he's not short of a bob or two,' said Maya. 'What an odious man. How are you, Sean?'

'Good thanks. I've just been speaking to Adila. We're going to be charging Laing with the attack on Lisa.'

'Brilliant news. That's a huge relief. Did you ask him about Trevor Dawlish?'

'Yes, he's got a cast-iron alibi. He's been working in London and only came back up here ten days before he met Lisa, so the dates don't fit.'

'Who's interviewing Hanford?'

'Malone and Amy Lund from MIT again. We did think about using another DS in view of his animosity towards Amy, but DCI Chambers seems to think it would be a good strategy to keep her in there. I'll let you all know how it goes.'

As Malone and Lund settled down to reinterview Hanford, his solicitor provided them with the information no detective wants to hear.

'My client strenuously denies all the accusations against him. He does however acknowledge, and is at pains to apologise, for his erroneous actions towards DS Lund...'

'You provoked me and you know it,' Hanford interjected. 'But I apologise for attempting to hit you. It's out of character for me.'

'Really?'

The solicitor gave Hanford a warning look, punctuated with

a raised eyebrow. 'For the duration of this interview my client will be providing a "no comment" response.'

Malone resisted the urge to mutter 'for fuck's sake' and they proceeded to start putting the questions to Hanford. Both detectives carefully monitored his body language. Although he repeated 'no comment' autonomously again and again, his body was throwing off subconscious clues to his emotions. A pursed lip, flushed face, dilated pupils and the twitch of a jaw muscle were obvious indicators of what he thought to the line of questioning. One thing was clear from their mute detainee, the account provided by Bernadette had really got his back up.

Maya hadn't been back to the office long herself when Tara returned, laden down with exhibit bags.

'How did you get on; did you find anything of interest?'

'The clothing he was wearing, which Kym gave me the screenshot of from CCTV, was a nightmare.'

'Why?'

'The guy must wear some kind of imagined uniform. He has twelve pairs of chinos and five pairs of khaki gilets. Weirdo.'

'Anything else?'

'Yes. Take a look at these.' She spread a collection of evidence bags onto the desk. Maya studied the contents. There were several pairs of cufflinks, two pairs of expensive-looking watches and an 18-carat gold Masonic ring.

Maya and Tara eyed each other. 'They're the ones taken from Trevor's cabinet in the study, aren't they?'

'Looks like it.' Maya grinned. 'Well done, Tara. I think we're getting very close to nailing the bastard.'

After a lengthy and very vocal consultation with his solicitor, Hanford eventually conceded to answer the questions put to him. Spending time in his cell at Beech Field custody had been all the encouragement he needed to start talking. His solicitor continued to advise him to provide no-comment answers, but that meant taking the risk that he'd be charged and remanded while he waited for the trial to take place. Not only did the thought of prison unnerve him, but he also had his business interests to think of. He concluded the best thing to do was tell the truth.

He arrived in the interview room bristling with discontent, already looking a much older, washed-out version of himself.

'About Bernadette,' he said as he jabbed the tabletop with his finger, before either of the detectives even had a chance to ask a question. 'I want to put the record straight right now on that score. Yes, we were sleeping together, but I was not blackmailing her. If you must know, she came on to me.'

'Really?' Lund said as a smile danced in the corner of her mouth. 'A woman over thirty years your junior, who's madly in love with her husband and in your own words "wouldn't say boo to a goose", seduced you?' She made no attempt to mask the repulsion in her voice.

Hanford puffed his chest out. 'It may surprise you to know that I'm not immune to female attention, far from it. I have a high standing within the community, a lot of women find success a real turn-on.'

'With respect, you're a local councillor with an antiques business that's doing okay. You're hardly Richard Branson. More like a middle-class Derek Trotter. If you don't mind me saying so.'

Hanford didn't reply to Lund, choosing instead to glare at her, while he chewed the inside of his mouth.

'Tell us about it,' said Malone as he leaned towards Hanford in a conspiratorial man-to-man gesture. 'How did the relationship start and how long has it been going on?'

Hanford gave a wry smile. 'About six months. I had to pop to the town hall to meet a business acquaintance. She was heading out for lunch as I was walking back to the shop and we got chatting. She mentioned one of the street lights had gone off outside her house and I said I'd email the highways department and get it repaired.'

'Did you know her address?'

'Not then, no. She wrote it down for me, along with her mobile number so I could let her know the outcome.'

'Have you ever been to her house?'

'No.'

'Following the unexplained death of Rose Dawlish, our crime-scene investigators carried out a thorough examination of her house. A lot of forensic evidence was recovered from the scene, so I'll ask you again, is there any reason why we would find your DNA or fingerprints within that address.'

Tersely, he repeated, 'No.'

'When was your next communication with Bernadette?'

'I texted her to let her know I'd reported the faulty light. She was very grateful, jokingly commented I was her knight in shining armour.'

Malone could feel Lund tense next to him, she was clearly bursting with a retort, but professionalism kept her restrained and silent.

'I replied saying that, ironically, I had the head from an old suit of armour in the shop. She said she'd love to see it and would also like to look around for ideas for Trevor's birthday present.'

'And?'

'She doesn't work Wednesdays, so she said she'd come then. And believe me she did,' he said with a lascivious grin as he cackled at Malone and his solicitor.

'And the affair started that day?'

'Yes. I'm sure you don't need me to provide you with step-by-step descriptions of the events leading up to our, shall we say, consummation?'

'Not this close to lunchtime, no,' said Lund dryly. 'We can always revisit that at a later date if necessary. So how regularly did you see each other after that?'

'Most Wednesdays.' He suddenly switched on Lund, a flash of anger in his eyes as he looked her up and down disgustedly. 'I know what you're thinking, sat there looking like the judge, jury and executioner. You think I forced her, don't you? Well, I didn't. She was more than willing. And it wasn't just sex. Don't get me wrong, that was good. Would have preferred her to moan and move a bit more but at my age beggars can't be choosers.'

'How romantic. So, what else was there between you?'

'I genuinely enjoyed her company. She was quiet, but fun. She loved hearing all about me and my business and the history behind some of my stock.'

'She massaged your ego.'

'No. She was genuinely pleased to see me and spend time with me.'

'And did it not bother you, knowing she was going home to Trevor?'

'That ineffectual arsehole, no. It suited me. I don't want a serious relationship with anyone. I'm happy to get my back scratched now and then, and Bernadette was doing that. All this bullshit that I blackmailed her, it's a lie. She was a willing participant. More than bloody willing.'

'We had our crime-scene investigators search both your home and workplace,' said Malone.

'And?'

'As part of that search, I would like to refer you to close-up photographs of exhibits TC29 to TC36 inclusive. Do you recognise these items?'

Hanford craned forward as Malone displayed the images, fan-shape, like a pack of cards across the desk. 'Yes, those items were given to me by Bernadette.'

'For what purpose?'

'To sell.'

'When?'

'A few weeks ago. She brought them to my house, I was surprised to see her at first, as she'd already ended it by then. I thought she'd changed her mind about us sleeping together. But she wanted cash for those things.'

'She sold you sentimental jewellery belonging to her husband while he was missing?' Lund asked doubtfully.

'Bernadette had told me before how she was struggling for money. It wasn't easy for her, she earned peanuts and Trevor's wage must have been a joke. Plus, there was the added expense of the old woman. I gave her a nice payout for the lot. I've been bloody generous to her. I treated her lots of times when we were together.'

'To gifts?'

'No, I'm not stupid, just money. Even someone as naïve as Trevor would notice if his wife started wearing a new dress or necklace. I gave her cash now and then. It's less effort than having to waste time thinking of what to get or spending time shopping for it.'

'How much?'

'Does it matter? A couple of hundred here and there so she could treat herself. I don't want to brag, detective, but it's loose change to a man of my worth. And not wanting to sound crass' – he eyed Lund with a wolfish grin – 'it wasn't much more than I'd spend on a decent prostitute. And I genuinely liked her, so...' He splayed his hands indifferently on the table.

'When did it go sour? If what you're telling us is true, and incidentally, we will be going through your phone records, CCTV and bank account with a fine-toothed co–'

'You can have access to all of that, I've nothing to hide,' Hanford interjected.

'Why do you think she is now accusing you of blackmailing her and, potentially, making you look like the number-one murder suspect?'

'Guilt?'

'We need more information than just one-word answers,' snarled Malone.

'Okay, so she ended it, out of the blue. Told me she was pregnant and didn't want to carry on the affair. Guess she didn't like the thought of my cock nudging her baby's head if I carried on shagging her. Women can be very irrational and oversensitive at times.' He eyed Lund, goading her, but her face refused to disclose any disgust or annoyance.

'And what did you do?'

'Nothing at first. It didn't bother me. Then I was heading into the town hall to drop some paperwork off, and I suddenly thought Trevor had the right to know. Maybe it was a guilty conscience on my part, but we're brothers in the same Lodge, and my loyalty lies there when all is said and done.'

'Nothing more important than brotherly code,' said Lund.

Hanford held his palm up in her direction without even looking her in the eye. 'Women don't understand. Shut up, I'm talking.'

Hanford sighed as he rubbed his eyes. 'I wasn't even one hundred per cent sure at that point that I was going to tell him. I don't know, it just seemed instinctive. I asked reception to tell me where his room was. He looked pleased to see me. I told him we needed to talk, but somewhere more private. He said he was on his way to the precinct and invited me to join him.'

Hanford sighed. 'I don't mind admitting I felt like a total shit. He was babbling away, the most animated I'd ever seen him. Usually, I'd have to instigate a conversation with Trevor, but he was full of it. Told me he wanted to get a few treats for Bernadette as it was their wedding anniversary. I congratulated him, then commented how it would be a double celebration this year. With the baby on the way.'

Hanford suddenly silenced himself as he stared awkwardly at the tabletop.

'And?'

He turned to his solicitor and then Malone and Lund before he answered. 'He looked gobsmacked and asked me to repeat myself. Twice.'

Hanford puffed out his cheeks. 'I apologised and said I hoped I'd not pre-empted the announcement. He asked me how I knew, and I said I'd heard it on the grapevine. I had to make something up on the spot so told him I'd overhead the chat while passing the clerical room where Bernadette worked. Made a comment about clucking hens.

'It was excruciatingly awkward. He clearly knew nothing

about the baby. He soon forgot about the shops. We walked in an awkward silence, he followed me aimlessly as I headed back to the shop, we were near Stour Bridge and he stopped at the canal and sat on a bench.

'I asked him if he was okay, and he just nodded. Then he asked me what I had wanted to talk about, and I made some excuse about Masons' business. I told him he seemed distracted and it was nothing that couldn't wait. By then I just wanted to get away from him to be honest, plus I was meeting a client at the shop so couldn't stop even if I wanted to, which I didn't.'

'Could the baby be yours?' asked Malone.

Hanford snorted. 'Doubtful at my age. Don't get me wrong, I've still got it,' he said, winking at Lund, 'but I'm slightly past my prime.'

'It's still possible though,' said Malone. 'You've admitted to sleeping with her and now you're telling us she was pregnant and Trevor didn't know, which infers he may not be the dad.'

Hanford shook his head. 'Not possible. We always used protection.'

'Always?'

Hanford turned to his solicitor and grinned before leaning towards Malone. 'Ever heard of the umbrella treatment?'

'No, enlighten me.'

'When I was about eighteen, I found out that a girl I'd been with had the clap. These days they'll just treat you with antibiotics and have done with it. Back in the day, they'd stick a swab in your urethra to check if you had it first.'

'Thanks, I think I've heard enough.'

Hanford laughed. 'Hurt like hell and I've never ridden without a johnny since. That baby is definitely not mine. And if it is Trevor's, I'm telling you, he knew absolutely nothing about it.'

THEN

Trevor

Trevor Dawlish had never been an angry man. It wasn't in his nature. He was renowned for being mild-mannered. He was studious, polite, thoughtful, dependable, and honest.

Honest? Well, most of the time...

The majority of the time.

He had his "little-white-lies". Okay, and one black lie. That didn't make him a duplicitous person, surely.

He protected secrets and held his counsel, but didn't everyone?

He wasn't harming anyone with the confidences he kept.

Up until now.

Now he could harm someone.

Now, he was raging with an intensity so strong it was a physical burn. A pain so raw and visceral, nothing he thought or did could shake it off.

He was hurting.

He was shaking, fists clenched so hard, his fingernails buried into the palms of his hands leaving half-moon furrows in the flesh.

Right now, Trevor felt like he could kill.

And, as God was his witness, he'd smile while he was doing it.

As God was his witness, he would sing his exaltations as he squeezed out every last breath of the person who had wronged him. And then he would shatter every single bone in their body.

With shaking hands, he reached for his mobile phone and called Bernadette. She answered straight away. 'Hi, is everything okay?' He detected concern in her voice and it made his stomach churn. It was unusual for him to call her through the day.

'Bernadette, are you pregnant?'

There was a silence on the line, but the pounding of his own heartbeat was deafening. Eventually, in her soft voice, sounding even more timid than usual, she replied.

'Yes. I was going to tell you this evening. How did you know?'

'It doesn't matter how I know. How far along are you and why didn't you tell me earlier?'

'I'm twelve weeks. I didn't want to tell you straight away in case something happened. My first scan is next week. I was going to tell you tonight. It's my anniversary gift to you.' She giggled nervously.

'Look, I know how worried you are about having a baby, but nothing is going to happen to it, Trevor. Everything's going to be fine. What happened to your little brother, isn't going to happen to our baby. It's going to grow up to be strong and healthy, just like its daddy. Try and get away as soon as you can so we can talk about it, okay?'

He had so many questions but couldn't trust himself to speak anymore. He needed to talk to her in person, to read her face while she answered his questions. 'Okay, bye. Love you,' he added habitually before disconnecting the call.

He was still shaking and now bile was rising in his throat. He knew Bernadette wanted a baby despite his reservations. They had been 'trying' but with no success. She had suggested they visit the doctor so they could both get checked out, but he had made excuse after excuse to put her off, assuring her it would happen in its own time.

He felt guilty knowing he had kept the truth about his infertility from her. His parents had told him that he'd been born with undescended testicles. They had descended by the time he was six months old. After reading up about it when he was in his early twenties, he had been to see his GP, who had referred him for tests which proved he was infertile. It had come as a relief, as losing his baby brother had been the most painful experience in his life. Until now. He'd never told his parents or Bernadette and he'd had to learn to live with the guilt.

But now it was clear that Bernadette was keeping a secret of her own. A much bigger, dirtier secret than his. He could feel his rage building as his heart simultaneously broke whilst he came to terms with the betrayal. He didn't know whether to scream or cry. He couldn't face the thought of going home and seeing her. He didn't think he could cope with her lies. And what would this do to Mum? The betrayal would be hard on her too. It would kill her.

He thought fleetingly of phoning Jonathan Forbes. He was the closest friend he had since his dad had died, but if he spoke the words out loud to someone, it meant they were true, and denial was a tempting option right now.

He heard footsteps crunching along the gravel canal path. He looked up and saw a familiar face walking towards him. He smiled at his soon-to-be killer.

68

The air in the conference room crackled with anticipation. DCI Chambers could normally silence the room with a stony glare, but today there were too many pockets of conversation as detectives swooped on each other's updates like seagulls on chips.

'Can I have your attention please?' bellowed Chambers. 'Right, I just want to bring you all up to speed. As you know, Hanford claims he and Bernadette were in a sexual relationship for six months, during which time he has "gifted" her a substantial amount of money.

'Enquiries with the bank have just confirmed this and he has handed over his mobile phone which shows conversations of a sexual nature between him and Bernadette. Hanford also claims that he doesn't think Bernadette's baby is Trevor's. He was adamant that Trevor didn't even know about it, so we need to know who else she has been in a relationship with. We've had confirmation today from Trevor's medical records that he was infertile.'

There was a stunned silence around the room.

Chambers turned to Adila. 'This, of course, means that the

grieving widow hasn't been entirely honest with us, and we need to know what else she's hiding.'

'Is Hanford still in the frame for Trevor's murder though?' Sean said. 'He was the last person to see Trevor and we only have his word for the fact he left Trevor on the canal bank safe and sound. He certainly has a motive, too, if he was sleeping with Bernadette.'

'At this stage he is still very much a suspect. We do have a witness who was able to confirm that he met Hanford in his shop, as planned, at 1300 hours on Tuesday 5 October. He said there was nothing about his demeanour or appearance that suggested he'd been in any physical confrontation.'

'He's a slippery bastard though,' said Lund. 'He's the type that could kill someone and not turn a hair.'

'The problem we have,' offered Maya, 'is that we have no forensic evidence from Trevor's body to link to his killer, he was too decomposed.'

'Obviously Bernadette has been treated as a witness up to now. It looks like we'll have to interview her,' said Redford.

Chambers nodded. 'I agree.' She turned to Sean and Turner. 'I'd like you two to conduct the interview as you've both dealt with her previously. I know tables have turned, meaning that the circumstances are now stacked against her, but I'm aware, from what I've heard, that she's incredibly vulnerable and we do need to consider that, particularly as she's also pregnant.'

The two men nodded.

'Can we offer anything else forensically?' asked Kym.

'I can't see anything we may have overlooked. My only thought is Hanford's bedding. Did we seize that?'

Maya shook her head. 'It wasn't part of the strategy because at the time, although she claimed she was being blackmailed, the sex was consensual. Putting Bernadette in his bed just proves what they've both told us.'

'Also,' Malone said, 'Hanford went to great pains to tell us that he uses condoms. It's unlikely, although not impossible, that the baby isn't Hanford's either.' Both he and Lund shuddered at the memory of the conversation.

'It would be a moot point anyway. Finding his semen in his bed still doesn't progress the investigation,' Maya said.

Chambers tapped her teeth with her pen. 'I think we'll get Laurel back in. She might be able to shed light on who the unidentified prints belong to. It might be an innocent visitor or workman, or it could be another of Bernadette's lovers. Either way, I want to know.

'Also, we can provide Laurel with the latest evidence about Bernadette and see how she reacts. It might jog her memory. I'm still keen to know who it was she saw running away from the Dawlishes' house that morning. Let her see a photo of Hanford so we can find out whether or not it was him.'

Maya suddenly had a thought. 'There were tester pots of paint on the desk in Trevor's study. They'd been used on the wall in there. If Trevor isn't the dad, then why would they be turning his office into a nursery. And I assume, looking at the neutral, lemon colours, that's the intention. Also,' she said, turning to Jack, 'remember there was a spot of paint on Rose's slipper. The one wedged under the stairlift.'

Jack had the grace to look embarrassed, considering how he had dismissed any discussion about the paint when they were at the scene.

Chamber's face lit up for the first time since the briefing had started. 'That's very interesting. Especially if that happened since Trevor went missing. Did we recover the tester pots?'

'Yes, but because it wasn't deemed pertinent at the time they've just been booked into property. If I'm honest, I just exhibited them on a whim, because of the paint on Rose's slipper. I'll get them out of the property system today and have them submitted to the lab for chemical treatment as a priority, hopefully get some fingerprints.'

'Excellent. Thank you, Maya.'

'Also,' said Maya, 'we can search the clothes that were seized off Hanford, to check if there's any paint on them. Even if they've been washed, there may well still be traces.'

Chambers grinned. 'We're cooking on gas, people. Adila, can I ask you to go and speak to Bernadette's sister please? She might be able to shed some light on our illusive widow's private life. We'll have a chat with her and Laurel before we put the latest evidence to Bernadette. Let's see if we can find out who the daddy is.'

69

Stacey's eyes widened with shock when she opened the door to Adila.

'What's happened? Is Bernadette okay? Please don't tell me something bad has happened to my sister?'

Adila smiled reassuringly. 'She's fine. Sorry to have scared you, but I just wondered if I could have a very quick chat. I promise I won't keep you.'

'Come on through.' Stacey led Adila through to the lounge where she perched anxiously on the edge of an armchair. She was the mirror image of her sister, and shared the same nervous, flighty mannerisms.

'Bernadette seems to have settled back at home okay. I was surprised she was ready to return so soon.'

'She said she wanted her own space,' Stacey said tersely.

Adila raised an eyebrow. 'Did you argue?'

'No,' said Stacey a little too quickly. 'She just needs her privacy apparently.'

'Maybe it's because of the pregnancy. Hormones and the nesting instinct.'

'Probably.'

'How does she seem about the baby?'

'Really happy. It's all she's ever wanted. A husband and children. She was starting to get so despondent about it because they'd been trying for a while, and nothing has happened until now.'

'Was Trevor happy too?'

'Yes,' said Stacey unconvincingly. She wiped a hand over her face. 'It's difficult for Trevor. Do you know about his little brother?'

'I do. It's tragic. Difficult to come to terms with, I can understand his reservations. But he was happy about the baby?'

'I mean, I suppose so. I always feel a bit sorry for dads, especially when it's the first baby. All the attention is on mum and how she's feeling, etc. Bernadette didn't really say much about what he thought. But then again, she's had so much on her plate.'

'Oh, she has, bless her,' said Adila with more conviction than she felt. She was still struggling to come to terms with the fact that Bernadette wasn't the weak, vulnerable woman she had portrayed herself to be. Adila prided herself on having a strong bullshit detector and was annoyed that she'd allowed herself to be fooled.

'Can I just ask you about the night Rose died? When Bernadette stayed over here. Just run me through the events of that evening again. You invited her for tea, is that right?'

Stacey frowned. 'Is there something I need to know about?'

'There's nothing for you to be concerned about. Some new information has come to light and my boss has just asked me to dot the i's and cross the t's.' She rolled her eyes for good measure. 'I just do what I'm told,' she said apologetically.

Stacy visibly relaxed. 'Bernadette intimated the invitation if I'm honest. I feel guilty for not thinking to invite her earlier myself. She rang to say how difficult things were with Rose and how tired she was and that she'd not eaten properly. She made a joke about how much she was craving my lasagne.

'That was when she told me she was pregnant. Obviously, I was thrilled for her and then subsequently worried that she wasn't eating properly so insisted she come over that night. I knew she'd want to talk about how she was going to cope with the pregnancy and baby on her own. Such a worry.' Stacey shook her head despondently.

'To be honest, after dinner things are a bit of a blur. After we'd eaten, Bernadette said she was feeling a bit unwell. Morning sickness and a headache. I was really concerned when she told me that, because I wasn't feeling great myself and I was worried there might have been something wrong with the food.

'Bernadette had brought a bottle of wine for me, and I'd had a couple of glasses. I don't mind admitting, they went straight to my head. It was a relief when Bernadette said she was going to bed, because I could hardly keep my eyes open. Must have been a bug or something.'

'And Bernadette stayed all night.'

Stacey frowned. 'Well, yes. She told you that. She was up before me. She woke me up with a strong coffee. Good job she did too, otherwise I think I could have slept until lunch.'

'Can I ask if you know how Bernadette and Trevor were doing financially?'

'Oh, I couldn't say. She's a very private person. She'd never talk outside of her marriage about something as personal as money. That said, she's never asked me for any financial help, and they both worked, so I assume they were both comfortable.'

'This is a delicate question, particularly in light of Trevor's death, but would you say they were a happy couple?'

'Yes. Again, Bernadette was quite secretive, but they seemed to be.'

'Secretive?'

'I mean, private.'

'Okay. Is there any chance she could have been seeing someone else?'

Stacey let out an incredulous laugh. 'I wouldn't have thought so for one moment. Why do you ask?'

'Oh.' Adila rolled her eyes. 'Just my boss, you know. Is there anything else at all you can think to tell me about Bernadette, Trevor or Rose?'

'Nothing. Nothing at all. They were just a normal family. It's so tragic. I'm just so glad Bernadette has the baby. I've told her I'll help out and support them both as much as I can.'

Adila smiled. 'That's kind of you. One thing I've learnt in this job is that family need to stick together more than ever at a time like this. I'm glad Bernadette has you. Here's my card. If anything else does spring to mind, however obscure or insignificant it may seem to you, please give me a ring and let me know.'

Stacey showed Adila out and waved her to her car. The cold weather prevented her remaining on the doorstep to watch her drive away. Adila reached for her phone and called Redford straight away.

'Boss? Assuming it's not already been done, it might be worth running Bernadette's registration plate through ANPR on the evening Rose died. It sounds like her sister was out for the count that night. Bernadette could well have left the address and returned home without Stacey even knowing.'

70

Laurel had always been against any mention of prison reform. She was of the opinion that prisons were like holiday camps. Her brief foray in Styal prison had changed her mind. In fact, she had begun to reconsider the moment she'd been bundled into the GEOAmey prisoner transport van. She was horrified to discover that the majority of the women around her were addicts, victims of horrific abuse or mentally ill. She was certain half of them belonged in hospital rather than prison.

The squalor was horrendous and the food inedible. The constant noise had her on edge. Shouting, screaming, crying, threats and the continuous banging of cell doors. The small shred of sanity she was clinging on to, broke the moment she saw a woman self-harming by trying to reopen a slash wound to her throat using a plastic knife.

Laurel had never been more terrified in her life, and she wished more than ever that she had not failed her own suicide attempt. She had been right to try and take her life that night, death would be better than this. The thought that she might be found guilty of killing Rose and permanently imprisoned, made her feel physically sick.

She could have wept and kissed the floor of Beech Field custody suite when she was transported back there for her interview. Admittedly, she was still locked up, but in comparison to the prison, it looked and smelt like a five-star hotel. She was a shadow of her former self since she'd last been here.

Her weight loss was evident, and she looked diminished and haunted. She had her hands wrapped around a paper cup of hot chocolate, which compared to what she'd been consuming the last few days, tasted like heaven. She had a consultation with Purcell again before the formal interview began.

Adebayo took the lead. He smiled warmly at her to put her at ease. He was all too familiar with the shell-shocked look of someone who had just experienced their first taste of prison life.

'How are your injuries?' He nodded towards her wrists. The Medacs nurse at Beech Field had surveyed and re-bandaged her when she'd arrived from Styal. Although medical care was an option there, Laurel wasn't considered a priority, so she hadn't been seen by a nurse.

'Getting better, thank you,' she said quietly.

'We just want to share some new information with you and see if you can help.'

'Help? I assumed I was being accused of something else.'

'You may recall on our previous interview that we asked you if you knew this man, Simon Hanford.' Adebayo showed Laurel a photograph.

'No, I don't recognise him. If we have ever met, I don't recall.'

'Could he be the man you saw leaving the Dawlishes' address? The man you assumed was Trevor?'

Laurel frowned. 'How tall is he?'

'About six foot two.'

'Then no. He looks too slim. Trevor, or the man I thought was Trevor had a stockier build and was about five foot eight. He did have a hood up, though, so I didn't see his face fully. All I can tell you is, he had dark hair.'

'Can you think who else it may have been? Did the Dawlishes have any other visitors, or could it have been a workman?'

'No. I'm the only person who ever called round. I told you, they were a very introverted family. And it would have been too early for a tradesman, not that they've had anyone in. Trevor was a very handy man. In all the years I've lived there I've never known there to be any home repairs he's not been able to do himself.

'He's helped me out a lot, too, when things have needed fixing. The dear, dear man.' She looked solemnly down at the table; her eyes looked red but were void of tears as if she was all cried out.

'Anyway, the missing jewellery, I thought you were working on the assumption it was a burglary. Assuming you searched my house again and didn't find it there,' she said dryly yet without her usual spirit.

'We found the items at Hanford's address. They weren't stolen, Bernadette sold them to him. It also transpires they were sleeping together.'

Laurel's head shot up and her eyes widened.

'Bernadette was having an affair? No.' She sat open-mouthed, shaking her head. 'The baby?'

The question hung in the air. Malone cleared his throat before answering. 'This is where it gets a little awkward. Trevor was infertile so it can't be his. Hanford claims he used protection. There's a possibility that Bernadette was seeing a third man.'

Laurel was gobsmacked. 'What a bitch. Bernadette though, are you absolutely sure?' she asked incredulously.

Malone nodded. 'Seemed she had us all fooled and isn't the butter-wouldn't-melt type we all thought.

'Which is why it's important that you tell us anything that might help. Are you sure there were no other visitors at the address, especially on her day off? I know you work, but you've said you work from home at times. Or did she mention anyone's name to you regularly in conversation, somebody from work perhaps?'

'I've not seen or heard of anyone else. I'm genuinely shocked. I assume you've checked with the other neighbours?'

'Yes, they've not seen or heard anyone else coming or going either and unfortunately, we have no CCTV. On the night Rose died, you've admitted to having a wander around the house.'

Laurel nodded as she began to blush, recalling how she'd masturbated on Trevor's office chair.

'Did you go into the study?'

The blush deepened and she felt a feeling of mortification creep up her spine. Did they know what she had done? *Please God, don't let there have been a webcam in there or something.* She nodded again, unable to trust herself to speak.

'Did you notice tester pots of paint on the desk or samples painted on the wall?'

The relief was palpable. 'No, it was all in order as you'd expect for Trevor. What has Bernadette said, why has she not admitted to who she was sleeping with? They could have killed Trevor and Rose.'

Adebayo smiled. 'She doesn't know that we're aware, yet. We've got detectives ready to go and speak to her. I think it's going to be a very interesting conversation.'

Laurel wasn't the only other person recalling what the study looked like the last time she had been at the Dawlishes. Maya had submitted the tester paint pots to the lab with a request that fingerprint treatment be carried out as a matter of urgency. Ewan, one of the lab assistants, had just emailed her to confirm the exhibits had arrived safely and he was going to work on them straight away.

She had decided to revisit the scene photographs she had taken at the Dawlishes' house, to see if she noticed anything amiss that might now be pertinent given the latest information. She had scrolled through the photographs twice, scrutinising each image, convinced that there must be something pertinent that could assist the investigation. She had a niggling doubt similar to what she had felt on previous cases. She had long since learnt to trust her instincts and wasn't going to stop scouring through the photographs until she found what she was looking for.

Eventually she spotted it as she clicked on images of the Dawlishes' bathroom. Bathrooms were rarely of much interest during a murder investigation, other than to screen taps and other surfaces for blood. The seventies avocado suite adorned with pink bathmat and shower curtain looked uninspiring and she was ready to click on the next image, when the clue she was looking for stood out so obviously, she was surprised she'd not noticed it on the day.

71

The CID office was a hub of activity. So many extra people were squeezed into the open-plan office that people were doubled up at desks. The air buzzed with pockets of conversation and ringing phones, the police radio, as always, a continuous chorus in the background. Looking around to see who she could grab to talk to, Maya spotted Adila and Sean stood in a corner with Jack and Redford. Adila caught her eye and indicated for her to come over. As much as she was reluctant to be anywhere near Jack, her professionalism took priority.

'Maya,' said Adila excitedly, 'we've just had a huge breakthrough. ANPR cameras have picked up Bernadette's car driving back to the Dawlishes the night Rose was killed.'

'Really? The plot is certainly thickening. How did she leave the address without the sister not knowing though?'

'I strongly suspect she slipped something, most likely the sedatives she'd been prescribed, into her sister's wine to knock her out for the night.'

'That's brilliant work, well done. You've pissed on my chips though, as I thought I'd had a breakthrough but certainly not as huge as that.'

'What have you got?' asked Redford.

'First of all, the tester paint pots are at the lab being examined for prints as we speak. Secondly, I've been looking back through the scene images. In the bathroom, there are two toothbrushes in the holder.'

Adila frowned. 'Bernadette's and Rose's?'

'No. Rose wore a full set of dentures. She soaked them in her room every night ready to put back in when she woke up. And Trevor's was seized when he was initially reported missing, wasn't it?'

Sean nodded.

'Which suggests whoever Bernadette's latest amour is, he has been staying with her overnight in the family home. I suspect that Bernadette handed his toothbrush over, which is why we never had Trevor's DNA on the vulnerable person's database.'

'Bloody good effort.' Redford grinned.

'Although, if it is the new man's toothbrush, he's not on the database either. We seem to be two steps forward, one back all the time.'

'Some CCTV would help,' grumbled Sean.

'You bloody kids and your CCTV,' quipped Redford. 'Back in my day we didn't have CCTV, or DNA come to that. We caught the bad guys through good old-fashioned coppering.'

'How soon after you started did Faulds propose fingerprints as a method of identification?' Sean smiled.

'Cheeky sod.'

Maya paused. 'That is odd, isn't it? The lack of CCTV at the canal. We know Hanford was most likely giving the staff in there a backhander to keep an eye on his business. Perhaps whoever he's been dealing with knows more about his comings and goings and might even know about his relationship with Bernadette? He may have seen her visiting Hanford at the shop or even leaving the town hall together.'

'I don't think it's a useful line of enquiry at the moment.' Jack sniffed. 'Our resources are stretched enough following concrete leads. We haven't got the time to go chasing after your whims.'

Maya bit back a retort but Redford interjected, 'Now hang on, Jack. It would make sense. It's a good suggestion and I respect Maya's judgement. Hanford's a slippery fucker and as yet, we've not managed to track down anyone who can tell us much about him. Adila, can you drop in, see what you can find out, if anything?'

Jack sighed and left, glaring at Maya before he stomped away.

'The manager in there, a bloke called Patrick Karim, is a miserable fucker, just to give you the heads-up.'

'We work with Jack,' she said, grinning, 'so I'm used to it.'

Adila was shown to the CCTV room and was grateful that she'd been prewarned by Sean, as the atmosphere in the room was frostier than the weather outside. The room itself was hot though, unpleasantly so, and she wondered if the discomfort of the heat added to the moody atmosphere. She presented her warrant card to a pale-looking youth sat closest to her.

'Boss in?' she asked succinctly.

He pointed a curled, E.T.-like finger towards the corner of the room. Adila approached the desk with her warrant card still in her hand and saw a surly-looking dark-haired man hunched over his desk, wearing a thick, navy-blue hoodie.

'Patrick Karim? I'm...' She got no further. He suddenly launched himself from the desk. Adila wasn't quick enough to deflect the blow as his fist suddenly smashed into her face. She could hear her nose crunch sickeningly, as her head snapped back, sending a spasm of pain up her neck. It was agony, and her vision blurred as she struggled to maintain her balance.

She could make out the figure of him fleeing the room, and her coppers instinct took over as she started to race after him, despite the overwhelming discomfort and stream of blood that was already pouring down her front. Another man who had clearly witnessed the assault, was ahead of her, screaming obscenities at Karim who was running towards the car park, whilst shouting into his mobile phone.

She closed in on them quickly, but the lank-haired man was over six foot, and his height gave him an added advantage as he suddenly lunged forward and rugby tackled Karim to the floor. Karim attempted to fight him off, but the man smashed his face repeatedly into the floor, temporarily stunning him.

Adila took over as she pulled at Karim's arms so she could cuff him while reading him his rights. The corridor was brimming with staff now and she could hear one of them already shouting up on the police radio asking for backup. She swiped at her bloodied face with her sleeve as she kept pressure on Karim's back to keep him pinned to the floor, until the van arrived to take him to custody.

Karim's mobile phone lay on the floor and the man who had helped her, picked it up and held the screen towards her.

'Hello? Patrick? Hello? Are you there?'

Adila recognised the voice of the panicked woman and all the clues fell into place when she saw Bernadette Dawlish's name on the caller ID.

72

After receiving Patrick's panicked phone call, Bernadette had already begun to hurriedly gather some belongings together and was loading them into the boot of her car, ready to make her escape. When Sean and Turner arrived at the address, she flew at them both like a wild cat, her demeanour completely changed as she tried to claw at their faces and fight her way into the car.

It was like meeting a stranger compared to the sorry, snivelling woman they had both encountered previously. Whereas Laurel had been a shadow of her former self, Bernadette's character grew tenfold. It was as if they'd both swapped personalities. Laurel had become anxious and timid, where Bernadette was argumentative and arrogant.

Even her voice had changed. The nervous, soft voice was louder, the northern accent accentuated making her sound streetwise and brash; the antithesis to the image she had portrayed previously. She was racially abusive towards Adebayo and when the police van came to transport her to the custody suite for interview, she banged around in the caged area of the van, screaming obscenities at the driver.

She calmed slightly as she was led to the custody officer's desk to have her rights explained. This wasn't unusual for aggressive prisoners to accept defeat once they were brought in as it was obvious that in here, there was nowhere for them to go. Particularly, if like Bernadette, this was the first time they had been arrested as the setting was alien and somewhat daunting.

The suite was painted in the typical corporate blue of the rest of the police station. Opposite the holding cell stood a tall, horseshoe-shaped desk where the prisoners were processed. Closest to the desk was a cell with floor-to-ceiling windows, where any vulnerable prisoners at risk of self-harm could be easily monitored.

The custody sergeant was perched on a tall chair as he tapped details into the computer screen. He was surrounded by posters explaining prisoners' rights and advice for those with drug or alcohol addiction, which Bernadette pointedly ignored. She stood looking surly and aggressive, almost comical in her floral skirt, ankle socks, flat shoes and long beige cardigan. Her attitude certainly didn't match her mumsy outfit.

The duty solicitor was a doughy man with a grey comb-over and sharp, rodent-like teeth. Bernadette immediately took a dislike to him. Sean and Turner anticipated that Bernadette, the new Bernadette, would give a no-comment interview, but it seemed she was only too happy to talk.

'Where's Patrick?' she asked sullenly once they were seated in the interview room.

'He's due to be questioned in another police station.' For a brief moment there was a glimpse of the old Bernadette as her eyes began to fill with tears and her lower lip trembled. 'Is he okay?' she asked softly.

'Fine. He's doing much better than Trevor,' said Sean.

She scowled petulantly and turned away.

'So, I assume the baby is Karim's?' asked Turner.

Bernadette smiled proudly. 'Yes.'

'We knew it couldn't be Trevor's because he was infertile.'

'What? What do you mean infertile? Did he know?' Bernadette exploded as she suddenly leapt to her feet, balled fists planted on the table.

Turner eyed her with a steely look before firmly telling her to sit back down. He then explained about Trevor's medical records, whilst Bernadette visibly seethed. At one point she even turned to glare at the solicitor as if it were all his fault. 'I can't believe he lied to me all those years,' she spat, the irony clearly lost on her.

'We did, of course, wonder if it was Simon Hanford's.'

She visibly baulked.

'He didn't blackmail you, did he, Bernadette? From what we hear you were a willing participant, who was treated quite generously by your lover.'

'Hardly willing, he's repulsive and incredibly egotistical. He was a convenience, that's all. It was Patrick's idea. We needed money so I could get away from Trevor and that bloody house and start again. I told you at the time, I'd do anything for the man I love.'

'And nothing says romance more than sleeping with another man for money so you can fund your new lifestyle,' said Sean.

'What would you know?'

'I know a lot, Bernadette, and I can't quite believe I was taken in by your grieving widow act. According to Laurel, Trevor really loved you.'

'Trevor had no spark. He was a nice man, a lovely man, but there was no passion. It was okay at first, but he promised me much more than he delivered. All that mattered to him was the Masons and his bloody mother. Even she was okay at first until the dementia started kicking in. I'm a victim of circumstance.' She looked petulant as she plucked at a thread on her cardigan, musing for a while before she continued to speak.

'I would probably have stayed happy and ticked along with Trevor and Rose, but then I met Patrick and I found out what it was *really* like to love someone. To want someone. It's like he unlocked something inside me that I didn't know existed. Feelings that I never knew were possible to feel.'

'Stacey said all you'd ever wanted was a husband and kids.'

Bernadette suddenly looked panicked. 'You've spoken to my sister? Behind my back?'

'Yes. She was very helpful. Told us all about the night you slept over at her house, except it sounds like she was the only one doing the sleeping. Our ANPR cameras have tracked your vehicle from just after 8.30pm and again at 2am on the bypass near your home. Stacey also stated that it was you who suggested the dinner invitation. Did you slip some of your sedatives in the wine you took for her?'

'Only two,' she said sulkily.

'So, it was premeditated. You gave yourself an alibi so you could sneak back home with your lover and kill Rose.'

'We didn't kill Rose. She fell in the night. Her death was an accident.'

Sean let out a caustic laugh which Bernadette ignored as she continued. 'We just wanted to be together. I'd been slipping Rose the sedatives I'd been prescribed so Patrick could come and go without her hearing him. I think they might have made her feel woozy and that caused her to fall down the stairs. She saw Patrick and assumed he was Trevor – she was clearly confused. That's why she fell.'

'You did a poor job of staging the fall. Our SOCO, Maya, spotted straight away that there was something amiss with the positioning of the slipper and the stairlift.'

'She's wrong. It was an accident. Can she prove otherwise?'

'Rose had clearly been neglected by you before her death.'

'I tried my best to look after her, but she was hard work. And she wasn't my responsibility, she was Trevor's mum, not mine. She was a burden. A problem that wouldn't fit in my new life with Patrick and the baby. It was a blessing in disguise for all of us that she fell.' Bernadette cradled her stomach. 'This is my priority now; *this* is my future. The baby and Patrick. *My* family.'

'I assume it was Karim who Laurel saw leaving the house the morning she thought it was Trevor?' Turner asked.

'That interfering cow. Yes, I told him to leave early before anyone saw him. But we got, well, let's just say distracted and he left a bit later than intended.'

'Laurel said that you made a show of a cabinet in the study being emptied that day.'

'Yes, we'd been through it looking for anything of value we could sell. Obviously, we were going to clear it out when the time was right for the baby anyway. It was Patrick's idea for me to take the stuff to Hanford and flog them.'

'This leads us to the million-dollar question, who killed Trevor?' Sean asked as he smoothed down a fresh page in his policy book, pen poised. 'Was it you, Patrick or both of you.'

Bernadette looked nervous. 'I don't know all the details. I told Patrick I couldn't bear to hear it. And he agreed, said I'd be better off not knowing. All he said was that he met Trevor on the canal bank and he started attacking him out of the blue. Patrick was covered in bruises afterwards. He tried to get Trevor off him and, in the process, accidentally strangled him. It wasn't his fault. It was all Trevor's doing.'

Sean turned to the solicitor. 'Do you deal with a lot of accidental strangulations?'

'I think this is my first,' he mumbled. He had been looking

decidedly uncomfortable throughout the interview, physically leaning away from Bernadette who clearly intimidated him.

'It's true. He didn't mean to kill him. Just to get him off. He was devastated when he realised what he'd done. He really didn't mean to. He was crying when he told me.'

'Sounds like he's as good at faking crocodile tears as you are,' Sean said cynically.

'As well as the paint, Maya also observed another discrepancy at your house. The extra toothbrush, Karim's toothbrush. It didn't occur to her at first, it was only when she'd reviewed the scene photographs. She pointed out that Rose soaked her dentures overnight, so there should only have been one toothbrush in the bathroom. Yours – because you'd handed Trevor's to the police officer who took the initial missing from home report, didn't you?'

Bernadette shifted awkwardly in her seat.

'Except,' continued Sean. 'We now know that it wasn't Trevor's, was it? I assume you'd already binned that. It was Patrick's. Your lover had already moved in the night he killed your husband, hadn't he? You really didn't leave any time for the grass to grow, did you?'

Bernadette refused to look at him, turning instead to concentrate on something on the wall.

Turner looked at Sean. 'Any more questions?' Sean shook his head. 'Fine, in light of what you've told us, Bernadette, we'll be officially charging you soon. Obviously, Patrick is being interviewed at the moment too, so we may have a few more questions once we have details of his account.'

Bernadette inched forward in her seat. 'But at least I can go home now?' she said hopefully.

'Go home?' said Sean. 'You're going nowhere, it's highly likely you'll be remanded in custody.'

'Patrick too?'

'Yes. You do realise the severity of the situation, don't you? Two people have been murdered. Your husband and mother-in-law. And you really think we're going to just let you both go back home?'

'But I'm pregnant. I thought if I told you the truth about Trevor, we'd be allowed to go home. That we'd just have to come back when it was time to go to court. Patrick said everything was going to be okay, that I'd be okay because of the baby. None of this is my fault.'

The realisation of the seriousness of the situation suddenly dawned on her as brash Bernadette faded away to be replaced by naïve, timid Bernadette. 'I... what I just said... none of it is true. Patrick and me, we haven't done anything. I don't know anything.' She turned to her solicitor, wide-eyed and pleading. 'Tell them they have to let me go home now. Please?'

Sean eyed her levelly, his voice low. 'Laurel Miller was right about you. You really are thick.'

Turner terminated the interview and Bernadette was led back to the custody desk so they could get her keys and take her to her cell. What they didn't realise was that Laurel had just been back to the Medacs room to be given more painkillers for her wrists. She was being accompanied back to her cell when she spotted Bernadette. Before anyone could intervene, she drew back her hand and slapped her hard across the face. The sound resonated across the custody suite so sharply it caused people to wince.

A scuffle ensued as people rushed forward to separate the two women quickly before it could escalate. 'That was for Trevor, you ugly, boring, dim-witted slag,' snarled Laurel.

'Did you see that? Did you see it?' Bernadette asked Sean incredulously, as she held her hand protectively to her face. 'She hit me. She actually hit me, and I'm pregnant. She'll get done for that, won't she?'

'Common assault is a minor charge. She has no previous police record and hugely mitigating circumstances, so probably not, no.'

He winked at Laurel as he guided Bernadette back towards her cell.

73

Redford had called into the SOCO office to update Maya and the others about Bernadette and Karim's arrest. He gave them a quick precis of Bernadette's interview so far. He told them about Karim's involvement in Trevor's death, but how she was still maintaining that Rose's death was accidental. He also asked that, prior to Karim's interview, arrangements could be made for his and Adila's injuries to be photographically recorded.

Maya had made her way to the custody suite where Karim was being held. She checked in with the custody sergeant and Karim was brought out of his cell. He oozed aggression and surliness and barely looked Maya in the eye.

'I can see you have facial injuries; do you have any others I need to be aware of?' Maya asked as she primed her camera.

'I've got a cut on my forearm,' he muttered. He began to slip off his navy-blue zip up hoodie and Maya winced. The garment smelt of body odour and was clearly long overdue a wash.

'Here, let me help.' Reluctantly she reached out to take the hoodie from him so she could rest it on the seat next to her when something caught her eye. She could barely express her excitement as she surreptitiously eyed the clothing again before her attention turned to his trainers.

Both items contained spots of buttercup yellow paint.

Adila had taken painkillers for her injuries, but it was Maya's latest discovery that really helped detract from her own discomfort as she geared up to interview Karim. He sat next to his solicitor in the interview room wearing a grey top and jumper and oversized black plimsolls that had been given to him by the custody sergeant.

'What's going on? Why have you taken my clothes and trainers?' He griped.

'We'll get to that later,' said Adila as she battled to suppress a grin.

Karim glared at her and Lund. 'Where's my woman?'

'I assume you mean Bernadette unless, like her, you have others on the go?'

'What do you mean by that?'

'We know she was sleeping with Simon Hanford.'

Karim grunted indifferently. 'It was a financial transaction, that's all. Bernadette was willing to do it for our sake, so we could get some money together for our fresh start. Where is she?'

'She's been interviewed at Beech Field police station. She's provided us with quite a lot of information. We just need to hear your side of things and then you can fill in the blanks.'

'What has she said?' Karim looked panicked. 'My Bernie isn't the brightest, she can misunderstand situations, it takes her a while to cotton on. You lot better have not been putting words in her mouth.'

Adila leaned forward and arched an eyebrow. 'You look worried, Patrick?'

'No, I'm not, it's just that Bernie doesn't always think before she speaks.'

Lund suppressed her grin. 'She's been quite chatty.'

He visibly winced as he wiped a hand across his swollen face as he realised Bernadette had inadvertently thrown him under the bus. He should have made it clearer to her that if this happened, if their plan was uncovered, that they just needed to keep their mouths shut. He should have worked out a cover story before now. His phone call to let her know the police were onto them had been too little too late. His arrogance had been his downfall.

He was also cursing himself for panicking. He had known the moment Adila approached him waving her warrant card that they'd been caught out. If only he hadn't reacted the way he had and tried to get away. He should have just answered her questions and denied everything. He could have ridden it out and then they could have made plans to get away sharpish.

'Tell me about how you pushed Rose Dawlish.'

'I didn't. I was nowhere near her. She fell in the night. We think she caught her foot in the chairlift and fell.'

'And you just left her there? Didn't get help, didn't try to resuscitate her?'

He shrugged. 'We panicked. It was obvious when we found her, she was dead. And yes, we should have phoned someone, but we realised how it would look, me being in the house with Bernie. But it was an accident, a horrible mistake, it was not murder.'

'That's for the court to decide,' Adila said. 'You met Maya earlier. She was the SOCO who photographed your injuries.'

'What about her?'

'She is also the SOCO who attended the Dawlishes' when Rose was found dead at the bottom of the stairs.'

Karim huffed impatiently. 'So what?'

'To Maya, it was immediately obvious that Rose's death had been staged. The way the slipper had been wedged under the chairlift wasn't an accident. What you claim, never happened, did it?'

Silence.

'Maya noticed smudges of paint on Rose's slipper. That paint matched sample pots that had been used in Trevor's study.'

Karim's telltale sign of annoyance was obvious as a muscle pulsed in his jaw.

'And Maya also recognised the same colour paint on the cuffs of your hoodie. You really need to wash your clothes more frequently. *That* is the reason your clothing and footwear have been seized.'

Karim's solicitor turned to him. 'I suggest a moment's consultation.'

Karim shook his head. 'It's okay. Right, fine. We didn't find her at the bottom of the stairs. I was helping her to the toilet and she fell. It was an accident. I knew no one would believe that, so I moved the slipper to highlight the fact it was a mishap.'

Lund raised an eyebrow as Adila scribbled some notes. 'A mishap, really. Is that the best you can do? Moving on then, Bernadette has also told us that you, in her words, "accidentally strangled" Trevor.'

Karim groaned and he turned to his solicitor who shook his head. 'I've advised you all along to make no comment to any of these allegations. Whether you choose to follow my advice or not is completely up to you.'

'Come on, Patrick,' Lund goaded. 'Make it easy on yourself. You'll get a considerably reduced sentence if you plead guilty. We have a witness statement from Simon Hanford. It'll help in the long run if you tell us the truth. I know you love Bernadette, but she's not the brightest, is she?

'Do you really want to take the chance of having her stood in court being cross-examined by a barrister? That's a big gamble. She's already sold you out, mate, and that was after a relatively brief interview with my colleagues. A barrister would have a field day with her, and you know it.'

Karim's solicitor was about to speak, but he was silenced with a raised hand. 'Okay. I'll admit it. I pushed Rose. But it wasn't intentional. It was spur of the moment. I've been under a lot of pressure. I wasn't in my right mind. Diminished responsibilities.' He turned to his solicitor who gave an imperceptible nod.

Adila and Lund exchanged a look as they acknowledged he was going to tell the truth but was already planning his mitigation.

'Tell me about Trevor, what happened there?'

'I saw him and Hanford on the CCTV cameras and followed them. I thought I'd erased the footage of the two of them together, but I can only assume in my haste, that I didn't. I watched Hanford head towards his shop, but Trevor stayed by the canal. I held back for a bit and watched him. He was clearly upset about something and I guessed Hanford had told him about Bernadette. Trevor rang Bernie and I waited until he finished the call and then I went to talk to him.

'He was agitated and started to confide in me about the baby and how it wasn't his because he couldn't have kids. He was rambling on about whether or not he could forgive Bernie and move on. Said he'd be willing to bring up another man's baby if it meant they could stay together. I wasn't expecting that response, never in a million years.'

'How did that make you feel?' Lund asked.

'I was fucking fuming. The thought of him with my woman

and baby? No chance. It was bad enough Bernie sleeping with Hanford to get money for us. I snapped. Told Trevor that the baby was mine and to do the decent thing and walk away.'

He wiped a hand across his face. 'I honestly didn't think he'd react the way he did. He came for me and we got into a scuffle. I'd never had him down as a fighting man, but he wouldn't back off. He was even getting the better of me at one point and I wasn't having that. I grabbed Trevor in a headlock, self-defence like, and the next thing I knew he dropped to the floor and I realised I'd gone too far. I wasn't aware I was squeezing him around the neck, I was trying to stop him from struggling and getting at me.

'And it was an accident. I panicked and pushed him into the canal. I spotted his phone on the ground and took it back to the town hall with me. I left it in his room on the desk. His wallet was there too, so I pocketed that. How was I supposed to know he had a bloody bank card on him?'

'About his wallet, where is it now? We know it was in the address up until the night Rose was killed,' Adila asked.

'I saw it on the way out. I knew it had a bit of cash in it, so I took it. It's not like Trevor was going to need it anymore.'

'A thief as well as a killer. You're building quite the criminal CV. Then what happened, after you left the canal bank?' Lund asked.

'I went back to work as normal and then afterwards, when the old woman was out for the count, I called round to see Bernie and told her what I'd done. Obviously, she was shocked at first and a bit upset, but I explained it was an accident and that at least it meant we could be together. That nosy bloody neighbour of hers, that Laurel was away for the night, so I stayed and that's when we started to make a plan about reporting Trevor missing.'

'Did you honestly think you'd get away with it?' Lund asked.

He shrugged arrogantly. 'Well, yeah. We thought after a while the police would give up on a missing person of his age and when we had enough money, we'd move away and start somewhere new together.'

'Which was why you got rid of Rose, she was an inconvenience?'

He shook his head vehemently. 'I *told* you, that was unintentional, spur of the moment.'

'So what was the plan?'

'Like I said. Go along with the ruse that Trevor was missing. I didn't expect his body to bob back up. I thought it would stay at the bottom of the canal.'

'Really? Well, that was naïve of you. You should have done your research. Unfortunately for you dead bodies don't lie neatly and conveniently at the bottom of the canal, they have a habit of floating back up,' Adila said.

He ignored her and carried on. 'I noticed all the police activity on the CCTV and listened in to the police radio. I rang Bernadette and told her to ring up and say Trevor was back home, to carry the ruse on.'

'I've listened to the 999 call. It's very convincing. I assume it was your idea for Bernadette to claim she'd been assaulted?'

'Yes. It would all have been okay if he hadn't had that bloody bank card on him.'

'Don't be so sure. None of it was plausible, Laurel Miller for one never believed the claim that Trevor assaulted Bernadette. It wasn't in his nature; he would have never hurt her in a million years.'

'That bitch, Laurel. She should be grateful I'm in here. All the shit she's put my girl through over the years, I'd have gone for her next given half a chance.'

'Next? I thought you stated that the deaths were accidental?'

Karim paled as his solicitor looked at him, tutted and shook his head. 'Laurel inadvertently helped with your plan, though, didn't she? The morning she saw you leave the house and assumed you were Trevor. It was you Bernadette was mooning after that morning, wasn't it?'

'I'm not answering anything else. That's all I have to tell you. Can I go now?'

'No!' Adila said indignantly. 'What is it with you and Bernadette both assuming you've committed little more than a shoplifting offence? You're looking at *two* murder charges. Neither of you will be going home for a very long time, are you both really so stupid?'

The solicitor opened his mouth to object, but Adila continued as she eyed Karim with bemusement. 'And you do realise that your baby will be born in prison and most likely go into care. I only hope it goes to a decent family, to kind, loving parents who aren't twisted liars.

'I hope it never finds out who its biological parents are and goes to a family as loving and kind as Trevor and Rose Dawlish were.'

74

To say Maya and the rest of the team were feeling jubilant was an understatement. Although they had eventually got to the bottom of what happened, there was now a mountain of work for CID to do to prepare for court. It was the evening Maya had planned to stay at Dominique's for their early Christmas celebration, but she needed to write a statement detailing her involvement in Trevor's body recovery and her examination following Rose's death. Knowing it would mean finishing late, she stepped into the back office to call Dominique, who answered on her first ring.

'Are you on your way? I've already started on the Baileys?' she said excitedly.

Maya laughed. 'You big kid. Look, I'm really sorry, Mama, but I need to tie up some loose ends for a job I've been involved with. Because I'm not going to be in the next few days, I really need to do it tonight. It means I'm going to be late. Do you mind?'

'Of course not. I completely understand.'

'Listen, don't wait up because I don't know how long I'm

going to be. Make sure you lock up properly though,' she added as an afterthought.

The hours flew by. Chris was also working late as he'd picked up an assault and was finishing his paperwork. They worked in a companionable silence and were both surprised how late it had suddenly got when Nicola arrived for the night shift.

Maya eagerly filled her in on the developments of the case.

'You were right,' Chris said to Maya. 'You said that murder was motivated by either love or money.'

Maya smiled. 'It's Laurel I feel sorry for. It sounds like she really loved him. Just think, if she'd made a move earlier, they may well have got together and Trevor and Rose wouldn't have been murdered. They could have been genuinely happy together.'

'You're right,' said Chris. 'I assume if Trevor did like Laurel, which he may have done because they were good friends and he did a lot for her, he never made a move pre-Bernadette because he was too shy.'

Nicola sighed. 'I can't believe she never told him how she felt. I mean, I know it would be embarrassing if you told someone you cared for how much you liked them and it wasn't reciprocated. But life's about taking chances, isn't it? Imagine never telling your potential soulmate how much you care and never getting a shot at real love. Everybody deserves to be happy.'

The words resonated for Maya. She found her thoughts drifting to Spence. As Chris and Nicola continued to chat, her mind wandered. As much as she tried to deny it, she still liked him. A lot. Whether it was the exhilaration of the case finally being solved, the impending festive season, or Nicola's words, she didn't know, but the next thing she knew she had composed a text telling him how much she missed him and wanted to have an honest and open discussion about whether there was a future for them. She sent it before she had a chance to change her mind.

'What are you grinning at?' asked Chris.

'Nothing. Come on, let's go. We can leave Nicola in peace.'

They walked out the building together and Maya waved to Chris as she climbed on top of the Bonneville. She was on tenterhooks waiting for Spence to reply, but she also knew he would be working so he might not pick the message up until much later. She pulled her visor down against the lashing rain as she drove out of the car park.

Her thoughts were consumed with Spence as nerves suddenly hit her. She turned onto the dual carriageway. She had acted spontaneously and was now beginning to regret it. She accelerated. She'd never be able to face him again if he rejected her. She was so distracted that the bend took her by surprise.

She was going too fast and she'd not leaned into the curve. The dual carriageway was a treacherous stretch of slush and ice. She knew what was going to happen seconds before it did as she lost control of the bike and was thrown from it. She screamed as she was flung across the carriageway. Sprawled across the asphalt, she looked up and was horrified to see headlights hurtling towards her.

75

Marcus heard Anthony arrive home. He carried the freezing air in with him as he entered the lounge and shook off his coat. Marcus looked up from his newspaper, his face illuminated by the little Christmas tree. 'Did you get petrol?' he asked.

In reply, Anthony placed the green fuel container on the table. They could hear the liquid sloshing about inside. Then he pulled a sturdy silver Zippo lighter from his pocket. He grinned as he flipped the hinged lid and sparked up. Marcus nodded his approval as Anthony peeled off his gloves and sat down at the table. He looked worried and Marcus commented as much.

'I've been thinking, I'm not happy about this.'

'Why, we've talked about it enough.'

'It's just too risky for you.'

'Piece of piss. We've planned it to the nth degree. Nothing can go wrong. Not for us anyway.' Anthony's doubt started to irritate him. 'Look, mate, this is all we've talked about since I got out of prison. It's long overdue.

'Maya and Dominique are the reason I got sent to prison. They are going to pay for that. Think of all the years we've spent apart because of them. Mum died without me having a chance to say goodbye to her. I haven't spent all these months pretending to be a Holy fucking Joe to lull them into a false sense of security and convince the probation I've changed for nothing. Not doing this isn't an option just because you're losing your nerve. It's going to happen and it's going to happen tonight.'

An angry looked flashed across Anthony's face. 'I'm not losing my nerve, far from it,' he said indignantly. 'I've got the fucking stuff, haven't I?'

'Then what's wrong?'

Anthony sat up straight and rubbed his chin. 'Just shut up and listen a minute. I've got an idea, a slight change of plan.'

76

Maya and the Bonneville were stretched across the road as the headlights continued to descend towards her. She was in pain, but she knew she had to move. Rain lashed at her as she scrambled across icy water to safety. Mercifully, she heard the sound of brakes and saw hazard lights come on as the car, and others behind it, slowed to a stop.

'Are you okay, try not to move,' a woman called as she dashed from her car. She rushed to Maya's side and spoke reassuringly. Maya was about to answer her when she heard a familiar voice.

'Maya? Are you okay? I saw you head off like a bat out of hell. What happened?' Chris rushed to her side as the woman stepped away and called the emergency services.

'It's my own stupid fault, I wasn't concentrating. I was too busy thinking about something. I didn't realise I'd picked up speed and was too late to judge the bend.' She had never been more grateful to see him.

'Are you hurt?'

'Yes, all down my right side, and I think I've broken my arm.' She was in agony and shivering in shock as much as pain.

'It's all right, love, I'm here. Just try and stay still.' He turned to the woman who confirmed ambulance and traffic police were on the way.

'How's the bike?' Maya asked.

'Sod the bloody bike, let's just concentrate on you,' Chris said.

The woman returned with an old picnic blanket and a golf umbrella, which she passed to Chris so he could keep Maya dry.

'They said they'd be here as quick as they can. Are you bleeding at all?' asked the woman.

'Not as far as I know.'

A small crowd began to gather around them as concerned motorists, and downright nosy ones, came to check on Maya. Chris, as always, took control, asking people to return to their vehicles unless they could do anything to help. More blankets were handed over to Maya and for Chris who was lain on the ground next to her so he could talk to her and keep her calm. Maya concentrated on taking measured breaths, so she could breathe through the pain and ward off the ensuing panic.

'What were you thinking about to let yourself get so distracted? You seemed fine when we left.'

'It was something Nicola said that made me text Spence. I really like him and I want to know if there's any chance of us having a future together.'

'Not if you keep flinging yourself off motorbikes, there's not. But I'm glad to hear it. You two should have got it together months ago.'

'What if he says no?'

'Then he's a bloody fool. Forget about it for now, just concentrate on staying still. We'll get you patched up in no time.'

She grinned at him weakly as she gritted her teeth against the pain, willing to hear the sound of sirens.

77

He was dressed all in black, wearing clothes that had been purposefully padded out. That way if he was captured by any CCTV cameras, they would see the build of a much bulkier man. That was the thing about prison. Rather than it being the opportunity for rehabilitation, it was an education, to learn from others and know how to get away with future crimes, and Marcus had certainly picked up enough tricks over the years.

He had a plain black rucksack slung on his back. Something else he had been told – avoid any logos which could be picked up on CCTV. Not that he was planning on keeping the bag. Once he'd done what he needed to tonight, he was going to dispose of it straight away. The brothers had gone through the plan so many times it was foolproof. He was confident he was going to get away with murder. They would finally get revenge for all the time Marcus had spent in prison.

All the signs were there that tonight was going to be a success. He didn't need the pocket torch; the moon was so bright it illuminated his way as he silently slipped round the back of Dominique's house. He removed the mole grips from the rucksack and used them to snap the kitchen door lock. He jumped as the clicking sound seemed to ring out like a gunshot. His breath caught in his throat, his heart pounding as he froze, waiting for any sign of movement from within the house or neighbouring properties. Nothing.

His racing heart gradually slowed as he began to calm himself. He recalled what he had been told, the noise would sound no louder or intrusive than a key being turned in the lock. Understandably his senses were heightened, which is why he had become so easily alarmed. Everything would go to plan as long as he took his time and kept his head.

He eased the back door open and let himself in. At this stage he paused. He needed to know they were definitely in bed asleep and hadn't heard him so far. The seconds felt like minutes as he stood poised in the kitchen. He was so still, he realised he was even holding his breath. Nothing, no sign of movement. He was good to go.

A light was glowing from the hall. How considerate of them to leave it on and show him the way. He eased the mole grips back into the rucksack, slowly and carefully. He couldn't afford to risk rushing and accidentally drop something. He couldn't afford to wake them up. He wanted them to die in their beds. To burn in damnation before they even reached the gates of hell. Mother and daughter taken together. It was almost biblical.

He eased the petrol canister out of the bag and unscrewed the top. He began to pour it on the kitchen worktops, flinching as the splashing sound seemed to roar like a crashing wave. He felt better as he moved across the hall. The carpet silently soaked up the accelerant. He stood still for a moment, listening out for any movement, but all was quiet. Silent night, indeed, he thought to himself.

He moved into the lounge and left a trail across the carpet and included the sofa and bottom of the curtains. He even splashed some up the Christmas tree, confident that would go up like a dream with all the tinsel and other embellishments. He shook the container to see how much was left and was pleased to see he had been suitably sparing and had slightly less than half left. He would need to coat the stairs and landing with the rest. That way, if Maya or Dominique did wake up, there would be no way out.

The fire would take hold so quickly, they wouldn't stand a chance. He smiled to himself as he took one careful step after another. He was careful to plant his feet on the edges of the stairway to hopefully minimise any creaking floorboards. He concentrated on distributing the petrol on the centre of each step.

Splash,

splash,

splash.

78

Dominique's full bladder woke her. Once Maya had phoned her to say she would be finishing work late, she'd polished off a bottle of mulled wine herself and several more glasses of Baileys. Now she had a dry mouth, thick head and an urge to urinate that she was trying to ignore because she was comfy in bed. She didn't relish the prospect of a cold toilet seat. She glanced at her alarm clock and saw that it was half-past midnight. She'd not even been asleep that long. She rubbed her eyes and stretched, suddenly alert to a familiar creaking sound.

She strained to listen, wondering if she'd imagined it. She habitually slept with her bedroom door slightly ajar, so if there was a noise, she would hear it. After a heartbeat, she heard it again. It was unmistakable. It sounded like the stairs creaking. She smiled to herself. Typical of Maya to be so thoughtful. It sounded like she was sneaking up the stairs so she wouldn't wake her up.

She swung her legs out of bed and was about to call out to Maya when something caused her to freeze. She could smell something. Something that, despite being familiar, made her blood run cold. It certainly shouldn't be here in the house. It was unmistakably petrol. She willed herself to stay calm despite the fist of fear that suddenly gripped her chest.

She sat still on the bed as she continued to listen. The creaking continued and she could hear a splashing sound. All her senses were heightened as she concentrated on keeping her breathing quiet and calm. It sounded and smelt like someone was pouring petrol on her stairs. She knew she needed help, but cursed herself when she realised she'd left her mobile downstairs.

She needed to get out and she needed to get out now before whoever was splashing petrol around her house decided to ignite it. She thought of Maya. What if she was home? She would need to get out too. She thought about crying out, to warn her but if she was asleep, she might not hear her straight away. But the intruder would. Marcus would. And she knew he wouldn't think twice about sparking a lighter. How had she been so naïve to think he wouldn't come after them? Maya had been right, that bloody letter, all that shit about him being born again was a ruse to make her think he wasn't a risk to them.

Instinct took over as she leapt from the bed. She wrenched the door open screaming at the top of her lungs as she came face to face with the intruder who was three stairs away from the top. Dressed in black with a balaclava covering his face, she could only make out a pair of familiar eyes. She was more consumed with the sight of the petrol can.

Time seemed to stand still as he threw the canister at her. The remains of petrol splashed onto her feet and pyjama bottoms. He reached in his pocket and produced a silver Zippo lighter. He flicked back the hinged lid and that was all Dominique needed to see to force her from her shocked reverie. She sprang into action.

Screaming again, she leapt across the landing and picked up the cumbersome hoover. It took a herculean effort to lift it as high as she could, but adrenaline had kicked in. She grunted as she hurled it at her assailant. He had no chance. Because he was lower than her, balanced precariously on the edge of the step, the weight of the hoover struck him across his chest, causing him to barrel backwards down the stairs, the lit Zippo still in his hand as he fell.

She heard the flames make a whumping sound as they began to lick greedily at the petrol. Dominique screamed as they swept up the stairs; the smoke alarms also began to shriek. Her mind was consumed with thoughts of Maya as she ran into her old room, which was furthest away from the stairs.

Relief flooded her as she took in the sight of the empty bed. Thank God she wasn't home yet. Her relief was short-lived. The fire was already gaining a threatening pace and would undoubtedly soon reach the landing, and she knew she'd lost any chance to use the stairs. Not only were they well alight but *he* was down there. She could hear him scream and move around downstairs. Even if she could survive the fire, he would no doubt be armed with a knife or God knows what else, waiting for her to flee the house.

Terror gripped her as she slammed the bedroom door shut. She pulled the duvet and pillows from the bed, stuffing them around the bottom of the door to prevent any smoke billowing in. She knew it would soon be futile as the flames continued to take hold, the more at risk she was of being engulfed in the inferno. She had no phone and at half-past midnight on a Monday night, how likely was it that her neighbours would realise what was going on and call for help? They'd most likely be asleep.

She reached for the handle of the bedroom window. It

wouldn't open. She tried it again and again. It was locked. She began to panic as she frantically searched the window ledge for the key. She couldn't remember where she had put it. She'd probably not opened the window to air the room since early October during the sudden warm spell.

She banged uselessly at the glass, screaming for help as she choked back tears. All she could hear from outside the room was the incessant beeping of the smoke alarm in competition with the crackling and popping sound as the fire began to grow, devouring everything in its wake. Despite her efforts with the duvet, she could already see and smell thick black smoke creeping through the door and her eyes were streaming.

Frantically, she looked around the room. Her eyes landed on the old, boxy-looking CD player that lived on the bedside table. She picked it up and used it to smash against the window. Nothing happened at first, the glass barely fractured whereas the CD player took the brunt of the damage.

She continued to hammer it against the glass but blow by blow it fell apart whilst the window remained relatively unscathed. Smoke silently crept into the room. Sooty, sinister fingers crept around the door frame ready to choke the breath from her body. Dominique began to cough as she instinctively remembered to drop to the floor where there was more air.

She scrambled to the wardrobe and pulled it open. She pushed bags and boxes aside, looking for something she could use to break the window. The noise outside the bedroom door was terrifying now and she knew that every second meant she was growing closer to potentially burning to death.

Her fingers closed on the straps of an old motorbike helmet. It was one Dominique's dad had bought for Maya not long before he died. She gasped grateful thanks as she carried it over to the window and began to use it to pound against the double-glazed unit as she coughed and spluttered.

Smoke continued to fill the room. Grim Reaper-black, it stained the pure white walls with its filthy tongue. It had become a being. A pummelling fist desperate to force its way down her throat and fill her lungs. It was getting hard to breathe. Sobbing, she continued to pound away at the window with the helmet.

'Thank God!' she gasped as first the interior then exterior panel of glass gave way. The winter air rushed in as sweet as nectar. She gulped in greedy breaths as she swept as much glass as she could from the window ledge before scrambling onto it. She began to scream and shout for help as she clung to the window frame, too scared to even notice the shards of glass that dug into her hands and feet.

She shouted again and again, but the silence echoed back at her. The cul-de-sac below remained still. She could feel her legs begin to tremble as she heard the roar of the fire taking hold. She screamed again and again. Terror gripped her and she was unable to hold her bulging bladder as it succumbed to the fear.

She could hear a window pop, a sign of how ferocious the heat was downstairs. The house was being slowly but surely devoured. She looked down at the garden below. If she could jump and throw herself in the direction of the rhododendron bush, maybe that would break her fall and allow her to scramble away from the burning house.

Her vision swam as she looked down again at the path below. Stood here, clutching precariously onto the window frame, it seemed so far. But the smoke was beginning to bellow out from behind her as well as underneath, leaving her with no other choice. Then, blessedly, she noticed lights coming on in houses across the cul-de-sac. Her neighbours had heard her!

She continued to cry out regardless, when suddenly a large explosion from somewhere in the house silenced her mid-scream. The smoke bellowed forward violently, like a murky tidal wave and she was horrified to see flames beginning to lick around the bedroom door.

She had no choice.

She gritted her teeth and braced herself.

Then she jumped.

79

Maya lay on the hospital bed in silence as the doctor studied her X-rays.

'Consider yourself very lucky, young lady,' he said as he eventually took a step back from the bed. He then realised how crass his words sounded under the circumstances and coughed nervously.

'What I should say is, other than your arm, nothing else is broken. You've a fair few scratches and bruises. No doubt you'll be sore for a few days, but I can arrange for you to collect some painkillers before you leave.'

'That's good news then, isn't it?' Chris said more cheerily than he felt. He had been clutching onto Maya's good hand since he arrived and was showing no signs of letting go anytime soon. 'Thanks for your time, doctor,' he added as he nodded his goodbye.

Maya remained silent in the bed; her gaze fixed on a stain in the corner of the cubicle.

'Can I get you anything, love?' Chris asked for what felt like the hundredth time since he had arrived.

Maya shook her head mutely.

'Tea, hot chocolate?' he persisted. 'Even that chicken soup from the machine is okay. Well, it's not great, but you know it's warm and it tastes and smells a bit like poultry...' He tailed off, aware he was rambling but desperate to say or do something to help his friend.

As they had waited for the ambulance, he had tried to phone Dominique, but had got no answer. He had offered to go to her house and let her know what had happened and drive her to the hospital, but Maya had said she was probably already in bed and not to disturb her.

Chris wished more than anything that he had insisted. That he had called at Dominique's. That he had woken her up and brought her to the hospital with him. Then at least she would have been safe.

He had waited in the hospital cubicle while Maya had been taken for an X-ray of her arm. When her phone started to ring, he had answered it, seeing Nicola's name flash up on the display. He had listened, wide-eyed and with growing horror as Nicola explained about the fire as she'd heard the job come through on her night shift and realised it was at Dominique's address.

He could barely comprehend what he was hearing as she rambled on about a severe head injury and smoke inhalation. He had broken the news to Maya as gently as he could, once she'd returned from her X-ray. She had listened with a similar expression on her face to how he must have looked when Nicola said the words.

She had barely spoken since. Now, she lay in the hospital bed looking fragile and broken. It hurt his heart to see her so lost. He gently squeezed her hand. He reached across and brushed a curl from her face as he muttered to her gently. 'Anything you need, kid, just let me know, eh?'

Her large brown eyes brimmed with tears as she turned to look at him.

'I want to see Mama.'

He nodded and stood up. 'I'll see what I can do.' He leant down and gently kissed her on the forehead, before heading towards the nurses' station.

Her gaze followed him as tears streamed down her face.

80

Chris had borrowed a wheelchair off one of the nurses so he could transport Maya round the hospital. It was too far to walk, and she was too bruised and battered, as well as emotionally exhausted. It seemed strange to arrive at the 'customer' side of Rose Cottage. Despite the endless visits he had made to the mortuary over the years, he had been fortunate never to have to attend the viewing gallery. He hoped to God he would never have to again.

He pressed the buzzer and was relieved to see Morticia's friendly, familiar face. He gave her a weak smile as she greeted them warmly. Ever the professional when it came to dealing with the grieving side of death.

'Please come in, both of you,' Morticia said as she held the door open and beckoned them both in. 'How are you feeling, Maya?'

Maya looked at her blankly as she gave a small shrug. 'Sore. Numb. I just want to see my mother.'

'I understand. Come through, everything is ready, so I won't keep you.' Morticia gestured towards the viewing-room door as she slipped back through the mortuary entrance. They were immediately joined by a tall, wiry-looking man with greying wavy hair.

'Maya, Chris?'

They both nodded. 'James Harper, MIT Syndicate 2. I spoke to you before,' he said to Chris, who nodded as they shook hands. Harper gave Maya a well-worn sympathetic smile. 'I know how tough this is, but I'm sure you appreciate that we need you to identify the body, although under the circumstances, I know it will prove difficult.'

Chris helped Maya climb out of the wheelchair and he linked her arm as she hobbled over to the viewing window. Morticia's voice sounded muffled over the two-way speaker.

'Are you ready?' she asked as her hand hovered on the sheet.

Maya nodded at first, before swallowing drily and confirming in a voice thick with emotion, 'Yes.'

Morticia slowly pulled the sheet away. Maya's eyes were glued to the face in front of her. She couldn't speak. She just stared.

After several agonising moments, Morticia replaced the sheet over the body as she smiled apologetically. 'It doesn't matter how many bodies we see in the mortuary. When we're in the viewing gallery and it's a parent, it's difficult.'

Chris held Maya while she cried hysterical tears and repeated again and again, 'I want my mother.'

81

Maya had finally fallen asleep. Chris had persuaded the nurses to let him stay with her, and under the circumstances, they had agreed. He sat in a hospital chair, with his head back, resting his eyes. He must have started to drop off himself, until a sudden noise caused him to sit up, alert and primed. Sleepy eyes peered at him from the hospital bed. They flickered shut again, before opening again and staring silently at him dazed and confused.

'It's okay,' he murmured. 'You're safe. Everything's okay.' His heart hammered with relief as he leant forward and gently placed a hand on Maya's shoulder. He shook it gently at first, then a little firmer to raise her consciousness.

'Maya. Maya, love, wake up. Dominique has opened her eyes.'

Maya sat up and smiled at Dominique. 'That was a big nap, how are you feeling now?'

'Sore,' said Dominique hoarsely. 'How are you?'

Maya let out a dry laugh. 'Same.'

Chris got up to pour Dominique some water and held the

glass while she took a sip. 'It's my pelvis that's shattered, not my hands,' she said, amused despite the pain.

'Whist, woman. Let me help you. I'm getting quite used to all this nursing. You're giving me enough practice between the two of you. There might be a career change in the offing for me, what do you think, Maya?'

'No offence, mate, but I think your bedside manner is more suited to the dead than the living, stay as you are, eh?'

'When I saw you before, I sensed you wanted to tell me something, until the analgesic knocked me out. You were clearly upset. What's happened?'

'I've been worried sick about you. I've broken my arm; our family home has been destroyed by fire. Of course I'm upset.'

'I can tell when something's wrong.'

'It'll keep until you're feeling a bit stronger and not as drugged up.'

'Maya?'

Chris caught Maya's eye and nodded. 'Tell her, she needs to know and she's going to find out soon enough anyway.'

'Tell me what?'

Maya let out a weary sigh. 'Before we came to see you, we were asked to go to the mortuary to identify the body. MIT are investigating and needed to know as a matter of urgency.'

'I understand. That can't have been easy.'

'It's not that. The body. It's not Marcus.'

Dominique froze, her eyes wide with shock. She squeezed her eyes shut as she brought her hands up to her head and strained to think. She recalled the events of the fire. It was too soon and too terrifying, but she needed to go back to the moment she left her bedroom. She saw him on the stairs. Dark clothing. Balaclava. Familiar eyes.

'Tony,' said Maya filling in the blanks. 'Or should I say, Anthony. I recognised him straight away as being the man I saw at mid-week communion. I'd explained that if it had been Marcus, I might not recognise him with it being so long since I last saw him, but the body in the mortuary, the man who started the fire, it's definitely Anthony.'

'Jesus,' breathed Dominique. 'Yes. It's been so long since I've seen him too. And he was wearing glasses... but the one physical similarity they shared was their eyes. They both had Lily's vicious smile too. Oh God, Maya. You were right all along. Of course they were going to come after of us. I've been so stupid and naïve. I realised the moment I woke up and smelt the petrol.'

She lay back against the pillows while she came to terms with the news and recalled the events. 'I threw the hoover at him, you know the heavy one. I was terrified. At that stage I didn't know whether you were in the house or not.'

Maya reached for Dominique's hand as she relayed what she'd been told. 'Anthony was found outside in the back garden. It looks like he's endured quite a serious head injury in the fall, but despite that he managed to get out, to get away from the fire. He sustained burns to his lower legs but somehow managed to extinguish them.

'It looks like he'd made it to the garden before he collapsed. The fire was so strong that even outside, where he lay, the smoke would still have got to him from the open back door. We'll know more after the post-mortem.'

Maya fell silent. She exchanged a glance with Chris. He reached for her shoulder and patted it reassuringly. Then she sat and waited. It took several seconds. Dominique started; her eyes widened again, this time with the sheer terror that mirrored Maya's own.

'If Anthony was killed in the fire, then that means...'

Maya nodded. 'Marcus isn't dead. He's still out there somewhere.'

82

Marcus was pacing the flat cursing himself. Anthony should have been back ages ago. His lack of presence could only mean one thing. Something had gone wrong. He swore as he walked into the kitchen and took another swig of vodka straight from the bottle. He tried to ring his mobile phone again but knew it would be futile. Anthony wouldn't be able to answer it if he'd been arrested.

He knew it had been a mistake letting him take his place and do the job. But Anthony had insisted. He said it was his duty as the older brother. That if anything went wrong, Marcus would be straight back inside. If he was perfectly honest, that thought did make him panic and he eventually conceded. He had been confident that Anthony could handle it, they'd gone through the plan so many times, how to disguise their appearance, how to snap a lock, avoiding making noise once inside the house.

He took another gulp of vodka and looked at the time. He couldn't afford to wait around any longer. If Anthony had been arrested, the police would be around here in no time. He needed to go, and now. He packed lightly and quickly, including the emergency stash of money that Anthony had gathered just in case something like this happened and he needed to get away quickly.

He slipped the much-coveted photo out of its frame and pocketed it along with the plastic lily. Then he opened a drawer and pulled out the biggest knife they had. He carried it over to the coffee table where his Bible was sat and with a scream raised his hand and thrust the blade through the front cover.

He took one last look round the little flat that had been his home for such a short, but incredibly precious time.

Then he left.

83

Maya saw Chris glancing towards the door again. She noticed how tired he looked. She was exhausted herself, and in pain, but she knew the adrenaline was keeping her awake. James Harper from MIT had arranged for a uniformed patrol to come and sit outside Dominique's room until Marcus had been located and arrested. This had come as a huge relief to her. Maya hadn't disclosed the fact that she was terrified to return to her own apartment, and Harper hadn't advised her whether she should also consider herself at risk.

'You should go,' she said to Chris. 'You look as knackered as I feel.'

'Yeah, I'll make a move in a bit.'

'Go now, there's no need to wait. Honestly, Chris, I can't thank you enough for everything you've done. You're a true friend, I don't know what I'd do without you.'

Chris looked towards the door again and grinned. 'You can thank me later,' he said as he suddenly stood up. Maya turned to the door confused as to what he had just said and her heart lurched at the sight of Spence, stood in the doorway.

Chris dropped a kiss on the top of her head. 'I'll speak to you soon.' He glanced towards the bed where Dominique was sound asleep. 'Look after her for me,' he said as he shook Spence's hand before he left.

Spence's face was a mask of concern. His wavy hair looked ruffled and in contrast to his usual smart appearance, he looked thrown together in a hoody and joggers. She had never been so relieved to see him. He embraced her carefully, kissing her cheek before he stood back to survey her.

'How are you both?' he asked quietly as he sank into Chris's chair.

'Sore, shocked, stressed but glad we're both alive despite us both having shattered bones. I can't believe you're here, how did you find out?'

'I didn't get your message until late. Obviously, I rang you back straight away and Chris answered because you'd nodded off. He told me everything. I would have been here sooner, but I drove to the twenty-four-hour supermarket to get you some toiletries and a change of clothes. You're coming back to The Eagle with me. I don't want you going home until that maniac's been arrested.'

'But what about Helen. Won't she mind?'

'Helen who comes in the pub? No, why would she, what's any of this got to do with her?'

'I thought you two were an item. I saw you kiss; she was all over you.'

'You would have seen her kiss me, it wasn't reciprocated. She's very flirtatious and a good laugh, but that's it. She's really not my type.'

'What is your type?'

'You, Maya. You're my type. You're the only one I want. The only woman for me.' He reached for her hand and they sat grinning inanely at each other.

'I thought you weren't interested. I thought you'd friend-zoned me. Helen said you'd told her we were just friends and weren't interested.'

'She told me that's what *you'd* said. Devious mare, well she's barred from now on.' They smiled and he leant forward to press his forehead against hers. 'What about you and Jack? I was surprised to get your message after I saw you leave with him.'

'Too much alcohol and I was jealous after seeing you with her. And then you wouldn't answer my question.'

'I was scared if I told you how I felt, you'd knock me back.'

'Never. And for the record, nothing happened between Jack and I. He did stay the night, but that was all.'

'So are we doing this, me and you? Are we finally going to give us a chance?' he asked softly as he stroked her cheek with his hand.

Maya replied with a kiss.

84

By the time police arrived at the Naylors' flat, Marcus was long gone and a manhunt was underway. His photograph was shared far and wide, but other than a few false leads, it seemed like he had successfully gone to ground. It wasn't helped by the fact that the photograph was an old one and didn't represent how Marcus now looked with longer hair, a beard and a heavier build.

Maya had decided to stay with Spence until her arm was better and she could ensure her apartment was reinforced with added security features. This would include a panic alarm which would go through to the local police station if activated, resulting in an immediate police response. Staying at The Eagle wasn't just a practical decision, it suited the pair of them as they'd been inseparable since the moment they left the hospital together.

Dominique had been advised she would need to stay in hospital for a minimum of three weeks until she would be considered fit to be discharged. At least this would give Maya time to arrange some alternative accommodation for her.

Elaine had attended the scene at Dominique's house in

company with the fire investigators. For now, the property was boarded up pending an evaluation by the loss adjusters from Dominique's insurance company. Maya knew from working on the number of arsons that she had, that some personal effects may have survived the fire, but it depended on the intensity of the heat, the smoke damage followed then by the water damage from the firefighter's hoses. She had asked Spence to drive her to the house so she could see the extent of the damage for herself.

Tears filled her eyes as they pulled up outside the house. It was shocking to see such a devastating blackened shell. The usually pristine front garden was cluttered with burnt debris, which the fire brigade had dragged out of the house to ensure nothing could reignite. She climbed out of the car and straight away, the smell of charring assaulted her nostrils. Spence was at her side in an instant as he put his arm around her and gently pulled her into his chest.

'It's horrific,' she mumbled. 'Much worse than I thought it would be. Mama's going to be devastated.'

'I know, but the main thing is she got out of there. She's okay and so are you. It's just stuff, love.'

'I know what you're saying, but it's more than just stuff. It's a home, a lifetime of photographs and other sentimental things.'

He held her as she sobbed into his chest, wincing at the devastating sight. Like Maya, it looked so much worse than he had imagined too. He was kicking himself for not driving by first so he could see for himself and then prewarn her.

Then something in the garden caught his attention and he frowned. 'The neighbours know that Dominique is okay, don't they?'

Maya looked up at him as she wiped her eyes. 'Yeah, I rang Jean next door on the night to let her know and so she could tell the others. Why?'

'It looks like someone has left a flower. It's sick, like leaving a bouquet at a scene where someone has died.'

'Well, someone did die. Where are you looking?'

Spence pointed to the plastic lily and Maya inched open the garden gate and stepped precariously over the debris to below the front window. Her stomach lurched violently. Marcus had been here. He may have slithered back to the gutter afterwards, but he had taken a chance to come back here and leave a threatening message for her and Dominique. It showed how clearly dangerous and deranged he really was.

He would be after revenge now even more than ever. Marcus Naylor's threat had been received and well and truly understood. He may have gone to ground for now, but one day he would be back.

And he would be coming for them.

THE END

ACKNOWLEDGEMENTS

Thanks to the team at Bloodhound, especially Ian Skewis for his editing expertise and constructive criticism. Also, thanks to my readers and for the kind comments from those who have read *Definitely Dead*, the first in the Maya trilogy.

Huge thanks to my dear friend and boss, Lindsy Slamon, for continuing to support me and once again giving her valuable time to read and comment on an early draft and for highlighting any glaring errors. Also, to my partner in crime, Graham Bartlett, author and police advisor, for his invaluable advice and observations. You two are the best.

Special thanks to Ian (AKA Trig), for advising me on the procedure followed by the underwater search unit – that was an interesting conversation to have while at the hairdressers!

To my husband, Gary, and my friend and fellow author, Christie Newport, for also taking the time to read and advise on an early draft. Thanks to my friends and family who continue to support my writing journey and for being really understanding when I have to cancel nights out because of edits or deadlines – Jeanette, I mean you! A special thanks to my Swanwick family for your support and friendship, especially Sharon and Liz.

And finally, as always, my eternal thanks to Gary, Sophie and Elissa for all your love and support. None of this would happen without you three behind me. You make me so proud and I love you all so much.

A NOTE FROM THE PUBLISHER

Thank you for reading this book. If you enjoyed it please do consider leaving a review on Amazon to help others find it too.

We hate typos. All of our books have been rigorously edited and proofread, but sometimes mistakes do slip through. If you have spotted a typo, please do let us know and we can get it amended within hours.

info@bloodhoundbooks.com

Printed in Great Britain
by Amazon